The
Dinosaur
Tourist

The Dinosaur Tourist

CAITLÍN R. KIERNAN

Subterranean Press • 2018

First Edition

ISBN
978-1-59606-882-7

Subterranean Press
PO Box 190106
Burton, MI 48519

subterraneanpress.com
www.caitlinrkiernan.com
greygirlbeast.livejournal.com
Twitter: @auntbeast

Manufactured in the United States of America

For Christopher Geissler and Derrick Hussey
And also for Sonya Taaffe, friend, constant reader, and fellow siren.

Table of Contents

The Beginning of the Year Without a Summer 9

Far From Any Shore 25

The Cats of River Street (1925) 41

Elegy for a Suicide 63

The Road of Needles 71

Whilst the Night Rejoices Profound and Still 89

Ballad of an Echo Whisperer 105

The Cripple and the Starfish 119

Fake Plastic Trees 133

Whisper Road (Murder Ballad No. 9) 151

Animals Pull the Night Around Their Shoulders 163

Untitled Psychiatrist No. 2 175

Excerpts from *An Eschatology Quadrille* 187

Ballad of a Catamite Revolver..207

Untitled Psychiatrist No. 3 221

Albatross (1994)..235

Fairy Tale of Wood Street 249

The Dinosaur Tourist (Murder Ballad No. 11)....................................267

Objects in the Mirror 283

I'm in God's garden.
I'll make it a forest.
The Editors, *In This Light and On This Evening*

The Beginning of the Year
Without a Summer

This day and this night are a coin. Flip it, and in rapid succession first one thing and then the other, in constant, indecisive revolution. I am standing at the bottom of a steep paved road where the eastern edge of the cemetery meets the dirty slate-colored river, the Seekonk River, and it's a cold day in early May. As a lifelong Southerner, only recently transplanted to New England, that's a concept I'm still not comfortable with, cold days in early May. Standing here, looking out across the choppy waters of Bishop Cove, across almost four hundred yards to the opposite shore, the day seems even colder than it is, the wind sharp enough to peel back my skin and remind me how terrible was the winter. How terrible and how very recent and how soon it will return. The wind rattles the branches all around, and I reluctantly button my cardigan and hug myself. I look up into the stark face of the wide carnivorous sky, squinting at all that merciless blue, not a brushstroke of cloud anywhere at all. What sort of god permits a sky like that? It's a question I would ask in all seriousness, were I not an atheist. The trees sway and shudder in the wind like unmedicated epileptics. The new leaves are still bright, their greens not yet tempered by summer and inevitable age. This is the *face* of the coin, this afternoon at the edge of the cemetery. I'm not alone. There's a young woman sitting only a few feet away. She sits on the hood of her car and smokes cigarettes and talks as if we are old friends, when, in fact, we've only just met and only by the happenstance of our both having arrived at this spot at more or less the same time on the same cold, windy day in early May. She's at least twenty years my junior, dressed in a T-shirt and jeans, not even a sweater, as though this is a much warmer day than it is. There's a big padded camera bag on the hood beside her.

There are swans in the water.

"You teach?" she asks me, and I say that yes, I do.

"But I'm not a very good teacher," I add. "I didn't get into science to teach."

"You're at Brown?"

Around us, the trees sway and creak. The river laps against the shore. The swans, hardly even seeming to notice the wind, bob about on the waves and dip their heads beneath the water, foraging in the shallows. I notice that their long necks are dirty from all the sediment stirred up by the waves and the currents and by their hungry, probing bills. Their white feathers seem almost as if they've been stained with oil.

I point at the birds and ask the girl, "Is that why it's called Swan Point?"

She shrugs, stubs her cigarette out against the sole of her boot, then flicks the butt towards the river.

"You shouldn't do that," I tell her. "They're poisonous. Birds and fish eat them. Fish eat them, and then birds eat the fish. In experiments, the chemicals from a single filtered cigarette butt killed half the fish living in a one-liter container of water. Plus, they're made of non-biodegradable acetate-cellulose. Every year, an estimated 1.6 billion pounds of –"

"Jesus, yeah, okay," she says and laughs. "This isn't a classroom. You're not on the clock, professor."

"Sorry," I say, not meaning it, not sorry at all, but I'm embarrassed, and so I apologize anyway.

This is the *face* of the coin.

The coin is in the air, turning and turning, ass over tit.

"I don't know why it's called Swan Point," the girl says, and she lights another cigarette. For only an instant, a caul of grey smoke hangs about her face before the wind takes it apart. "I never bothered to ask anyone. I just like coming here. I've been coming here since I was a teenager."

The wind, blowing up off Narragansett Bay, smells like low tide on mudflats, like sewage, like sex, primordial and faintly fishy. It roars across the water, ruffling the feathers of the swans, and it roars through the trees, giving them fits. I dislike the wind. Not as much as I dislike that blue sky hanging above me, and not as much as I dislike the cold, but enough that I wish I'd waited for a less blustery day to wander down to this spot I've glimpsed on other drives and walks through the cemetery. One of the swans turns its head towards me, seeming to glare with its tiny black eyes, such tiny eyes for so large a bird. It only watches me a few seconds before turning its attention back to feeding, and maybe it was only my imagination that it was ever watching me at all.

"They don't actually belong here," I say.

"What?" the girl asks. "What don't belong here?"

"Those swans. I mean, that particular species of swan. *Cygnus olor.* They're an invasive, introduced to North America from Europe back in the 1800s."

"Yeah," the girl says without looking at me. "Well, they don't hurt anyone, do they? And at least they're pretty to look at."

"They're that," I agree. "Pretty to look at, I mean."

"Someone murdered one last fall," she says. Not killed. She says *murdered.* "Broke its neck, then nailed it to a tree." And she points to a large red maple not far away. "That tree there. Drove a nail through the top of its skull, and one through each shoulder. Wait, do swans have shoulders?"

"Yeah," I tell her. "Swans have shoulders."

"Okay, well, that's what they did, whoever killed the swan. Almost like they were crucifying it, you know. There was a reward offered by the cops or the SPCA or someone like that. Two thousand dollars to help them catch the person who murdered the swan. The reward started off at fifteen hundred, but went up to two thousand. I gotta tell you, I could have used that money. But I don't think they ever caught the person responsible, the swan murderer. Who the fuck would do something like that? Who the fuck is sick enough to nail a swan to a tree?"

I don't have an answer for her, and I don't offer one. The sky had been bad enough without the mental image of a swan nailed to a tree.

"You know about birds," she says, then takes a long drag off her cigarette.

"It was just the one?" I ask her. "Only one swan was killed?"

"As far as I know," she replies. "Of course, who's to say the sick fuck didn't kill more of them, and all those others were just never found."

"What an awful thing," I say. "What a terrible, awful thing." And I'm wishing that she hadn't told me, that she'd kept it to herself, wondering why she felt the need to tell a stranger about a *murdered* swan.

She shrugs again and exhales smoke. "I hope it was senseless," she says, "because I'd hate to know the logic that would lead a person to break a swan's neck and then nail its corpse to a tree. I'd prefer to believe there was no reasoning at all behind an act like that, that it was completely fucking thoughtless."

The coin that is on one side a day and on the other a night flips.

I close my eyes and rub at my eyelids, at the bridge of my nose, wanting to change the subject, but at a loss as to how I can do so.

And the tumbling coin turns its face away from me. Tails. So, I'm camped out on a settee upholstered with sky-blue velvet that, like everything else in this house has been worn smooth and threadbare. The very floors beneath my feet are threadbare, having been so long trammeled by so many feet and with such force that the varnished pine boards seem to me exhausted and ready to shatter into splinters. The only light in the room, way up here on the third floor of the house, comes from tall cast-iron candelabras spaced out along the high walls, but it's plenty enough that I can see the dancer. The heavy drapes have been drawn against the July night, against the moon and the prying stars. In one corner of the room, there's a quartet: cellist, violist, the two violins. The air is thick with an incense formulated in accordance with Ayurvedic principles; in this instance, a hand-rolled tattva incense from some nook or cranny of the Himalayas, herbs, resins, gums brought together in the service of *air,* and my nose wrinkles at the almost overpowering reek of patchouli. I'm drinking beer. I don't even know what brand. It was placed in front of me, and I'm drinking it, and I'm watching the dancer as she whirls and swoops and bares herself for unseen Heaven beyond the ceiling of the room, beyond the attic, the roof of the house, the shingles. The beer is flat and going warm and tastes like fermented cornflakes. But that's okay. No one comes to this house to drink, this house hidden deep within the squalor of Federal Hill. My head hurts, and I pop two Vicodin, washing them down with the flat beer, and I wait for the tall, dark-complexioned man sitting beside me to say something. To say whatever it is he's going to say next.

That turns out to be, "So, does Providence agree with you? I trust you're settling in well?"

"I am," I reply. "As well as can be expected. I miss Birmingham."

The man sips his whiskey and bitters and nods his head. "I've never been so far south as that. Fact is, I've never been any farther south than Pittsburgh."

"You should remedy that," I tell him and smile. Despite my headache, I'm in good spirits, my mood buoyed by the dancer, by the musicians as they draw the strains of the second movement of Bedřich Smetana's "Z mého života" from their instruments, and buoyed also by simply being here, in the house. The house itself is a tonic.

"You miss the heat?" he asks.

"I miss the heat," I reply, nodding my head, "and I miss the fieldwork, getting my hands dirty, the grit under my nails, the sweat, all that. But I have a good job here. I shouldn't complain so much."

The dancer comes very near the sky-blue settee then, and her white hair, plaited into a single braid that hangs down past her ass, swings like the tail of a beast. Her eyes meet mine, but only for an instant, half an instant. They are such a vivid, unreal shade of blue, lapis lazuli, ultramarine, that I know they must be contacts. Her bare, callused feet hammer the boards, and then she's gone again.

"She came to us all the way from Amsterdam," says the man, and he nods towards the dancer. I don't know the man's name, but I know better than to ask. "She's quite talented, yes?"

"Very much so," I say, knowing that the time for small talk is passing. The coin is turning, rotating as it's carried up and away from the surface of the world, vainly seeking escape velocity. We've sat here almost an hour now, me nursing my beer, him drinking scotch after scotch. For a time he talked about my work, in such a way that I could tell he wanted to impress me. He'd even read the papers in *Nature* and the *Journal of Vertebrate Paleontology,* and he asked specifically about the fauna from the Tuscaloosa Formation, about the basal hadrosauroids *Eolophorhothon progenitor* and *Tuscaloosaura psammophilum,* the tyrannosauroid *Phobocephalae australis,* and the little nodosaur, *Heliopelta belli.* However, he wasn't especially interested in what these discoveries from the Alabama Black Belt meant to paleontology and our understanding of the Late Cretaceous of the Appalachian subcontinent; he was, instead, fascinated by the nomenclature, the meanings of the binomina, the process of choosing and publishing names. Regardless, it was honest interest, and I appreciated that very much. There are few things I find more tiresome, more entirely exasperating, than politely feigned curiosity.

The book is resting on the settee between us, a small antique photo album that was already a century old when I was born. I gently touch the flaking red-leather cover with the fingers of my left hand.

The dancer passes very near again, naked except for her borrowed feathers.

The man glances at her, then me, then at the book.

"We all thought it was lost forever," he says. "We had every reason to believe exactly that after the fire, after the purge, what with all the years that came and went with no one having heard even a rumor the book might have survived the flames." He doesn't yet touch it. That'll come later, when it is finally no longer my burden.

"Your mother would be proud," the man says. "She was a strong, fine woman, a brilliant woman, and it is a crime she was denied her time as the book's keeper."

"When I was a kid," I say, not exactly changing the subject, "when I was very young, she would tell me stories of Providence. She'd tell me stories of this house and of the city, and she'd tell me stories of the swans and the river."

"I wish I could have met her," he says and smiles. I dislike his smile. His lips are pale and thin. One could look at his smile and be forgiven for thinking that he has too many teeth. "But, as I understand it, she never traveled, and, as I've said –"

"– you've never been farther south than Pittsburgh."

"Exactly," he says. "Now, please, tell me again of the day you found the book."

I'm wishing the Vicodin would kick in, impatiently waiting for the opioid rush to wash away my headache. I'm not exactly in the mood to repeat that story, how I found the photo album. I would far rather simply hand the book over to this man with too many teeth, this man who will be a proper guardian, and then watch the dancer and listen to the music. But I am a guest here, no matter my pedigree and no matter that I've come bearing so marvelous a gift. For now, I am a guest. And it would be a breach of etiquette to beg off. The observation of proper etiquette is very important here. It's only a story, even if it really happened, and it's a small thing to ask of me to tell it again. I have another sip of my flat beer, thinking back to how I told him the story before and trying to decide if I want to tell it the same way the second time around.

"It's not actually a random phenomenon," the man says.

"What isn't?" I ask him.

He leans over, depositing his empty glass on the floor at his feet. "A coin toss," he says as he sits up again. "So long as the initial conditions of the toss are known – velocity, angular momentum, position, etcetera – then it's a problem that can be modeled in Lagrangian mechanics. If you are intent on burying yourself so deeply in this metaphor, you ought to understand its limitations."

On the shore of the Seekonk River, a city of narrow houses at my back, I'm listening to a young woman who hasn't introduced herself talk about dead swans. In the house on Federal Hill, a man who can see my thoughts is asking me to tell him a story he's already heard from me twice.

"A practiced magician," he continues, "an accomplished illusionist, he can control a coin toss with a surprising degree of precision." And then the man laughs and taps the side of his nose. *A word to the wise. Just between you and me.*

The girl sitting on the hood of the car lights another cigarette.

The dancer spins.

"Please," says the man sitting beside me on the settee. "I'd love to hear it again."

I almost ask him for something stronger than the beer, but only almost.

"Well," I begin, "there was this one fellow kept stopping by the site. That pretty much always happens, the curious locals. If you're lucky, they just want to have a look at what you're up to, find out why someone would be rooting around in Farmer Joe's back forty or what have you. If you're lucky, they don't start in about Noah's Flood or the evils of the great lie of evolution. When they do, of course, you have to be polite and listen, nod your head, not get into arguments, because you never know who any given ignorant redneck might be related to. He could well be the first cousin of the guy who's given you permission to dig on his land. Anyway, this one guy, he wasn't like that. He'd studied some geology at Auburn, and he asked intelligent, thoughtful questions."

"And he told you about the train?" the man asks me, as though he doesn't already know the answer.

"He did," I reply. "He told me about the boxcars."

The dancer pirouettes, making three full turns on the ball of her left foot. The feathers along her arms and shoulders rustle like dead leaves, and I'm surprised that I can hear them over the music. I wonder if it's some trick of the room's acoustics, if it's a happy accident or by design. And, for the second time, I begin telling the man about the abandoned railroad cars and the dead crows. He seems to take great delight in the tale. I can't help but feel, now, that the coin has risen as high as it possibly can, and all of its momentum has been spent. At any second, I think, gravity will reclaim it, reasserting its primacy, and the coin will begin its rapid, inevitable descent.

Call it.

Kopf oder Zahl.

"Heads," says the girl at the eastern edge of Swan Point Cemetery. "I always hated the way that Granddad would cut off the heads of the ducks he killed and nail them to the boathouse wall. But it was how he kept up with what he'd shot over the season."

"I've never heard of anyone doing that," I say, and I check my watch. I have a four o'clock lecture, and it's already a quarter to three.

"Well, he'd do it every year," the girl says. "It's how me and my sister learned to tell mallards from mergansers, eiders from wood ducks, sitting out there with my grandfather's grisly little menagerie. Swans, they're not ducks, are they?"

"They're in the same family," I tell her, "but they're more closely related to geese than to ducks."

An especially strong gust of wind rolls off the river, and I turn my back to it. To the river and the wind. My ears are beginning to hurt from the cold. *How can this be May?* I think. *How can this possibly be May?* For a dizzying moment or so, I have trouble recalling the last time that I was truly warm.

"Can I tell you a story?" the girl asks. The wind doesn't seem to be bothering her the way it does me, or not bothering her as much, which, I admit, makes me angry.

"About your grandfather's boathouse?" I ask, turning up the collar of my cardigan and wishing I had a wool cap with me.

"No, no," she says. "I told you all there was to that. This is something else. But, I don't know, maybe they're connected somehow. At least, they seemed to be connected in my head." And, as she talks, she unzips her camera bag and takes out a Pentax K1000 35mm. It's refreshing to see someone as young as her using film instead of digital. She slips the strap around her neck, then checks the settings and peers through the viewfinder, aiming the camera nowhere in particular.

"Doesn't the wind bother you?" I ask her.

"I don't mind. It's not so bad today. It was worse yesterday."

"You were raised here?"

"No, I'm from Maine, not far from Portland."

I tell her that I've never been to Maine, and she tells me that I haven't really missed much.

"Anyway," she says, "the story, I won't get into it, not if you don't want to hear or don't have the time. I saw you check your watch." She lowers the camera and looks at me. "It's just, the thing with the murdered swan, and then Granddad's boathouse, you know the way shit reminds you of other shit, like dominoes getting knocked over. Free association. Whatever."

"Yeah," I say. "I know how that is. Sure, I've got time to hear a story."

"Okay, well, when I was eight, that summer, not long after my eighth birthday, there was a whole week in July when I kept finding feathers in my bed. Me and my mom both found them."

A few feet from shore, three of the swans, moving in what could pass for perfect unison, dip their heads and long necks beneath the dark river.

"Every night, I'd turn back the sheets, and the bed would be full of feathers."

"You didn't have a feather mattress, I assume."

"No, and besides, it wasn't like that. What do they stuff feather mattresses with? Chicken feathers? Duck feathers? No, these were all different sorts of feathers. Blue jays, cat birds, crows, mockingbirds, robins, even seagulls, and there were some sorts we never did figure out what they were. I'd turn back the covers, and there would be dozens of feathers in my bed. Jesus, it was weird. And it went on for a whole week, like I said. Dad was in Italy on business –"

"Italy? What does your dad do?"

"Did. He's retired."

"What did your dad do?"

"He was an engineer, but that doesn't have anything to do with the story, except that he was away when this happened. At first I thought it was my sister putting the feathers in my bed. She was a year older than me. We had a huge fight when I accused her of doing it, and Mom sent her to stay with my grandparents for a few days."

"Same grandparents had the boat house?" I ask.

"No, that was my father's parents. These were my maternal grandparents. But it didn't matter. The feathers showed up, anyway, without her being there. Every night, a handful of them, all those different colors and shapes, and my mother kept having to change and wash the sheets, because she was paranoid about birds carrying diseases. My bed smelled like Lysol..."

The girl trails off for a moment, watching the swans bobbing on the rough, wind-tossed river. "What do you call a group of swans?" she asks.

"That depends. If they're flying, you call a group of swans a wedge, because of the formation they fly in, because it's wedge shaped. If they're not flying, like these swans," and I motion towards the river, "a group of swans is called a lamentation."

"That's sort of melodramatic, don't you think?" she says, then lifts her camera again and spends a few seconds watching the swans through the viewfinder.

"So, it wasn't your sister," I say, prompting her to continue.

She lowers the camera again and nods. "No, it wasn't my sister. It kept happening after she left, and never mind there was no way she'd ever have gathered up *that* many feathers. It really scared my mother. Me, I was mostly just annoyed and angry and wanted to know who was playing such a stupid trick on me. I even thought maybe my mom was doing it and just pretending it was upsetting her. That was even dumber than blaming my sister, of course, but at the time I either didn't realize it or, you know, just didn't care."

I look back up at that insatiable too-blue sky. "But then it just stopped, after a week?"

"No, something happened first, then it stopped after a week."

The dancer's bare and busy feet have made a percussive instrument of the floor, and I have the distinct impression that she's setting the tempo and the string quartet is having trouble keeping up. Her feet are dusted white with resin.

The coin is falling now.

"What was that?" I ask. "What happened?"

The girl takes a drag off her cigarette, then begins fussing about with the lens of her camera.

"I was sitting at my desk," she says, "the little desk in my room where I sat and did my homework and stuff. I was sitting there after breakfast one morning reading a book – I don't recall what the book was, I sort of wish that I did – and a raven flew into the window. It hit the glass so hard it was like a gun going off. *Bam!* Scared the shit out of me, and I screamed, and –"

"It killed the raven," I say, interrupting her.

The girl laughs. "Fuck yeah, it killed the raven. It even cracked the windowpane. Crushed the poor thing's skull, I guess. Broke its neck, at the very least. Cracked the window and left a smear of blood on the glass, it hit so hard." And she laughs again. It's a nervous, uneasy sort of laugh. "How fast do ravens fly?"

"I don't know," I tell her. "But there were no more feathers in your bed after that? That's what made them stop appearing?"

She turns her head and stares at me. "Yeah, there were no more feathers in my bed after that, and at the *time,* that's how it seemed to me, that somehow the death of the raven had made whatever was happening stop. Like, I don't know, like a sacrifice?"

"But that's not what you think now?"

"I don't know. Questions of causation and correlation and what have you, right? But something else happened that same day, the same day the raven smacked into my bedroom window."

"And what was that?"

The wind blows, and I smell the salty, noisome bay.

Drops of sweat fall from the dancer's naked body and speckle the dusty floor.

"I got my period. My first period. I was only eight, but..." And again she trails off and sits smoking and pretending to adjust the Pentax's aperture settings.

"You were young," I agree, "but it happens."

"Mom, she blamed hormones in milk and beef and stuff, but, like I said, causation and correlation. Who fucking knows. Point is, that day a raven went kamikaze on my bedroom window, *and* I got my period, *and* the creepy thing with the feathers in my bed stopped. And that was that. It's not a very satisfying ending to a story."

"Usually, the world doesn't come with satisfying endings attached," I tell her, and she shrugs and begins taking photographs of the feeding swans.

On the third floor of the house on Federal Hill, I sit with the smiling man on the blue settee, the antique photo album between us, and he listens to me tell my own story.

"I never did learn how or why or by whom all those railroad cars had been moved where they were, but there were about a dozen of them, half swallowed up by the kudzu vines, miles from the nearest tracks. They were all boxcars, except for that caboose."

"That's where you found the book?" he asks.

"Yeah."

"Is it true what they say about kudzu, how fast it grows?"

"Up to a foot a day, maybe more," I say. "It was introduced into the US in 1883, from Asia. It doesn't belong here. Anyway, the vines were so thick I think we never would have gotten into the caboose if we hadn't had machetes."

"But you did have machetes, and you did get in," says the man.

"Yes, on both counts."

...and in rapid succession first one thing and then the other, in constant, indecisive revolution...

The man lays his hand on the cover of the book, so that I can no longer see it, which, I discover, makes it easier for me to tell him about the caboose. I dream about it most nights and suspect that I always will. Knowledge comes at a price, my mother would have said, and often that price is our sense of well being. Or our innocence. Or our ability to sleep without nightmares.

"I was surprised that the kudzu hadn't gotten inside," I say.

"Maybe something kept it out," replies the man, and he leans forward a bit, watching the dancer intently now.

"The windows weren't broken out, which is nothing short of a miracle. No telling how long it had been sitting there. Decades. But the windows weren't broken out, and the rear door opened as easily as if the hinges had just recently been oiled. There was a pot-bellied stove, bunks, a desk. The walls were painted a muddy sort of mint green, and photographs of naked women had been cut out and tacked up and pasted all over them."

"Kids," the man whispers, the smile returning to his thin lips.

"And there were the birds," I say.

"'When you have shot one bird flying,'" says the smiling man, "'you have shot all birds flying.' That's Ernest Hemingway. You dislike talking about the birds. I can tell. I'd not thought you'd be squeamish about a thing like that."

I don't reply right away. I want to deny the charge, his casual accusation that I don't have the stomach for the life that has been passed down to me. But I don't. I let the charge stand. He would know my denial was a lie, and, more importantly, I would know it was a lie.

"We counted the bodies of seventy-five crows," I say, instead. "Some were hardly more than skeletons, sort of mummified, skin and feathers stretched over bone. Others couldn't have been dead more than a few hours. Each one had been nailed to the mint-green walls with three two-penny nails. One nail through the back of the skull, and –"

"It must have been very hot," the man whispers. "It must have been very hot inside the caboose."

"It was late summer. August. Dog days. Yes, it was very hot."

"But you're used that that," says the man.

"The book, it was lying on a shelf above the brakeman's desk. There was nothing else on the shelf, just the one book. It was dusty, but it wasn't moldy, which is at least as unlikely as none of the windows being broken out."

"Maybe it hadn't been there very long."

"Maybe not. There's no way to know, and I don't suppose it matters."

"Not in the least."

I take a small sip of my flat beer, because my mouth has gone very dry. I can taste the incense now, hot and cloying, as much as I can smell it. The music and the rhythmic tattoo of the dancer's feet on the floor have grown inexplicably, uncomfortably loud. I glance towards the book, mostly hidden from view by the man's hand, but I don't have to *see* the book to see it. The image of it is worked into my mind, tooled there as surely as the grotesque patterns worked into its tooled leather cover, that album with its gilded fore edge and the cracked leather binding stained red and black like dried blood on the feathers of dead crows. There is a single word blind stamped into the spine, and there's a brass hasp and a staple, but no lock to keep it shut. Anyone can open the book and see what's inside.

Anyone can turn a page.

Or flip a coin.

"Well, you've brought it home," says the man, "which is really all that matters."

By the polluted river, at the eastern edge of Swan Point Cemetery, the girl smokes cigarettes and sits on the hood of her car, snapping pictures.

I say that I should be going, and she nods and takes another photograph.

"Do you believe in evil?" she asks me.

"I do," I reply, without giving the matter a second thought. "I haven't been left with much choice in the matter."

"Well, I believe in evil," she says. "Murdering a swan, nailing it to a tree, that's evil, pure and fucking simple."

Before the music began, and before I took the book from my satchel and presented it to the man who seems to have too many teeth when he smiles, before *that,* the dancer knelt on the floor, and she bowed her head, and everyone assembled in the room watched as the alabaster feathers were inserted beneath her skin. The hollow quill tips of primary and secondary flight feathers, the feathers of swans, had been fitted into seventy-four 22-gauge hypodermic needles, and then the needles were artfully arranged in rows along her shoulders and forearms. I was surprised that the piercing had taken only half an hour. She had not been given wings, but only the suggestion of wings, a shaman's trick that she could fly and yet still be bound by the same cruel gravity that pulls a coin toss back towards earth.

And now the fourth movement has ended, and the musicians are waiting patiently for what comes next. The dancer has stopped dancing. She stands perfectly still at the center of the room, her counterfeit wings folded modestly across her breasts, the candlelight painting her with flickering shades of yellow and white and orange. And the woman who gave her those wings reappears from the shadows; she carries a ballpeen hammer and three heavy forty-penny nails. She whispers something to the dancer, kisses her on the cheek, and then they walk together to the north end of the room, where a sturdy cross carved of red maple has been erected.

"A shame your mother can't see this," says the man, and he picks the book up off the sky-blue settee and sets it in his lap. He has taken the weight of it from me and made it his own, and for that I might almost be moved to worship him as an atheist's god. "A crying shame," he says.

The dancer, the evening's surrogate, never utters a sound. Her whole life has prepared her for this moment and led her here, and she faces her fate with the dignity and poise of a swan.

"You're an ornithologist?" asks the girl as she stubs out another cigarette on the sole of her boot. This time, she doesn't flick the butt towards the river, but places it into an empty film canister.

"No," I say. "I'm a paleontologist. That's what I teach."

"But you know a lot about birds."

"I suppose I do," I reply.

"Well, maybe we'll run into each other again," she says. "I come here a lot."

We exchange goodbyes, and then I turn and walk to my own car, parked farther from the water, and she goes back to taking pictures of the swans. The insistent wind is behind me, pushing me along, urging me forward.

The man with the book in his lap looks away from the spectacle just long enough to offer me a wink and to tap the side of his nose again.

A word to the wise.

He has the black eyes of a crow.

"She was a fine woman, your mother," he says.

And the world spins, like a tossed coin, moving in constant, indecisive, predictable revolutions, and I hold it in the palm of my hand.

THE BEGINNING OF THE YEAR WITHOUT A SUMMER

More than anything else, this story was inspired by a trip to Swan Point Cemetery on April 22, 2014. Despite the temperature being somewhere in the sixties Fahrenheit, the wind off the river was very cold. The next day I wrote in my blog, "We [Kathryn and I] visited bookshops at Wayland Square, had breakfast at the Classic Cafe on Westminster, and ended up at Swan Point Cemetery, where we did, in fact, see a flock of swans in the choppy waters of the dirty Seekonk River." The part of this story that pleases me the most is the four taxa of fictional dinosaurs I created for it – *Eolophorhothon progenitor, Tuscaloosaura psammophilum, Phobocephalae australis,* and *Heliopelta belli.* As of this writing, no one (to my knowledge) has yet discovered dinosaur remains in the Upper Cretaceous-aged Tuscaloosa Formation of the Gulf Coastal Plain, but hope springs eternal.

Far From Any Shore

...out there past men's knowing, where the stars are drowning and whales ferry their vast souls through the black and seamless sea.
— Cormac McCarthy

It fits easily into the palm of my hand, no larger than a baseball or a small red apple. It isn't quite so round as either of those things, the "Venus of Gove County," which Jackson took to calling the artifact the day after it was unearthed from the chalky badlands just south of Castle Rock, Kansas. Every time I lift it from the cardboard box, from that simple excelsior-lined cradle, I'm surprised at its light weight. Though carved of something that looks very much like a greenish-grey soapstone, the object weighs hardly anything at all. It might well have been fashioned not from any stone, but from balsa wood. I hold it, and I close my fingers tightly about it. I feel, or I only imagine I feel, an icy, thrumming tingle that resonates through the flesh and bones of my hand and then moves gradually up my arm. If I hold it long enough, I can hear the ocean, and this seems to me precisely the same auditory illusion I've imagined when holding a conch shell up to my ear. Seashell resonance, it's called, and you can get just exactly the same effect simply by placing an empty glass to your ear, or nothing more than your cupped hand. But where's the romance in that? I can never bring myself to handle the thing for very long, Jackson's Venus, and so I either set it down on the table in front of the motel window or I return it to its box. This time, the former. I pour another shot of Jack into the plastic cup I've been drinking from, on and off, since I checked into the room, shortly before dawn. I know that I'm drunk. I have a second bottle of whiskey, still unopened, and I intend to keep drinking until both bottles are empty. The alcohol isn't helping, but I don't know what else to do. I've set it on the table, and in the sliver of sunlight getting in through the narrow slit where the closed drapes do not quite meet, the thing on the table seems oily. It isn't the least bit oily to the touch, but there it sits shimmering, regardless, showing off all the motley hues of motor oil spilled into a puddle of water. I shut my eyes, because I can only ever watch it for just so long.

"It isn't what it looks like," Joanna Fielding said, rolling it about in her callused hands. We three sat together by Coleman lamplight, the night after Jackson brought it into camp. "Whatever it is," she said, "it sure isn't that."

"When I was a kid," said Jackson, "when I was in seventh grade, I found a rock shaped like a penis. Not just the penis, mind you, but the balls, too. I found it in a chert pit not far from my house. Now, it wasn't anything but a siltstone concretion, but –"

"A pseudofossil," Joanna said, interrupting him.

"Well, of course. Right. A pseudofossil. But it sure as hell *looked* like a dick, you know? Next day, I took it to school with me, and a teacher confiscated it. At the end of the day, when I asked for it back, he said no, and he also told me he'd call my parents if I brought the matter up again. He accused me of having carved it."

"Yeah, well, whatever it is," Joanna said again, "it isn't what it looks like."

A warm, grass-scented wind blew across the prairie, blowing out of the summer night and rattling the tarp above our heads, rustling the tents. Jackson shook his head and laughed.

"Probably, it's a coprolite," he said. "That's what makes the most sense. We get it back to the lab and run a couple of tests, it's going to turn out we've got nothing here but a lump of calcium phosphate. Seventy-three million years ago, a mosasaur or a plesiosaur or just a shark came along and took a dump, and here we are gawking at fossilized shit, like it's the image of Jesus Christ or Elvis Presley on a grilled-cheese sandwich."

In my motel room, behind closed eyelids, the three of us laugh at that, and Joanna passes the ugly thing back to Jackson. He makes a joke about the Cardiff Giant, and what if some hayseed hick farmer had found this during, say, the Great Depression? Why, just imagine driving merrily along in Granddad's rattletrap Model T, and here's a hand-painted plywood sign stuck up at the side of the road: Venus of Gove County! Carved by Adam in the Garden of Eden! See it now! Just 5¢ a head! And we laugh, like we'd laughed at the grilled-cheese joke. We laughed because we're scientists, and our enlightened, educated minds don't project superstitious nonsense onto oddly shaped rocks. We don't fall for the trickery of pareidolia. Rationality wins out every time over optical illusions and misleading pattern recognition; I know there's no ocean inside a conch shell. The wind snatched at our laughter and dragged it off into the night to haunt the ears of mule deer, jackrabbits, and pronghorn antelope.

Here in the motel there's a noise, and I open my eyes and squint through the daylight shadows towards the bathroom. The door's shut, and I try to recall whether it was shut when I came in or if I closed it. And I wonder why I didn't turn on any of the lights before I drew the drapes shut. I sit very still, listening, but I don't hear anything else, and after five minutes or so I reach for the remote and switch on the little flat-screen Toshiba TV facing the bed. It flickers obediently to life, tuned to a reality show about wealthy rednecks in the Louisiana bayous. I sit and stare at it for more than half an hour, because that's better than sitting and staring at the thing from the cardboard box, the thing Charlie Jackson dug out of the chalk more than two days ago now. My heart's racing, my mouth is cottony, and my palms are sweating, even though the AC's cranked all the way up to the highest setting.

"I saw something like this once," said Joanna Fielding.

It was almost midnight when I took the pickup and left camp, following roads that were hardly more than rutted, washed-out cattle trails winding between the Niobrara canyons and cornfields, following the only path out of that desolate landscape, bumping and swerving back to narrow county highways and, eventually, northwards to I-70. The cardboard box rode in the passenger seat next to me, hidden from view beneath a wool blanket. At Grainfield, I should have turned west, back towards Boulder, back towards the mountains. Instead, I stopped at the Sinclair station (one of the few I've ever seen that still has the once-iconic green dinosaur on its sign) and topped off the tank. Moving on autopilot, force of habit, I crossed the street to a diner and ordered breakfast, eggs and bacon and grits, but didn't eat any of it. I drank two cups of bitter coffee. The waitress watched me the whole time, as if she expected me to rob the place. There were seven black stars tattooed on the back of her left hand. I paid the bill, bought a pack of Camels from a vending machine, and then I took the interstate east – I think I never will know why – and I kept right on driving until I was across the county line and into Missouri.

Once, a state trooper appeared in my rearview mirror, as if from nowhere, as if some phantom spat out by the night, but I minded my Ps and Qs, kept my eyes on the truck's speedometer and after a few miles he (or she) passed me.

"I was in San Francisco," Joanna said, "back in the mid nineties, and I saw something like it. Not *exactly* like it, but what I saw in Berkeley, that's what first crossed my mind when Charlie brought it into the camp yesterday."

"What was it?" I asked her. "What was it you saw in Berkeley?"

Lying on the stiff Motel 6 mattress, I'm pretending I can get some sleep. The television is talking to itself, doing a shit job of keeping me company, a shit job of drowning out my restless thoughts. The room smells like air freshener, antiseptic spray, Ivory soap, clean linen, and, very faintly, of cigarette smoke, despite the no smoking signs and the smoke alarms. Out in the sun-drenched parking lot, I can hear cars coming and going. I hear a maid roll her cart past my door. And then I hear that noise from the bathroom again, and then a third time after that. But I don't get up to see what, if anything, is making it. I lie still, and my heart is beating louder than the crawling voices of the idiot swamp people on the television, basking in their unlikely, fleeting, grotesque fame.

"It was on display at the Hearst Museum," said Joanna Fielding, avoiding my question. "I have a friend there, an ex, and I was in town for a few days, and she and I met for lunch. We're still good friends. We've stayed on good terms. She had a curatorial position there."

Joanna was rambling, but I didn't hurry her.

"It was in a tall case all by itself, next to a display of Tlingit and Haida religious artifacts. The label said it had come from marine dredgings off the coast of Prince of Wales Island. It was almost the exact same size and shape as what Charlie found."

My exhausted thoughts are jumbled up and melting with the yammering voices on TV. And I hear Jackson say, *I just need some sleep, man. Just a few hours, and then my head will be clearer, and I can figure out what to do. What happens next.* I hear *him* say those words, but I'm pretty sure the sentiment is mine.

"So," I asked Joanna again, "what was it, the artifact from Alaska?"

She frowned and shook her head.

"They were calling it a fetish, something shamanistic, maybe a spirit totem. It was black. Deep jet black, supposedly carved from argillite." And then she laughed a nervous laugh and lit a cigarette. She blew smoke rings towards the Coleman lantern and a huge moth swooping crazily about the flaring propane light. "It turned up in 1937," Joanna continued, "during a canal expansion for a ferry, pulled in with all the sand and clay and everything else by the trailing suction hopper." She tapped ash into the grass at her feet. To the south of camp, there was thunder and a flash of heat lightning.

"You ask me," she said, "Charlie should just put it right back where he found it and cover it over, bury it."

I open my eyes and roll over, rolling towards the window, away from the bathroom. The digital alarm clock says it's 3:46 p.m., and I wonder where the hell all those hours and minutes have gone. Have I been dozing, dreaming of Joanna Fielding telling me her story about the Alaskan artifact? My eyes come to rest on the thing from the chalk, sitting where I left it on the table. Somehow, I'm surprised that it's still there. Probably I was wishing (without knowing I was wishing) that it would be gone. I could get up and get dressed, couldn't I? Get in the truck and start driving again, and I could spend my life forgetting it and forgetting what I've done because of it.

No, I can't. Why even bother thinking a thing like that, when I fucking well fucking know better?

I'm thirsty. Suddenly, I'm so awfully thirsty. I sit up and rub at my face, and then I stare at the clock, and then I stare at the table.

"It was about a hundred feet downslope from the excavation," Jackson said, when he'd come into camp with the thing, when I'd asked him exactly where he'd found it. "I marked the spot. It was already mostly weathered free. At first, I thought it was nothing but a badly eroded mosasaur vertebra. Just junk. In fact, I was pretty *sure* that's what it was, until I started digging and got it out of the ground."

"You should have left it alone," Joanna said. "You should have left it out there." Except, no, she said that later. The next day, I think. "You should have left the fucking thing where you found it."

Charlie was eating saltine crackers with a can of sardines packed in Tabasco sauce, and he looked up from his lunch.

"You're telling me you'd have left it?" he asked her. "Seriously? You expect me to believe that?"

She didn't reply.

I can hear two people arguing out in the parking lot, a man and a woman; they're speaking Spanish. Never mind the smoke alarm and the motel's rules, I want a cigarette. But when I check the pocket of the shirt I was wearing last night, all I find is a crumpled pack and some brown scraps of tobacco hiding inside. My mouth tastes like ass, and I consider taking a shower. But then I'd have to open that door I can't remember whether I shut or not. And if I *did* shut it, I might have had a damn good reason.

"*No me preguntes porqué,*" says one of the Spanish speakers, the woman.

"*Era el océano. He visto el mar,*" the man replies.

I root about in my knapsack and find a clean T-shirt and jeans, a cleanish pair of underwear, and a Tiger's Milk bar that'll have to pass for lunch. Or dinner. I sit cross-legged at the foot of the bed, barefoot, my reflection in the bureau mirror staring back at me while I eat. I look like hammered shit, as my grandfather would have said. As my dad would have said. I use my fingers to comb at my hair, as if it matters. The woman in the mirror could easily be fifty, instead of thirty-five. That look in her eyes, I've seen it in photographs of veterans from Afghanistan and Iraq.

"*Porqué habla demasiado algunas personas,*" says the woman in the parking lot.

"*Yo no sé. Nunca habló conmigo,*" the man replies.

The rumpled woman in the mirror crumples the Tiger's Milk wrapper and tosses it at the wastebasket. And misses. I reach into the knapsack again and pull out my iPad. I try hard to focus, to shut out the voices from the other side of the motel door *and* my memories of everything that happened in camp *and* the siren-song lure of Jackson's Venus, still sitting on the table, but I might as well be trying to put toothpaste back into the tube.

Why haven't I stuck the fucking thing back in the cardboard box?

I hear that noise from the bathroom again and close my eyes. The noise seems more urgent, more persistent, than before, as if it's getting fed up with me ignoring it. But fuck it. Fuck the bullshit echoes in my head. I close my eyes, and there we are, on the bright day after Charlie found his Venus, his Madonna of the Late Cretaceous epicontinental seas, Blessed Virgin Mother of the Western Interior Basin, the three of us walking through the tall grass back to the ten foot by ten foot hole we've dug in the chalk. We've exposed the skull and forelimbs and most of the vertebral column of an exquisitely preserved little mosasaur, only the second known specimen of *Selmasaurus kiernanae*. With luck, the back flippers are in there somewhere, and we just haven't found them yet. Coupled with the *Pteranodon* skull we found the week before, it'll have been a very profitable trip. I watch where I put my feet, keeping an eye out for prairie rattlers. Behind me and to my right, Charlie Jackson is chattering like it's any other day in the field, telling a dirty joke about jackalopes. There seems to be no end to his reserve of jackalope jokes. Joanna is walking a little ways in front of us, apart from us;

---

she hasn't said a word since we left camp. There's a Marsh pick in her left hand, swinging like a pendulum. Me, I want to talk about the dream I had the night before. But I know that's the very last thing I'll ever do.

The afternoon air smells like rain and ozone, though there's not a cloud visible anywhere in the wide, wide west Kansas sky.

The day is long and hot, and we move a few hundred pounds of overburden, but we don't find the hindlimbs of the mosasaur, just a few oyster shells and fish bones. We work mostly in silence, and several times I catch Joanna Fielding staring off towards the spot where Charlie found the thing that's now sitting on the table in my motel room. She looks lost and afraid.

I open my eyes.

"*A continuación, gire no pálido, caracol amada,*
"*Pero venir y unirse a la danza.*"

I almost go to the window and push the drapes aside to get a look at the man and woman in the parking lot. I consider opening the door and asking her why she's begun quoting Lewis Carroll. Why in creation would she be doing that in a motel parking lot, during the heat of the day? I don't go to the window, and I don't open the door; I only *almost* do.

That last afternoon in the field, I only *almost* asked Joanna Fielding what she was thinking, gazing out across the gullies. Her eyes were near to the same shade as the blue-white sky, and, I thought, just as desolate. The woman watching me from the mirror has eyes like that, even though her eyes are green.

I do a Google search and turn up an article in the archives of the *Wrangell Sentinel,* dated June 17, 1937, a brief account of the foundering of the dredger *Sweet Leilani* at the mouth of Cross Sound off Chichagof Island. One week earlier, it had been working some two hundred and fifty miles southeast, off Prince of Wales Island, clearing a channel for a ferry. The ship went down with all hands onboard, no survivors. The weather was good, and the ship sent no distress signal. Very little wreckage was recovered.

The label said it had come from marine dredgings off the coast of Prince of Wales Island. It turned up in 1937, during a canal expansion for a ferry. That's what Joanna told us, and all I have to do is add two and fucking two.

In the same paper, one week and a day later, there's the captain's obituary. *Captain Sternberg was an avid collector of aboriginal artifacts, and his widow will be donating his collection to the Lowie Museum in Berkeley, Calif.* I check Wikipedia and see that in 1991 the Lowie Museum of Anthropology was rechristened the Phoebe A. Hearst Museum of Anthropology.

"Hay otra orilla, ya sabes,
"Tras el otro lado."

"Shut up," I whisper. "Please, just shut the hell up. I don't need to hear this."

Outside, the man and woman laugh, one laugh high and shrill, the other low and rumbling like distant thunder, a laugh pregnant with threat. The insistent noises coming from the bathroom, almost constant now, are nothing at all like laughter. They're the same noises I heard the night that Joanna Fielding died, sounds that are wet and hollow and, if sound can be said to be cold, then this sound is very, very cold, like sound rising up from below the weight of a salty mountain of deep-sea water.

"She's sick," Charlie Jackson says. Charlie Jackson *said*. Sitting here, time is coming apart all around me, raveling. No, that's not quite right. Time has been coming apart around me for days, but I'm only now becoming acutely aware of my, what – temporal dissociation? Temporal dysphoria? There's no precedent, I don't think, and so there's no proper diagnosis. But I suspect, maybe, the crew of the *Sweet Leilani* might have felt something like this, in the hours before the ship sank in the frigid depths of Cross Sound. I have to assume that Joanna and Charlie felt it, too. I wonder about the employees at the Hearst Museum, and if visitors who've peered into the case containing the Prince of Wales Island artifact have felt it.

"Madre Hydra," says the woman in the parking lot. *"Limosna para Madre Hydra. Limosna para el abismo."*

Alms for Mother Hydra.
Alms for the abyss.

"There was a photograph," says (said) Joanna Fielding, "displayed there with the thing the dredger found. A very similar fetish – if that's what those things were – from a dig in Tell Mardikh, in Syria. It was dated to 2700 BC. The two pieces, I swear they could have been carved by the same hand, they were that similar."

"And what I found, you're saying it looks like –" Charlie began (begins).

"Only almost," says (said) Joanna, interrupting him, emphatic. "Only almost."

"It's just a goddamn coprolite," Charlie told (tells) her. "You'll see."

I need to piss, but that means opening the bathroom door. I consider pissing in the wastebasket. Really, what possible goddamn difference does it make. I'm a murderer now, and pissing in the wastebasket of a Motel 6 in Columbia, Missouri must certainly constitute an inconsequential transgression. It's even lined with a plastic bag. I promise my aim will be better than when I tossed the Tiger's Milk wrapper.

"She needs a hospital," Charlie says. "Right? We need to get her to a hospital." That was about five hours before he was also bedridden, too weak to leave his tent.

"It's not a disease," he says. "I don't think it's a disease, and I don't think it's a spider bite or anything like that."

I relieve myself in the wastebasket. I wipe with a handful of napkins I found beside the coffeemaker.

"I had the dream again," says Charlie Jackson.

"Yeah, well, keep it to yourself, please," I reply. I'm trying to make the day's entry in the field logbook. I've written nothing about what Charlie found, and I won't.

"She's sick," he says. "Her eyes, Jesus, her eyes are all wrong."

That was the night I stopped him from smashing the artifact with a crack hammer. I still can't say why I didn't let him do it.

After I piss, after I've pulled my jeans up and fastened them and poured myself another plastic cupful of bourbon, I go to the table by the window. I sit and pick up the object, the artifact, the thing, *it*. At once, there's the thrumming sensation pulsing up my arm and the sound of the sea in my ears. The thing from the chalk bears a passing resemblance to the famous Venus of Willendorf, but much rounder, less pear-shaped. The breasts, if those are meant to be breasts, are gigantic, and I imagine I can make out the pubic area, *le mont de Vénus*. The faceless head is absurdly small, and ringed about with what might be plaited rows of hair, but which put me much more in mind of the suckered arms of an octopus or squid. And arranged around the ludicrously swollen belly are a dozen or so dimples that, to me, look all the world like bulging eyes. This afternoon, afternoon now become almost evening, it seems heavier in my hand that ever it has before.

On the other side of the door, out on that sunbaked plain of asphalt and automobiles, the woman all but chants:

Sin usted, ¿no es cierto, ¿verdad,
¿No le gustaría, ¿no unirse a la danza?
Sin usted, ¿no es cierto, ¿verdad,
¿No le gustaría, ¿no unirse a la danza?
And this time, I'm the one who laughs.
Will you, won't you...?

I set the thing back down on the table, then glance towards my pack. My gun's in there, the .22 Colt my father left me. It would be so easy to put an end to this, or, more precisely, to remove myself from the unfolding equation. I've begun to believe something has been set in motion here that will long survive me, just as it has survived Charlie and Joanna. A man dug a lump of stone out of the earth. A butterfly flapped its wings. And now there is a whirlwind, long forestalled, to be reaped. The thought of squeezing that trigger almost brings me solace, but I haven't the courage, and I can't allow myself to pretend that I'll find it. I look back at the carving – I will say that, *carving,* because I also will not allow myself to pretend that it's only a coprolite or a concretion or any other common and unremarkable geologic phenomenon. It is precisely what it appears to be. It is a carving, sculpted by a sentient being, more than seventy million years before the evolution of man. Whatever is to come, I won't hide in brittle denial. I am still a scientist, even now.

"Maybe something was sprayed on the fields," says Charlie. "A pesticide that we're having a bad reaction to, I don't know. Something poisonous, maybe even hallucinogenic. Something we've been breathing for days that's gotten into our water and our food, messing about with our heads." And he talks (talked) about crop dusting, spray drift, volatilization drift, chlorinated hydrocarbon pesticides dissolving in and being stored in fatty tissue, DDT, damage to the nervous system by organophosphate insecticides. "Did you know," said Charlie, "that upwards of ninety-five percent of all applied pesticides actually fucking miss their intended target and instead end up falling on people, wildlife, lakes and rivers, the soil? Dow and Monsanto try to cover all that shit up, but people know. It's all over the internet. And Jesus, don't get me started in on what it's doing to the bees."

"You're beginning to sound like some nut from that Art Bell radio show," I told (tell) him.

"Fuck you," he said (says).

The phone in my room starts ringing; I'm not about to answer it. Who would possibly be calling me. No one knows I'm here. The phone rings twenty times, and then there's five minutes or so of silence before my cell phone begins to buzz. I let it.

"You're dreaming, too," said Charlie, lying there in his sleeping bag, dying fast and delirious. "You won't tell the truth, but I know you're dreaming the same dream as me and Jo. I've seen you down there, walking the ruins, wandering hallways in the mansions of Poseidon."

"Shhhh. Be quiet. Don't talk."

He was running a fever of 105°F. He'd shat himself, and there was red blood and mucus in his stool.

"You need to rest," I said, and then I managed to get a few swallows of Gatorade in him, but he threw it all right back up again.

"It doesn't make you sane," he said. "It doesn't make you brave, or better than us, lying like you're doing."

And then he told me to get rid of the artifact, the take it back where he'd found it, to do what Joanna had asked him to do two days earlier.

Two days, or three. I'm no longer sure how long it has been.

Finally, I left him in his tent and sat watching a storm pass by ten or twenty miles south of the camp, towering thunderheads, anvils of water vapor and flickering electric fingers. Their undersides were black as the boils on Charlie and Joanna's bodies. I could taste the rain, but I knew it would come nowhere near us. I thought, *We've been quarantined by all that is clean and natural. We're being shunned.* There were no calls of nocturnal birds that night, no lonely coyote songs; I didn't even hear crickets and katydids. *We've been set apart, and the prairie and the sky are holding their breath.*

"*Se puede realmente no tienen idea de*
Qué maravilla será
Cuando nos llevan y nos tiran,
Con las langostas, en el mar!"

"It was my *favorite* book when I was a little girl," says (said) Joanna, burning alive in her own fever. "I memorized passages and would recite them to my parents and my brother, who were almost always patient and would listen. I memorized all of 'Jabberwocky,' 'The Lobster Quadrille,' and 'The Walrus and the Carpenter.' I learned them in English, French, Latin, and Spanish." And she recited:

"*The sea was wet as wet could be,*
The sands were dry as dry.
You could not see a cloud, because…"

Joanna stops (stopped, has not yet begun to speak), mid verse, and she said (says, will say) to me, raving, "She loves *you* most of all. Lucky girl, lucky, lucky girl. I am all green with envy. You'll live to see the rising of the waters, the ninth wave, gathering half the deep, roaring, and all the waves will be in a flame. You'll see the clock turned back, deep timewards, lucky, lucky girl. *Tiefer, tiefer. Irgendwo in der tiefer.* You'll see Laramidia and Appalachia restored to bracket serpent-haunted tides, the night of first ages restored, monstrous and free, and Mother Hydra will take your hand and lead you through the welcoming, unlit fathoms."

I wanted to slap her. I wanted to hold my hand over her mouth and force the lunatic's words back down her throat. But, instead, imagining it mercy, I let her rant until she passed out again. Then I sat with the sleeper. The boils on her forehead and cheeks that had at first looked so much like inguinal buboes and had made me fearing it was bubonic plague, her blood – and Charlie's, too – swarming with a devouring bacterial lode, *Yersinia pestis* taking them apart. And so it might not have been the thing from the chalk at all, but only flea bites, fleas from prairie dogs and pocket gophers. I had no idea why or how I'd been spared, only *lucky, lucky girl.*

The tent reeked of vomit and shit, saltwater and dead fish.

"She'll tear a hole in the sky," Joanna said, an hour later. "You'll see," and then a boil on her left hand had burst, skin splitting like overripe fruit, and an eye as black as the bottommost bottom of the sea had opened and turned its gaze towards me.

Beyond the door to my hotel room, as a bloated, bloody Missouri sun falls down towards the simmering horizon, I hear dancing feet, happy dancers cavorting on the pavement to greet the coming night. The man and woman are no longer alone out there.

Sin usted, ¿no es cierto, ¿verdad,
¿No le gustaría, ¿no unirse a la danza?

Beyond the closed door to the bathroom, something rolls ponderously about and splashes and sings in the ancient voices of whales of species extinct twenty million years. Something unnamable has been born, and I'm afraid I was, unconsciously, its midwife. It fed from Joanna Fielding's dreams and fever, and it fed from Charlie Jackson, and I carried it, fetal, along a darkened interstate, spiriting it away from its cradle, its prison, and out into a not-entirely unsuspecting world. I know now there are those who have been waiting for – this will sound like a line from a shitty horror film – waiting for a sign. They're out there in the dusk, calling me to dance the world's end tarantella.

I put the barrel of the .22 to what was left of Joanna's face, and she smiled, showing me a mouthful of crystalline barracuda teeth. I squeezed the trigger once, twice, three times, the shot echoing across the stillness of the prairie. And then I did the same with Jackson. I cannot even know if I were merciful. I acted out of horror as much as anything, seeing human beings so reduced, or merely so altered. I could not have left them there, unable to die despite my earlier certainties that their deaths were imminent. So I squeezed the trigger, again and again, and I left them lying where I shot them, and I called it murder. I hadn't the energy or the presence of mind to bury the corpses, though, in retrospect, I can hardly bear the thought that coyotes and buzzards and maggots are feeding on that corrupted flesh, spreading the contagion. I know in my heart and my guts and in the recesses of my lizard hindbrain that it *is* a contagion – organic, mnemonic, visual, tactile, older even than the strata of blue-grey shale and yellow chalky limestone that preserved its ceramic Venus of Gove County vector, something infinitely communicable that has slept since the stone that entombed the beautiful petrified skeletons of our *Selmasaurus* and *Pteranodon* was only carbonaceous silt and clayey slime.

Outside, a ring of lights around the parking lot has awakened, bathing an unseen bacchanal in soulless white sodium-halide glare. The sun has gone down in the west, and the moon's hungry eye has come to keep watch.

Extraña es la noche en la que se alzan las estrellas negras.
Y extrañas son las lunas que giran en los cielos.
Pero más extraña todavía es la
Perdida Carcosa.

What, I wonder, is happening at the Hearst Museum?

And wherever that artifact from Syria has been kept all these years, are there also dancers gathering there?

Not seven requisite seals for an apocalypse, but only three for *this* Second Coming. Though, of course, there may well have been another four somewhere, or even another hundred, discovered down millennia and never brought to the attention of scholars and priests, science or newspapers. I screw the cap off the Jack Daniel's bottle and refill my cup with the last of the bourbon; when I swallow, it's a comforting fire in my chest. I drink and consider making a run to the liquor store just down the street, but I have a feeling the revelers would never let me pass. I am, after all, their fatted calf, their sacrificial goat, caged here and awaiting the appointed moment when angel trumpets sound, and the lamb with seven horns and seven eyes is called from her motel room and released to open the book, *her* book. I have brought them the final piece in a puzzle. The whirlwind in the thorn tree. Alpha and Omega. Four white horses breaking at the crest of a tsunami reaching out to the spaces between galaxies.

Ah, God, how I wanted to make sense here at the end. How I wanted linear narrative and compositional coherence, here at the end. The end which I understand is truly only the *beginning of the beginning,* and *I* began these pages with my mind so much more intact, didn't I? But the recollections of camp, the sounds leaking from behind the two closed doors that flank me, the dreams and alcohol, the thing squatting on the table, all have conspired to undo the stingy scraps that remained of my sanity.

Pero no quiso unirse a la danza.
Por lo tanto, no lo haría, no podría, no lo haría,
No podría, no unirse a la danza.
¿No, no podría, no lo haría,
No podría, no podría participar en el baile.

The television has gone to static. White noise. Not even a test pattern. I only almost switch it off.

Someone knocks on the door to my room, rapping impatient knuckles, and they whisper promises that I have nothing to fear from them, nothing whatsoever. That never again will I need to be afraid. *Please come out and play. Please come out and dance.* But he or she – I cannot tell which, and it certainly doesn't matter – didn't sit vigil while Joanna and Charlie were gnawed and twisted and refashioned. They didn't see the lightning tongues licking at the tall, waving grass or feel the Kansas prairie recoiling from their footsteps. They didn't wait alone by the glow of a Coleman lantern, wrapped in the arms of the quietest, stillest night in human history.

Before it's over, I want to get this down:

The day before Jackson found his demon, we worked happily, so carefully brushing and digging away sediment from permineralized bone, with whisk brooms and trowels, dental picks and hawkbill linoleum knives, and Joanna smiled and gazed up at the blistering summer sun. It painted her brown cheeks and chestnut hair and caught in the facets of her sky-blue eyes. And she said, "We're lucky, you know? We're the luckiest people on earth, kneeling here at the bottom of the sea. When I think about it, *really* think about it, that's where I am in this moment, because once upon a time, a hundred, two hundred meters of inland sea were stacked up overhead, pressing down."

Jackson called her a hopeless romantic.

"It's my church," she replied. "So, I kneel."

There.

On the table, the carving has begun to ooze what looks like transmission fluid and smells like puke.

A crowd has gathered out there, singing, cavorting, waltzing, fucking, bleeding, calling down that hungry moon, and now the soft body of something without a spine or even any definite form – I know this, for I saw it in the dreams I refused to share with Charlie Jackson – is slamming itself against the bathroom door. Because I might be a reluctant messiah, but it's on beyond eager to break free and join the dance.

Will you, won't you, will you,
Won't you, won't you join the dance?
Will you, won't you, will you,
Won't you, won't you join the dance?

I finish my drink and drop the cup to the scabby beige carpet, and then I go to open the bathroom door.

With thanks to Yolanda Espiñeira Martínez.

FAR FROM ANY SHORE

A fairly straightforward nod to both Robert W. Chambers and H.P. Lovecraft. Someday, I may screw up my courage and explain the whole *"Selmasaurus kiernanae"* thing (see also "Interstate Love Song [Murder Ballad No. 8]," *Black Helicopters,* and the cover of *Beneath an Oil-Dark Sea: The Best of Caitlín R. Kiernan Volume Two*). Maybe. Or maybe it can be a mystery for the ages. This story was written in June and July of 2014.

The Cats of River Street
(1925)

1.

Essie Babson lies awake, listening to the soft, soft murmur of the Manuxet flowing by on its way down to the harbor and the sea beyond. Unable to find sleep, or unable to be found *by* sleep, she listens to the voice of the river and thinks about the long trip the waters have made, all the way from the confluence of the Pemigewasset and the Winnipesaukee, and before that, the headwaters at Franconia Notch and faraway Profile Lake in the White Mountains of New Hampshire. The waters have traveled hundreds of miles just to keep her company in the stillness of this too-warm last night of July. Or so she briefly chooses to pretend. Of course, the waters of the river, like all the rest of the wide world, neither know nor care about this sleepless spinster woman, but it's a pretty thought, all the same, and she holds tightly to it.

Some insomniacs count sheep; Essie traces the courses of rivers.

"You're still awake?" asks her sister, Emiline.

"I thought you were asleep," Essie sighs and turns over onto her right side, rolling over to face Emiline.

"No, no, it's too hot to sleep," Emiline replies. "I'm so tired, but it's really much too hot. I'm sweating on my sheets. They're soaked right through with sweat."

"Me, too," says Essie. "Mine, too."

There's only a single window in the second-story bedroom, and both storm shutters are open and the sash is raised. But the night is so still there's no breeze to bring relief, to stir the stagnant air trapped inside the room with the two women.

"Think about the river," Essie tells her sister. "Shut your eyes and think about the river and how cool it must be, out there in the night. Think about the harbor and the bay."

"No, I won't do that," Emiline says. "You know I won't do that. Why would you even suggest such a thing, when you know I won't."

Essie shuts her eyes. The room smells of perspiration and dust, talcum powder, tea rose perfume, and the potpourri they order from a shop in Boston. The latter sits in a bowl on the chifforobe: a salmagundi of allspice, marjoram leaves, rose hips, lavender, juniper and cinnamon bark, with a little mugwort thrown in to help keep the moths at bay. Emiline insists on having a bowl of the potpourri in every room in the high old house on River Street. She dislikes the smell of the Manuxet and the fishy, low-tide smells of the bay, whenever the wind blows from the east, and also the muddy odor of the salt-marshes, whenever the wind blows from the west or south or north. Essie has never minded these smells, and sometimes they even comfort her, the way the sound of the river sometimes comforts her. But she also rarely minds the scent of the potpourri. Tonight, though, the potpourri is cloying and unwelcome, and it almost seems as if it could smother her, as if it means to seep up her nostrils and drown her.

Emiline is deathly afraid of drowning, which, of course, is why it was foolishness to suggest that thinking on the river might help her to sleep.

Essie rolls onto her back once more, and the box springs squeak like a bucket of angry mice.

"I'm going to buy a new mattress," she says.

And, again, Emiline says, "It's much too hot to sleep." Then she adds, "It's very silly, lying here, not sleeping, when there's work to be done."

"Yes, in the autumn, I think I will definitely buy a new mattress."

"There's really nothing wrong with the mattress you have," says Emiline.

"You don't know," Essie replies. "You don't have to sleep on it. Sometimes I think there are stones sewn up inside it."

"I should get up," whispers Emiline, and Essie isn't sure if her sister is speaking to her or speaking to herself. "I could get some baking done. A pie, some biscuits. It'll be too hot to bake after sunrise."

"Em, it's too hot to bake now. Try to sleep."

Then the door creaks open, just enough to admit their striped ginger tom Horace into the bedroom, and Essie listens to the not-quite inaudible padding of velvet paws against the white-pine floorboards. Horace reaches the space between the women's beds, and he pauses there a moment, deciding which sister he's in the mood to curl up with. The moonlight coming in through the open window is bright, and Essie can plainly see the cat, sitting back on its haunches, watching her.

"Well, where have you been?" she asks the ginger tom. "Making certain we're safe from marauding rodents?"

The cat glances her way, then turns its head towards Emiline.

Emiline calls Horace their "tough old gentleman." His ears are tattered, and there are ugly scars crisscrossing his broad nose and marring his flanks and shoulders, souvenirs of the battles he's won and lost. The sisters have had him for almost seventeen years now, since he was a tiny kitten, since they were both still young women. They found him one afternoon in the alley out back of the Gilman House, hiding behind an empty produce crate, and Emiline named him Horace, after Horace Greeley. It seemed an odd choice to Essie, but she's never asked her sister to explain herself. It isn't a bad name for a cat, and the kitten seemed to grow into it.

"Well, make up your mind," Essie says. "Don't take all night."

"Don't rush him," Emiline tells her. "What's the hurry. It's not as if we're going anywhere."

Downstairs, the grandfather clock in the front parlor chimes midnight.

And then Horace chooses Emiline. He leaps – a little stiffly – up onto her bed and, after sniffing about the quilt and sheets for a bit, lies down near her knees. Essie feels slightly disappointed, but then the cat has always preferred her sister. She sighs and stares up at the fine cracks in the ceiling plaster, concentrating once again on the soft, wet sound of the Manuxet flowing between River and Paine streets. Across from her, Horace purrs himself and Emiline to sleep. After another hour or so, Essie also drifts off to sleep, and she dreams of tall ships and the sea.

2.

The brass bell hung over the shop door jingles, and Bertrand Cowlishaw – proprietor of River Street Grocery and Dry Goods – looks up from his newspaper just long enough to note that it's the elder Miss Babson who's come in. He nods to the woman as she eases the door shut behind her. Though the shades are drawn against the noonday heat, and despite the slowly spinning electric ceiling fan, it's stifling inside the dusty, dimly-lit shop.

"And how are you today, Miss Babson," he says, then turns his attention back to the front page of a two-week old edition of the *Gloucester Daily Times*. Bertrand remembers when it wasn't so hard to get newspapers from Gloucester and Newburyport and even from as far away as Boston in a timely fashion. He remembers when the offices of the *Innsmouth Courier* were still in business, and also he remembers when it quietly folded amid rumors of threats from elders of the Esoteric Order, of which it had frequently been openly critical.

"A bit out of sorts, Bert," she replies. "Emiline and me, we're having trouble sleeping again. It's the heat, I suppose. You'd think it would rain, wouldn't you? I can't recall such a dry summer." And then she picks up a can of peaches in heavy syrup and stares at the label a moment before setting it back on the shelf.

"Hot as Hades," Bertrand agrees, "and dry as a bone, to boot. You got a list there, Miss Babson?"

She tells him yes, she certainly does, and takes her neatly-penned grocery list from a pocket of her gingham dress. It's written on the back of a letter from a cousin who moved away to Gary, Indiana several years ago. Essie goes to the counter, stepping around a barrel of apples piled so high it's a marvel they haven't spilled out across the floor, and she gives the envelope to Bertrand.

"I confess, we haven't had much of an appetite," she tells the grocer. "And neither of us wants to cook, the house being as terribly hot as it is."

While Bertrand examines the list, Essie steals a glance at his newspaper, reading it upside down. The headline declares SCOPES FOUND GUILTY OF TEACHING EVOLUTION, and there's a photograph of William Jennings Bryan, smug and smiling for the press. Farther down the page, there's an article on a coal strike in West Virginia and another on the great-grandnephew of Napoleon Bonaparte. Essie Babson tends to avoid news of the world outside of Innsmouth, as it never seems to be anything but unpleasant. In all her forty years, she's not traveled farther from home than Ipswich and Hamilton, neither more than six miles away, as the crow flies.

"Let's see," says Bertrand, as he gathers the items from her shopping list and places them in a cardboard box. "Condensed milk, icing sugar, one can of lime juice, baking powder, raspberry jam, a dozen eggs, a can of lima beans. We do have some nice fresh blueberries, as it happens, if you and –"

"No, no," she tells him. "Just what's on the list, please."

"Very well, Miss Babson. Just thought I'd mention the blueberries. They're quite nice, for baking and canning."

"It's really much too hot for either."

"Can't argue with you there."

"You'd think," she says, glancing again at the July 22nd *Gloucester Daily Times,* "people would want to be properly educated, in this day and age. Even in Tennessee, you'd think people wouldn't put up such a ridiculous fuss over a man just trying to teach his students science."

"Folks can be peculiar," he says, reaching for a box of elbow macaroni. "And when it comes down to religion, people get pigheaded and don't seem to mind how ignorant they might look to the rest of the world. Five cans of sardines, yes?"

"Yes, five cans. Emiline and I enjoy them for our luncheon. And soda crackers, please. Mother and Father, they were Presbyterians, you know. But they prided themselves on being enlightened people."

"Folks can be very peculiar," he says again, adding an orange tin of Y & S licorice wafers to the cardboard box. "And we are talking about Tennessee, after all."

"Still," says Essie Babson.

Just then, Bertrand Cowlishaw's fat calico cat – whose name is Terrapin – leaps from the shadows onto the counter, landing silently next to the cash register. Terrapin isn't as old as Horace, but she isn't a youngster, either. Bertrand has been known to boast that she's the best mouser in all of Essex County. Whether or not that was strictly true, there's no denying she's a fine cat.

"And what about you, Turtle," says Essie Babson. "Has the weather got you out of sorts, as well?" She always calls the cat Turtle, because she can never remember its name is actually Terrapin.

The cat crosses the counter to Essie, walking over Bertrand's paper and the smug newsprint portrait of William Jennings Bryan. Terrapin purrs loudly and gently butts Essie in the arm with its head.

"Well, then I'm glad to see you, too."

"Molasses? I don't see it on the list, but –"

"Oh, yes please. I must have forgotten to write it down."

Essie scratches behind Terrapin's ears, and the cat purrs even louder. Then, apparently tired of the woman's affection, she retreats to the register and begins washing her front paws.

"Horace," says Essie, "has been acting a little odd."

"Maybe it's the full moon coming on," replies Bertrand. "The Hay Moon's tonight. The tide'll be high."

"Maybe."

"Animals, you know, they're more sensitive to the moon and the tides and whatnot than we are."

"Maybe," Essie says again, watching the cat as it fastidiously grooms itself.

"Well, I'm pretty sure I have everything you needed. If you're absolutely certain I can't interest you in a pint or two of these blueberries."

"No, that's all, thank you."

Bertrand Cowlishaw brings the box to the counter, and Essie checks it over, checking it against her list to be certain nothing's been overlooked. The cat meows at Bertrand, and he strokes its back and waits patiently until Essie is satisfied.

"I'll have Matthew bring these around to you just as soon as he gets back," the grocer tells her. "He had a delivery over on Lafayette, but he shouldn't be long."

Matthew Cowlishaw is Bertrand's only son. Next year, he goes away to college in Arkham to study mathematics, astronomy, and physics, which has always been the boy's dream, and Bertrand has reluctantly given up his own dream that Matthew would one day take over the store when his father retired. His son is much too bright, Bertrand knows, to spend his life selling groceries in a withering North Shore seaport.

"When it's cooler," Essie Babson says, "I'll bake some sugar cookies and bring some around to you. I will, or I'll have Emiline do it. She needs to get out more often. But it's much too hot to bake in this heat. It surely won't last much longer."

"One can only hope," replies Bertrand. He licks the tip of his pencil, tallies up her bill, and writes it down in his ledger book. He rarely ever uses the fancy new nickel-plated machine he bought last year from the National Cash Register Company in Dayton, Ohio. It's noisy, and the keys make his fingers ache.

Essie gives Terrapin a parting scratch beneath the chin, and the cat shuts its eyes and looks as content as any cat ever has.

"You take care," says Bertrand Cowlishaw.

"Just hope we get a break in this weather," she says, then leaves the shop, and the brass bell jingles as the door opens and swings shut behind her. Bertrand goes back to his newspaper, and Terrapin, having gotten her fill of humans for the time being, leaps off the counter to prowl among the aisles and barrels and bushel baskets.

3.

Frank Buckles sits in his rocking chair on the front porch of his narrow yellow house on River Street, sweating and smoking hand-rolled cigarettes and drinking the bootlegged Canadian whiskey he buys down on the docks near the jetty. He stares at the green-black river flowing between the grey granite-and-mortar quay walls built half a century ago to contain it and keep the water flowing straight down to the harbor, a bulwark against spring floods. The river glistens brightly beneath the summer sun. He dislikes the river and often thinks of selling the house his grandfather built and getting a place set farther back from the Manuxet. Or, better yet, moving away from Innsmouth altogether, maybe all the way up to Portland or Bangor. Sometimes, he thinks he wouldn't stop until he was safely in the Maritimes, where no one had ever heard of Innsmouth or Obed Marsh or the Esoteric fucking Order of Dagon. But he isn't going anywhere, because he lacks the resolve, and what few tenuous roots he has, they're here, in this rotting town the outside world has done an admirable job of forgetting.

Lucky them, thinks Frank Buckles, as he shakes out a fresh line of Prince Albert, then licks the paper and twists it closed. He lights the cigarette with a kitchen match struck on the side of his chair, and for a few merciful seconds the smell of sulfur masks the musky stink of the river. It isn't so bad up above the falls, back in the marshes towards Choate and Corn and Dilly islands, where the waters are broad and still. When he was young, he and his brother Joe would often spend their days in those marshes, digging for quahogs and fishing for white perch, steelhead, and shad. Back there, away from the sewers that spill into the Manuxet below the falls, it was easy to pretend Innsmouth was only a bad dream.

But then in April of '18, both he and his brother were drafted, and they were sent off to the French trenches to fight the Huns. Joe died less than five months later in the Meuse-Argonne Offensive, blown limb from limb by a mortar round. The very next week, at the Battle of Blanc Mont Ridge, Frank lost his left foot and his right eye, and they shipped what was left of him back home to Massachusetts. Joe's remains were buried in Lorraine, in the American cemetery at Romagne-sous-Montfaucon, in a grave that

Frank has never seen and never expects to see. That his brother was killed and he himself was mangled only weeks before the end of the war to end all wars is a horrible irony that isn't lost on Frank. And now, seven years have gone by, and both his mother and father have passed, and Frank spends his days sitting on the porch, drinking himself numb, watching the filthy river roll by. He spends his nights tossing and turning, lying awake or dreaming of murdered men tangled in barbed wire and of skies burning red as blood and roses. Sometimes, he sits with a shotgun pressed to his forehead or his mouth around the muzzle, but he hasn't got that much courage left anywhere in him. He wonders if there would be time to smell the cordite before his soul winked out, if he would taste it, how much pain there would be in the split second before his brains were sprayed across the wall. He has a stingy inheritance that might or might not be enough to see him through however many years he's left to suffer, and he has the narrow yellow house on River Street. Sometimes, he sobers up enough to do odd jobs about town.

Frank exhales a steel-grey cloud of smoke, and the breeze off the river immediately picks it apart. The breeze smells oily, of dead fish and human waste; it smells of rot.

This is Hell, he thinks. *I'm alive, and this is Hell.* It's an old thought, worn smooth as the cobbles along the breakwater.

"Is it better to be a living coward,
Or thrice a hero dead?"
"It's better to go to sleep, my lad,"
The Colour Sergeant said.

One of the three tortoiseshell kittens – two female, one male – that have recently taken up residence beneath his porch scrambles clumsily up the steps and mews at him. It can't be more than a couple or three months old. He has no idea where the kittens came from, whether they were abandoned by their mother, or if the mother were killed. She might have gotten a belly full of poison left out for the rats. She might have perished under the wheels of an automobile. It could have been a hungry dog, or she might have run afoul of the tribes of half-feral boys that roam the streets and alleys and the wharves, happy for any opportunity to do mischief or cruelty that comes their way. It might simply have been her time. But it hardly matters. Now, the kittens live beneath the porch of his narrow yellow house.

The first is followed by a second, and then the third, the brother, comes scrambling up. The trio is thin and crawling with fleas. The little tom has already lost an eye to some infection or parasite. To Frank, that makes him a sort of comrade in the great and barbarous shitstorm of the world. Frank has been told that a male tortoiseshell is a rare thing.

"What's it you three want, eh?" he asks them, and they loudly mewl in tandem. "That so?" he replies. "Well, people in Hell want ice water, or so I've heard."

One of the tortoiseshell girls parks herself between his boots, and she begins playing with the tattered laces. When the kittens first showed up, he seriously considered herding them all into an empty burlap potato sack from the pantry, putting a few stones in there to keep them company and weight it down, then dropping the sack into the river. It's what his father would have done with the strays. But the thought passed almost as soon as it had come. Frank Buckles knows he's a sorry son of a bitch, but he's not so heartless that he'd send anything to its death in those foul waters.

He scratches at the stubble on the chin he hasn't bothered to shave in days and stares down at the kitten. Ash falls from his cigarette, but it misses the cat.

"Yeah, okay," he says. "How about you moochers just give me a god-damn minute." Then he gets up and goes inside the dark house. The kittens all line up at the screen door, waiting and watching for Frank's return. After only five minutes or so he comes back with a third of a tin of Holly-brand canned salmon and a chipped china saucer. He empties what's left into the dish and gives it to the hungry kittens. They fall upon it with as much ferocity as any cat has ever shown a fish, living or dead. In only a few moments the saucer is licked clean.

"Greedy little shits," Frank mutters, tossing the empty tin at the Manuxet before sitting back down in the rocker. The chair was built by his paternal grandfather, as a gift to his grandmother, before he signed up with the 8th Massachusetts Volunteer Militia, left his pregnant wife behind, and marched off to die at the hands of a pro-succession mob in Baltimore, on the 19th day of April 1861. His grandfather made many chairs and cabinets and tables, and sometimes Frank Buckle wonders where they've all gone, how many have survived the sixty-four years since the man's untimely death.

The kittens, their hunger sated for the time being, have all disappeared back beneath the porch, to the cool shadows below.

"Yeah," Frank mutters, "beat it. The lot of you. Stuff your faces and leave me here holding an empty can. Lotta gratitude that is, you bums."

Lithe and supple lads they were
Marching merrily away –
Was it only yesterday?

Frank Buckle, he sips his illegal whiskey, and he rocks in his grandmother's chair, and he watches the demon sun shining bright as diamonds off the greasy river. He reminds himself that there's always the shotgun he keeps beside his bed, and he tries not to think about where that burning river leads.

4.

She was only fourteen years of age when Annie Phelps took a keen interest in the things that wash up along the sands and shingle beaches of Innsmouth Harbor, the breakwater, and the marshy shorelines to the north and south of the port. The strandings and junk, the flotsam and jetsam of commerce and mishap, the remains of dead and dying creatures, fronds and branches of the kelp and algae forests that grow below the waves. As a child, her parents didn't exactly encourage her boyish fascinations, but neither did they exactly discourage them. When she was eighteen, she would have gone away to study natural history and anatomy and chemistry at a university in Arkham, maybe, or Boston, or even Providence. But there wasn't the money for her tuition. So, she stayed at home, instead, and cared for her ailing mother and father.

Annie didn't marry, preferring always the company of women to that of men. There is talk that she enjoys much more than their platonic company. However, in a shadowed and ill-starred place like Innsmouth, there are always far darker rumors than whispers of Sapphic passion to provide the grist for clothesline gossips. She was twenty-eight years of age when the influenza of '18 claimed Charles and Beulah Phelps, and afterwards she sold their listing Georgian house on Hancock Street and took up residence in three adjoining rooms in Hephzibah Peabody's boarding house on River Street. Her study and bedroom both have excellent views of the gurgling Manuxet.

Annie Phelps makes a modest living as a seamstress and a typist, keeping back most of the income from the sale of the house on Hancock for that proverbial rainy day. But her passion has remained for those treasures she finds on the shore, and hardly three days pass that she doesn't find time to make her way down to the fish markets or past the waterfront, where few women dare to venture alone, to see what the boats or the tides or a fortuitous storm have hauled in to arouse her curiosity. Most of the fishermen and fishmongers, the sailors, boatwrights, deckhands, and dockworkers, know her by sight and let her be.

This day, this sweltering late Monday afternoon in July, she sits at her father's old roll-top desk, in her study, a small room lined with shelves loaded down with books and jars of biological specimens she's pickled in solutions of formaldehyde. There are squid and sea cucumbers, eels and baby dogfish. Among the books and jars, there are also the bones of whales and dolphins, the jaws of a Great White shark, the skull and shell of a loggerhead sea turtle. There are also fossils and minerals sent to her by correspondents – of which she has many – from as far away as Montana, California, and Mexico. The pride of her collection is an enormous petrified whale vertebra from the Eocene strata of Alabama, fully two feet long. She pays Mrs. Peabody a little extra to allow her to keep this cabinet of oddities, but that doesn't prevent the old woman from regularly grousing about Annie's peculiar collection or the unpleasant odors that sometimes leak from beneath her door.

Annie Phelps has four cats: a black-and-white tom she's named Huxley; a fat grey tom with one yellow eye and one blue eye, whom she's named Darwin; a perpetually thin calico lady, Mary Anning; and, finally, the skittish young girl she christened Rowena after a Saxon woman in *Ivanhoe*. When she's not entertaining a friend or a lover, the cats are all the companionship she needs, even if the apartment is rather too small for all five of them, and even though they claw her mother's already threadbare heirlooms and leave the rooms smelling of piss. The cats are another thing she pays Mrs. Peabody extra to overlook. Were it not for the fact that it's getting harder and harder to find lodgers, the landlady likely would not be willing to make these concessions to Annie's eccentricities.

On this afternoon, she sits drinking a lukewarm glass of lemonade, spiked with a dash of Jamaican ginger, the jake she gets from a pharmacist over on Federal. Annie is very careful how often she imbibes, because she's well aware of the cases of paralysis, and even death, that have resulted from excessive use of the extract.

Darwin and Huxley are both perched on the back of the roll-top. Darwin has scaled a stack of monographs on malacology and the hydromedusae of coastal New England. Meanwhile, Huxley has wedged himself between one of her compound microscopes and a copy of Lyell's *Geological*

Evidences of the Antiquity of Man. Both cats are purring loudly and watching as she composes a letter to Dr. Osborn at the American Museum. Occasionally, she'll send him a few of her more intriguing specimens and is proud that some have become permanent additions to the museum's collections in Manhattan.

"What will he think of this piece, Mr. Darwin?" she asks the cat. "Frankly, I think it may be the most fascinating and curious object I've sent him yet."

Darwin shuts his yellow-green eyes.

"Yes, well, what do you know, you chubby old fool?"

Annie stops writing and stares at the jawbone in its cardboard box, cradled in wads of excelsior. It's a bit worn from having been rolled about in the surf, but is unbroken and still has all its teeth. At first glance, she took it for the jaw of a man or woman, some unfortunate soul drowned in the harbor or the cold sea beyond the Water Street jetty. But that impression was fleeting, lasting hardly longer than the time it took her to pick the bone up off the sand. It's much too elongate and slender to be the jaw of any normal human being, and both the condyle and the coronoid process all but absent. The mental protuberance of the mandibular symphysis is almost blade-like. But the teeth are the strangest of all the strange jawbone's features. Instead of the normal adult human complement of four incisors, two canines, and eight molars, the teeth are homodont – completely undifferentiated – and more closely resemble the fangs of a garpike than those of any mammal.

Standing at the edge of the murky harbor, low waves sloshing insistently against the shore, Annie Phelps was briefly gripped by an almost irresistible urge to toss the strange bone away from her, to give it back to the sea from whence it had come. To be rid of it. She squinted through the mist, out past the lines of ruined and decaying wharves, at the low dark line of rock that the people of Innsmouth call Devil Reef. Growing up, she heard all the tales about the reef, yarns of pirate gold, sirens, and sea demons, and she knows, too, of the locals who compete in swimming races out to the granite ridge on moonlit nights, a sport sponsored by the Esoteric Order, a religious sect who long ago took over the Masonic Hall at New Church Green.

But she didn't throw the bone away. She carefully wrapped it in newspaper and added it to her basket with the other day's finds. Annie Phelps is a rational woman of the twentieth century, a woman of science and reason, even if her circumstances mean that she will never be more than an amateur naturalist. She is not bound by the fearful, superstitious ways of so many of the people of the town, all those citizens of Innsmouth who mistake the effects of inbreeding, disease, and poor nutrition among the Marshes, Eliots, Gilmans, Waites, and other old families of the town for some metaphysical transformation brought about by the secretive rites and rituals of the Order of Dagon – as certainly a witch-cult as any described in the scholarly works of Margaret Murray. Growing up, she heard all that bushwa, and she sometimes feels anger and embarrassment at the way so many of her neighbors live in terror of whatever goes on inside the dilapidated, pillared hall.

"It certainly isn't a fossil," she says to Huxley, ignoring the less-than-useful Mr. Darwin. "There's no sign whatsoever of permineralization. It's no sort of reptile, and I don't believe it's a fish, neither cartilaginous or osteichthyan. But I can't believe it came from a mammal, either."

If the cat has an opinion, he keeps it to himself.

Annie writes a few more lines of her letter –

I am very grateful for the copy of your description of Hesperopithicus, *though I must confess it still looks to me very like a pig's tooth.*

– and then she glances at the jawbone again.

"The water gets deep out past the reef," she says to Huxley and Darwin, "and who knows what might be swimming around out there."

The cats purr, and Huxley begins vigorously cleaning his ears.

The enclosed specimen has entirely confounded all my best attempts at classification. Beyond the self-evident fact that it resides somewhere within the Vertebrata, I'm entirely at a loss.

Sometimes, Annie dares to imagine she will one day find something entirely new to science, and Dr. Osborn – or someone else – will name the new animal or plant after her. She stares at the jaw and considers a number of appropriate Latin binomina, if it should prove to be something novel, finally settling on *Deinognathus phelpsae*, Phelps' terrible jaw. She likes that. She likes that very much.

But then she feels the prickling at the back of her neck and along her forearms, and the sinking, anxious feeling she first experienced the day she found the bone, and she quickly looks away and tries to focus on finishing the day's correspondence:

…and at any rate, I hope this letter finds you well.

Outside, there's a sudden commotion, a loud splashing from the river, and Annie sets her pen aside and goes to the window to see what it might have been. But there's nothing, just the waters of the Manuxet swirling past the boarding house, dark and secret as the coming night.

"Someday," she says to the cats, "I'm gonna pack up and leave this place. You just watch me. Someday, we're gonna get out of here."

5.

Ephraim Asher Peaslee closes his wrinkled eyelids, sixty-one years old and thin as vellum paper, sinking into the sweet rush and warm folds of the heroin coursing through his veins. All the world bleeds to white, and he could well be staring into the noonday sun, patiently waiting to go mercifully blind, so bright does the darkness around him blaze. But it doesn't blind him. It doesn't ever blind him, and neither does it burn him. He lies cradled in the worn cranberry velvet of the chaise lounge in the parlor of his house at the corner of River and Fish streets, directly across from the shattered arch of the Fish Street Bridge. The heavy drapes are drawn, like his eyelids, against the last dregs of twilight, against the rising Hay Moon, Corn Moon, Red Moon, goddamn Grain Moon, whichever folk name suits your fancy. None suit his. The moon is a cruel cyclopean eye, lidless, watchful, prying, and this night it will drag the sea so far inland, swelling the harbor and tidal river all the way back to the lower falls. It won't be the kindly, obscuring white of his opiate high, but will lie orange and bloated, low on the horizon. It will scrape its cratered belly against the sea, hemorrhaging for all the bloodthirsty mouths that lie in wait, always, just below the waves. Oh, Ephraim Asher Peaslee has seen so *many* of those slithering, spiny things, has drowned again and again in their serpent coils. He's been kissed by every undertow and riptide, dragged down screaming to bear witness to abyssal lands no human man ever was meant to see. Right now, this evening, he pushes back against those thoughts, awakened by the rising moon. He tries to cling to nothing but the heroin, the forever white expanse laid out before him after the needle kiss. The radio's on, "I'll Build a Stairway to Paradise," and the music makes love to his waking alabaster dream. *It's madness to be always sitting around in sadness, when you could be learning the steps of gladness.* He folds his bony hands in supplication, in prayer to St. Gershwin and the ghost of Guglielmo Marconi and the Crosley Model 51, that they have graced him with this balm, a sacred ward against the memories and the nightmares and the long hours to come before dawn. God bless, and take your choice of gods, but surely, please, bless the pharmaceutical manufacturers in faraway eastern Europe, in Turkey and Bulgaria, god bless the Chinese farmers and poppy fields, where moralizing tyrants have not yet obliterated his ragged soul's deliverance from the abominations of Innsmouth. Pray a rosary for the white powder that ferries him away to Arctic wastes, Antarctic plains, where water is stone and nothing can swim through those crystalline rivers. *I won't open my eyes,* thinks Ephraim Asher Peaslee. *I won't open my eyes until morning, and maybe not even then. Maybe I will never again open my eyes, but fall eternally, perpetually, into the saving grace of the heroin light.* Then he hears the rising moon, a sound like the sky being torn open, like steam engines and furnaces, and he turns his face into a brocade pillow, wishing he were able to smother himself, but knowing better. He's a failed suicide, several times over; a coward with straight razor and noose. And trying not to hear the moon or the sluice of the rising tide, trying only to drown in white and ancient snow and the fissured glaciers that course down the basalt flanks of Erebus, there is another sound, past the radio – *Dance with Maud the countess, or just plain Lizzy. Dance until you're blue in the face and dizzy. When you've learn'd to dance in your sleep, you're sure to win out –* past crooning and tinny strings, there is the thunder, earthquake, sundering purr of Bill Bailey, his gigantic Maine Coon, twenty-five pounds if he's an ounce. Bill Bailey, raised up from a kitten, and now he comes heroic, thinks the heroin addict hopefully, to pull my sledge up the crags of a dead and frozen volcano in the South Polar climes, Mr. Poe's Mount Yaanek, where the filthy, unhallowed Manuxet never, never will do them mischief on this hot August night. Risking so many things – his shredded sanity not the least of all – Ephraim Asher Peaslee opens his eyes, letting the world back in, releasing his desperate hold on the white. He rolls over, and Bill Bailey stands not far from the cranberry chaise, watching him, waiting cat-patient, those amber eyes secret filled. "You hear it, too, don't you? We ought to have run. We ought to have packed our bags and taken that rattletrap bus away to Newburyport. They'd have let us go. They have no use for the likes of us. They'd be *glad* to be rid of us." The cat merely blinks, then sets about licking its shaggy chocolate coat, grooming paws and chest. "You *do* hear it, I *know* you do." And then, close to tears and disappointed by the cat's apparent lack of concern, by Bill Bailey's usual pacific demeanor, the old man once more turns away and presses his face into the cushion. Sure, what has a cat to fear from the evils of an encroaching, salty sea? A holy temple child of Ubaste, privy to immemorial knowledge forever set beyond the kin of loping apes fallen from African trees and the grace of Jehovah. Bill Bailey purrs and bathes and does not move from his appointed station by the chaise. And Ephraim Asher Peaslee tries to give himself back to the white place, but finds that, in the scant handful of seconds it took him to converse with the cat, the luminous White Lands have deserted him. Left him to his own meager devices, none of which are a match for the monsters the mad and unholy men and women of the Esoteric Order see fit to call forth on nights when the moon sprawls so obscenely large in the Massachusetts heavens. Their oblations and devotions that rot and gradually discard their human forms, sending those lost souls tumbling backwards, descending the rungs of the evolutionary ladder towards steamy Devonian and Carboniferous yesteryears, muddy swamp pools, silty lagoons, dim memories held in bone and blood and cells of morphologies devised and then abandoned two hundred and fifty or three hundred million ago. Ephraim Asher Peaslee of No. 7 River Street shuts his eyes more tightly than, he would say, he ever has shut his eyes before, skating his hypodermic fix down, down, *down,* but not down to the sanctuary of his white realms. Some door slammed and bolted shut against him, and, instead, he has only clamoring, fish-stinking recollections of the waterfront, the docks where beings no longer human cast suspicious, swollen eyes towards interlopers. Grotesque faces half glimpsed in doorways and peering out windows. Shadows and murmurs. The squirming mass he once caught a fleeting sight of before it slipped over the edge of a pier and, with a plop, was swallowed up by the bay. The chanting and hullabaloo that pours forth from the old Masonic Hall. All of this and a hundred other images, sounds, and smells burned indelibly into his mind's eye. Shuffling hulks. Naked dancers on New Church Green, seen on stormy, starless nights, whirling devil dervishes. *All you preachers who delight in panning the dancing teachers, let me tell you there are a lot of features of the dance that carry you through the gates of Heaven!* So many other citizens might turn their heads and convince themselves they've seen nothing, and anyway, what business is it of theirs, the pagan rites of the debased followers of Father Dagon and Mother Hydra? Oh, old Ephraim Asher Peaslee, *he* knows those names, because he can't seem to shut out the voices that ride between the crests and troughs. Out there, as night comes on and the last scrap of sunset fades, he prays to his own heathen deities, the narcotic molecules in his veins, the radio, to keep him insensible for all the hours between now and dawn. And Bill Bailey stands guard, and listens, and waits.

6.

When even the solar system was young, a fledgling, Pre-Archean Earth was kissed by errant Theia, daughter of Selene, and four and a half billion years ago all the cooling crust of the world became once more a molten hell. Theia was obliterated for her reckless show of affection and reborn as a cold, dead sphere damned always to orbit her intended par-amour; she a planet no more, but only a satellite never again permitted to touch the Earth. And so it is that the moon, spurned, scarred, diminished, haunts the sky, gazing spitefully across more than a million miles of near vacuum, hating silently – but not *entirely* powerless.

She has the tides.

A dance for three – sun, moon, and earth.

She can pull the seas, twice daily, and twice monthly her pull is vicious.

And so she has formed an alliance with those things within the briny waters of the world that would gain a greater foothold upon the land or would merely reach out and take what the ocean desires as her own.

For the ocean, like the moon, is a wicked, jealous thing.

Hold that thought.

Cats, too, have secrets rooted in antiquity and spanning worlds, secret histories known to very few living men and women, most of whom have only read books or heard tales in dreams and nightmares; far fewer have for themselves beheld the truth of the lives of cats, whether in the present day or in times so long past there are only crumbling monuments to mark the passage of those ages. The Pharaoh Hedjkheperre Setepenre Shoshenq's city of Bubastis, dedicated to the Cult of Bast and Sekhmet, where holy cats swarmed the temples and were mummified, as attested by the writings of Herodotus. And the reverence for the *Tamra Maew* shown by Buddhist monks, the breeds sacred to the Courts of Siam, the *Wichien-maat, Sisawat, Suphalak, Khaomanee,* and *Ninlarat.* In the Dream Lands, the celebrated cats of Ulthar, whom no man may kill on pain of death, and, too, the great battle the cats fought against the blind and loathsome, toad-like beasts on the dark side of the moon.

Cats upon the moon.

Star-eyed guardians whose power and glory has been forgotten, by and large, by humanity, which has come to look upon them as nothing more than pets.

The stage has been set.

Here's the scene:

All the cats of Innsmouth have assembled on this muggy night, coming together at a designated place within the shadowed, dying seaport at the mouth of Essex Bay, south of Plum Island Sound, and west of the winking lighthouses of Cape Ann. The sun is finally down, and that swollen moon has cleared the Atlantic horizon to shine so bright and violent over the harbor and the wharves, over fishing boats, the meeting hall of the Esoteric Order of Dagon, and over all the gabels, balustrades, hipped Georgian and slate-shingled gambrel rooftops, the cupolas and chimneys and widow's walks, the high steeples of shuttered churches. The cats take their positions along the low stone arch of Banker's Bridge, connecting River Street with Paine Street, just below the lower falls of the Manuxet. They've slipped out through windows left open, through attic crannies and basement crevices, all the egresses known to cats whose "owners" believe they control the comings and goings of their feline charges.

The cats of Innsmouth town have come together to hold the line. They've come, as they've done twice monthly since the sailing ships of Captain Obed Marsh returned a hundred years ago with his strange cargoes from the islands of New Guinea, Sumatra, and Malaysia. Strange cargoes and stranger rituals that set the seaport on a new and terrible path, as the converts to Marsh's transplanted South Sea's cult of Cthulhu called out to the inhabitants of the drowned cities beyond Devil Reef and far out beyond the wide underwater plateau of Essex Bay. They sang for the Deep Ones and all the other abominations of that unplumbed submarine canyon and the halls of Y'ha-nthlei and Yoharneth-Lahai. And their songs were answered. Their blasphemies and blood sacrifices were rewarded.

Evolution spun backwards for those who chose that road.

And even as the faithful went down, so did the Deep Ones rise.

On these nights, when the spiteful moon hefts the sea to cover the cobble beaches and slop against the edges of the tallest piers, threatening to overtop the Water Street jetty, on *these* nights do the beings called forth by the rites of the Esoteric Order seek to slip past the falls and gain the wetlands and the rivers beyond Innsmouth, to spread inland like a contagion. On *these* nights, the Manuxet swells and, usually, is contained by the quays erected when the city was still young. But during *especially* strong spring tides, such as this one of the first night of August 1925, the commingled sea and river may flood the streets flanking the Manuxet. And things may crawl out.

But the cats have come to hold the line.

None among them – not even the very young or the infirm or the very old – shirk this duty.

Essie and Emiline Babson's tom Horace is here, as is shopkeeper Bertrand Cowlishaw's plump calico Terrapin. The three tortoiseshell kittens have scrambled out from beneath Frank Buckle's front porch to join the ranks. All four of Annie Phelps' cats – Darwin and Huxley, Mary Anning and Rowena – are here, and a place of honor has been accorded Mister Bill Bailey, the heroin addict Ephraim Asher Peaslee's enormous Maine Coon. Bill Bailey has led the cats of Innsmouth since his seventh year and will lead them until his death, when the burden will pass to another. *All* these have come to the bridge, and five score more, besides. The pampered and the stray, the beloved and the neglected and forgotten.

By the whim of gravity, the three heavenly bodies have aligned, sun, moon, and earth all caught now in the invisible tension of syzygy, and within an hour the Manuxet writhes with scaled and slimy shapes eager and hopeful that this is the eventide that will see them spill out into the wider world of men. The waters froth and splash as the Deep Ones, hideous frog-fish parodies of human beings, clamber over the squirming mass of great eels long as Swampscott dories and the arms of giant squid and cuttlefish that might easily crush a man in their grip. There are sharks and toothsome fish no ichthyologist has ever seen, and there are armored placoderms with razor jaws, believed by science to have vanished from the world aeons ago. Other Paleozoic anachronisms, neither quite fish nor quite amphibians, beat at the quay with stubby, half-formed limbs.

The conspiring moon is lost briefly behind a sliver of cloud, but then that obstructing cataract passes from her eye and pale, borrowed light spills down and across the Belgian-block paving running the length of River and Paine, across all those rooftops and trickling down into alleyways. And there are those few, in this hour, who dare to peek between curtains pulled shut against the dark, and among them is Annie Phelps, distracted from her reading by some noise or another. She sees nothing more than the water growing perilously high between the quays, and she's grateful she has nothing of value stored in the basement, not after the flood of '18, when she lost her entire collection of snails and mermaids' purses, which she'd unwisely stored below street level. But she sees nothing more than the possibility of a flood, and she reminds herself again how she should move to some village where there would be crews with sandbags out on nights like this. She closes the curtain and goes back to her books.

Two doors down, Mr. Buckles sits near the bottom of the stairs, his 12-gauge, pump-action Browning across his lap. He carried the gun in France, and if it was good enough to kill Huns in the muddy trenches it ought to do just damn fine against anything slithering out of the muck to come calling at his door. The shotgun is cocked, both barrels loaded; he drinks from his bottle of bourbon and keeps his eyes open. Even in the house he can smell the stench from the river, worse times ten than it ever is during even the hottest, stillest days.

On Banker's Bridge, Bill Bailey glares with amber eyes at the interlopers, as they surge forward, borne by the tide.

Farther up the street, Essie Babson looks down at the river, and she sees nothing at all out of the ordinary, despite what she plainly *hears*.

"Come back to bed," says Emiline.

"You didn't hear that?" she asks her sister.

"I didn't hear anything at all. Come back to bed. You're keeping me awake."

"The heat's keeping you awake," mutters Essie.

"Have you seen Horace?" Emiline wants to know. "I couldn't find him. He didn't come for his dinner."

"No, Emiline. I haven't seen Horace," says Essie, and she squints into the night. "I'm sure he'll be along later."

Bill Bailey's ears are flat against the side of his head. The eyes of all the other cats of Innsmouth are, in this moment, upon him.

Above his store, Bertrand Cowlishaw lies in his bed, exhausted from a long, hot afternoon in the shop, by all the orders filled and the shelves he restocked himself because Matthew was in and out all day, making deliveries. Bertrand drifts uneasily in that liminal space between waking and sleep. And he half dreams about a city beneath the sea, and he half hears the clamor below the arch of Banker's Bridge.

Bill Bailey tenses, and all the other cats follow his lead.

Something hulking and only resembling a woman in the vaguest of ways lurches free of the roiling, slippery horde, rising to her full height, coming eye to eye with the chocolate Maine Coon.

Its eyes are black as holes punched in a midnight sky.

Ephraim Asher Peaslee floats, coddled in the gentle, protective arms of Madame Héroïne; after a long hour of pleading, he's been permitted to reenter the White Lands, where neither the sea nor the moon nor their demons may ever come. He isn't aware that Bill Bailey no longer sits near the cranberry velvet chaise lounge. And the radio is like wind through the branches of distant trees, wind through a forest in a place he but half recalls. He is blissfully ignorant of the rising river and the tide and the coming of the Deep Ones and all their retinue.

The scaled thing with bottomless pits for eyes opens its mouth, revealing teeth that Annie Phelps would no doubt recognize from the jaw she found on the shingle. Dripping with ooze and kelp fronds, its hide scabbed with barnacles and sea lice, the monster howls and rushes the bridge.

And the cats of Innsmouth town do what they have always done.

They hold the line.

They cheat the bitter moon, with claws and teeth, with the indomitable will of all cats, with iridescent eyeshine and with a perfect hatred for the invaders. Some of them are slain, dragged down and swallowed whole, or crushed between fangs and gnashing beaks, or borne down the riverbed and drowned. But most of them will live to fight at the next battle during New Moon spring tide.

Bill Bailey opens the throat of the black-eyed beast that once was a woman who lived in the town and cared for cats of her own.

Mary Anning is devoured, and Annie Phelps will spend a week searching for her.

One of the kittens from beneath Frank Buckles' front porch is crushed, its small body broken by flailing tentacles.

But there have been worse fights, and there will be worse fights again.

And when it is done and the soldiers of Y'ha-nthlei and Dagon and Mother Hydra have all been routed, retreating to the depths beyond the harbor, beyond the bay, when the cats have won, the survivors carry away the fallen and lay them in the reeds along the shore of Choate Island.

When the sun rises, there is left hardly any sign of the invasion, or of the bravery and sacrifice of the cats. Some will note dying crabs and drying strands of seaweed washed up along River and Paine streets, but most will not even see that much.

The day is hot again, but by evening rain clouds sweep in from the west, and from the windows of the Old Masonic lodge on New Church Green the watchers watch and curse. They say their prayers to forgotten gods, and they bide their time, patient as any cat.

THE CATS OF RIVER STREET (1925)

It is odd that I somehow managed not to write a story about cats until the summer of 2014. Cats have been my companions all my life. Indeed, I cannot clearly recall a time, even in early childhood, when there wasn't at least one around. And yet they are almost entirely absent from my fiction. "The Cats of River Street" was written in July and August, when it occurred to me that a cat story set in Innsmouth would be fun and a fitting tribute to Lovecraft's own love of felines. This one is dedicated to Cat Tail (1975–1977), Mouse Trap Morgan (1977–1980+) and all her many kittens, Charles Darwin Fat-Kitty (1982–1985), Meg (1985–2006), Charles (1985–1995), Velvet Elvis (1990–?), Sophie Joe (1989?–2006), Hubero P. Wu (200?–2017), Sméagol (aka Linus Bean Thumbknuckle) 2005–2012), Selwyn (2012–), and Lydia (2017–).

Elegy for a Suicide

This is the story of the hole in the ground.

"Our souls are damned," E says, and she folds open the pearl-handled straight razor. I know that she doesn't believe in souls, and I know, too, that she knows I know. But it's a game, a staple of this pantomime. The stainless-steel blade catches the bathroom light and flashes it back. The razor is one of the lovers she's not yet found the courage to fuck. There are a lot of those, but the razor is the most immediate, the most precious, and, I would say, the most cheated. She taunts the razor at the very precipice of orgasm. It may as well be the soft pad of her index finger pressed against my clit, the way she folds that razor open, then trails vulnerable flesh along metal, almost, *almost* slicing. Only ever *almost*. Only ever until tonight, but I'm getting ahead of myself, and I don't see how that will profit anyone. E studies every minute detail of the blade. She is intimately familiar with its history, knows it like she knows the inside of her eyelids, and I understand this familiarity is crucial to…what? This is a ritual, I suppose. Did I ever suppose that before this moment?

"W.H. Morley and Sons, Clover Brand –" and she pauses to point out to me the tiny clover stamped into the narrow *tang,* there before the deadly-sweet *shank,* sharp as her grey eyes. "– and the handle only looks like old ivory or bone."

The handle is yellowed, like a mouthful of nicotine-stained teeth.

"French Ivory celluloid," she says and shuts off the tap. The water in the tub steams in our cold bathroom. The window above her, the width of a grave, has completely fogged over. Nothing outside worth seeing anyway. "Manufactured in Austria, 1923, between the wars. There on the handle, I believe that's one of the lotus-eaters of, maybe, the Isle of Djerba or the country of the Gindanes." E pauses, then adds, "A lotophage."

I know she got all that last bit off Wikipedia, because E's a lazy scholar. But, yes, there *is* the figure of a nude woman molded or carved, I don't know which, into the handle. The nude woman's arms are upraised, and above her is a single flower stained red. I don't know if it was stained red when it left the factory. Morley and Sons wherever in Austria. But now there is that splotch of red, rather like an invitation. The woman stands inside the blossom of a second flower, though it *isn't* stained red. The flowers look nothing like lotus.

She's still talking. She doesn't need an audience to listen.

She doesn't need an assembly for her oratories.

"'Why are we weigh'd upon with heaviness,

And utterly consumed with sharp distress,

While all things else have rest from weariness?'"

She holds the razor up to the light and reclines in her hot bath. I sit on the toilet seat while she recites Tennyson. I don't look at her, because then I can't pretend nothing has changed and that there's any going back to before the hole. The Hole. And I'm tired of looking at her face, and I'm sick of seeing the razor. I count the filthy, once-white hexagonal tiles of the floor.

"It'll all be a pretty story when you're done," she says, and I shake my head.

"I'm never writing this."

"Of course you will."

"You're seriously fucking deluded."

"Oh, you'll write about it. You'll never see a god again. You'll write about it."

She laughs, and I wince – no, I actually do wince – because I know she's absolutely goddamn right. However this goes, I'll write it down. I'm already composing sentences in my head, sick fuck that I am. I stare at the tiles, and I listen to her razor soliloquy, and I think back on the way it begins, a day faded down almost to twilight, the day when we found the damned thing. That's more than a month ago, far back in January. We're picking our way through the snow-scabbed, brown-weeded wastes on the western bank of the Seekonk River. Near the old railroad leading out to that towering drawbridge that's been raised since sometime in the 1970s. It's a rust cathedral, girders and bolts instead of flying buttresses, but it's still a cathedral. E's looking through the trash, because it's something she does. Me, I'm just along for the ride, freezing my ass off and wishing she'd get bored and announce that it's time to head back towards Gano Street and town.

I'm trying not to shiver. E says only pussies shiver.

We come upon a sheet of corrugated tin or aluminum, and she reaches down and pulls it back to reveal a barren patch of ground. The soil is black and no weeds grow there, and so at first it strikes me as barren. But, in point of fact, there's pale mold and a riot of tiny brown-capped mushrooms that have grown in the shadow E has now taken away. She leans close, asking herself aloud if maybe they're a psychedelic species, packed with psilocybin.

"Hey, you know, we could pick them, take them back to the apartment and find out," she suggests.

"Of the many ways I would rather not fucking die, poisoning myself by eating toxic mushrooms is high on the list."

E scowls. "Pussy," she says. She's tossed the sheet of tin – or aluminum – aside and is on her knees now at the very edge of that not-quite-barren patch of ground. She begins to pick one of the brown mushrooms, but then something *else* catches her eye. It catches my eye a few seconds afterwards. She's almost always the first to notice anything even just the slightest bit out of place. And this is out of place.

In the tub, E's moved on to James Joyce, episode five of *Ulysses*.

"It's really goddamn tiresome," I say so quietly I'm hardly even whispering. I'm only breathing out syllables. "Do it or don't fucking do it, but it's really goddamn tiresome the way you go on and on and on."

"You want me to do it," she says.

"I want you to shut the fuck up, that's what I want. I want you to get out of that tub and dry off and throw the razor in the trash and let's never talk about it ever again."

"You don't want much, do you?" she asks. "Think it's going to go away?" she asks and raises her left arm so I have to see what's happening to her. So I have to gaze directly at the corruption eating at her.

Below the sheet of corrugated metal, there in the mold and mushrooms, there is a hole. It can't be more than four inches across. I can't recall how to calculate diameter, but the hole can't be more than five inches across, so it certainly isn't a very big hole. And while it *is* a hole in the ground, it isn't a *dirt* hole. The edges are pink and puckered and fleshy, and its rim puts me more in mind of an enormous asshole than anything else. A sickly shade of pink, like a burn scar, like proud flesh with blue-white veins, and it looks wet and sticky and warm.

Gotta be another sort of fungus, I think. What else would I think?

I tug at the back of her hoodie, like that was going to do any good.

"What the hell...?" she begins and trails off.

I go back to counting the hexagons. "There are these places called hospitals," I say. I say again.

"You seriously think this is anything that doctors can fix?"

"I seriously fucking think we don't know whether they could help or not," I say, and she laughs and splashes.

"An apocalypse of the flesh," E smiles. I do not have to look at her face, and the corruption that has also taken hold there, to know that she's smiling. "Do you know the original meaning of *apocalypse?* Not a catastrophe. Not the end of the world. It means revelation, a vision, a sudden insight."

She goes back to describing the razor.

"I have to die to finish it," E tells me. Again.

"I'm calling an ambulance."

"No you're not," she says. She's right.

There in the weedy patch on the bank of the Seekonk, E whispers, her voice filled all at once with awe and curiosity. With, I suppose, apocalypse. She whispers, "Oh my god, what *is* that?"

"One of the nastiest things I have ever seen," I answer, even if I am well aware the question was rhetorical. She doesn't want to know. E never wants to know, because knowing would serve no end but erasing a mystery.

She scoots closer to the hole, smushing mushrooms beneath the knees of her jeans, scraping up the scum of mold with denim.

"Seriously. It's disgusting. Just leave it the fuck alone."

But I'm too late, and she's already touched the outermost edge of the hole, and it quivers like Jell-O. No, I'm not too late, because she wouldn't have listened anyway. Where E touched the hole, a dime-sized crimson blister has formed.

"Jesus," I hiss. "Please. You don't have any idea what that shit is."

"Exactly," E replies, and she almost sounds sensible. "It's warm," she says, so I was right about that. Then she lays her left hand down flat against the pink whatever it is. "It's warm…and it's sort of pulsing. Or throbbing."

For a moment I honestly believe I'm going to vomit.

The mirror on the medicine cabinet door has also steamed over. I wish my eyes could do the same. The pills are in there, the ones she's been taking for the pain, eating them for a week now. Eating them like candy. I have asked her how much it hurts. I only have to see her arm, that patch on her right cheek, and the inside of her thighs to know it must fucking hurt like fucking hell.

She's talking about the razor again.

"They didn't have the nerve, either," says E. "They must have done this, pretty much the same thing as this, trying and unable to make it stop."

"You don't know that."

"I might. The voices are getting louder, and they have an awful lot to say."

"Then stop listening."

"When a god talks, you don't stop listening."

When a god talks. I'm not about to have that argument again. It's not that I lose. You can't lose an argument with a brick wall.

"It's got plans, right? Maybe I'm holding this razor, and maybe I even want to use it. I think that person before me definitely also kept trying, but it has plans."

E put her arm into that hole, and she pulled out the straight razor.

"Zombie ants," I say to her. Now, I mean – here in our bathroom, not back on that day at the hole. "I told you about the zombie ants. Maybe they think a god's talking to them, too."

"Fucking ants don't think shit," she replies.

Zombie ants.

Ophiocordyceps unilateralis, a fungus that grows in tropical jungles all around the world. Its spores get into an ant, and somehow they force it – rewire its fucking tiny ant brain – to bite down on a leaf, into a particular vein at a very specific height off the ground. And the zombie ant just hangs there, and the fungus kills it, changes its exoskeleton, until fruiting bodies have filled up its head. The dead ant's head bursts, spreading more spores, infecting more ants, making more zombies.

"Gods don't talk to bugs."

"You think you're anything *more* than a bug to this thing?"

E slides down until only her face is left above the steaming water. A new crimson blister appears below her right eye. I begin to say something that isn't an argument, as if I haven't already tried that, as well. *I love you, and I'm watching while some kind of parasite, some kind of cancer, is eating you alive, and you won't let me help you.*

Why haven't I called an ambulance? Good damn question, right? Is the god from that hole muttering in my ears, too?

I count tiles and listen to the faucet dripping.

She's started in all over again about the razor being like a lotus flower. You eat the flower, and then there's peace. You draw the blade down your forearms and across your wrists, or you cut to the chase and open up your throat, and there's no more pain. Only, of course, that's not what her new god wants. Suicide would interrupt the cycle.

E reaches down into that hole, which is a lot deeper than I would have thought. She reaches in, and something changes about her expression. Just as though somebody flips a switch. But I can't *describe* the change. I've tried. Fuck all knows I've tried. Her face changes, her expression, and, a few seconds later, when she withdraws her hand she's holding the antique Austrian razor. She raises it, opens it, and the blade glints faintly in the last of the daylight. Her arm glistens, wet with whatever that stuff the red blister's secreting.

"Oh my god, it's beautiful," E says. "Who the hell would have just left something this cool lying in a hole?"

I'm supposing that god wasn't talking to her yet.

"You're *not* going to keep that."

"Shit yeah, I am."

E stands before the tall mirror in our bedroom, nude as she is in the bath. Her back is to me, and yet I can watch her eyes. Even scarred, she is as beautiful now as she has ever been. I see her, front and back. I see her, shattered and whole. She says a god is whispering in her ear, but I'm watching Hell devour her. She has become a tiny boat on a vast sea of paradoxes, and I can only watch. Standing here before the tall mirror, she smiles and plays with her left nipple. I don't think I've ever seen such joy in her eyes, such complete delight. The razor is lying nearby, atop the chest of drawers.

"Fuck me," she says, but I don't want to. I can hardly stand the thought of touching her, because if I touch her then I'm also touching it.

"Remember that night out on the Cape?" I ask, changing the subject. "The night we watched the Perseids from Newcomb Hollow Beach?"

My iPhone buzzes and I answer it. It's work, wanting to know why I'm late again.

"Star fall, phone call," E smiles at me from the mirror.

Is this all a game to her? Do the zombie ants think that they're playing some sort of game? E says that bugs don't think.

"Tomorrow," I promise the voice at the other end of the line, even though I know the promise is a lie. "I'll be in tomorrow. I'm sure I'll feel much better by then."

A week ago I'd have been terrified of losing my job; now it's something that seems to exist in a time and a place I'll never get back to, not ever again.

If I was *ever* there.

"We should go back to that beach," E says, masturbating for her reflection. "Next July, we should go back there and watch the sky again." The tone of her voice hasn't changed. She doesn't sound like someone masturbating, and I wonder if she knows she's doing it. Maybe this is another compulsive act, like all the baths. Something she's only dimly conscious she's doing, but that the god in her head needs to complete the cycle. I can't turn away. It doesn't matter what she's becoming, what's becoming of her, she's still beautiful, and I still adore the sight of her.

"Yes," I tell her. "We'll go back there."

Her hand stops moving, and she frowns – but only very, very slightly. If I hadn't spent the last two years with her, I might not know she was frowning.

"I don't want to leave," she says, and I say I don't want her to leave, either.

"Maybe," she says, "if I used the razor–"

"You'd be leaving, either way," I reply. "It's only two different doors." And that's assuming that the shit from the hole wouldn't be just as happy with her corpse as with a living host. That's assuming a goddamn lot.

"I can't remember why I did it. Isn't that odd?"

A drop of pinkish slime drips from between her legs and spatters the floorboards between her bare feet. I want to burn the building down.

"All I remember is that it seemed very urgent. Like, all my life had been such a waste right up until then, but if I just reached inside that hole everything would have meaning, finally, forever and forever."

"But you don't feel that way anymore?"

She never answers the question. Her smile comes back, and she turns her back to the mirror. "Fuck me," she says. And that's what I do. Doesn't matter how much the corruption that has taken root on her – *in* her – body disgusts me. I make love to her, knowing that I am also making love to it. I more than half expect, in the moment that we both come, only seconds apart (which never happens), that I'll hear the god inside her skull, too.

She lies beside me on sheets that needed to be washed a month or so ago, and she stares up at the ceiling. Her eyes look glassy. I notice that it's spread to her throat, and I can't remember if it had before we had sex. It's moving fast now. It's impatient to be born, and maybe that orgasm was the last bit of adrenaline it needs to bite down hard on that leaf and hold on. I talk to her, but she doesn't talk back. She only nods a few times, shakes her head once or twice. I ask if it hurts, and she doesn't nod or shake her head, but I go to the bathroom and get the pills from the medicine cabinet.

I bring her the pills and a glass of water, and E takes three of them, then lies down again.

"Do you want the razor?" I ask, and E shakes her head. But I go to the chest of drawers and get it for her anyway. I put it in her hands, which are as limp as a ragdoll. Then I get dressed and go out, telling myself there are a few things that we urgently need from the market, and that she'll only take a nap while I'm gone.

I can be awfully good at lying to myself.

"I won't be gone long. Get some rest. I'll fix dinner when I get back."

E nods and smiles sleepily.

In the weeds near the Seekonk River, she's already started scratching at the hand she put into the hole. I want to go back there and cover it up again. *We should have,* I think. *We should have left it exactly the way that we fucking found it.*

I'm gone longer than I meant to be, because I run into a friend, and you'd never know from our conversation that this day was any different from any other. It's dark by the time I get back to our street, and it's begun snowing. Fat flakes drifting down to earth like falling stars, like spores, like gods tumbling from imagined heavens. By morning, there will be almost a foot blanketing Providence.

I knew perfectly well that E would be gone, but it still takes me by surprise.

Somewhere soon there will be another hole in the ground.

At least she left the razor lying on the bed, and I sit holding it for a long, long time, staring at that yellowed French Ivory celluloid handle, wishing that the flowers truly were lotuses.

ELEGY FOR A SUICIDE

I shouldn't have to explain this one, at least not to the constant reader. Everything I write is, to one degree or another, autobiography – only sometimes it's more obvious than others. This story was written in August 2013.

The Road of Needles

1.

Nix Severn shuts her eyes and takes a very deep breath of the newly minted air filling Isotainer Four, and she cannot help but note the irony at work. This luxury born of mishap. Certainly, no one on earth has breathed air even half this clean in more than two millennia. The Romans, the Greeks, the ancient Chinese, they all set in motion a fouling of the skies that an Industrial Revolution and the two centuries thereafter would hone into a science of indifference. An art of neglect and denial. Not even the meticulously manufactured atmo of Mars is so pure as each mouthful of the air Nix now breathes. The nitrogen, oxygen – four fingers N_2, a thumb 0_2 – and the so on and so on traces, etcetera, all of it transforming the rise and fall of her chest into a celebration. Oh happy day for the pulmonary epithelia bathed in this pristine blend. She shuts her eyes and tries to think. But the air has made her giddy. Not drunk, but certainly giddy. It would be easy to drift down to sleep, leaning against the bole of a *Dicksonia antarctica,* sheltered from the misting rainfall by the umbrella of the tree fern's fronds, by this tree and all the others that have sprouted and filled the isotainer in the space of less than seventeen hours. She could be a proper Rip Van Winkle, as the *Blackbird* drifts farther and farther off the Lunar-Martian rail line. She could do that fabled narcoleptic one better, pop a few of the phenothiazine capsules in the left hip pouch of her red jumpsuit and never wake up again. The forest would close in around her, and she would feed it. The fungi, insects, the snails and algae, bacteria and tiny vertebrates, all of them would make a banquet of her sleep and then, soon, her death.

> *...and even all our ancient mother lost*
> *was not enough to keep my cheeks, though washed*
> *with dew, from darkening again with tears.*

Even the thought of standing makes her tired.

No, she reminds herself – that part of her brain that isn't yet ready to surrender. *It's not the thought of getting to my feet. It's the thought of the five containers remaining between me and the bridge. The thought of the five behind me. That I've only come halfway, and there's the other halfway to go.*

Something soft, weighing hardly anything at all, lands on her cheek. Startled, she opens her eyes and brushes it away. It falls into a nearby clump of moss and gazes up with golden eyes. Its body is a harlequin motley of brilliant yellow and a blue so deep as to be almost black.

A frog.

She's seen images of frogs archived in the lattice, and in reader files, but images cannot compare to contact with one alive and breathing. It touched her cheek, and now *it's* watching *her.* If Oma were up and running, Nix would ask for a more specific identification.

But, of course, if Oma were on line, I wouldn't be here, would I?

She wipes the rain from her eyes. The droplets are cool against her skin. On her lips, on her tongue, they're nectar. It's easy to romanticize Paradise when you've only ever known Hell and (on a good day) Purgatory. It's hard not to get sentimental; the mind, giddy from clean air, waxes. Nix blinks up at all the shades of green; she squints into the simulated sunlight shining down between the branches.

The sky flickers, dimming for a moment, then quickly returns to its full 600-watt brilliance. The back-up fuel cells are draining faster than they ought. She ticks off possible explanations: there might be a catalyst leak, dinged up cathodes or anodes, a membrane breach impairing ion-exchange. Or maybe she's just lost track of time. She checks the counter in her left retina, but maybe it's on the fritz again and can't be trusted. She rubs at her eye, because sometimes that helps. The readout remains the same. The cells have fallen to forty-eight percent maximum capacity.

I haven't lost track of time. The train's burning through the reserves too fast. It doesn't matter why.

All that matters is that she has less time to reach Oma and try to fix this fuck-up.

Nix Severn stands, but it seems to take her almost forever to do so. She leans against the rough bark of the tree fern and tries to make out the straight line of the catwalk leading to the port 'tainers and the decks beyond. Moving over and through the uneven, ever shifting terrain of the forest is slowing her down, and soon, she knows, soon she'll be forced to abandon it for the cramped maintenance crawls suspended far overhead. She curses herself for not having used them in the first place. But better late than fucking never. They're a straight line to the main AI shaft, and wriggling her way through the empty tubes will help her focus, removing her senses from the Edenic seduction of the terraforming engines' grand wrack-up. If she can just reach the front of this compartment, there will be an access ladder, and cramped or not, the going will surely be easier. She'll quick it double time or better. Nix wipes the rain from her face again and clambers over the roots of a strangler fig. Once on the slippery, overgrown walkway, she lowers the jumpsuit's visor and quilted silicon hood; the faceplate will efficiently evaporate both the rain and any condensation. She does her best to ignore the forest. She thinks, instead, of making dockside, waiting out quarantine until she's cleared for tumble, earthfall, and of her lover and daughter waiting for her, back in the slums at the edge of the Phoenix shipyards. She keeps walking.

2.

Skycaps launch alone.

Nix closes the antique storybook she found in a curio stall at the Firestone Night Market, and she sets it on the table next to her daughter's bed. The pages are brown and brittle, and minute bits of the paper flake away if she does not handle it with the utmost care (and sometimes even when she does). Only twice in Maia's life has she heard a fairy tale read directly from the book. On the first occasion, she was two. And on the second, she was six. It's a long time between lifts and drops, and when you're a mother who's also a runner, your child seems to grow up in jittery stills from a time-lapse. Even with her monthly broadcast allotment, that's how it seems. A moment here, fifteen minutes there, a three-week shore leave, a precious to-and-fro while sailing orbit, the faces and voices trickling through in 22.29 or 3.03 light-minute packages.

"Why did she talk to the wolf?" asks Maia. "Why didn't she ignore him?"

Nix looks up to find Shiloh watching from the doorway, backlit by the glow from the hall. She smiles for the silhouette, then looks back to their daughter. The girl's hair is as fine and pale as corn silk. She's fragile, born too early and born sickly, half crippled, half blind. Maia's eyes are the milky green color of jade.

"Yeah," says Shiloh. "Why is that?"

"I imagine *this* wolf was a very charming wolf," replies Nix, brushing her fingers through the child's bangs.

Skycaps launch alone.

Sending out more than one warm body, with everything it'll need to stay alive? Why squander the budget? Not when all you need is someone on hand in case of a catastrophic, systems-wide failure.

So, skycaps launch alone.

"Well, I would never talk to a wolf. If there were still wolves," says Maia.

"Makes me feel better hearing that," says Nix. A couple of strands of Maia's hair come away in her fingers.

"If there were still wolves," Maia says again.

"Of course," Nix says. "That's a given."

Her lips move. She reads from the old, old book: "Good day, Little Red Riding Hood," said he. "Thank you kindly, wolf," answered she. "Where are you going so early, Little Red Riding Hood?" "To my grandmother's."

Nix Severn's eyelids flutter, and her lips move. The home-away chamber whispers and hums, manipulating hippocampal and cortical theta rhythms, mining long- and short-term memory, spinning dreams into perceptions far more real than dreams or déjà vu. No outbound leaves the docks without at least one home-away to insure the mental stability of skycaps while they ride the rails.

"You should go to sleep now," Nix tells Maia, but the girl shakes her head.

"I want to hear it again."

"Kiddo, you know it by heart. You could probably recite it word for word."

"She wants to hear you read it, fella," says Shiloh. "I wouldn't mind hearing it again myself, for that matter."

Nix pretends to frown. "Hardly fair, two on one like this." But then she gently turns the pages back to the story's start and begins it over.

The home-away mediates between the limbic regions and the cerebral hemispheres, directing neurotransmitters and receptors, electrochemical activity and cortisol levels.

There was once a sweet little maid...

Shiloh kisses her brow. "Still, hell, I don't know how you do it, love. All alone and relying on make-believe."

"It keeps me grounded. You learn the trick, or you washout fast."

The skycap's best friend! Even better than the real thing! Experience the dream, and you might never want to come home.

The merch co-ops count on it.

"You could look for work other than babysitting EOTs," whispers Shiloh. "You have options. You've got the training. There's *good* work you could do in the yards, in assembly or rollout."

"I don't want to have this conversation again."

"But with your experience, Nixie, you could make foreman on the quick."

"And get maybe a quarter the grade, grinding day and night."

"We'd see you so much more. That's all. And it scares me more than you'll ever know, you hurtling out there alone with nothing but make-believe and plug and pray for waking company."

Make haste and start before it gets hot, and walk properly and nicely, and don't run, or you might fall.

"The accidents –"

"– the casts hype them, Shiloh. Half what you hear never happened. You know that. I've told you that, how many times now?"

"Going under and never coming up again."

"The odds of psychosis or a flatline are astronomical."

Shiloh rolls over, rolling away. Nix sighs and closes her eyes, because she has prep at six for next week's launch, and she's not going to spend the day sleepwalking because of a fight with Shiloh.

...and don't run, or you might fall.

The emergency alarm screams bloody goddamn murder, and an adrenaline injection jerks her back aboard the *Blackbird*, back to here and now so violently that she gasps and then screams right back at the alarms. But her eyes are trained to see, even through so sudden a disengage, and Nix is already processing the diagnostics and crisis report streaming past her face before the raggedy hitch releases her.

It's bad this time. It doesn't get much worse.

Oma isn't talking.

"Good day, Little Red Riding Hood..."

3.

Of course, it *isn't* true that there are no wolves left in the world. Not strictly speaking. Only that, so far as zoologists can tell, they are extinct in the wild. They were declared so more than forty years ago, all across the globe, all thirty-nine or so subspecies. But Maia has a terrible phobia of wolves, despite the fact that "Little Red Riding Hood" is her favorite bed-time story. Perhaps it's her favorite *because* she's afraid of wolves. Anyway, Shiloh and I told her that there were no more wolves when she became con-vinced a wolf was living under her bed, and she refused to sleep without the light on. We suspect she knows perfectly well that we're lying. We suspect she's humoring us, playing along with our lie. She's smart, curious, and has access to every bit of information on the lattice, which includes, I'd think, everything about wolves that's ever been written down.

I have seen wolves. Living wolves.

There are a handful remaining in captivity. I saw a pair when I was younger, when I was in my twenties. My mother was still alive, and we visited the bio in Chicago. We spent almost an entire day inside the arbore-tum, strolling the meticulously manicured, tree-lined pathways. Here and there, we'd come upon an animal or two, even a couple of small herds – a few varieties of antelope, deer, and so forth – kept inside invisible enclo-sures by the leashes implanted in their spines. Late in the afternoon, we came upon the wolves, at the end of a cul-de-sac located in a portion of the bio designed to replicate the aspen and conifer forests that once grew along the Yellowstone River. I recall that from a plaque placed somewhere on the trail. There was an owl, an eagle, rabbits, a stuffed bison, and at the very end of the cul-de-sac, the pair of wolves. Of course, they weren't pure-bloods, but hybrids, watered-down with German shepherd or husky genes or whatever.

There was a bench there beneath the aspen and pine and spruce culti-vars, and my mother and I sat a while watching the wolves. Though I know that the staff of the park was surely taking the best possible care of those precious specimens, both were somewhat thin. Not emaciated, but thin. "Ribsy," my mother said, which I thought was a strange word. One I'd never before heard. Maybe it had been popular when she was young.

"They look like ordinary dogs to me," she said.

They didn't, though. Despite the fact that these animals had never lived outside pens of one sort or another, there was about them an unmis-takable wildness. I can't fully explain what I mean by that. But it was there. I recognized it most in their amber eyes. A certain feral desperation. They restlessly paced their enclosure; it was exhausting, just watching them. Watching them set my nerves on edge, though my mother hardly seemed to notice. After her remark, how the wolves seemed to her no different than regular dogs, she lost interest and winked on her Soft-See. She had a glass conversation with someone from her office, and I watched the wolves. And the wolves watched me.

I imagined there was hatred in their amber eyes.

I imagined that they stared out at me, instinctually comprehending the role that my race had played in the destruction of theirs.

We were here first, they said without speaking, without uttering a sound.

It wasn't only desperation in their eyes; it was anger, spite, and a promise of stillborn retribution that the wolves knew would never come.

Ten times a million years before you, we feasted on your foremothers.

And, in that moment, I was as frightened as any small and defenseless beast, cowering in shadows, as still as still can be in hope it would go unnoticed as amber eyes and hungry jaws prowled the woods.

I have wondered if my eyes replied, *I know. I know, but have mercy.*

That day, I do not believe there was any mercy in the eyes of the wolves.

You cannot even survive yourselves, said the glittering amber eyes. *Ask yourself for charity.*

And I have wondered if a mother can pass on dread to her child.

4.

Nix Severn reaches the ladder leading up to the crawlspace, only to find it engulfed in a tangle of thick vines that have begun to pull the lockbolts free of the wall. She stands in waist-high philodendrons and bracken, glaring up at the damaged ladder. Briefly, she considers attempting the climb anyway, but is fairly sure her weight would only finish what the vines have begun, and the resulting fall could leave her with injuries severe enough that she'd be rendered incapable of reaching Oma's core in time. Or at all.

She curses and wraps her right hand around a bundle of the vines, tugging at them forcefully; the ladder groans ominously, creaks, and leans a few more centimeters out from the wall. Nix lets go and turns towards the round hatchway leading to Three and the next vegetation-clogged segment of the *Blackbird.* The status report she received when she awoke inside the home-away, what little there was of it, left no room for doubt that all the terraforming engines had switched on simultaneously and that every one of the containment sys banks had failed in a rapid cascade, rolling backwards, stem to stern. She steps over a log so rotten and encrusted with mushrooms and moss that it could have lain there for years, not hours. A few steps farther and she reaches the hatch's keypad, but her hands are shaking, and it takes three tries to get the security code right; a fourth failure would have triggered lockdown. The diaphragm whirs, clicks, and the rusty steel iris spirals open in a hiss of steam. Nix mutters a thankful, silent prayer to no god in whom she actually believes because, so far, none of the wiring permitting access to the short connecting corridors has been affected.

Nix steps through the aperture, and the hatch promptly spirals shut behind her, which means the proximity sensors are also still functional. The corridor is free of any trace of plant or animal life, and she lingers there several seconds before taking the three, four, five more steps to the next keypad and punching in the next access code. The entrance to Isotainer Three obeys the command and forest swallows her again.

If anything, the situation in Three is worse than that in Four. As if the jungle weren't slowing her down enough, she comes upon a small pond, maybe five meters across, stretching from one side of the hull to the other. The water is tannin stained, murky, and half obscured beneath an emerald algal scum, so there's no telling how deep it might be. The forest floor is quite a bit higher than that of the 'tainer, so the pool could be deep enough she'd have to swim. And Nix Severn never learned to swim.

She's sweating. The readout on her visor informs her that the ambient temperature has risen to 30.55°C, and she pushes back the hood. For now, there's no rain falling in Three, so there's only her own sweat to wipe from her eyes and forehead. She kneels and brushes a hand across the pond, sending ripples rolling towards the opposite shore.

Behind her, a twig snaps, and there's a woman's voice. Nix doesn't stand or even turn her head. Between the shock of so abruptly popping from the dream-away sleep, her subsequent exertion and fear, and the effects of whatever toxic pollen and spores might be wafting through the air, she's been expecting delirium.

"The water is wide, and I can't cross over," the voice sings sweetly. "Neither have I wings to fly."

"That isn't you, is it, Oma?"

"No, dear," the voice replies, and it's not so sweet anymore; it's taken on a gruff edge. "It isn't Oma. The night presses in all about us, and your grandmother is sleeping."

There's nothing sapient aboard but me and Oma, which means I'm hallucinating.

"Good day, Little Red Riding Hood," says the voice, and never mind her racing heart, Nix has to laugh.

"Fuck you," she says, only cursing her subconscious self, and stands, wiping wet fingers on her jumpsuit.

"Where are you going so early, Little Red Riding Hood?"

"Is that really the best I could come up with?" Nix asks, turning now, because how could she not look behind her, sooner or later. She discovers that there *is* someone standing there; someone or something. Which word applies could be debated. *Or rather,* she thinks, *there is my delusion of another presence here with me. It's nothing more than that. It's nothing that can actually speak or snap a twig underfoot, excepting in my mind.*

In my terror, I have made a monster.

"I know you," Nix whispers. The figure standing between her and the hatchway back to Four has Shiloh's kindly hazel-brown eyes, and even though the similarity ends there, about the whole being there is a nagging familiarity.

"Do you?" it asks. It or she. "Yes, I believe that you do. I believe that you have known me a very, very long while. 'Whither so early, Little Red Riding Hood?'"

"I've never *seen* you."

"Haven't you? As a child, didn't you once catch me peering in your bedroom window? Didn't you glimpse me lurking in an alley? Didn't you visit me at the bio that day? Don't I live beneath your daughter's bed and in your dreams?"

Nix reaches into her left hip pouch for the antipsychotics there. She takes a single step backwards, and her boot comes down in the warm, stagnant pool, sinking in up to the ankle. The splash seems very loud, louder even than the atonal symphony of dragonflies buzzing in her ears. She wants to look away from the someone or something she only *imagines* there before her, a creature more canine than human, an abomination that might have been created in an illicit *sub rosa* recombinant-outcross lab back on earth. A commission for a wealthy collector, for a private menagerie of designer freaks. Were the creature real. Which it isn't.

Nix tries to open the Mylar med packet, but it slips through her fingers and vanishes in the underbrush. The thing licks its muzzle with a mottled blue-black tongue, and Shiloh's eyes sparkle from its face.

"Are you going across the stones or the thorns?" it asks.

"Excuse me?" Nix croaks, her throat parched, her mouth gone cottony. *Why did I answer it. Why am I speaking with it at all?*

It scowls.

"Don't play dumb, Nix."

It knows my name.

It only knows my name because I know my name.

"Which *path* are you taking? The one of needles or the one of pins?"

"I couldn't reach the crawls," she hears herself say, as though the words are reaching her ears from a great distance. "I tried, but the ladder was broken."

"Then you are on the Road of Needles," the creature replies, curling back its dark lips in a parody of a smile and revealing far too many sharp yellow teeth. "You surprise me, *Petit Chaperon rouge.* And I am so rarely ever surprised."

Enough...

My ship is dying all around me, and that's enough, I will not fucking see this. I will not waste my time conversing with my id.

Nix Severn turns away, turning much too quickly and much too carelessly, almost falling face first into the pool. It no longer matters to her how deep the water might be or what might be lurking below the surface. She stumbles ahead, sending out sprays of the tea-colored water with every step she takes. They sparkle like gems beneath the artificial sun. The mud sucks at her feet, and soon she's in up to her chest. *But even drowning would be better,* she assures herself. *Even drowning would be better.*

5.

Nix has been at Shackleton Relay for almost a week, and it will be almost another week before a shuttle ferries her to the CTV *Blackbird,* waiting in dockside orbit. The cafeteria lights are too bright, like almost everything else in the station, but at least the food is decent. That's a popular myth among the techs and co-op officers who never actually spend time at Shackleton, that the food is all but inedible. Truthfully, it's better than most of what she got growing up. She listens while another EOT sitter talks, and she pokes at her bowl of udon, snow peas, and tofu with a pair of blue plastic chopsticks.

"I prefer straight up freight runs," Marshall Choudhury says around a mouthful of noodles. "But terras, they're not as hinky as some of the caps make them out to be. You get redundant safeguards out the anus."

"Far as I'm concerned," she replies, "cargo is cargo. Jaunts are jaunts."

Marshall sets down his own bowl, lays his chopsticks on the counter beside it.

"Right," he says. "You'll get no kinda donnybrook here. None at all. Just my pref, that's it. Less hassle hauling hardware and whatnot, less coddling the payload. More free for dream-away."

Nix shrugs and chews a pea pod, swallows, and tells him, "Fella, here on my end, the chips are chips, however I may earn them. I'm just happy to have the work. Those with families can't be choosers."

"Speaking of which…" Marshall says, then trails off.

"That your concern now, Choudhury, my personal life?"

"Just one fella's consideration for a comrade's, all."

"Well, as you've asked, Shiloh is still nagging me about hooking something in the yards." She sets her bowl down and stares at the broth in the bottom. "Like she didn't know when I married her, like she didn't know before Maia, that I was EOT and had no intent or interest in ever working anything other than offworld."

"Lost a wife over it," he says, as if Nix doesn't know already. "She gave me the final notice and all, right, but fuck it. Fuck it. She doesn't know the void, does she? Couldn't know what she was asking a runner to give up. Gets wiggled into a fella's blood, don't ever get out again."

Marshall has an ugly scar across the left side of his face, courtesy of a coolant blowout a few years back and the ensuing frostbite. Nix tries to look at him without letting her eyes linger on the scar, but that's always a challenge. A wonder he didn't lose that eye. He would have, if his goggles had cracked.

"Don't know if that's the why with me," she says. "Can't say. Obviously, I do miss them when I'm out. Sometimes, miss 'em like hell."

"But that doesn't stop you flying, doesn't turn you to the yards."

"Sometimes, fuck, I wish it would."

"She gonna walk?" he asks.

"I try not to think about that, and I especially try not to think about that just before outbound. Jesus, fella."

Marshall picks up his bowl and chopsticks, then fishes for a morsel of tofu.

"One day not too far, the cooperatives gonna replace us with autos," he sighs and pops the white cube into his mouth. "So, gotta judge our sacrifices against the raw inevitabilities."

"Union scare talk," Nix scoffs, though she knows he's probably right. Too many ways to save expenses by completely, finally, eliminating a human crew. *A wonder it hasn't happened long before now,* she thinks.

"Maybe you ought consider cutting your losses, that's all."

"Choudhury, you only *just* now told me how much choice we don't have, once the life digs in and it's all we know. Make up your damn mind."

"You gonna finish that?" he asks and points at her bowl.

She shakes her head and slides it across the counter to him. Thinking about Maia and Shiloh, her appetite has evaporated.

"Anyway, point is, no need to fret on a terra run, no more than anything else."

"Never said I was fretting. It's not even my first."

"No, but that was not my point, fella." Marshall slurps at the broth left in the bottom of her white bowl, which is the same unrelenting white as the counter, their seats, the ceiling and walls, the lighting. When he's done, he wipes his mouth on a sleeve and says, "Maybe it's best EOTs stay lone. Avoid the entire mess, start to finish."

She frowns and jabs a chopstick at him. "Isn't it rough enough already without coming back from the black and lonely without anyone waiting to greet us?"

"There are other comforts," he says.

"No wonder she left you, you indifferent fuck."

Marshall massages his temples, then changes the subject. For all his faults, he's pretty good at sensing thin ice beneath his feet. "It's your first time to the Kasei though, that's true, yeah?"

"That's true, yeah."

"You can and will and no doubt already have done worse than the Kasei 'tats."

"I hear good things," she says, but her mind's elsewhere, and she's hoping Marshall grows tired of talking soon so she can get back to her quarters and pop a few pinks for six or seven hour's worth of sleep.

"Down on the north end of Cattarinetta Boulevard – in Scarlet Quad – there's a brothel. Probably the best on the whole rock. I happen to know the proprietress."

Nix isn't so much an angel she's above the consolation of whores when away from Shiloh. All those months pile up. The months between docks, the interminable Phobos reroutes, the weeks of red dust and colonist hardscrabble.

"Her name's Paddy," he continues, "and you just tell her you're a high fella to Marshall Mason Choudhury, and she'll see you're treated extra right. Not those half-starved farm girls. She'll set you up with the pinnacle merch."

"That's kind of you," and she stands. "I'll do that."

"Not a trouble," he says and waves a hand dismissively. "And look, as I said, don't you fret over the cargo. Terra's no different than aluminum and pharmaceuticals."

"It's *not* my first goddamn terra run. How many times I have to –"

But she's thinking, *Then why the extra seven-percent hazard commission, if terras are the same as all the rest?* Nix would never ask such a question aloud, any more than she can avoid asking it of herself.

"Your oma, she'll –"

"Fella, I'll see you later," she says, and walks quickly towards the cafeteria door before he can get another word or ten out. Sometimes, she'd lay good money that the solitudes are beginning to gnaw at the man's sanity. That sort of shit happens all too often. The glare in the corridor leading back to the housing module isn't quite as bright as the lights in the cafeteria, so at least she has that much to be grateful for.

6.

Muddy, sweat-soaked, insect-bitten and insect-stung, eyes and lungs and nostrils smarting from the hundreds of millions of gametophytes she breathed during her arduous passage through each infested isotainer, arms and legs weak, stomach rolling, breathless, Nix Severn has finally arrived at the bottom of the deep shaft leading down to Oma's dormant CPU. The bzou has kept up with her the entire, torturous way. Though she didn't realize that it *was* a bzou until halfway through the second 'tainer. Sentient viruses are so rare that the odds of Oma's crash having triggered the creation of (or been triggered *by*) a bzou has a probability risk approaching zero, at most a negligent threat to any transport. But here it is, and the hallucination isn't an hallucination.

An hour ago, she finally had the presence of mind to scan the thing, and it bears the distinctive signatures, the unmistakable byte sequence of a cavity-stealth strategy.

"A good quarter of an hour's walk further in the forest, under yon three large oaks. There stands her house. Further beneath are the nut trees, which you will see there," it said when the scan was done. "Red Hood! Just look! There are such pretty flowers here! Why don't you look round at them all? Methinks you don't even hear how delightfully the birds are singing! You are as dull as if you were going to school, and yet it is so cheerful in the forest!"

Oma knows Nix's psych profile, which means the bzou knows Nix's psyche.

Nix pushes back the jumpsuit's quilted hood and visor again – she'd had to lower it to help protect against a minor helium leak near the shaft's rim – and tries to concentrate and figure out precisely what's gone wrong. Oma is quiet, dark, dead. The holo is off, so she'll have to rely on her knowledge of the manual interface, the toggles and pressure pads, horizontal and vertical sliders, spinners, dials, knife switches…all without access to Oma's guidance. She's been trained for this, yes, but AI diagnostics and repair has never been her strong suit.

The bzou is crouched near her, Shiloh's stolen eyes tracking her every move.

"Who's there?" it asks.

"I'm done with you," Nix mutters and begins tripping the instruments that ought to initiate a hard reboot. "Fifteen more minutes, you'll be wiped. For all I know, this was sabotage."

"Who's there, skycap," the bzou says again.

Nix pulls down on one of the knife switches and nothing happens.

"Push on the door," advises the bzou. "It's blocked by a pail of water."

Nix pulls the next switch, a multi-boot resort – she's being stupid, so tired and rattled that she's skipping stages – which should rouse the unresponsive Oma when almost all else fails. The core doesn't reply. Here are her worst fears beginning to play themselves out. Maybe it was a full-on panic, a crash that will require triple-caste post-mortem debugging to reverse, which means dry dock, which would mean she is utterly fucking fucked. No way in hell she can hand pilot the *Blackbird* back onto the rails, and this far off course an eject would only mean slow suffocation or hypothermia or starvation.

Nix takes a tiny turnscrew from the kit strapped to her rebreather (which she hasn't needed to use, and it's been nothing but dead weight she hasn't dared abandon, just in case). She takes a deep breath, winds the driver to a 2.4 mm. mortorq bit, and keeps her eyes on the panel.

"Alright," she says. "Let's assume you have a retract sequence, that you're a benign propagation."

"Only press the latch," it says. "I am so weak, I can't get out of bed."

"Fine. Grandmother, I've come such a very long way to visit you," Nix says, imagining herself reading aloud to Maia, imagining Maia's rapt attention and Shiloh watching from the doorway.

"Shut the door well, my little lamb. Put your basket on the table, and then take off your frock and come and lie down by me. You shall rest a little."

Shut the door. Shut the door and rest a little...

Partial head crash, foreign-reaction safe mode. Voluntary coma.

Nix nods and opens one of the memory trays, then pulls a yellow bus card, replacing it with a spare from the console's supply rack. Somewhere deep inside Oma's brain, there's the very faintest of hums.

"It's a code," Nix says to herself.

And if I can get the order of questions right, if I can keep the bzou from getting suspicious and rogueing up.

A drop of sweat drips from her brow, stinging her right eye, but she ignores it. "Now, Grandmother, now please listen."

"I'm all ears, child."

"And what big ears you have."

"All the better to hear you with."

"Right...of course," and Nix opens a second tray, slicing into Oma's comms, yanking two fried transmit-receive bus cards. *She hasn't been able to talk to Phobos. She's been deaf all this fucking time.* The CPU hums more loudly, and a hexagonal arrangement of startup OLEDs flash to life.

One down.

"Grandmother, what big eyes you have."

"All the better to see you with, *Rotkäppchen*."

Right. Fuck you, wolf. Fuck you and your goddamn road of stones and needles.

Nix runs reset on all of Oma's optic servos and outboards. She's rewarded with the dull thud and subsequent discordant chime of a reboot.

"What big teeth I have," Nix says, and now she *does* turn towards the bzou, and as Oma wakes up, the virus begins to sketch out, fading in incremental bursts of distorts and static. "All the better to *eat* you with."

"Have I found you now, old rascal?" the virus manages between bursts of white noise. "Long have I been looking for you."

The bzou had been meant as a distress call from Oma, sent out in the last nanoseconds before the crash. "I'm sorry, Oma," Nix says, turning back to the computer. "The forest, the terra…I should have figured it out sooner." She leans forward and kisses the console. And when she looks back at the spot where the bzou had been crouched, there's no sign of it whatsoever, but there's Maia, holding her antique storybook…

…the home-away releases Nix Severn, slowly, gently drawing her out of the dream. She opens her eyes to the staccato *pop* of the chamber's latches and the hiss of hydraulics as the canopy of the sleep tube retracts.

"Good morning, Nix," Oma purls through the clips covering the skycap's ears.

The EOT's illumination settings are still on low, easy on Nix's eyes, but they're dry and she rubs them, anyway. For a heartbeat, a heartbeat or two, she doesn't recall any of the dream – not the terraforming that had almost destroyed the *Blackbird,* not the bzou, not a girlfriend who walked out on her two outbounds ago, not the daughter they never had or the wolves she never saw at the Chicago bio…none of it.

"Fuck," she says. "Jesus, Oma, what the hell was that?"

"Is there a problem?" the computer replies, its voice perfectly concerned.

"You need to recalibrate or some shit, okay? I don't need fucking *nightmares.*"

"I'm extremely sorry, Nix. I've no idea how such an unfortunate discrepancy could have possibly occurred. I'll begin recalibration at once."

"It's okay," Nix says, even though it isn't. "Accidents happen." She shuts her eyes and waits another five minutes before getting up from the cradle.

Little Red Cap, where does your grandmother live?

"Nix, the day's navigational and five by five are waiting. I'll have your breakfast ready as soon as you're ready."

"Thank you, Oma," Nix replies. And she almost manages to make it to the shower stall before she begins crying.

THE ROAD OF NEEDLES

This story has a somewhat complicated history. A fairly straightforward retelling of "Little Red Riding Hood," it actually began life in January 2013 as a script for one of the Dancy Flammarion graphic novels, the second chapter of *Alabaster: Grimmer Tales* (Dark Horse, 2014, originally serialized in the now-defunct *Dark Horse Presents*). A month later, after finishing the first third of the script, I set down and wrote out a prose version of the story, in which Dancy becomes Nix Severn and there's a great deal more worldbuilding and general what have you, and then I sold the story to Paula Guran for *Once Upon a Time: New Fairy Tales* (Prime Books, 2013). And *then* it won the 2014 Locus Award for Best Short Story, which surprised no one more than me. But wait. There's more. After finishing "The Road of Needles," I found that I wasn't happy with the very last bit, where Nix wakes up from the home-away induced nightmare and we learn it was all a dream. While I think this is actually a much more solid and certainly bleaker ending, it's also a more cliché ending. Then again, clichés become clichés for a reason, usually because they work, and therefore, all these years later, I have decided to restore the original ending. I may regret it later on, but what the hell.

Whilst the Night Rejoices
Profound and Still

Remember thee!
Ay, thou poor ghost, while memory holds a seat
In this distracted globe. - Hamlet

1.

Of course, the first colonists brought their own sacred days and traditions with them. When their Bussard ramjets and shimmer sails descended from the black into the orange Martian atmosphere, they carried with them the religions and celebrations of Earth. But Mars is not Earth, and beliefs erode as surely as anything. One or another belief adapts to the needs of those who need them, or the belief dies off altogether, to be supplanted by a new, more useful, more appropriate *weltanschauung.* So it was with the colonists children's children's children and with the generations that followed after. Worlds turned – more than a hundred years for Earth, almost two hundred for Mars – and the old ways were duly supplanted. Meanwhile, across the void, the cradle of mankind rotted away under the weight of half-recollected calamities, and the supply freighters ceased their comings and goings. No one was left to remind the colonists, who were now Martians, of the world their ancestors had forsaken hoping for better lives so far away. The elaborate terraforming schemes of corporations and governments were only ever half-implemented, at best, and outside the sanctuary of the domes, the planet stayed more or less as it had been for three and a half billion years.

Beáta is thinking none of these thoughts as she sits at her gourd stall halfway down the dusty boulevard. She is thinking only that it has been a good year for the farms and the foundries, and that the people of Balboa have coin to spend on the march, which means they have money to spend on her gourds and candles and wards. It will be a proper Phantom March, which is never a guarantee. Beáta is always prepared for the lean times.

The boulevard smells of incense, sweets cooling in candy molds, the leafy hydroponic wares of the greens merchants, modest cauldrons of precious, bubbling sugar. And the starchy meat of her gourds, two of which she's split long ways so that customers may see for themselves she is offering the best on the row.

"Buy'em dry, buy'em raw," she calls out over the clamor. "Fresh for stew or holl'er for the light. Buy'em dry or buy'em raw."

If all goes well in the scant hours remaining before the march, she'll have sufficient roll to cover both rent on her stall and on her one-room coop five blocks over in the genny district, where the hundred plus wind turbines raised above the dome's roof run day and night, night and day, twenty-four months a year. She'll still owe some back rent, but who in the genny district doesn't? The landlords know well enough to tolerate a modicum of tardiness or watch the empty coops pile up, empty and even less profitable than tenants who only pay when they can.

"Buy'em dry, buy'em raw..."

The customers come and go, glittering and painted in their march finery, and Beáta happily watches as her stock of gourds diminishes. At this rate, the lot will be gone an hour *before* the march. Which means she'll be able to close shop and climb onto one of the balconies or squeeze into the press filling up the bleachers. As a gourd seller, she has a certain status among the citizens of Balboa, and respectful folks wouldn't begrudge her that much.

Two women stop and carefully survey her wares, then she sells them a pair of yellow-brown gourds, dried, hollowed, already fitted with beeswax candles, already fitted at their tops with jute loops. The two women immediately attach the gourds to their rosaries of olivine and hematite beads strung on strands of transgen hagfish silk. The women have likely inherited the rosaries from their mothers, who inherited them from their mothers before them, and so on. New strings can be purchased at stalls along the boulevard, but the oldest are the most prized, and Beáta can tell by the cut of their clothes that these are women of tradition. They do not even haggle over her asking price, and they tip. For Beáta, tips are rare as blue turnips are to sugar-beet farmers, as they say. The women thank her, offer well wishes from the Seven Ladies of the Poles and the Seven of the Wells, and then vanish once more into the crowd. Beáta grins, which she rarely does, because she's ashamed of the teeth she's missing right up front and all the rest going lickity split. But even a gourd merchant hasn't the cachet to land a health patron, not in times like these, so she makes do with the teeth she has left, and only smiles when she can't help herself.

"Fresh for stew or holl'er for the light. Buy'em dry or buy'em raw."

Beáta Copper's first Phantom March – at least the first she can recall – she was five years old, and her mothers took turns holding her up on their shoulders so she could watch the mummers over the heads and hats of the other celebrants. To her eyes, the boulevard seemed to have caught fire, all those lanterns swinging side to side, twirling roundabout, the gourd lanterns in the march and those scattered in amongst the crowd. It was not so simple to put her at ease when the rods came along, but then they were *meant* to frighten the children. The worst of the four was Famine, three stories tall, its many-jointed limbs and its toothsome jaws worked by twenty puppeteers. Famine, its hungry gaze blacker and colder than a winter's night on the Niliacus. Not even Old Man Thirst could trump Madam Famine. Beáta wanted to look away, but her mothers wouldn't permit it. Yes, the march is celebration and reverence, but it is also a grim reminder of the gifts and of the frailty of day-to-day existence in this and any dome.

"Buy'em dry or buy'em raw."

At her Phantom Eve tuition in the week before, she'd been *taught* of the famines that had gripped Mars in the long seasons after contact with Earth was lost. How half the planet's population had died before the horticulturists and water miners had managed to establish the United Provision Syndicate as a functional and effective body. She watched tapes of the complete ruin of Paros and Sagan, of the refugee camps, little terror shows of light and shadow flickering across the temple screen. The pictures from Sagan were the worst, because that dome had been so big and had needed so much to survive. The albino priestess had talked about the Seven Sol War, when Sagan had raided nearby Barsukov in a desperate attempt to save itself by stealing from another failing dome. In the end, the skins of both craters had been breached, and almost everyone had died one sort of death or another, most quickly from suffocation and decompression. She had been taught that honoring the Seven and the Seven was the only way to insure that those dark seasons never, ever came again.

"The goddesses smile on us, and they hold the Four at bay," said the white-haired priestess, "but only through our worship and only through our conservation of their bounty, which we wring from soil, earth, and sky. Waste is the one evil in the world. All wrongdoing is waste, in one way or in another. We remember this against our undoing."

Thirty-two years on, Beáta still believes that, sure as she believes fertilizer stinks. But she pays as much respect to the scientists and laborers of the UPS and never fails to pay her dues, even if it means the rent goes wanting.

"...or holl'er for the light."

A produce inspector makes his last obligatory rounds before the hymns that signal the march's commencement, and when he stops at Beáta's stall, she gives him a fat, uncarved gourd on the cuff, the pick of what she has left.

"Now, Beá, you wouldn't be trying to grease me, would you?" he asks, admiring her gift, turning it over and over in his thin hands.

"Ain't no need in that, sir, not seein' as mine's the cleanest on the street," she assures him, spreading her arms wide to indicate every vegetable remaining at her stall. "Not a yea big speck of the phako or scourge anywhere to be seen."

"Then you're as kindly and as responsible as ever," he says, tossing the gourd up and catching it twice for luck, once for the Poles and once for the Wells. "Clean bill, Beá, as usual. And all the blessings upon you."

"As on you, inspector."

He tips his cap and moves along to the next stall over, a fellow she knows from her own neighborhood. He sells neatly bound bouquets of collards and kale.

Outside the dome, the sun sets, twilight spreading out and filling up the canyons of the Corprates to the west, washing over the plains and channels surrounding Balboa. Drowning the craters. Beáta is visited by and makes sells to a handful of stragglers, and all but five of her smallest gourds are purchased. She makes an offering of them, tossing them into the boulevard to be trampled beneath the feet of the mummers, then draws the awning, ties it down, and goes to find her place among the devout.

2.

Before he switches off the electric, Jack carefully snaps the antique clip into the even more antique crank box and then presses the ON switch. The sound that leaks from the speakers isn't *exactly* music. There might be music hidden somewhere in it, but it was recorded – decades ago – to mimic the wild voices of the goddesses, the wail of the global perihelion dust storms, the shudder of the dome against the gales. Once the lights are out, there's only the flickering, dim glow from the peanut-oil lantern. The darkness is heavy and warm and musty.

Of course, he's not alone in the attic. There must always be three and ideally no more than three. Miranda and Dope already sit cross-legged on the plastic floor, waiting for him. In their way, these three twelve-year-olds are enacting a ceremony as sacred and crucial to the community's safe passage through Phantom Eve as the coming procession. Here, on the night before the March, all the children below the dome must gather in thrices to do their part, a duty that must be performed precisely and in all seriousness. Each of the three has already sliced the tip ends of their index fingers and squeezed blood into the lantern.

Jack takes his place with Miranda on his left, Dope on his right, and he's wishing two things: that he hadn't drawn short this year and that there was another boy in the attic with him. Isn't having to assume the role of teller bad enough without also being the only XY?

Miranda takes a deep breath and begins reciting the invocation to the Seven and the Seven, and when she's finished Dope murmurs the ward against the Four. Dope hardly ever raises her voice above a whisper, because she stutters sometimes. Jack waits patiently, his eyes on the lamp's wick, his mind running over all the details of the tale he's chosen.

"Your turn," Dope murmurs when she's done, and Jack glares at her.

"Don't you think I know? Think I'm simple?"

"Nuh-nuh-no," she whispers.

"Shit. Think I don't *know* my part?"

"I'm suh-suh-suh-"

"Stop it, Jack," Miranda scowls. "She didn't mean nothing by it. She's just nervous is all. Tell me you ain't."

Jack shakes his head. "Might be nervous, but I know my part."

In the lantern light, Dope's face is still pale as cheese, and Miranda's is nearly the same red-brown as the desert. He wants to get up and shut off the crank. Not because he's scared, but who wants to hear those noises? Who in his right mind? They've already worked their way beneath his skin and are coiling, cold and dense, down in his gut.

"Sorry, Dope," he says, even if he isn't, and then he begins the tale.

The crank sings its wordless, disharmonious song.

"Was back at the start of the Seven Sol War, see, and it isn't a coincidence that the Seven and the Seven took offense, when Sagan turned on its sister. The Seven knew to the final hour how long the fighting would go on, see. They knew, and that pissed them off just about as bad as they ever get pissed off, because they saw how it would make the Four even stronger than they were already."

He pauses, watching the lantern, wondering if there's anything he can leave out without breaking the rule. There isn't, but that doesn't stop him from wondering, or from wishing there were.

"But they waited," he continues. "They waited until the cannons had done their worst, and the Saganites had breached the containment gates to loot what was left of Barsukov, even if that wasn't much. That was the irony. Most of what they came to steal they'd managed to destroy in the war, so the prize was lost by their own hands.

"And there were the Four, slitherin' about the skin of Barsukov and getting in the souls of the invaders. Waste, you see, that's the only evil in all the world, just like they say at temple mass. And the militia from Sagan, what had they done but waste pretty much all of a larder that was meager even before they showed up?"

"Even if that wasn't their intent," chimes in Miranda, because her family is descended from Saganite refugees, and she can get defensive. "It was desper –"

"Did *you* draw," sighs Jack. "I sure don't *remember* you drawing, but maybe I'm mistaken."

The crank box roars and titters from across the attic, and Jack wishes he'd turned the volume down a bit.

Miranda apologizes.

"So," Jack says, "regardless of their *intent,* the militia did the worst thing possible when, as it was, there was so little to go around. Before they got inside, they scorched the ground. They burst cisterns, fouled reservoirs, even burned crops and grain silos. Hell, by the time the looting started, hardly a rat's squat left in there *to* loot. This made them angry, those men and women from the north, and so they killed even more, and so it wasn't only the battles that killed folks."

"I don't like this puh-part," murmurs Dope, but Jack ignores her.

"And that's when the Seven and the Seven swept down from their towers at the poles, and up from the wells, too. They'd foreseen it all along, how the invaders would do themselves more harm than good – though, even if they hadn't, the Seven would have come upon them anyhow. Waste is waste, whether it's a human life or a stalk of wheat.

"Now, back on Earth, in the old days, there used to be these big snakes. Not like any old rock viper or hedge green. No, sir. These snakes, they were so big could stretch from one side of a dome to the other with hardly any space left over past the ends of their noses. Got hungry, they'd squeeze anything to death they wanted. Anything. Can't remember what they were called, those snakes, but that's what they'd do."

"Boads and ambakandees," says Miranda.

"Pitons," adds Dope. "Them, also."

Jack glares at his companions, then goes on with the tale.

"And that last night of the war, the Seven and the Seven came down and settled over Barsukov, and they wrapped themselves as tight around the dome as those big Earth snakes would have done. The Four, who'd been busy and distracted, what with feeding on the dead and dying and the bloodthirsty, saw too late the fate rushing over them. They didn't have a chance to flee before the goddesses began to squeeze in. That's when the dome busted. *That's* when the worst of the dying started."

There's a clacking noise from the crank, and Dope jumps, which sort of makes Jack feel better.

"After all, when the people under siege saw how they were going to lose, some of them burned their *own* terraces and ponics, poisoned their *own* water, just so the Saganites wouldn't get at it. And waste is waste, right, no matter who commits it. So, the Seven and the Seven, they went and squeezed like them giant Earth snakes, and the dome started coming apart. So ferocious was their anger, that of the goddesses, that the Four fled back to their caverns down deep below Arsia Mons, leaving the conquerors *and* the conquered to their fates. Was almost a full week before rescuers from the south reached Barsukov, and most those people didn't die the day the dome came down, they'd already perished by the time help arrived. Only a hundred or so got into the bunkers, a few dozen more air-locked and radsafe in private shelters. Some of the wealth-off, in-clover folk, those few were.

"They say, and it's gospel, when the rescuers were still coming across the Hydaspis, they actually *saw* all the Ladies, still swirling about the crumpled mess left of Barsukov, and they looked a thousand times more terrible than the Four. Rescuers almost damned turned back then and forgot the distress signals, cause sure the people must have had coming to them what they got, if the Ladies were so riled.

"They had to decide, weighing the lives of whoever – if anybody – might have survived against the will of the Seven and the Seven. We'd have done the same."

The crank box squeals loudly enough that Jack has to pause until he can once more be heard over the cacophony. You can buy new clips, the sound clean and adjusted – same as you can buy new playbacks, instead of relying on half-century old cranks that should have gone to the reprocess plant before he was born. But Jack's family grows potatoes and cabbages, and there's never money for luxuries.

"Respect the grace of the Ladies," his mother says, "and be glad for what we have. Don't mope for what we don't."

And he tries.

"The captain of the team, he went so far as to halt the rescuers then and there, and was gonna be a vote, to go on or turn back. That's when the birds came flying overhead, those huge black birds died out long, long ago, and all we have are pictures. Ravens, so they were called on Earth. Shouldn't have been able to fly here in the thin air, naturally, and sure shouldn't have been able to breathe or – shit, you both know – but, still, there they were. And not ghost birds, neither. *Genuine* ravens, their ebon feathers shining in the sun. The rescuers figured had to be a sign. But was it a sign to turn back, or was it a sign to finish what they came to do?"

"I'd huh-have turned back, you bet," murmurs Dope.

"Fine thing then you weren't the priestess who read the significance of those ravens. She met with the captain in this dragger, and she told him that – even in their fury – the Seven and the Seven were not without mercy, and by their hands had the miracle of the birds been sent from the past of Earth and the memory of man to beckon him and his team on despite the terror of the sight before them. He listened. Course he listened, because that's what we do when a priestess talks."

In the dark attic, Jack finishes the sacred duty imparted upon him by drawing short. He tells of the heroism and the pardoning of the surviving Saganites by vote of the dome councils. He tells of how the ruins were abandoned to wind and dune and of the survivors of the war who didn't live to see the brassy foil shimmer of Balboa's skin.

"So it was the Ladies did show us how even in the most sour crannies of our hearts is there something worth salvation. But down to this day, to this very day, prospectors and surveyors and the like who have cause to pass by those ruins, they can hear the bombs, and the crash of the broken Barsukov comin' down. Worst of all, they tell of the shrieks of the dying swept to and fro across the flats."

He knows that maybe that last part's true, and he knows maybe it isn't. But he also knows that Phantom Night is more than a celebration of the life that will return beyond the long Martian winter. It's reverence of the dead, and it's time to send a few shivers through the soul, as well. Fear is the twin of Determination, that they dance always locked arm in arm, and there will not ever be the one without the other. When his tale is done, the three children bow their heads, and once the clip has run out and the crank automatically shut off, they recite the janazah, the specific fardth al-kaifāya demanded on that night to insure the community will see another year and to beseech another ten score years farther along. It is the task of the young to pray for the future. When Jack and Miranda and Dope are finished, they quietly exit the attic, and Jack pulls the trapdoor shut behind them and locks it. The clip is in his pocket, and he'll place it beneath his bed, where it will rest undisturbed until the conclusion of the March and the festivities.

3.

In the strictest sense, the temple wasn't built. Rather, it was found and then made the *cradle* for an elaborate construction. At least, as elaborate as the dome could manage, post-cutoff. The temple began as a cavern, discovered beneath the northwestern perimeter of Balboa during the digging of a basement vault for a genetic repository by the local office of the Provision Syndicate. Unlike the caverns on the flanks of Arsia Mons, this one is not an ancient lava tube, but was carved through sedimentary rock by an underground river long before the first multicellular life evolved on Earth.

Within the temple, scaffolding, catwalks, and stairwells spiral downwards from the surface, affording access to the structure's various levels. On the uppermost tiers are the plazas for public prayer and the classrooms. The monks and priestesses have their spartan dwellings on the mid-levels. And at the very bottom is the series of interlinked ceremonial chambers. As Phantom Night is the most important of the year, the central chamber is the largest and the one with which the greatest care has been taken. But it isn't ostentatious, as waste is the one evil in all the world. In accordance with the holy writ of the Seven and the Seven, it is functional, sufficient to its purpose and no more.

As is the custom, this year's avatars have been chosen by the drawing of lots from men and women between the ages of sixteen and twenty-three. They are the ones who must enact the most critical of all the observances of Phantom Night. They are the ones who will tread the line between *waste* and *sacrifice,* a hairline that exists only in the heart of humanity.

Beneath the sandstone roof of the cavern, at dawn on the day of the March, the drums sound like an old clip recording of thunder and cannon fire. Their rhythmic tattoo bruises the air and batters the bodies of the avatars. Seven plus seven daughters for the Polar Ladies and the Ladies of the Wells, and four men to represent the Four. Within a central ring the men stand on pedestals that have been placed at north, south, east, and west. Upon a low dais of polished basalt, placed *precisely* at the center of the circle, the women stand hand-in-hand, a ring with their backs to the men.

In a bamboo cage suspended ten feet above the dais is a single priestess, the highest appointed on that year, the Junon. Unlike the avatars, she isn't nude, but wears a heavy robe of the coarsest jute and a cap of thistle vine.

Flutes and strings join the drums, and the braziers are lit. Soon, the chamber quickly smells of sage, coriander, clove, and burning stalks of wheat. The smoke is drawn upwards through the natural chimney of the temple. Those who live nearby are blessed with the scent before the scrubbers remove it from the air. The avatars chosen to represent the Seven and the Seven turn to face the avatars chosen to stand in for the Four. In unison, the women recite the Litany of Preservation, and then the men jeer and curse them. Now the hands of the Seven and the Seven hang at their sides.

Overhead, the Junon dips her left hand into a gourd and sprinkles water upon the heads on the women. Then, with her right, she scoops up a mixture of fine dust from dunes near the poles and ground human bone, and this, too, she sprinkles on the heads of the daughters. She gazes down at the avatars, and her face is both solemn and angry.

"Until the coming of the fleets, the Four held sway over the world, and during the days of darkness did they bring upon us the full force of their wickedness and destruction.

"Until the coming of the fleets, the Seven and the Seven slept in their towers of ice and in their deep places, for there was no need of them. But we came from the stars, and we *brought* need. We came, it seemed, only to destroy ourselves, as we had always done on Earth, and the Four gathered to feast upon us. But the Seven and the Seven were awakened by the cries of the righteous and the just, by those who cherished life above all else and who were not wasters.

"They awoke and did do war against the Four, and drove them deep below, and bound them there."

Each of the women steps off the dais, taking one step towards the outer ring, four of them taking a step towards the men. The women bow their heads, and the men continue with their carefully rehearsed insults.

"And so they delivered us," the priestess says, shouting now above the rising music. "But this covenant can last only so long as we remain true and show our respect and squander nothing which is precious! And as *all* things are precious, we squander *nothing,* or surely the Four *will* be once more released to ravage the world!"

The women take another step forward, wait, and then take five more. Now four of them are very near the heckling men who stand at the rocks arranged at the Four Quarters. At the feet of those four women are daggers planted in the hard-packed dirt, blades of black volcanic glass and iron hilts forged in the temple furnaces. The women stoop and draw the blades from the floor, and the men fall silent.

"Here, in this sacred place and on this morning, we remember the battle the Ladies bravely and selflessly fought on our behalf. In this hour, we offer our gratitude. We do this with no hesitation and with no regret."

The Junon falls silent then, her part done. And the four women descend upon the avatars of the Four with the scalpel-sharp daggers. The only resistance offered by the men is pantomime, but their pain and screams are real. Their wails rise, as the smoke from the incense rises, though few above will hear them, so deep is the cavern.

A pair of monks emerges from among the musicians, each bearing a guttering torch, and they turn the Junon's bamboo cage into an inferno. Her robes, her hair, her skin, all drenched with oil, burn with flame as hungry as any of the Four, and her screams are added to those of the men.

The ten daughters who were not fortunate enough to draw the crimson tiles turn to watch the slaughter of their brothers. All but two among them are young enough to have another opportunity for that honor next year.

But nothing here is wasted.

Nothing.

After the four women have eaten, whatever is left of the men will be gathered by the monks, and – along with the Junon's ashes – will be dispersed among the people of Balboa to fertilize gardens throughout the dome. The four women kneel, and their ten sisters repeat the Litany.

Beneath every dome across the planet the ceremony is coming to a close, and beneath every dome the bells above temples ring out across an indebted populace.

4.

The dead of Mars are not buried. In the living memory of all the inhabitants of all the domes and that of all those who live on the out farms, mines, and wellingsteads, have never the dead been buried. Instead, carved stones are erected beneath the orange-blue sky, carved stones marking a birth, a life, and a death, but signifying the final resting place of no one. The deceased are not ever tossed aside, but composted and so resurrected – bone and sinew, blood and organs – to nourish those who will come after.

Honor lies only in continuation, and the only hope for immortality lies in repurposing.

Almost a quarter mile beyond the dome's west gates and locks and cargo hatches of Balboa, on a low rust-colored hill, is the vast field of monuments. Always, the wind blows between the stones, but on Phantom Night it blows with the voices of the dead. Even if few have heard these voices for themselves, few doubt the truth of the tales.

One night each twenty-four months, the dead come awake. But not to *haunt* the living. One night a year the dead come awake to howl reassurance across the planum. To whistle and sing thin, papery songs. To be grateful that the heirs to their incarnations are faithful and have kept the covenant to insure the Seven and the Seven keep the Four at bay. This is how the dead celebrate.

The dead sing.

And the living tell tales of the ghost songs.

The sun sets.

On the boulevard, the March begins.

5.

In their rooms three stories above the revelers, two women lie in bed. Earlier, they were among those who visited Beáta Copper's stall to buy their gourd, and they are the mothers of a girl child named Miranda. The women do not number themselves among the believers, not in the strictest sense. For them, the ceremonies of Phantom Night are the expression of metaphor. They might even use the word *superstition,* in the company of like mind individuals. Yet they also do not doubt the value of these ceremonies. Life is nothing easy, and whatever eases the passage is to be cherished, so long as it doesn't encourage waste. Like the faithful, they find no greater wrong against humanity than waste. So, in their own ways they observe the night. For example, there are few greater affirmations of life than sex.

Beryl sits up and gazes towards the open doors leading out onto their balcony. She's a school teacher, and her partner is employed at the windworks. Together, they can afford a good room above the streets, and they can afford to raise a daughter. Beryl sits and watches the not-darkness of the evening outside. The revelers are chanting, laughing, cheering, and soon enough now the march will pass in front of their building. Miranda is down on the street with her friends, waiting to catch the sweets and baubles that will be tossed by the harlequins and waiting to shudder at the towering marionettes.

"We should go out now. It's getting late," Beryl says and turns to smile at her lover. "We don't want to miss the mummers."

"Are you very sure?" asks Aruna, whose skin is almost as dark as Beryl's is pale. "It may be we could show greater devotion to the Ladies if we had another tumble."

"It might be you ought get dressed," Beryl replies.

Aruna kisses the small of her back, then lets one finger trail gently up the length of Beryl's spine. "We can't have ours the only dark veranda, now can we?" she whispers.

"No, we can't," agrees Beryl, standing, pulling on a simple white shift with elbow length sleeves. "It would be a poor example."

Aruna makes an off color joke, but she follows her partner's example, gathering up her trousers and a gingham shirt, and they go together out onto the balcony. Beryl uses a pocket flint to light the candle set into the gourd, and then she hangs it from a hook on one of the doors. They sit together at the edge of the balcony, letting their legs dangle through the iron bars, as if they were as young as their daughter.

On this night all are young, as are as old.

On this night all simply *are*.

When she was twenty, Aruna drew a crimson tile, though she never talks about that dawn in the depths of the temple. She never brings up the subject, and Beryl never asks, though she's known for years. Beryl secretly hopes Miranda will be so lucky, even if her mothers do not accept the Seven and the Seven and the Four as literal fact, and even if they have raised their child to believe likewise.

"I can't see her anywhere," Aruna says, but that's hardly a surprise. It would be almost impossible to spot Miranda in the throng lining the boulevard.

"She's fine. You shouldn't worry."

"I'm not worried."

"*You* worry," Beryl replies, and Aruna knows it's pointless to argue.

Below them, there is the warm glow of hundreds of gourds, and the facades of every home and business are adorned with at least one – and sometimes several – soul lights. The sight of it makes Aruna sleepy, despite the noise, or it may be that she was sleepy before they stepped outside, and the glow is only making her sleepier. She lays her head on Beryl's shoulder.

"Stay awake," Beryl says immediately.

"I'm awake."

"You're awake now. Doesn't mean you'll be awake in five minutes."

"Doesn't mean I won't be."

Beryl turns and lightly kisses the top of Aruna's head. "I know you."

The drummers come first, escorted by the rows of temple monks, and for the time it takes them to pass, most of the onlookers fall silent. Beryl presses her face between the bars for a better view. After the monks will come the council and then a retinue of priestesses. The women who were fortunate enough to draw the fourteen select tiles this year will follow after, still nude and four of them still wearing the dried gore of their feasts. The Four will be on their heels, in turn pursued by the Ladies. By then, the crowd will be a cacophony.

But before the monks have passed, Aruna is dozing.

Beryl doesn't wake her, not even once the avatars have passed, the proxies of the Seven and Seven, shadowed by the dreadful puppets.

———— ➤ ————

WHILST THE NIGHT REJOICES
PROFOUND AND STILL

This story was written in October 2012, for a Halloween issue of *Sirenia Digest*. In my blog, I described it thus: "A sort of Samhain on Mars story. More of a Bradbury feel than my science-fiction stories that have a William Gibson feel, but not a pastiche. And not a riff on 'The Exiles.' Do any of my science fiction stories have a voice I haven't borrowed?" But, actually, five-plus years farther along, I think it might be a take on "The Exiles," after all.

Ballad of an Echo Whisperer

A gun shot.

A pirouetting shadow.

Steel wheels rolling on steel rails, rushing not quite smoothly, not silently, over gravel ballast and softwood crossties hewn long ago, then soaked in creosote to form this magic ladder stretching all the way from Penn Station to the city of New Orleans. I do call it magic, the railroad, all 1,377 miles of it. I lie in my narrow upper berth, the sleeper car swaying and jerking side to side beneath me, around me. We're racing northeast over Lake Pontchartrain not too long past dawn, heading home. Out there, the morning sun has set the estuary on fire, and the white inferno is too bright to look at for more than a few seconds without averting my eyes. There are already (or still) fishermen on the water in their fragile, bobbing boats, casting lines or reeling them in again.

How can they drift in the fire?

How can anyone bear that heat?

I haven't slept, because it was easier for me to stay awake all night than get up in time to make it to the Union Passenger Terminal on Loyola at six a.m. Now, I'll try to catch a few daylight hours of shut-eye, but first I'm watching as the *Crescent* sails over the lake. When I glance directly down, from this angle I can't see the tracks below me, not the rails and crossties and gravel ballast of the Norfolk Southern Bridge. I only see the brown-green water, as if the train has, even if only briefly, become another sort of boat. The impression is disconcerting. I'm not afraid of drowning, but I am afraid of being trapped inside a sinking train. I am afraid of burning alive on that blazing lake.

Below me, Annapurna is stretched out reading on the lower bunk. She slept last night, wise girl. Despite her name, she isn't Hindu; she's from Gloucester. Her parents just liked the name. No one ever calls her

Annapurna, except, she says, her family. She goes by Anna, and I've never called her anything else. Anna is stretched out beneath me reading by the light of the brackish lake of fire. I'm the writer, but Anna is the one who reads books the way some people eat popcorn. This morning, she's working her way through a volume of Thomas Hardy that she picked up in a bookshop on Dauphine Street. She'll read "A Mere Interlude" and "The Three Strangers"; I'll sleep.

I followed her to New Orleans, because she offered to pay for everything. She had business there, not me. Personally, I can do without the mid-August heat and the tourists who swarm the Vieux Carré, where she insisted on staying.

Anna is never a tourist. She prides herself on that. She'd never, for instance, attend Mardi Gras. She'd say "That's for locals, and it's for tourists who come to get drunk and catch beads and pretend they know what Mardi Gras is about. To pretend they belong. But I'm not a local, and I'm not a tourist."

Anna travels a lot, never a tourist and never a local, but, instead, passing through wrapped in this limbo she has created for herself. Sometimes, I wonder if she even sees the places she visits, and other times I suspect she experiences them more intimately than most and with a perspective she can only manage by keeping herself at arm's length. She's a photographer, and she's fortunate enough that she doesn't have to live off her art. Which isn't to say she isn't good at what she does; she's fucking brilliant. But she inherited a lot of money from an aunt or uncle (I've never been clear on which), so she has the luxury of not having to whore herself out to whoever is willing to pay.

"You're not a whore, William," she says.

"Close enough," I reply. "I'm selling my thoughts, not my body. That's the only difference. I'm a legal whore, maybe because thoughts are intangible and nowhere near as much fun as sex."

"Plenty of places it's illegal to speak your mind," she says. "To write down your thoughts for other people to read." She begins reeling off examples, and I concede her point.

This is a conversation from the dining car on the way down from Manhattan. It's an old, recurring conversation, and this time it recurs over dry salmon and a flavorless medley of steamed vegetables as we're leaving DC and entering Virginia. She abruptly changes the subject to Louisiana voodoo, and I pick at the desiccated fish on my plate while she lectures me about sympathetic magic, the African diaspora, Marie Laveau, and Papa Legba. I say hardly anything at all, because I don't know shit about voodoo. After dinner, when we're back in our sleeper compartment, she shoves a tattered paperback from one of her carry-ons into my hands – *The Spiritual Churches of New Orleans: Origins, Beliefs, and Rituals of an African-American Religion*. I flip through the pages and see that the two authors are anthropologists, one from Tulane and the other from Columbia University. Anna assures me it's thorough, trustworthy scholarship, and for a while I pretend to be interested in remedying my ignorance while she watches the night rushing by beyond the windows.

Then the porter comes round to fold out our beds, and I'm relieved that I can climb into my upper berth, set the book aside, and play Angry Birds on my iPad. Anna tips the man, because Anna tips almost everyone. She can afford to. The porter's name is Romalise. I ask him if he's from New Orleans or New York (from his accent, I suspect the former), and he confirms my suspicions – the Lower 9th Ward, to be precise – and he talks a few minutes about hurricanes Katrina and Rita, about how his family came back when so many others didn't, and about a Vietnamese restaurant where he was once a *Chef de partie* before the floods. When Anna and I are alone again, she explains that *Chef de partie* is really just a fancy phrase for line cook; I don't bother asking what it is that line cooks do. I'd rather be flinging vengeful pixel birds at snickering green pixel pigs.

In hindsight, that night seems so innocent, and lying here in my bunk peeking at the white, white burning expanse of Lake Pontchartrain, it also seems a lifetime ago. I know this because it's one of the last nights before I wander alone – long after midnight – down St. Peter towards Jackson Square and come to the black wrought-iron gate wedged in between a tobacconist and a shop that seems to specialize in the unlikely pairing of alligator skulls and Catholic tchotchkes. At first glance, this gate appears no different than any number of other such gates I've passed, most leading down short brick corridors or alleyways to modest courtyards. I almost keep walking, because there's a cool, half-hearted breeze breathed from the direction of the Square, cool air off the river; and so what if the sun's down, the night's still hot enough that I'm sweating like a pig. But I don't keep walking; I do stop.

Later – no, sooner than later – I'll regret not having continued on my way. Sooner than later, I'll regret having stopped at the black gates, *before* I stop at the gates. Can the present affect the past, and can the future affect the present? Retrocausality. The impossible only seems impossible until it happens.

I peer through the bars. The gate opens into an arched passage, no more than ten feet long, into one of the small courtyard gardens. The garden is lit, even at this late hour, and I can see carefully tended banana trees and night-blooming jessamine. The redbrick walls are mostly obscured by the clinging vines of bougainvillea and wisteria. There are voices, of women and of men and of people whose sex I can't discern.

There are voices, enough of them that the courtyard should be crowded with people. It sounds like a party. The voices, laughter and the clink of glasses, a live jazz band – trumpets, trombones, saxophones, clarinets, a drummer.

There are voices, but I can't see anyone. So I tell myself the party's inside, obviously, and only some acoustical trick, sound ricocheting off the walls and then up the passage to the black wrought-iron gates, is responsible for what I expected to see being at odds with what I *do* see.

It's almost three in the morning, and I wake Anna when I open the door to the hotel room we're sharing. I try to be quiet, but I bump into a suitcase that neither of us bothered to put in the closet or a corner or some other place out of the way. She switches on the lamp beside her bed, and I apologize for waking her.

"You look like you've seen a ghost," she says. Could I ask for a more clichéd greeting?

"It's just the heat," I reply. "It's still sweltering out there."

She squints at me and rubs her eyes. "They say it should be a little cooler tomorrow. There might be a thunderstorm or two in the afternoon."

"Doesn't it just get hotter down here when it rains?"

She looks annoyed and switches the lamp off again.

The next morning, before we split up and she heads to the Garden District and Lafayette No. 1, we get beignets and coffee from a place called Café Beignet. The crispy squares of fried dough come in a paper bag at least half filled with confectioners' sugar. The grease from the beignets has made lumps of some of the sugar, and Anna picks these out and eats them.

"It's a wonder you have a tooth left in your head," I tell her, and she ignores me and begins talking about the Karstendick tomb in Lafayette No. 1. We're here because her most recent obsession is cemetery ironwork, and Anna's informed me there are several superb examples of cast-iron tombs scattered around the city. Most date back well into the 19th century.

"In this climate, with the floods and all," I say, "it's pretty hard to believe they haven't all rusted away."

"You know, sometimes people *do* take care of shit." Then she goes on a bit about Gothic Revival influences and Doric columns, frieze embellishments and pintelles and downspout grotesques. I honestly try to pay attention, but the heat is distracting, and the talk of ironwork leads my mind back to the black gate and the courtyard.

Anna drops the bag of powdered sugar into a trash can and asks about the night before.

"You really did look pretty shook up," she says.

So, I commit a lie of omission and only tell her about staring into the courtyard and hearing an invisible party. She raises an eyebrow and frowns, clearly disappointed.

"That's all?"

"Yeah," I reply. "It was just a bit weird."

"We clearly have very different ideas of what constitutes weird." Then she suggests that the party was somewhere just out of sight, in one of the apartments opening out into the courtyard, and there was nothing more peculiar at work than echoes. Out of sight, but not out of earshot.

Great minds think alike and all that shit.

Anna flags down a taxi and leaves me standing on the corner of Bienville and Chartres. We've made plans to meet up for dinner at Tujague's. I don't know much worth knowing about restaurants, and so, whenever we travel together, I always let Anna choose. She's assured me I'll love the shrimp remoulade at Tujague's.

The Crescent Line speeds across Pontchartrain, and I turn my back on the rippling white fire and quickly drift off to sleep. I dream about the courtyard, and if I dream about anything else upon waking I'm unable to remember that I did. The dream is as good as video, faithfully reproducing even the most insignificant details of that night. Assuming any details are insignificant. Having written that, I realize how arrogant it is to claim that I can sort what is relevant from what is irrelevant.

So, the dream, as good as the night itself.

Conversely, the night, as good as the dream itself.

I press my face to the bars, straining for a better view of the courtyard. Now that I'm listening closely, the music rises and falls, as do the voices and Dixieland jazz, the rhythm makes me think of the wheels of trains against steel rails and also of waves rushing forward, then dragged back into the sea. A clot of drunken college students passes by, and they laugh. Probably, they're laughing at me, but I ignore them. And that's when I notice the shadows moving about in that counterfeit patch of jungle. Shadows that sway to the same cadence as the music and the jumble of conversation. Only, almost immediately, I realize I'm not seeing *shadows,* plural, but a *single* shadow. It washes to and fro, falling across the vine-covered walls and the drooping banana leaves. In no way does the shadow strike me as out of place in the empty courtyard.

It is, after all, only a shadow.

Same as the commingled voices are only voices and the jazz is only brass and percussion and woodwind.

You look like you've seen a ghost.

Do I? Do I really?

"William, I don't think you've heard a word I've said."

I glance back over my shoulder at St. Peter Street, but there's no sign of anyone who might have spoken. The street is empty. The voice was familiar.

On the way to New Orleans, I'm still awake at 2:51 a.m. when we pull into the Salisbury station, and the dimly-lit platform is deserted. No one's waiting to get on, but the *Crescent* stops anyway. I'm scribbling something on the third from the last page of a Moleskine notebook, and I stop scribbling and stare out at the depot. My head is filled with Pink Floyd, "Waiting for the Worms" spilling in through my earbuds. The volume's up too loud, because the volume's always up too loud. Fuck me if I know why, but I tap at the window with the eraser end of my mechanical pencil, three quick, sharp taps.

And then I see the black dog watching me from the platform. If I'd seen it a second earlier, I wouldn't have tapped against the sleeper compartment's window. I swear I wouldn't have. I don't know what sort of dog it is. When I get back to Boston, I tell myself, I'll figure that out. I *will* try. It might be a very large black lab. Or it might not be. I've never been a dog person, and so to me the dog is simply a big black dog. It's watching me, while I watch it, and its eyes flash a brilliant emerald green, shining back the light from the train. The dog is sitting near one of the closed doors to the station, its ears pricked forward; everything about the animal speaks to its attentiveness. It tilts its head to one side, and I almost shout down to wake Anna. Almost, but only almost.

"It's a dog," she'd say, groggy and angry. "Jesus God, William. You woke me up to see a goddamn *dog?* Do you even *know* what time it is?"

She wouldn't see what I see. She isn't meant to.

The dog that might be a black lab tilts its head to one side, and, on cue, a long shadow, cast by nothing I can see, pirouettes across the concrete. The dog lies down and rests its head between its paws. The shadow dances for me.

I force myself to look back at my notebook, and I don't look up again until the train is moving once more and there's nothing to see in the window but my reflection, superimposed over the blur of a North Carolina night.

A few days before we leave for New Orleans, I'm walking along Newbury Street at dusk. I hear someone call my name, and when I turn to see who there's an instant or two of vertigo. An instant or two when the familiar cacophony of the crowded sidewalk shrinks down to a whisper, and instead of exhaust fumes and hot asphalt I smell jessamine blossoms. I recognize the sweet aroma of the flowers because I'll smell it – *for the first time* – when I stand with my face pressed to the bars of an iron gate on St. Peter Street. On Newbury Street, I smell jessamine, and I see a large black dog padding away from me, snaking through the pedestrians. It isn't on a leash, and no one else seems to even notice it. Then the dog is gone, as is the smell of the flowers, and all is ordinary again.

Over breakfast, I tell Anna what I saw when the train stopped in Salisbury. Well, I tell her about the dog, not about the shadow. I haven't told anyone about the shadow.

"Maybe it lives at the station," she says.

"Lives there?"

"You know. The way some shops have cats. Like that. A train dog. Well, a train *station* dog."

"Maybe," I say, picking at a dry croissant I suspect was baked days before. I've smeared it with butter and strawberry jelly, but it stubbornly remains the Sahara Desert of croissants. "Probably."

Anna smiles and sips her steaming tea. The server pauses at our booth to ask if we need anything else, if everything's okay; I resist making a crack about the desiccated croissant. I have a habit of making snarky comments to waiters and what have you, and it drives Anna nuts.

"We're fine," she says. "Thank you."

When the server's moved on to the next booth, I pinch off a piece of the croissant and frown at it.

"Maybe Black Shuck's moved to Salisbury," Anna says to me. "Maybe –"

"Black Shuck?"

"You know. Ghost dogs? Hellhounds? Barghests?"

"Barghests?" I drop the pinched-off piece of croissant onto my plate. "You lost me."

"You truly do need to read a book every now and then," she sighs. "You write the things, the least you could do is read a few."

I wipe my hands on a paper napkin and lean back, watching as we rush past some bit of small-town trackside squalor. House trailers. Rusted cars precariously balanced on uneven stacks of concrete blocks. A scrubby brown lawn with a bizarre arrangement of life-sized plastic deer.

Meanwhile, in New Orleans, I peer through the wrought-iron gate on St. Peter, and the stingy breeze off the river stirs the banana leaves, lazily shuffling them about like the wings of enormous beetles. A woman is singing now, and the shadow sways in time to the "Basin Street Blues."

Now won't you come along with me
To the Mississippi?
We'll take a trip to the land of dreams
Blowing down the river, down to New Orleans.

Were the gate unlocked, I might find the courage to open it. I might also dance in that garden, with only a shade for a partner. Only an eclipse, and my own body's eclipse melding in a ghostly *pas de deux.* Oh, there's a word I haven't dared to use until now: *ghostly.* But wasn't it, that night? Even if I am not claiming the presence of an actual specter, in any conventional sense, surely this is a haunting. A haunted courtyard that's haunted me. A bruised place or moment that has, in turn, bruised me.

On our way home, Lake Pontchartrain also burns, not by sunrise, but by sunset. The *Crescent* speeds across that low span above marshes and then the big water proper. Our compartment is an even numbered compartment, so the windows face westward out across nothing at all but the low, flammable waves. The incandescent waves. This fire is not white morning, but the red-orange herald of twilight. I take a few photos with my Canon digital, and Anna warns me that it's terrible for the lens, aiming it directly into the sun that way. But I do, regardless, my sad-ass excuse for living dangerously. The sun is so bright and so much heat is filling up our compartment that it's very quickly becoming uncomfortable. Anna wants to move to the one across the aisle; it's empty, after all, and she can't imagine anyone will care. I say no, this is something I've never seen before, something I might never see again. She scowls and doesn't look at the lake. A tourist would gawk like I am gawking, and she is never a tourist.

The conductor – he must be a conductor – is moving through the sleeper car, letting people know we're only about forty-five minutes from arrival. Our door is open, and he pauses and points out across Pontchartrain.

"Beautiful, isn't she?" he asks.

Just then, we pass the remnants of what was once a pier, but is now nothing but a series of rotting pilings jutting unevenly from the water. There is another ruined pier after it, and then another. They put me in mind of broken, rotten teeth; I photograph them.

"First time in New Orleans?" he asks me, and I tell him that yes, it is. He smiles, then jabs a thumb over his shoulder, back towards that unoccupied compartment that Anna wanted to move to.

"From that side, you can see I-10 and the Twin Spans. Took a hell of a beating in the storm."

I don't have to ask which storm.

"Surge pulled the segments apart, yanked them loose and tossed them around like Lego blocks. Hard to believe a thing like that if you didn't see the aftermath. Fixed up good as new now, though."

I snap another photo, a chalk-white egret wading through a patch of cattails growing beside the tracks. The photo comes out nothing but a blur.

"So, you guys hear anything odd last night?" he asks. He's watching the lake, too, eyes shielded with his left hand. Anna wants to know what he means by odd.

"Had a couple of passengers say they heard something moving around, up and down the aisle."

"Something?" Anna asks him. "Not someone?"

"That's what they said. One lady said she thought maybe it was a dog. Maybe. We do allow some types of service animals. Seeing-eye dogs and what have you, but they aren't allowed to wander around loose like that. This lady, she said it was snuffling at her door the way a dog sniffs about. Said it sounded like a real big dog, too."

"I didn't hear anything," I lie. "But I'm a very sound sleeper," I also lie.

"I didn't hear it, either," Anna tells the conductor, and I assume she isn't lying. She wouldn't. It isn't like her. "Rules or no rules, maybe someone's dog got loose."

"Maybe," he says. "Asked around, of course, and no one would own up to it. But I figure they probably wouldn't."

I find it remarkable, even now, how so unremarkable a matter can strike me as simultaneously mundane and unnerving. But he'd said some*thing*, not some*one*. And I *had* heard it, and what I heard, I knew it wasn't a dog, same as I knew the black dog I'd seen back in Salisbury, the shadow's danc-ing partner, had been something *more* than a dog.

I sound like a madman. I know that. I don't believe that I am, but I wouldn't begrudge anyone who reads this the right to doubt my sanity.

After Salisbury, after I finally drift off to an uneasy sleep, and not too long before dawn somewhere in South Carolina, the snuffling noise the conductor will ask about wakes me. I lay very still, listening. Some*thing* brushes against the wall of our compartment with enough force that I can tell it's some*thing* larger than a seeing-eye dog. Unless maybe the blind are using Irish Wolfhounds these days. My back is to the door, and I don't turn to see if there's any*thing* to see. It lingers outside our compartment for, I guess, five minutes or so. At least, I listen to it for about that long; I can't say how long it may have been there while I was sleeping. And then it makes a grunting noise and moves along. Its footfalls are heavier than I'd expect from a dog.

The snuffling thing woke me from a dream of the dog I saw on Newbury Street.

"Well, you two enjoy your visit," says the conductor, and he smiles and leaves us with the blazing lake.

The night after I find the black gate and the courtyard, I take another walk, absolutely determined not to return to the garden and its waltzing shadow. I head down Royal and turn north at the intersection with Conti, turning away from Jackson Square and the river. I follow Conti Street past Bourbon and turn right at Dauphine, and by then I'm far enough from the courtyard that I've managed – at least consciously – to stop chewing over the events of the evening before. I have the shop windows and buskers, instead. I have a trio of drag queens – fellow tourists – who stop me and want to know how to get to a club called Oz. I have no idea whatsoever. They flirt with me, then wander off in search of the Yellow Brick Road. I watch them go, all platform heels and sequins and wigs, and I'm thinking, *Where does a train track begin and end?* Though clearly it is a *line,* does this one begin in Manhattan, or does it, instead, begin in New Orleans? Isn't this as relative to direction as determining the beginning of a circle?

I don't think a mathematician would say so.

But it seems that way to me.

A loop. An entirely unconventional Möbius strip, yes? Should I happen to *shout* within a three-dimensional Möbius, that sound would travel round and round and round. And if I shout along a straight *line,* the sound may echo back. So, *returning* to me either way.

A shout. Or dogs and shadows and unseen things that prowl the aisles of sleeper cars.

Over breakfast, on the way home, I say to Anna, "You never did tell me if you found that tomb you were looking for in Greenwood." I'm trying, trying, trying not to think about my dream of the black gate. Fortunately, Anna would almost always rather talk about her work than anything else. Sometimes, like now, I use this to my advantage, though it's a quality about her I greatly admire. She still has the sort of passion for her art that I lost a long, long time ago. She's said it annoys her that I never want to discuss my books and short fiction.

"The 1861 Edwards and Bennett," she nods. "Yeah, I found it. God, it's in beautiful shape, that one. Exquisite craftsmanship."

"So, it was a very profitable trip for you."

"Yes, indeed. Very, very. I'm thinking I may actually be able to get a gallery interested in an exhibition. Well, I was *hoping* that when I set up the trip, but don't count your chickens, right? Anyway, I sent Carlotta some shots, and she agrees we could land a show. She's excited."

Carlotta is Anna's agent, and is, by the way, a better agent than mine.

"Then at least I haven't suffered this abominable croissant in vain," I say, and she laughs.

"Your sacrifice will be duly noted, Brave William. As a matter of fact, I hereby dub thee *Sir* William of Mass Ave," and Anna picks up her butter knife and leans across the table. She taps a flat side of the blade against my right shoulder, my forehead, and then my left shoulder. Several people in the dining car notice and they laugh.

I sit up straighter and bow. "You are too gracious, My Lady. I shall uphold thy honor and my knightly vows, never flinching in the face of perilous pastries."

"Fais ce que tu veux, bon sire."

More laughter.

The laughter in the courtyard is high and shrill.

Despite my intent to avoid the gate, here I am again. Didn't I turn *right* on Conti, turning north, *away* from the river, away from that black wrought-iron gate? I'm absolutely fucking certain that I did. But here I am, regardless. I would have had to turn east – onto Dauphine or Burgundy – then turn south onto St. Peter. So, the French Quarter has gone Möbius, or, lost in thought, I blundered right back to the exact place I intended not to go. Yeah, I know the latter is the more likely, but I can't help believing the former is what actually happened.

The air carrying the laughter to me is so bloated with the cloyingly sweet smell of wisteria and bougainvillea that I cover my mouth and nose. I think I'd gag, otherwise. Wasn't it a pleasant, soothing smell only last night? But the voices are the same, and the laughter, and the jazz.

The woman singing.

Down in New Orleans, the land of dreams.

You'll never know how, how much it seems.

The shadow's there, swaying to the music. And if I don't want to be here, why don't I turn and walk away? Never mind the question of how I got here, leaving would be simple enough. But I stand with my face pressed to those black bars painted black, watching as the shadow sways and swoops and dips.

There's a single gunshot then. I know the sound of a gunshot, a pistol shot, and this isn't a car backfiring. And it isn't fireworks. It's a gunshot.

The shadow stops dancing. Wherever that party I can't see is going on, a woman has begun screaming and men are cursing. The trombones and clarinets and singer have all fallen silent, but I can hear glass breaking.

"Jesus," a man growls. "Jesus fucking Christ. Jesus fucking Christ."

I'm not alone on the sidewalk. Other people are passing the gate, but if any one of these passersby heard the gunshot, or the screams, they're busy minding their own business, pretending they've heard nothing at all.

The sky above Pontchartrain is on fire.

The blade of the butter knife is cold against my skin.

"William, you've not heard a word that I've said."

The sky is on fire.

"Have you?"

The garden gate is locked against me.

So, turn the little key.

A few days after we return from New Orleans, when Anna and I have each gone our separate ways until the next time she asks me to accompany her on a trip. Or calls to ask if I'd like to have dinner with her. Or see a movie. A few nights after we return from New Orleans, I wake from a dream that smelled of wisteria and jessamine and the faintest acrid stink of gunpowder. The shadow is dancing across the walls of my bedroom, and I can hear the snuffling sound, the sound from the train that *wasn't* a black dog, just outside my bedroom door.

In my upper berth, as we pull out of the Salisbury station, I tear a narrow strip from one of the violet *Crescent* line schedules, and twist it just so, then join the ends. I fold it into a Möbius strip. One end is joined to the other by the force on my right thumb and forefinger, so there's only the illusion of infinity. I release the paper. It flutters to the uncomfortable mattress and is nothing but a straight line again. A railroad track. A straight line is infinite. Only a matter of perspective makes it otherwise.

"Beautiful, isn't she?" the conductor asks, and I look up from the book of Thomas Hardy stories I was reading. I think he's talking about Anna, sitting there in the seat across from me. I look up, and she has her face pressed against the window, even though the light from the sunset on the lake is so bright I've had to pull the curtain on my side of the compartment shut. In the compartment across the narrow aisle, children are laughing so loudly that it's hard to hear what the conductor says next.

I close my book.

"Well, sir. You enjoy your visit," says the conductor, and he smiles and leaves me alone with the blazing lake.

The seat across from me is empty.

"William, you haven't heard a single word I've said."

It always was.

At the black gate I turn my head, slow as slow ever is, and there is no black dog watching me.

I turn back to the garden, and there is no shadow. There never was.

Turn the little key.

The party ends and the woman screams as moments echo, and I turn the key, squeeze the trigger, and the gun is a thunderstorm above the Vieux Carré.

----⟫----

BALLAD OF AN ECHO WHISPERER

In June 2013, I was a guest of honor at the World Horror Convention in New Orleans. During a heat wave. Daytime temperatures were exceeding 100°F, and so I stayed in the hotel until well after dark – when the temperature plummeted into the nineties – and then took long walks each night through the French Quarter. This story was inspired by those walks. And also by the morning sun off the waters of Lake Pontchartrain, not long after dawn, as the train ferried us back to a chilly New England excuse for summer. I sat down and wrote this story not long after the trip, in July of that year, for Ellen Datlow's *Fearful Symmetries* (ChiZine Publications, 2014).

The Cripple and the Starfish

Almost three thousand feet above sea level, the ruins of the Overlook Mountain House squat silent and barren on the crest of its namesake. It is a bleak, disowned place, left for timber rattlers and roosting birds, black bears and chipmunks, visited now only by the occasional sightseers curious and intrepid enough to make the two-hour hike from Woodstock. The hotel burned on a February night in 1923, and all that remains is a towering grey right-angle maze of cement poured in 1878, under the direction of architect and builder Lewis B. Wagonen of nearby Kingston, New York. These walls were raised one hundred and thirty-seven years ago, and ninety-two years ago the hotel burned. There is about this lonely place a mute and inescapable arithmetic – dates, altitude, time, geometry. It is the sum of its history, and little else remains. And, too, there are ghosts, of the fifteen women and men who perished in the fire and of four laborers who died during the hotel's construction. Though, by *ghosts* nothing more is meant than fading memory, lingering, voiceless echoes trapped forever in empty window casements and in reinforcing iron bars exposed by crumbling concrete and rusting down all the long decades since the fire. Lost souls with names that are nowhere now remembered, faces forgotten, whispers. In the summer, the ruins are wreathed in a riot of green – bracken and saplings and poison ivy, red oaks, mountain paper birch, balsam fir and red spruce, blackberry, blueberry, huckleberry.

But this is not summer. This is a freezing night late in January, and a storm front from Ontario has swept across the Great Lakes to dump its burden of snow on the peaks and ridges and deep glacier- and river-carved valleys of the Catskill Escarpment. The moon, waxing gibbous, is hidden behind the low violet-blue-oyster clouds racing by overhead, occasionally so low that they scrape their underbellies on the mountains, fog-shrouding secrets, concealing those who wish concealment. Those who have come;

those who have gathered. Another age might have pulled punches and called this a fairie court, though it is surely nothing of the sort.

All the same, there is a court here.

Below the open sky, where once were the second and third stories and the wide peaked roof of Mr. Wagonen's stately pleasure dome, sits the Queen of Blades, Madam of Keen Steel and Obsidian Massacres, most often known as the Lady of Silver Whispers (she has so, so many sobriquets, but not a proper name among them). She reclines upon her throne. She *names* it her throne, as does her retinue, the attendants and sycophants and hangers-on, but in truth it's nothing more than a broken-backed, mildewed récamier, the upholstery so threadbare and rotted that it hangs in faded strips the black and golden yellow of a yellowjacket wasp. She is naked, save the charcoal smears painted on her white skin, skin as pale and cold as the falling, drifting snow. Her eyes are rubies. Her lips are the deep, poisonous black of drooping clusters of belladonna berries, and her kiss is loaded with the same hyoscine, atropine, and hyoscyiamine compounds found in those very same deadly nightshades. Her nails are carved of cobalt glass.

The court teems around her, frenetic, freed on nights like this from their necessary seclusion, from the shadow sorceries that conceal them from the eyes of men – save on those rare instances when they choose to reveal themselves. They mutter delightful obscenities among one another, they argue philosophy and history and fashion, they prostrate themselves at her feet. Some among them caper and dance, fuck and engage in acts so perverse that no one would ever deign to call those acts mere fucking. Most nights here there is only hunger, their mutual craving shared and unsated, but not tonight. Tonight there has been a feast, a carload of unwary travelers whose Prius broke down on Route 212, three warm bodies stolen like children from their cribs – father, mother, daughter – and presented to the Lady of Silver Whispers. All here have drunk; not their fill, for there is not ever any genuine satiation. But the bill of fare was enough that the nagging emptiness has been dulled for a time.

They are not all her progeny. Some have come here from as far away as Chicago, Manhattan, Ottawa, Boston, Philadelphia, traveling long night-bound miles to witness her glory and to be counted among this number. One of these is a coal-haired woman named Marjorie Marie Winthrop, who was only nineteen years old the night the Overlook Mountain House burned. She's one of the youngest among the court, and she comes and goes, erratic as the weather. The Lady would never count her as loyal; Marjorie

Marie has always been too distant and consumed by her own hauntings and obsessions. Vampires are haunted, obsessed things, every one among them. But some, like Marjorie Marie, much more so than others. She sits on stairs that once led up to the hotel's wide south piazza, smoking, wrapped in the raw-bone wind and trying to recall how it felt to shiver.

She isn't alone on the stairs. The man with her was a colonel in the War Between the States, a Union soldier in Lincoln's army, and for decades he has loved Marjorie Marie, in the careless, detached way that vampires love. He sits with her, listening to the laughter and screams and catcalls of the court. His mother named him Hiram Levi, but somewhere down more than a century and a half of life and this existence stranded between life and the grave, somewhere and somewhen he sloughed that name off, like an old skin. Marjorie Marie knows him only as Willie Love, the name he adopted because of his fondness for the harmonicas, guitars, and the voices of the Delta Blues.

"You talk an awful lot," she says to Willie Love. She's soft-spoken, and her voice still carries a hint of a Southern Appalachian accent. "Sometimes, I think you're the wordiest dead man whom I've ever met."

Willie Love is always going on about writing books, though, to Marjorie Marie's knowledge, he's never set a single word down on paper. Instead, he seems to carry it all filed behind his carmine eyes.

He smiles and spares a quick glance at the swirling sky, then continues as if he hasn't been interrupted.

"I was saying, if we conceive of any given human being as the embodiment of the Taoist concept of yin and yang, and of the *taijitu* – which symbolizes yin and yang – each body being black and each soul being white – two distinct things that form a complete whole, distinguishable, divisible, but also intrinsically linked – then what occurs in our passage is that our souls have been, as it were, *inverted* – in part, the white turning to black – and then melded with our flesh. Refashioned, made *in*divisible, *in*extricable, *in*distinguishable."

"Inextricable," she says, and Marjorie Marie takes a long drag on her cigarette. The smoke reminds her of being alive and her breath fogging in the cold. Of course, she can't inhale the smoke. Her lungs have not drawn breath, haven't inflated, in all those one hundred and eleven years since her death at the hands of a pretty Romanian *moroi*. Even so, she *has* long since learned the trick of drawing the smoke into her mouth, then letting it leak slowly from her nostrils and lips. She doesn't feel the nicotine, as her ruined and transformed metabolism is entirely incapable of processing it. Those intoxicating molecules are not passed along through her sluggish circulatory system to cross the blood-brain barrier and act upon waiting acetylcholine receptor proteins in the adrenal medulla, the autonomic ganglia, and the central nervous system. But it helps, regardless, just having something in her mouth, something to take the edge off the endless oral cravings and keep her hands busy.

"Imagine," he continues, "the yin and yang as a paint bucket filled half with black and half with white paint. A stick is inserted into the paint, and it's stirred until it's not black and white, but only a uniform black."

"Wouldn't it come out grey, instead?" she asks him. "Not black, but grey?"

"You're being pedantic," he says.

"Yeah, but black and white make grey."

"Pedantic and too literal. It's a metaphor."

"Still, black and white make grey."

Then Marjorie Marie and Willie Love are both silent for a time, letting the cold night hang heavy between them, filled with the noise from the court. And the ceaseless wind. It's a wild night on the mountain, a wendigo's breath rattling through the trees and roaring across the snow gathered between their trunks, burying root and stone and last autumn's rotting leaves beneath crystalline dunes.

"Is there more?" she asks, finally.

"There's always more," he replies. "Isn't that the way it works?"

"I don't know. You're older than me."

"Older don't make me no way wise, girl."

Marjorie Marie has smoked her cigarette down almost to the filter; she drops the butt and grinds it out against the concrete step with the ball of her bare left foot. Then she lights another. The smoke, seemingly immune to the wind, hangs about her face like a question mark. She has the amber eyes of a lynx. She took her dinner from the mother, and the woman looked into those eyes, and the vampire looked into the woman's soul, her divisible soul that would soon be freed by her death.

Willie Love continues:

"So, yin and yang, and there's that dot of white in the black and, likewise, that point of black in the white half. I think of them as the eyes of the *taijitu*. When we died, you and me, those eyes were plucked from out their rightful places and swapped, so all the white was then in the white and all the black was then in the black. The inherent *balance* of yin and yang was pried apart. Violated. So, our bodies have no soul remaining to keep them alive and animate, and our souls have no body to tether them to the earth. But, instead of death, dissolution, whatever, our souls are tied down to – well, I'm not precisely sure what – a piece of magickal material, let's say. They are tied down, secreted away. What remains of our souls, now fused, returns as ghosts to haunt our corpses. Our bodies should be decaying to nothing but bones or less, right, right? Dust. But, no, *instead* they are puppeteered around by our fused black souls, and so long as we feed on the life of others –"

"It sounds to me, Willie, like you're rambling, just pulling this stuff outta your ass. We should go back to the party."

"You hate those fucks, and you know it," he sneers. "I know you know it. You don't want to be in there, not any more than I do."

"Whatever," she says, shrugs, and takes another drag on her cigarette.

"As I was saying," he continues, "let's take it just one step farther, and let us say that the process of our transubstantiation and rebirth, that it seared out the *eyes* of the yin and yang –"

"The black and white dots?"

"Right. The black and white dots. So the pieces of our bodies that were in our souls – existing there to maintain balance – are gone. And see, Marjorie Marie, this is why we cast no reflection, why holy water and crucifixes burn us, why our unhallowed flesh cannot bear the touch of sunlight. Because the pieces of our soul that existed within our bodies are gone. Hence no breath, no pulse, no heartbeat or blood pressure. No shitting, no pissing, no fucking ejaculations."

"You miss those, do you?" she smirks.

"Fuck you," he says, then laughs and tosses a dumpling-sized lump of shale towards a paper birch. It hits the trunk with an audible thump, audible at least to their ears, even over the cacophony of the wind and the Lady's bacchanal.

"I used to miss orgasms," she says, "but I got over that a long time ago."

"You were just a kid," he says. "A kid in nineteen aught four, at that. And unmarried. How many orgasms did you ever have?"

"A few," says Marjorie Marie, and she says it a little defensively. "I had a few. Enough to miss them for a time." And wanting desperately to change the subject, to divert his attention from whatever had passed for her sex life before her death at the hands of the Romanian vampire, she says, "There's more, isn't there."

"There's always more," he replies. "Isn't that the way it works?"

"You say so, yeah, that's the way it works."

She smokes, and Willie Love talks.

"Yeah, so maybe it goes like this. The magick of our passage, I mean. Rather than looking soulless, we look like haunted, possessed corpses."

"Speak for yourself, dead man."

"But there's something *different* about her," he says, lowering his voice to a conspiratorial whisper. And he turns his head and points back towards the Lady of Silver Whispers.

"Of course there's something different about her," says Marjorie. "Otherwise, she wouldn't *be* her, now would she? She'd be just be another one of us leeches. I figure it's cause she's older, because she's been around since God was in diapers."

"No," he says, frowning a slight sort of frown. "No, it's not so simple as that, I think. You look at her, or I do, and what I see is a *weak* vampire – because I'm only seeing the original black half of her, not the white and black made into one blackness. Whatever happened to her, she lost her soul. It wasn't fused like yours and mine. We assume she's like us, but she isn't. And what we see, that ain't the all of it. She's like an iceberg, and what we see is only *half* of what's really there to *be* seen. If you look hard, if you look really long and hard, you start to glimpse what's hidden below the surface."

"Honestly, I'd prefer not to."

"I know," says Willie Love. "I see how you are around her."

"She's a bag of spiders," says Marjorie Marie.

He laughs again, then adds, "You best be careful what you say aloud, girl. Don't ever think no one's listening in. There's always ears. There's always eyes. *De mortuis aut bene aut nihil,* as they say."

"I've made it this long, haven't I? And without you to play the good shepherd?"

There's a sudden, violent gust of wind, howling past at thirty miles per hour, thirty or forty or fifty, and trees bend and trees snap. Branches tumble to the ground, and snow devils whirl like dervishes in the Ulster County night. But that wind doesn't touch Marjorie Marie or Willie Love. Their life-in-death curse sets them well beyond the reach of the elements, and the gust parts for them like the Red Sea for *Moshe Rabbenu*. Not so much as a hair on Marjorie Marie's head is stirred by the blow's fury.

She shuts her eyes, bored with thinking on Willie Love's metaphysical prattling. He's not the first vampire she's known who cobbles together absurdities and nonsense in a topsy-turvy attempt to understand a thing that cannot be understood, not by minds that once were human. Minds that are still – for all their newfound alienness – not much *more* than the minds of humans. Marjorie Marie pushes his voice aside and lets her thoughts wander, instead, back through decades, through a century and then some, and she can hear the gentle conversations of the women and men, the privileged, monied families, who've come from bustling Eastern and Midwestern cities to spend lazy summer days and easy warm nights in the hotel, to gaze out at the majestic view. She sees them plainly, seated and standing, arranged along the south piazza at her back, attended by black servant boys with cool drinks. The women in their fine gingham and calico day dresses, hems lined with Irish lace, their wide hats adorned with feathers and silk flowers. The men in their tall beaver-skin top hats, playing checkers and cribbage and cards, string ties, bow ties, spats and frock coats. Billy Murray is singing "I'm Afraid to Come Home in the Dark" from the silver horn of a Victrola. It is a perfect summer day, and the fire that will bring down the Overlook Mountain House is more than two decades away. The new century holds in store horrors these people do not even begin to suspect, not from the gentle, sun-washed perspective of the south piazza. They are protected, momentarily, and the future is a slow train coming, with neither the wail of a steam whistle nor the rumble of steel wheels on steel rails to warn them of its murderous intent. They're babes left alone on the tracks.

"Did you hear that?" Willie Love asks, and she opens her eyes.

"I hear lots of shit, old man." And she does. She hears the fractal whisper of the spiraling snowflakes as they brush one against the other. She hears the heartbeat of a fisher cat sleeping in its den not far from the ruins. She hears the footsteps of a red fox, padding along a fallen log, as it stalks a rabbit, and she hears the lazy blink of an owl watching the fox. She hears the court, like a lesser storm raging beneath the clouds. She hears the flow of xylum sap in a maple's trunk.

"You'll have to be more specific," she adds.

"Never mind," he says. "It was nothing."

Marjorie Marie glances back over her shoulder towards the ragged throne of the Lady of Silver Whispers and all the noisy debauchery, and then she stares up into the falling snow and the low clouds, scanning the sky for any hint of dawn.

"They'll be at it all night," says Willie Love.

"Why the fuck do we even fucking come up here every year?"

"Where else, love, would we go?"

Baby dear, listen here –

I'm afraid to come home in the dark.

The fox pounces. The rabbit screams. The owl flies away.

"We're like the demons down under the sea, the tenants of Ol' Sheol," Willie Love says, and he lights the ragged stub of a cigar. "The flesh and life forces as one, rather than two discrete things. Which is, of course, *naturellement,* soulless in the way that *humans* understand souls. There is nothing remaining to transcend. Nothing has survived that is able, upon the final destruction of the flesh, to flee the body. There are nails, carpet tacks, hammered in all about the tatty edges of our vanquished élan vital."

"Willie, do you ever actually bother to think about this shit before it comes tumbling out of your mouth?"

Singing just like a lark,

There's no place like home.

But I couldn't come home in the dark.

"But," he goes on, undaunted, "this means there is still a consciousness, a spark, the *qì* if you wish – the Hebraic *ruah,* the *lüng* of Tibetan Buddhism, *ad infinitum, ad nauseam* – a *force* there animating the dead flesh, and the dead flesh can be both summoned and guided by magick the way a human soul can – if one is so disposed and has at his disposal the tools, the acumen, and the etheric, nether connections. Ergo, our souls didn't pass on to heaven or hell or whatever, whatever and whichever somewhere. We are, by the curse of our makers, no more than pretty, hungry birds with broken wings."

He rubs at his forehead, then just stares at her awhile.

"What?" she asks finally, his eyes beginning to make her uncomfortable.

"You're still out there rooting about for your own answers, however much you might mock my suspect conjectures."

And at first she doesn't reply. It's her own goddamn business and certainly none of his, and she has the decency to keep it to herself, not hold forth on the steps of the Overlook Mountain House, lecturing to her indifference and the freezing night and all passing nocturnal beasts.

"Marseilles?" he asks, pushing, apparently done torturing her with his treatise on the trapped souls of the undead.

"No," she says. "Not Marseilles."

"Well, sure as shit not that delusional cobblestone alleyway in le quartier du Montparnasse, within spitting distance or a stone's throw from Cimetière du Montparnasse. Not *that,* sweets, no matter how romantic would have been your undoing so near to the final resting places and narrow houses of Maupassant, Man Ray, Baudelaire, Samuel Beckett, Simone de –"

"It wasn't Marseilles," she says again, interrupting his catalog of those interred in Montparnasse Cemetery.

"I heard you went back to Bucharest," he says. "So, I just assumed –"

"Who told you I went back to Bucharest?"

Willie Love takes the damp, smoldering cigar stub from his mouth and frowns at her. "Well, did you? I thought you were past this, Marjorie?"

And for a week he never got home 'til the break of day.

At last poor Mabel asked the reason why.

Said Jones, "I'm goin' to tell the truth or die."

She rubs at her lynx-gold eyes, trying to drive away the unwelcome ghost of a song committed to an Edison hard black wax cylinder in 1907. That and all those mumbling, well-heeled Edwardian phantoms who haven't a clue how their time on earth has come and gone and will not come again.

"I spoke with Constantin Vasile," says Willie Love.

"You were checking up on me?" Marjorie Marie asks, not bothering to hide her incredulity or to mask the anger creeping into her voice. *Fuck this,* she thinks. *I was better off back there with the Lady's three-ring circus of freaks and fuckwits.*

"No, I wasn't checking up on you. There was another matter. And Constantin mentioned that you were in Bucharest, that you spent a few nights in his attic. He's worried about you."

In a workshop on Strada Pericle Gheorghiu, Constantin Vasile carves crucifixes and rosary beads and miniature wooden saints.

Marjorie Marie shuts her eyes again.

Baby dear, listen here –

I'm afraid to come home in the dark.

On the south piazza, a chubby red-headed man from Boston is complaining about Roosevelt's increasingly radical economic policies. No one seems to be listening to him. Children are laughing.

Was it Marseilles?

Wasn't it?

Here she has a jigsaw puzzle with a thousand pieces, does Marjorie Marie Winthrop, and she's never been especially good with puzzles. And, what's more, what's worse, this is a puzzle missing at least half its pieces.

Missing because they were stolen – those memories of her death – by the one who murdered her. Marjorie Marie doesn't know why. She's never had a chance to ask the bitch, the creature who's chosen never to be anything more substantial than a shadow at the corners of Marjorie Marie's vision.

She said she loved me. She said she loved me, and that she would not see me age and die and be lost to the world. So, she killed me, emptied my head, dragged me back from the void, and then abandoned me.

The Romanian vampire, whose name Marjorie Marie was forced to forget and has never has learned again – though not for lack of trying – used to send her letters, postcards, vials of perfume, jewelry, packages wrapped in brown butcher's paper that always found her, no matter where she was. But they stopped coming decades ago. For all Marjorie Marie knows, the woman is dead, having at last met her well-deserved undoing at the sharp end of a white-oak stake, purity punching its way through her rotten black heart. Maybe a hunter took her head. Maybe she was burned to ash and the ashes stirred with salt and holy water and scattered across the sea.

"Yeah," says Marjorie Marie, "I was in Bucharest."

"Well, did you find what you were looking for this time?" he asks, even though he knows she knows he already knows the answer.

Her existence has become convoluted sentences.

"It comforts me, that city does," she says, instead of answering his question.

"You're picking at scabs."

Above them, a thunderclap rumbles, like the wrath of an angry god, and Marjorie Marie thinks of Washington Irving's "odd-looking personages playing at nine-pins," attired in their "quaint outlandish fashion." *I could lie down beneath a tree,* she thinks. *I could turn my own Rip Van Winkle trick and sleep away a hundred years. I could dig deep, down past the burrows of groundhogs and the trails of earthworms, into the shale and limestone bones of the mountains, and there I could sleep until this world and all my regret and even the Lady of Silver Whispers has passed from the world.*

"Then why don't you?" asks Willie Love.

"Shit," she says, lighting another cigarette, the last from the pack of Camel Lights she took off the man from the car on 212. "You'd miss me too much."

But I could, thinks Marjorie Marie Winthrop. *I could do just that. Before too long, even Willie Love would forget me.*

"I might," he tells her. "But I might not."

The wind carries the ecstasy and smells and tastes of the court's orgy, and it carries the voices of the tourists on the south piazza. She can hear the roar of the flames that devoured the Overlook Mountain Hotel, the screams of those burning alive, the crash of the roof coming down in a shower of sparks that sailed away into the night, an ember cloud to rain charcoal and soot on the streets of Woodstock and Bearsville. Behind Marjorie Marie and Willie Love, the Lady calls for blood – not the blood of unfortunate mortals, but the blood of her own kind, so much richer, aged in dead veins that are as good as wine or whiskey kegs. It always comes to this, on these long winter evenings, that her appetite turns to cannibalism, and the illusion of immortality, the lie of life everlasting, comes crashing down for the one who loses the lottery.

She reaches into a velvet sack the deadly, sinful crimson of holly berries and draws out the astragalus bone of wild boar. The bag holds an assortment of foot bones from a dozen or more species and each has engraved upon it a Roman numeral. Likewise, a Roman numeral has been drawn with blue chalk upon the forehead of every one of the vampires who has answered the Lady's beck and call to gather with her in the ruins at the top of the mountain. They all came knowing the risk, the price of her company and of the pleasures of her court. But that doesn't make this moment any less terrible, and it doesn't diminish the dread in each unbeating heart as she hands the bone down to her hierophant to be read out. On the stairs leading up to the south piazza, Marjorie Marie and Willie Love fall silent. He chews at the stub of his cigar, and her left hand goes to the mark above her eyebrows: XVII.

"It's a razor-sharp, crap-shoot affair," whispers Willie Love, parroting the lyrics of a song he heard way back in 1995. He smiles. "There is no Hell," he says. And then, "There is no Hell like an old Hell."

They wait for the number to be read, and Marjorie Marie knows that there's some defeated sliver of her that is praying it will be her number, her time, her judgment justly handed down for her every misdeed and for daring to play roulette by coming to this high, haunted place on this stormy night.

"You're so full of shit," she says to Willie Love.

"That I am, dear heart. That I most assuredly am."

The Lady of Silver Whisper's jester plays on his tin penny whistle, and even above the storm, the notes are clear as lead crystal, C and F major, the rise and fall, manic cross-fingering, dry lips and breathless breaths blown through the wooden fipple. It's a ritual as old as her reign. It's a ceremony as immutable as the Stations of the Cross, the Lady's own *Via Dolorosa*.

"Twelve!" cries the hierophant, when the jester's song is finished.

"Twelve," echoes the Lady of Silver Whispers.

Marjorie Marie feels a shiver down her spine, ice in her atrophied guts, though she could not say if these sensations are born of relief or disappointment.

"'Prepare the table,'" says Willie love, "'watch in the watchtower, eat, drink: arise ye princes.'" And then he laughs a dry and humorless laugh.

Marjorie Marie turns and peers at him with those shimmering, unreadable lynx eyes of hers.

"Isaiah, Chapter Twenty-One, verses five through nine. 'Babylon is fallen, is fallen, and all the graven images of her gods he hath broken unto the ground.'"

Within the three-story cement walls of the Overlook Mountain House, beneath that roiling blizzard roof, the sacrifice is led through the muttering throng and up to the Lady's yellowjacket récamier. The sacrifice's name is Daciana Petrescu, who died in 1976 in Braşov. Marjorie Marie marvels briefly at the coincidence, that tonight the Lady would be treated to the blood of a Romanian, this tinker's daughter born in a Căldărari village on the banks of the wide Danube Delta. It will only seem a coincidence to Marjorie Marie, of course, striking only the wearisome nerves of her own obsessions. Daciana Petrescu doesn't struggle, and she doesn't cry out or protest in any way; she goes to her doom with dignity, head held high and whatever fear she may feel she doesn't let show. It will be a bad death, an ugly and violent death, a slow death, but she'll not give the Lady of Silver Whispers the satisfaction of seeing her terror or hearing her fear.

"She stole so much of you," says Willie Love. "Whoever she was, whether it was Marseilles or Paris. She mined your memories, scooped you out clean. She left you lost to fill in the gaps, to weave false recollections that may, perhaps, approach the truth, but which will never touch it."

"You're a bastard," she replies.

"Like Constantin, I worry for you."

The Lady's fangs sink into Daciana Petrescu's throat, tearing open the carotid, and what passes for her life is sprayed across the frozen crust at the her killer's bare feet. It wasn't her blood, anyway; easy come, easy go.

"I should leave," says Marjorie Marie. "I never should have come here, and I should go."

"Will you be back next year?" asks Willie Love, doing a shoddy job of disguising his anxiety that she might not, that he might never see her again.

"I should go," she says again, as if that's meant to count as an answer.

"We have expended our souls," he says. "Our creators, our executioners, they expended our souls, which are now one and the same as our flesh, in that implosion of yin and yang. And so, sweet, the only thing awaiting us is oblivion. Not Hell nor Heaven nor Purgatory. Not some pagan, pantheistic underworld. Only nothingness. Me, I take that as a scrap of comfort."

"I'm going now. Take care of yourself, Willie Love. Watch your shadow."

And then she breaks apart, the body of Marjorie Marie exploding into five hundred, six hundred, a thousand shrieking sparrows, a miraculous flurry of tiny bodies and frenetic wings. For a moment, all the Lady's court – and even the gore-lipped Lady herself – turns towards that mad twittering, and the dead man who was born Hiram Levi watches as the flock disappears into the snowbound sanctuary of the forest.

For Cybin Orion Nelsen, aka Nis Talio, and for India Onnalee Shore.

THE CRIPPLE AND THE STARFISH

Thanks to the generosity of Neil Gaiman, I spent most of the terrible winter of 2014-2015 snowed into a cabin in the Catskills, near Bearsville, New York. The cabin sits in the shadow of Overlook Mountain and the ruins of its grand hotel, and every night Kathryn and I lay in bed, listening to the wind howling down off the mountain. I imagined it as the voice of the wendigo. This story was written that January.

Fake Plastic Trees

"You're not sleeping," Max said. "You're still having nightmares about the car. When you're awake, it's what you think about. I'm right, Cody, aren't I?"

"Mostly," I told him, and then neither of us said anything else for a while. We sat together and stared at the ugly red river. It was Cody finally spoke up and broke the silence.

"Well, I was thinking," he said, "maybe if you were to write it down. That might help, I was thinking."

"It might not, too," I replied. "I already saw Doctor Lehman twice. I did everything he said, and that didn't help. How's writing it down supposed to help?"

"Well, it might," he said again. "You can't know until you try. Maybe you could get the bad stuff you saw out of your head, like when you eat spoiled food and throwing up helps. See, that's what I'm thinking."

"Maybe you ought to think less, Max. Besides, where am I supposed to get anything to write it on?"

He promptly handed me the nub of a pencil and some paper he'd torn out of the G to H volume of an encyclopedia in the sanctuary library. I yelled at him for going and ruining books, when there aren't so many left to ruin.

"Cody, we can always put the pages back, when you're done," he said impatiently, like I should have thought of that already without him having to explain it to me. "Only, they'll be better than before, because one side will have your story written on them."

"Who's gonna want to read my story?" I asked.

"Someone might. Someday, someone might. Anyway, that's not the point. Writing it's the point."

Sitting there on the riverbank, listening to him, it began to make sense, but I didn't tell him that, because I didn't feel like letting him know I didn't still think he was full of shit, and because I still don't think I can do this. Because it's my story doesn't mean I can put it into words like he wants.

"At least try," he said. "Just you take a day or two and give it a go." I told him I had too much to do in the greenhouses, what with the beans and corn coming on ripe, and he said he'd take my shifts, and no one would even care, because there's so little work right now at pumps and filters in the hydroplant.

"Oh, and while you're at it, put in how things went wrong with the world, so when things get better, people will know how it all happened."

I said that was just dumb. Other people have already written it down, what went wrong. The smart people, the people who weren't four years old on the first day of THE END of THE WORLD.

I stared at the shiny encyclopedia pages in my hands. If they'd been ripped out of a real encyclopedia, words would already have been printed on both sides, but they were just copies got made right after THE EVENT. See, that's how the olders always talk about it, and they say certain words and phrases like THE BEFORE and THE AFTER and THE EVENT and THE GOO as if they were being said all in capital letters. I stared at the pages, which were at least real paper, made from real wood pulp, and I told him if I do this I get more than a kiss. Max said sure, why not, so long as you're honest, and he kissed me then and told me I was prettier than any of the other girls in Sanctuary (which is bullshit), and then he left me alone at the edge of the river. Which is where I'm sitting now. Sitting, writing, stopping to toss a rock that's still a rock into the sludgy crimson river that isn't still a river, because most of the water went FACSIMILE twelve years ago.

The plasticine river moves by about as slowly as I'm writing this down, and I count all the way up to fifty-three before the rock (real rock) actually sinks out of sight into the not-water anymore. At least the river still moves. Lots of them went too solid. I've seen rivers that stopped moving almost right after the EVENT. These days, they just sit there. Red and hard. Not moving, and I've even walked on a couple. Some people call them Jesus Streams. Anyway, I walked all the way across a broad Jesus Stream on a dare. But it wasn't much of a dare, since I got a good dose of SWITCH OFF in me right away, back when I was four.

Okay. Fine, Max. So I'm *doing* this, even though it's stupid. And you better not welch on that bet or I'll kick your ass, hear that? Also, I'm not writing much about what happened. I shouldn't waste my time writing any of that stuff. I don't care what Max says, because that's all down on paper somewhere else. I don't even know most of it, anyway, that EVENT three-quarters of my whole life ago. What I know for sure doesn't take long to set down. I learned what they bother to teach about THE GOO in classes. They don't teach all that much, because why bother telling us about THE BEFORE and WHAT WENT WRONG so we got THE EVENT, when what we need to be learning is how to run the hydros and keep the power on, horticulture, medicine, engineering, and keeping the livestock alive (Max's dad used to oversee the rat cages before he was promoted to hydro duty, or Max would still be feeding pellets to rats and mice and guinea pigs). But, okay, Max:

THIS IS WHAT THEY TEACH YOU

Twelve years ago, in THE BEFORE, there were too many people in the world, and most of them were starving. There wasn't enough oil. There wasn't enough clean water. There wasn't enough of much of anything, because people kept having babies almost as fast as the rats do. They'd almost used up everything. There were wars (we don't have those anymore, just the rovers and sneaks) and there were riots and terrorists. There were diseases we don't have anymore. People started dying faster than anyone could hope to bury them, so they just piled up. I can't imagine that many people. Ma'am Shen says there were more than nine billion people back then, but sometimes I think she surely exaggerates.

Anyway, in the year 2048, in a LOST PLACE called Boston, in a school the olders call MIT, scientists were trying to solve *all* these problems, all of them at once. Maybe other scientists in other parts of the world at some other schools and some of THE COMPANIES were also trying, but SWITCH ON happened at MIT in Boston, which was in a place called New England. SWITCH ON, says Ma'am Shen, started out in a sort of bottle called a beaker. It gets called the CRUCIBLE sometimes, and also SEAL 7, that one particular bottle. But I'll just call it the bottle.

Before I started writing this part, I made Max go back to the library and copy down some words and numbers for me on the back of one of these pages. I don't want to sound more ignorant than I am, and it's the least he could do. So, in the bottle, inside a lead box, were two things: a nutri-ent culture and nano-assemblers, which were microscopic machines. The assemblers used the culture to make copies of themselves. Idea was make a thing you could eat that continuously made copies of itself, there'd be plenty enough food. And maybe this would also work with medicine and fuel and building materials and everything nine billion people needed. But the assemblers in the bottle were a TRIAL. So no one was sure what would happen. They made THE GOO, which Max's notes call polyvinyl chloride, PVC, but I'll call it plastic, cause that's what it's always called when people talk about it. People don't talk about it much, though I think they might have back before the SWITCH OFF really started working.

Okay, lost my train of thought.

Oh, right. The bottle at MIT. The bottle that was supposed to save the world, but did just the opposite. The assemblers (or so say Max's notes, and I can hardly read his handwriting) during the TRIAL were just four at the start, and four of them made four more of them. Those eight, though, because the production was exponential, made eight more assemblers. Thirty-six made seventy-two made 144 made 288 made 576 copies, then 1,152, 2,304, 4,608, and this was just in one hour. In a day, there were…I don't know, Max didn't write that part down.

The assemblers went ROGUE and obviously the bottle wasn't big enough to hold them. Probably not after a few million, I'm thinking. It shattered, and they got out of the lead box, and, lo and behold, they didn't need the culture to make copies of themselves. Just about anything would do. Glass (the bottle). Stone. Metal (the lead box). Anything alive. Water, like the river. Not gases, so not air. Not water vapor, which is one reason we're not all dead. The other reason, of course, is SWITCH OFF, which was made at another lab, and that one was in another LOST PLACE called France. People got injected with SWITCH OFF, and it was sprayed from the air in planes and then bombs of SWITCH OFF were dropped all over. The EVENT lasted two weeks. When it was more or less over, an estimated 78% of the global biomass and a lot of the seas, rivers, streams, and the earth's crust had stopped being what it was before and had become plastic. Oh, not all crimson, by the way. I don't know why, but lots of different colors.

I didn't know all these numbers and dates. Max's notes. What I know: my parents died in THE EVENT, my parents and all my family, and I was evacuated to Sanctuary here in Florida on the shores of the St. James crimson plastic river. I don't think much more than that matters about THE EVENT. So, this is where I'm gonna stop trying to be like the vandalized encyclopedia and tell the other story, instead.

The story that's *my* story.

Isn't that what Max wanted to start with?

MY STORY
(CODY HERNANDEZ' STORY)

I'm discovering, Max, that I can't tell my story without telling lots of other little stories along the way.

Like, what happened, the day that's still giving me the bad dreams, that was almost a year ago, which means it was about five years after most of the Army and the National Guard soldiers left us here because all of a sudden there were those radio transmissions from Atlanta and Miami, and they went off to bring other survivors back to Sanctuary. Only they never brought anyone back, because they never came back, and we still don't know what happened to them. This is important to my story, because when the military was here with us, they kept a checkpoint and barricades on the east side of the big bridge over the St. Johns River, the Sanctuary side. But after they left, no one much bothered to man the checkpoint anymore, and the barricades stopped being anything more than a chain-link fence with a padlocked gate.

So, the story of the Army and National Guard leaving to find those people, I had to get that out to get to my story. Because I never would have been able to climb over the fence if they hadn't left. Or if they'd left, but come back. They'd have stopped me. Or I'd probably never even have thought about climbing over.

Back in THE BEFORE, the bridge was called the Matthews Bridge. Back in THE BEFORE, Sanctuary wasn't here and where it is was part of a city called Jacksonville. Now, though, it's just the bridge and this little part of Jacksonville is just Sanctuary. About a third of the way across the bridge, there's an island below it. I have no idea if the island ever had a name. It's all plastic now, anyway, like most of the bridge. A mostly brown island in a crimson river below a mostly brown plastic bridge. Because of what the sunlight and weather do to polyvinyl chloride – twelve years of sunlight and weather – chunks of the bridge have decayed and fallen away into the slow crimson river that runs down to the mostly still crimson sea. The island below the bridge used to be covered with brown plastic palmetto trees and underbrush, but now isn't much more than a scabby looking lump. The plastic degrades and then crumbles and is finally nothing but dust that the wind blows away.

I wanted to know what was on the other side. It's as simple as that.

I considered asking Max to go with me, Max and maybe one or two others. Maybe the twins, Jessie and Erin (who are a year older than me and Max), maybe Beth, too. There are still all the warning signs on the fence, the ones the military put there. But people don't go there. I suspect it reminds them of stuff from THE BEFORE that they don't want to be reminded of, like how this is the only place to live now. How there's really nowhere else to ever go. Which might be why none of the olders had ever actually *told* me to stay away from the bridge. Maybe it simply never occurred to them I might get curious, or that any of us might get curious.

"What do you think's over there," I asked Max, the day I almost asked him to come with me. We were walking together between the river and some of the old cement walls that used to be buildings. I remember we'd just passed the wall where, long time ago, someone painted the word NOWHERE. Only, they (or somebody else) also painted a red stripe between the W and the H, so it says NOW HERE, same as it says NOWHERE.

"Nothing," he replied. "Nothing's over there anymore," and Max shaded his eyes from the bright summer sun. Where we are standing, it's less than a mile across the river. It's still easy to make out where the docks and cranes used to be. "You can see for yourself, Cody. Ain't nothing over there except what the goo left."

Which is to say, there's nothing over there.

"You never wonder about it, though?"

"Why would I? Besides, the bridge ain't safe to cross anymore." And Max pointed south to the long span of it. Lots of the tall trusses, which used to be steel, have dropped away into the sludgy river a hundred and fifty feet below. Lots of the roadway, too. "You'd have to be crazy to try. And since there's nothing over there, you'd have to be extra crazy. You know what suicide is, right?"

"I think about it sometimes, is all. Not suicide, just finding out what's over there."

"Same damn difference," he said. "Anyway, we ought'a be getting back." He turned away from the river and the bridge, the island and the other side of the river. So, that's why I didn't ask Max to cross the bridge with me. I knew he'd say no, and I was pretty sure he'd tell one of the olders, and then someone would stop me. I followed him back to the barracks, but I knew by then I was definitely going to climb the chain-link fence and cross the bridge.

Oh, I almost forgot, and I want to put this in, write down what I can recall of it. On the way home, we came across Mr. Benedict. He was sitting on a rusty barrel not far from the NOW|HERE wall. In THE BEFORE,

Mr. Benedict – Mr. Saul Benedict – was a physicist. He's one of our teachers now, though he isn't well and sometimes misses days. Max says something inside his head is broken. Something in his mind, but that he isn't exactly crazy. Anyway, there he was on the barrel. He's one of the few olders who ever talks much about THE GOO. That afternoon, he said hello to me and Max, but he had that somewhere-else tone to his voice. He sounded so distant, distant in time or in place. I don't know. We said hello back. Then he pointed to the bridge, and that sort of gave me the shudders, and I wondered if he'd noticed us staring at it. He couldn't have overheard us; we were too far away.

"It doesn't make sense," he said.

"What doesn't make sense?" Max asked him.

"It should have fallen. Steel and concrete, that's one thing. But after the bots were done with it…that bridge, it should have collapsed under its own weight. The plastic could never bear the load."

"The shape didn't change," I said.

"The shape isn't what I'm talking about, girl. The constituent *materials,* that's what I mean. Iron, steel, precompressed concrete, those materials, fine. But you can't build a bridge that size out of PVC and not have it fall down. It wouldn't hold up even long enough to be erected."

This is the thing about Saul Benedict: He asks questions no one ever asks, questions I don't understand half the time. If you let him, he'll go on and on about how something's not right about our understanding of THE EVENT, how the science doesn't add up right. I've heard him say the fumes from the outgassing plastic should have killed us all years ago. And how the earth's mass would have been changed radically by the nano-assemblers, which would have altered gravity. How lots of the atmosphere would have been lost to space when gravity changed. And how plate tectonics would have come to a halt. Lots of technical science stuff like that, some of which I have to go to the library to find out what he means. I'm pretty sure very few people bother to consider whether or not Mr. Benedict is right. Maybe not because they believe the questions are nonsense, but because no one needs more uncertainty than we have already. I'm not even sure I spend much time on whether or not he's making sense. I just look up words to see what the questions mean.

"But it *hasn't* fallen down," Max protested, turning back towards the bridge. "Well, okay. Some pieces broke off, but not the whole bridge."

"That's just the problem," Mr. Benedict said. "It hasn't fallen down. You do the math. It would have fallen *immediately.*"

"Max is terrible at math," I told Mr. Benedict, and he frowned.

"He doesn't apply himself, Cody. You know that don't you, Max? You don't apply yourself. If you did, you'd be an exemplary student."

We told him we were late for chores, said our until laters, and left him sitting on the rusty barrel, muttering to himself.

"Nutty old fart," Max said, and I didn't say anything.

Before I went to cross the bridge, I did some studying up first. In the library, there's a book about the city that used to be Jacksonville, and I sat at one of the big tables and read about the Matthews Bridge. It was built in 1959, which made it exactly one hundred years old last year. But what mattered was that it's about a mile and a half across. One morning, I talked Mr. Kleinberg at the garage into lending me his stopwatch, and I figured out I walk about three miles an hour, going at an easy pace. Not walking fast or jogging, just walking. So, barring obstructions, if I could go straight across it would only take me about half an hour. Half an hour across, half an hour back. Maybe poke about on the other side (which, by the way, used to be called Arlington) for a couple of hours, and I'd be back before anyone even noticed I'd gone. For all I knew, other kids had already done it. Even more likely, some of the olders.

I picked the day I'd go – July 18, which was on a Monday. I'd go right after my morning chores, during late morning break, and be sure to be back by lunch. I didn't tell Max or anyone else. No one would ever be the wiser. I filled a canteen, and I went.

It was easy getting over the fence. There isn't any barbed wire, like on some of the fences around Sanctuary. I snagged my jeans on the sharp twists of wire at the top, but only tore a very small hole that would be easy to patch. On the other side, the road's still asphalt for about a hundred yards or so, before the plastic begins. Like I said, I'd walked on THE GOO before, so I knew what to expect. It's very slightly springy, and sometimes you press shallow footprints into it that disappear after a few minutes. On the bridge, there was the fine dust that accumulates as the plastic breaks down. Not as much as I'd have expected, but probably that's because the wind blows it away. But there were heaps of it where the wind couldn't reach, piled like tiny sand dunes. I left footprints in the dust that anyone could have followed.

I glanced back over my shoulder a few times, just to be certain no one was following. No one was. I kept to the westbound lane. There were cracks in the roadway, in what once had been cement. Some were hardly an inch, but others a foot or two across and maybe twice as deep, so I'd have to jump over those. I skirted the places where the bridge was coming apart in chunks, and couldn't help but think about what all Mr. Benedict had said. It shouldn't be here. None of it should still be here, but it is. So what don't we know? How *much* don't we know?

I walked the brown bridge, and on either side of me, far below, the lazy crimson St. John's River flowed. I walked, and a quarter of a mile from the fence, I reached the spot where the bridge spans the island. I went to the guardrail and peered over the edge. I leaned against the guardrail, and it cracked loudly and dropped away. I almost lost my balance and tumbled down to the crimson river. I stepped back, trying not to think about what it would be like to slowly sink and drown in that...

And I thought about turning around and heading back. From this point on, I constantly thought about going back, but I didn't. I walked a little faster than before, though, suddenly wanting to be done with this, even if I still felt like I had to *do* it.

I kept hearing Max talking inside my head, saying what he'd said, over and over again.

Since there's nothing over there, you'd have to be extra crazy.

You know what suicide is, right?

Ain't nothing over there except what THE GOO left.

It took me a little longer to reach the halfway point than I thought it would, than my three-miles-an-hour walking had led me to believe it would. It was all the cracks, most likely. Having to carefully jump them, or find ways around them. And I kept stopping to gaze out and marvel at the ugly wasteland THE GOO had made of the land beyond the Matthews Bridge. I don't know if there's a name for the middle of a bridge, the highest point of a bridge. But it was right about the time I reached that point that I spotted the car. It was still pretty far off, maybe halfway to the other end. It was skewed sideways across the two eastbound lanes, on the other side of the low divider that I'm sure used to be concrete but isn't anymore.

But all the cars were cleared off the bridge by the military years ago. They were towed to the other side or pushed into the crimson river. There weren't supposed to be any cars on the bridge. But here was *this* one. The sunlight glinted off yellow fiberglass and silver chrome, so I could tell the nano-assemblers hadn't gotten hold of it, that it was still made of what the factory built it from. And I had two thoughts, one right after the other: "Where did this car come from?" And "Why hasn't anyone noticed it?" The second thought was sort of silly, because it's not like anyone really watches the bridge, not since most of the Army and National Guard went away. There it stands, in plain sight, but hardly anyone ever notices it.

Then I thought "How long's it been there?" And "Why didn't it come all the way across?" And "What happened to the driver?" All those questions in my head, I was starting to feel like Saul Benedict. It was an older car, one of the electrics what were already obsolete by the time THE EVENT occurred.

"Cody, you go back," I said out loud, and my voice seemed huge up there on the bridge. It was like thunder. "You go back and tell someone. Let them deal with this."

But then I'd have to explain what I was doing way out on the bridge alone.

Are you enjoying this, Max? I mean, if I've let you read it. If I did, I hope to hell you're enjoying it, because I'm already sweating, drops of sweat darkening the encyclopedia pages. Right now, I feel like that awful day on the bridge. I could stop now. I could turn back now. I could. I won't, but I *could*. Doesn't matter. I'll keep writing, Max, and you'll keep reading.

I kept walking. I didn't turn back, like a smarter girl would have done. A smarter girl who understood it was more important to tell the olders what I'd found than to worry about getting in trouble for being out on the bridge. There was a strong gust of wind, warm from the south, and the dust on the bridge was swept up so I had to partly cover my face with my arm. But I could see the tiny brown dust devils swirling across the road.

Right after the wind, while the dust was still settling, I came to an especially wide crack in the roadway. It was so wide and deep, and when I looked down the bottom was hidden in shadow. It didn't go all the way through, or I'd not have been able to see down there. I had to climb over the barricade into the eastbound lane, into the lane with the car, to get around it. I haven't mentioned the crumbling plastic seagulls I kept finding. Well, I figured they'd been seagulls. They'd been birds, and they were that big, that they might have been seagulls. They littered the bridge, birds that died twelve years ago when I was four.

Once I was only, I don't know, maybe twenty-five yards from the car, I stopped for a minute or two. I squinted, trying to see inside, but the windows were tinted and I couldn't make out anything at all in there.

The car looked so shiny and new. No way it had been sitting out on the weather very long. There weren't even any pieces of the plastic girders lying on it, no dents from decayed and falling GOO, so it was a newcomer to the bridge, and I think that scared me most of all. By then, my heart was pounding – thumping like mad in my chest and ears and even the tip ends of my fingers – and I was sweating. Not the normal kinda sweat from walking, but a cold sweat like when I wake up from the nightmares of this day I'm writing about. My mouth was so, so dry. I felt a little sick to my belly, and wondered if it was from breathing in all that dust.

"No point in stopping now," I said, maybe whispering, and my voice was huge out there in all the empty above and below and around the Matthews Bridge. "So, when they ask what I found, I can tell them all of it, not just I found a car on the road." I considered the possibility it might have been rovers, might be a trap. Them laying there in wait until someone takes the bait, then they ask for supplies to let me go. We hadn't seen rovers in a year or so, but that didn't mean they weren't still out there, trying to get by on scraps of nothing they found and whatever they could steal. Lower than the sneaks, the rovers, and turning down every invite to become part of Sanctuary. Ma'am Shen says they're all insane, and I expect that's the truth of it. I wished I'd brought a knife (I have a lockblade I keep in my footlocker), but that was dumb, cause rovers carry guns and bows and shit. What good's a knife for a fifteen-year-old girl out on her own, so exposed she might as well be naked. No chance but to turn around and run if things went bad.

I shouted, "Anybody in there?" At the very top of my voice I shouted it. When no one answered, I shouted again, and still nobody answered me. I hadn't thought they would, but it didn't hurt to try.

"You don't need to be scared of me," I called out. "And I ain't got nothing worth stealing." Which I knew was dumb, because if it was rovers they wouldn't be after what I *had* on my person, but what they could *get* for me.

No one called back, and so I started walking again.

Pretty soon, I was close enough I could make out the plates on the front of the vehicle, Alabama, which we all thought was another LOST PLACE, since that's what the Army guys had told us. On the map of what once was the United States hanging on the wall in the library, Alabama was colored in red, like all the LOST PLACES (which is most of the map). But here was a car from Alabama, and it couldn't have been sitting on the bridge very long at all, not and still be so shiny and clean. Maybe I counted my footsteps, after shouting and not getting an answer, but if so, I can't remember how many I took.

There was another gust of wind, and more swirling dust devils, and this time the bridge seemed to sway just a little, which didn't make my stomach feel any better.

Then I was finally at the car. Up close, it was a little dirtier than it had seemed to be from far away. There were a few dents and dings, a little rust, but nothing more than that. None of the tires were even flat. I stared at the tinted windows and waited for rovers to jump out and point their weapons at me, but that didn't happen. For the first time, I considered the possibility that the doors might all be locked, and I didn't even have anything with me to break out the windows. I looked past the car at the ruins of Arlington, and considered just sticking to my plan, forget the car for now, poke around over there a bit, then head home again. And yeah, tell the olders about the car, and take whatever punishment I'd have coming.

I leaned forward, peering in through the glass, but the tinting was too dark, even right up on it like that. I gripped the driver's side door handle, and it was very hot from the Florida sun. It was hot enough I almost pulled my hand back, but only almost. Instead, I gave it a quick twist to the left, and the tumblers clicked. Which meant it wasn't locked after all.

I took a deep breath and pulled up on the door, It came open easy as pie – like the olders say. It lifted, rising above my head, above the roof. The hinges didn't even squeak. There was only a soft whoosh from hydraulics and pistons. Scalding air spilled out of the car.

You know exactly what I found in there, Max. It seems wicked to write it down on these "borrowed" encyclopedia pages. It seems wrong, but I'll do it anyhow. Just in case you're right, because yeah, I want the dreams to stop. Dead people don't have dreams. Dead people probably don't have anything at all, so it's stupid me worrying like this, hesitating and drawing it out.

The door opened, and there were two people inside.

There was what was left of two people.

Like the might-have-been seagulls, THE GOO had gotten to them, and they were that same uniform shade of bluish green all live things go when the nano-assemblers get hold of them. I stepped back immediately, and turned my head away. I even thought I might puke. It's not that I'd never seen a person who'd died that way; it's just I hadn't seen any in a long, long time, and you forget. Or I'd forgotten. I covered my mouth, not wanting to be sick and have to see my half-digested breakfast spattered all over the road at my feet. I leaned forward, hands on knees, and took deep breaths and counted to thirty. Someone taught me to do that whenever I'm afraid I might throw up, count to thirty, but I can't remember who it was. Not that it matters.

When I felt a little better, I looked again. The woman was sitting with her back to the door, and her arms were wrapped tightly around the girl. The woman's fingers disappeared into the girl's hair, hair and hand all one and the same now. I figured they drove as far as they could, drove until they were too far gone to keep going. It takes hours and hours for the infected to die. As I said already, like the birds, they were the blue green that all infected living things become. But unlike the seagulls, the weather hadn't been at them, and the woman and the girl looked like they'd just been popped fresh out of a mold, like the molds they use in the machine shop to turn non-GOO plastic into stuff we need. Every single detail, no matter how fragile, was still intact. Their plastic eyebrows, each hair, their eyes open and staring nowhere at all. Their skin was almost exactly the color of Ma'am Lillian's teal-zircon pendant. Only completely opaque, instead of translucent.

Their clothes and their jewelry (I noticed the woman's silver earrings), those hadn't changed at all. But it didn't strike me odd until later, like the car being okay didn't really strike me odd, though it should have.

I still felt dizzy, even if the first shock of seeing them was fading. Even if I was just *seeing* them now, not seeing them and wanting to run away. I reached inside the car, and touched the back of the woman's neck. I shouldn't have, but I did. It was just a little bit tacky from the heat, a little soft, and I left fingerprints behind. I thought, you leave them out here long enough, shut up and baking inside that car, they'll melt away to shapeless globs long before the plastic has a chance to get brittle. I thought that, and pulled my hand back. I was relieved to see none of the PVC had come off on my fingers. But I rubbed them on my jeans anyway. I rubbed until it's a wonder my skin didn't start bleeding.

They looked like dolls.

They looked almost like the mannequins in the busted shop windows inside Sanctuary.

But they'd both been alive, flesh and bone and breathing, and it couldn't have been more than a few days before. A week at the most. I stared at them. I wondered which of them died first. I wondered lots of stuff there's not much point writing down. Then I glanced into the backseat. And right then, that's when I thought my heart my might stop, just stop beating like the girl's and the woman's had finally stopped beating. There was a cardboard box in the back, and there was a baby in a blanket inside the box. I don't know how the hell it was still alive, how it had been spared by THE GOO or by the heat inside the car, but it *was* still alive. It looked at me. I saw it was sick, from the broiling day trapped in the automobile, but goddamn it was alive. It saw me and began to bawl, so I rushed around to the other side of the car and opened that door, too. I lifted the cardboard box out careful as I could and set it on the bridge, and then I sat down next to it. I screwed the lid off the canteen and sprinkled water on its forehead and lips. I finally pushed back the blanket and took the baby in my arms. I'd never, ever held a baby. We don't have many in Sanctuary. And the ones we do have, the dozen or so, not just any kid can go picking them up. Just the mothers and fathers, the nurses and doctors. The baby's face was so red and sunburned so I sprinkled more water on its face. Its eyes were glassy, feverish, and it didn't cry as loudly as I thought it should have been crying. I sat there and rocked it, shushing it, the way I'd seen people do with babies. I sat there trying to remember a lullaby.

No need to draw this part out, Max.

The baby, she died in my arms. She was just too hot, and I'd come along too late to save her from the sun. Maybe me sprinkling the water on her had been too much. Maybe just seeing me had been too much. Maybe she just picked then to die. And I wanted to cry, but I didn't. I don't know why. I knew I ought to, and I still know I ought to have, but I just sat there holding her close to me like she wasn't dead. Like she was only asleep and was gonna wake up. I sat there staring at the blue-green plastic people in the front seat, at the sky, at the car.

In my bad dreams, there are wheeling, screeching gulls in that blue-white sky and it goes on forever, on out into space, into starry blackness, down to blue skies on other worlds without women and men and youngers, where none of these things have ever happened and where THE EVENT hasn't occurred and THE GOO will never reach. Where it's still THE BEFORE and will never be THE AFTER.

God and Jesus and angels and a day of judgment of wicked men, they all live and breathe inside the Reverend Swales' black book, and in the songs we sing on Sundays. Many other gods and devils live in other holy books. But on the bridge that day there was no god. In my dreams, there is no God. And I don't pray anymore. I don't think much of those who do.

You're saying, now that's not what happened, Cody. I can hear you, Max. I can hear you grumbling, plain as day, "Cody Marlene Hernandez, you're mixing it all up, and you're doing it on purpose. That wasn't the deal, you welcher."

Fine, you win.

I scrounged about and found a couple of other things inside the cardboard box. I hardly looked at them, just stuffed them into my pack. Carrying the dead baby in her blanket, I walked back across the bridge, quickly as I could, quicker than I'd come. It was a lot harder getting over the fence, with her in my arms, but I managed. I didn't drop her. I'd have fallen before I ever dropped her.

I spent a week in quarantine, just in case. Five men went out onto the bridge and brought back the plastic woman and the girl and buried them in the cemetery. They buried the baby there, too, after Doc Lehman did his autopsy. No one ever scolded me or yelled or revoked privileges for going out there. I didn't have to ask why. You get punished, you don't have to get punished all over again.

WHAT I'M WRITING DOWN LATER

Me and Max sat between the crimson river and the NOW|HERE wall, and I let him read what I wrote on the back of the torn-out encyclopedia pages. He got pissed near the end, and just like I thought he would, called me a welcher.

"The baby always dies in my dreams," I told him, when he finally shut up and let me talk again.

"I didn't say, 'Write what's in your dreams.' I said, 'Write what happened.'"

"It seemed more important," I told him and tossed a piece of gravel at the river. "What haunts me when I sleep, how it might have gone that day, but didn't. How it probably *should* have gone, but didn't."

"Yeah, but you went and killed that baby."

"No, I didn't. My nightmares kill the baby, not me. Almost every time I sleep, the nightmares kill the baby."

He chewed his lip the frustrated way he does sometimes. "Cody, I just ain't never gonna understand that. You *saved* the baby, but you go and have bad dreams about the baby dying. That's stupid. You waste all this energy getting freaked out about something didn't even happen, except in a dream, and dreams ain't real. I thought writing the truth, *that* would make you better. Not writing down lies. That's what I don't understand."

"You weren't there. You didn't hold her, and her so hot, and you so sure she was already dead or would be dead any second."

"I just won't ever understand it," he said again.

"Okay, Max. Then you won't ever understand it. That's fair. There's a lot about myself I don't understand sometimes. Doesn't matter the dreams don't make sense. Only matters it happens to me. It's all too complicated. Never black and white, not like SWITCH ON and SWITCH OFF, not like THE BEFORE and THE AFTER. I fall asleep, and she dies in my arms, even though she didn't."

He glared at the pages, chewing his lips and looking disgusted, then handed them back to me.

"Well, you don't win," he said. "You don't get any more than kisses, cause you didn't even talk about the map or the book, and because you killed the baby."

"I don't care," I replied, which was true.

"I was just trying to help you."

"I know that, Max. Don't you think I know that?"

He didn't answer my question. Instead, he said, "I'm going home, Cody. I got chores. So do you, welcher." I told him I'd be along soon. I told him I needed to be alone for a while (which is when I'm writing this part down). So, I'm sitting here throwing gravel at the sludgy crimson river people used to call the St. James River.

WHAT REALLY HAPPENED (FOR MAX)

Outside my dreams, the baby didn't die. The olders figured the car had only driven through Arlington and out onto the bridge the night before I found it. They guessed the girl and the woman got sick a couple of days before that, probably before they even got to Florida. They figured, too, the baby would have died of heat prostration and thirst if I hadn't found it when I did. "You did right," Ma'am Shen whispered in my ear when no one was watching or listening in. "Even if that wasn't your intent, you did right." We never found out the baby's name, so they named it Cody, after me.

The olders found something in the baby's blood. It's like SWITCH OFF, they say, but it's different. It's like SWITCH OFF, but it works better. You breathe it out, and it shuts off the nano-assemblers all around you. Maybe, they say, that's why the car didn't change, and why the woman and the girl's clothes and jewelry wasn't converted, too. But these new bots, they can't turn stuff back the way it was before.

And yeah, there was a map. A map of the United States and Mexico and Canada. Most of the cities had big red Xs drawn on them. Montreal, up in Canada, had a blue circle, and so did San Francisco and a few little town here and there. A red line was drawn from Birmingham, Alabama all the way to Pensacola. Both those cities had red Xs of their own. I found the red pencil in the box with the baby. And I found pages and pages of notes. In the margins of the map, there was a list of countries. Some in red, some in blue.

Turns out the woman was a microbiologist, and she'd been studying when the sanctuary in Birmingham was breached. That's what she'd written in her notes. They read us that part in class. "The containment has been breached." I also know the notes talk about the nanites evolving, and about new strains the SWITCH OFF doesn't work on, and new strains of SWITCH OFF that shut down THE GOO better than before, like what kept the baby alive. They know the scientist also wrote about how THE EVENT isn't over, because the bots are all evolving and doing things they weren't designed to do.

Of course, they also weren't designed to eat up the whole world, but they did.

Saul Benedict still frowns and asks his questions, and he says everything's even more uncertain than it was before I found the car.

But me, I look at that baby, who's growing up fine and healthy and breathing those new bots out with every breath, and sometimes I think about going out onto the bridge again with a can of spray paint and writing HOPE HERE in great big letters on the side of the car. So if maybe someone else ever comes along, someone who isn't sick, they'll see, and drive all the way across.

FAKE PLASTIC TREES

Ellen Datlow asked me to write a post-apocalyptic YA tale, and this story was the result. It marks only the second time anyone had asked me to write a story specifically for a YA audience (the first time was "The Dead and the Moonstruck," back in 2003). And I chose to write a tale of apocalyptic ecophagy by grey goo, inspired by Eric Drexler's *Engines of Creation* (1986). Nanotech is one of those things that scare the ever-loving shit out of me, humanity begging for its own undoing. The story was written in April 2011. I'm not sure why it's set in Jacksonville, Florida, except that I lived there for three years as a small child (1969–1972).

Whisper Road
(Murder Ballad No. 9)

It makes me think of skipping stones, the way the pale red light skips along above the treetops. It makes me think of finding a cobble on the beach, slate or granite or schist, no more than half the size of my palm, smoothed by ages of weather and not ground quite entirely flat. I put my thumb *here,* and I put my middle finger *here,* the weight of the stone cradled by my index finger. The stone hits the water, though the pale red light does not quite seem to touch the tops of the trees growing out beyond the edges of the cornfields. There is no moon tonight, no clouds, but no moon, either, and the light is very bright, silhouetted against the southern July sky. I ask Easter if she sees it, too. It's always good to be sure I'm not the only one. All too often I have found that I am the only one. Easter is messing around with the radio, looking for a station that isn't county music or preaching or hip hop, and she asks, "What? Do I see what?" I say, "If you'd look, you'd know what." Or she wouldn't, but, whichever way, I'd still have my answer. It skips like a grey slate cobble, that light, not moving smoothly along in its course, but buffeted from below, and I think how striking air and striking water are not necessarily so very different. Easter raises her head, and by the dashboard lights her bottle-blue eyes almost glow. It was her eyes that got me first; not her ass or her tits or the promise of what's between her legs, but those startling blue eyes. I take my right hand off the steering wheel and point out the open driver's side window. "Real low," I tell her. "Right above the treetops. If you see it, you'll know. If you see it, just tell me, so I know it isn't only me." And I can tell right away from her expression that she does, indeed, see the pale red light skimming along almost like a skipping stone on the waters of West Cove or Mackerel Cove or Hull Cove. But I still want to hear her say it out loud. She left the radio tuned to a blur of static, and I almost reach over and switch it off, but then she says, "Yeah, I see it. Don't you think it's probably an airplane? Or maybe a helicopter?" No, I reply, because it looks a lot more like a stone bouncing across water than it looks like either a helicopter or a plane, and, honestly, it doesn't *look* anything at all like a skipping stone. The comparison only comes to mind because of the way it's moving. *Behavior,* I think, *is not appearance.* "Then what is it?" Easter wants to know, as if I have the answer. And I catch a dull sliver of anxiety dug into her voice. That's hardly surprising, since the thing above the trees can't be too much more than half a mile away from us, half a mile from the edge of Tuckertown Road to that black wall of maples and oaks and pines. It can't be much more than a hundred feet above the treetops; maybe not even that. So, I don't fault her for sounding just a little bit nervous. Here it is past midnight, and we're the only car in sight. After that ugly piece of business back at the farm, we're both certainly worse for the wear, and now there's this thing that I'm pretty sure isn't a helicopter or an airplane, and she says, "I can't hear it. That close, don't you think we ought to be able to hear it, whatever it is?" I tell her I need a cigarette, please, and so she lights one and sets it between my lips. I breathe in smoke, willing the nicotine to clear my head, trying to concentrate on the road, because we just passed a yellow, diamond-shaped sign with the stark black outline of a buck printed on it. Wouldn't that be hilarious, a fucking deer dashes out in front of us, and we're both staring at a light in the sky. Next thing you know, bam, we're dead in the proverbial ditch, so there's our comeuppance. If you subscribe to notions of karma and fair play and the witches' threefold law, well, that would be our ironic just reward. "How fast are we going?" asks Easter, and I say, "You've got eyes, don't you?" But I glance at the speedometer, anyway, and the needle is sitting right at seventy. "Maybe you ought to slow down," she tells me. Maybe I should, I tell myself, because getting stopped for speeding would be almost as funny as hitting a deer. I ease my foot off the gas pedal, and the speedometer needle promptly retreats to sixty-five, sixty, fifty-five. "Hey, Chaz," says Easter, "it's slowing down, too," and when I look I see that she's right. Out there across the field, the pale red light hasn't moved on ahead of us, like it should have. We aren't trailing along behind, as we should now be doing. "What the fuck," she says. "What the fuck would do that?" Like I should know. Like I do know, but I've decided at this late date to start keeping secrets from her. "Can you please find a station?" I ask. "The static's getting on my nerves. I hate that sound. I've always hated that sound. It's like hearing ants." Easter switches off the radio, and I say fine, yeah, that works, too. We pass a turnoff for some or another nameless dirt road and a couple of big trees very briefly block our view of the thing in the sky. "Maybe we should stop," she says, and I ask her what good she thinks that would do. "It might keep going, Chaz. It might pass us by, if we were to stop now. You could pull over there," and she points through the windshield towards a place up ahead where the shoulder is a little wider and paved with gravel. "You could just pull over, and we could see if it keeps going." She sounds a lot more afraid than she did only a minute before, that strained brittleness that comes before panic starting to creep into her voice. And I realize that I find this more disconcerting than the sight of the thing in the sky, because Easter is the one who never loses her shit. Not really. I couldn't count all the times she's talked me down. I wouldn't care to try. Back at the farm, when the dogs started barking and I reached for my gun, she was there to say, "No, no, Chaz. It's okay. They're just dogs. People will think it was a coyote set them off. Or just a skunk. Or a raccoon. There are lots of things out here to make dogs bark at night. No one even notices. No one gives it hardly more than a passing thought." But barking dogs are one thing, and that pale red light skimming along above the trees, well, that's another altogether. I don't pull over, and we rush past the gravelly place at the side of the road. Easter makes a small, uneasy noise, and she takes the cigarette from my mouth and sits smoking and watching the strange light out beyond the cornfield. "Just a little farther," I tell her. "That Jehovah's Witness church, that's not too far from here. I can pull over there, if you'd like." The tip of the cigarette flares in the dark, and she exhales a grey cloud; the wind through the open windows pulls it apart. "They don't believe in blood transfusions. Jehovah's Witnesses, I mean. Did you know that?" she asks me, and I say no, I didn't. "Well, it's true. They don't. They believe that blood is sacred, so it's some sort of blasphemy or something, some kind of unholy desecration, to get a blood transfusion. So, they'll just let their people bleed to death and shit. No, I don't think we should stop there. We should find somewhere else to stop." And fine, I tell her. We won't stop at the church. We'll keep going. "They won't allow organ transplants, either," she says. "Because, when you get someone else's heart, or their liver, or their kidneys, you're inevitably gonna get some of their blood in the bargain. It can't be helped, and so they're also against organ transplants. They'd rather let people die." I take my eyes off the road long enough to see that the red light is still out there, pacing us. Skipping. Skimming. And then the landscape on my left abruptly changes, and the fields are replaced by a merciful tangle of trees growing too closely together, grape vines, greenbriers, bracken, and I actually breathe a sigh of relief. *Now it can't see us,* I think. *Now it'll get bored and go away, find some other car to follow.* For a moment, neither I nor Easter says a word. I don't look at her, but I can feel her blue, blue eyes staring past me at the open driver's side window, staring towards the welcome, concealing sanctuary of the woods outside the window. "You okay?" I finally ask her, more to break the silence than anything else. She laughs a not entirely convincing sort of laugh and says, "Jesus in Heaven, what the fuck is wrong with us? Sure, that was weird. That was really fucking weird, but what the fuck is wrong with us, freaking out like that over a goddamn airplane or a helicopter." And I tell her it's just we're both still keyed up after the scene back at the farm. That it's probably nothing but the adrenaline making us jump at shadows. "Well, we gotta calm down," she says. "We're not ever gonna get to Hartford, or anywhere else, if we don't get a grip and get our shit together." I tell her we'll be fine, everything's gonna be right as rain, and now she's opening the glove compartment, digging around for the bottle of Percocet she keeps stashed in there. Back at the farm on Whisper Road, she was the one doling out calm and reassurances, and the comforting words sound funny coming from me, as unconvincing as that laugh of hers. She finds the bottle and dry swallows two of the pastel yellow pills; she offers me one, but I say no. Not when I'm driving. When I'm driving I don't drink and I don't smoke weed and I don't take pills, and Easter says, "Suit yourself." And then she says, "There's a place you can pull over at Worden's Pond. It's not much farther, a little parking lot with a dock for fishermen and kayaks and stuff. We can stop there, just long enough to catch our breath." That sounds good, I reply. That sounds perfect. So, we'll stop at Worden's Pond. Easter puts the prescription bottle back into the glove compartment and slams it shut, because the latch is busted and if you don't slam it, the door doesn't stay closed. She flicks the cigarette butt out the window. In the rearview, I see it hit the road and die in a bouncing flurry of orange sparks. "Maybe it was a drone," she says. "I've never seen one at night, so maybe that's what it was. I don't know what they'd look like in the dark, but they might look like that. I was reading a magazine article about using drones to catch illegal deer hunters. You know, poachers. And to spot forest fires and check on power lines – all sorts of other everyday things you might not know about drones getting used for. I bet that's what it was. I bet it was just a drone." Maybe so, I tell her. Maybe that's exactly what it was. And I'm also thinking, *I expect the police use them, too,* but I keep that to myself. The police aren't looking for us. No one's looking for us. Not yet. No one saw us, and, besides, it'll be at least another day or two before anyone goes poking around the farm and calls the cops. It might have been longer, if she'd let me kill the dogs. Those dogs get hungry, they'll attract attention, no matter what Easter says about no one out here paying any mind to barking dogs. But when I told her I was going to kill them, the beagle and the German shepherd, she said she'd leave me if I did. She helped me tie up the man and the woman, and she watched me cut their throats, but then when I say I need to put down a couple of mutts to save our hides, to buy us time, she tells me she'll walk if I do. I don't know if she really meant it, but I didn't kill the fucking dogs. "Isn't it crueler to leave them here to starve?" I asked her, and she replied, "They won't starve. Someone will find them." And then someone will be looking for us, only I didn't say that. "We used to swim in Worden's Pond," says Easter, "when we were kids, my brothers and me. My brothers used to catch turtles and water snakes there." We pass the church – the Kingdom Hall, according to the sign hanging out front – and the woods on our left give way to open fields again. I taste foil, and for a few seconds my heart is a long-distance runner thudding in my chest. "Don't look," Easter tells me, as if I have some choice in the matter. Of course I look, but there isn't anything out there to see. No pale red phantom skipping along. Nothing but dry-stone walls and alfalfa and more rows of tall corn, then a black line of trees to mark the boundary of someone's toil, marking off the southern edge of the fields. I think about how those cornstalks would rustle out there in the dark, whenever the wind stirs, and it gives me a shiver. "It's gone," I say, not feeling even half as relieved as I should. "Whatever it was, it's gone now. Relax. Find something on the radio." Easter turns her head to see for herself, cause maybe after the way things went back on Whisper Road, my word isn't good enough for her anymore. I said no one was gonna get hurt, and then they did, and so I can't exactly blame her for losing faith. But I want to, whether blaming her is right or wrong. It'll be a long, long time before I'm over losing her trust. "It's gone," she says, like an echo, and I say, "Like I told you, huh?" She turns away from me then, turning head and shoulders to stare at the summer night from the vantage point of her own window. "We should stop anyway," she says. "Just to clear our heads." I nod and tell her, "Fine, sure, we'll stop anyway," even though I only want to keep driving. The tires are making music, the steady lullaby hum of rubber against asphalt, and what matters now is putting as many miles behind us as quickly as possible – get out of Rhode Island, get up to Hartford, ditch this car, get some fucking sleep, then figure out what comes next. Easter has friends in Hartford, people she says will be sympathetic to our situation – for the right price. She switches the radio on again, and this time it only takes her a moment to find the college station out of Kingston. They're playing the Rolling Stones, "Start Me Up," a song I know from my father's old records. "Leave it there," I say to her. "That's good. You sure we need to stop now? Can't be more than twenty, twenty-five miles from here to the state line. We could stop then, stop and piss and top off the tank. Get some coffee." But she stubbornly shakes her head, no, "No, I need to stop *before* that, I need to get some air." As if all the air in South County isn't blowing in through her open window, whipping at her long hair, roaring in our ears. I can smell the ocean on that air, the ocean and cooling tar and fresh-cut hay. And then she adds, "I need to wash my hands." Easter looks down at her open palms. She washed her hands back at the farm after I killed those two, washed her hands twice in the kitchen sink with scalding hot water and liquid dishwashing soap, Palmolive or Dawn or Joy or something like that. I finally had to tell her to stop it, that she was gonna scrub all the skin off if she didn't, and we needed to get the fuck out of there. I couldn't have her going all Lady Macbeth on me, especially when she wasn't the one who held the knife and there wasn't a drop of blood on her anywhere. I check the speedometer, the gas gauge, the odometer, the clock. I almost tell her she can wait to wash her hands again, that it won't kill her to wait, but then I lose my nerve. I'm a goddamn coward when it comes to Easter. "It wasn't necessary," she says, "what you did." And I tell her, "Well, it seemed pretty necessary at the time. But now it's done, and there's no point being sorry for something that can't be undone. That's just what happened. That's just the way it went." She rubs her palms together, wrings her hands, then glances past me at the place where the pale red light isn't skipping along beneath the sky and above the trees. "They got kids," she says. "I saw photographs. Kids and grandkids, and all I'm saying is it wasn't necessary, and you promised no one would get hurt. I've never done anything like that before, that's all. I'd never seen anything like that done." I say, "You've seen it in the movies, lots of times. You've seen it on TV." And she says, "That isn't the same. That isn't the same at all." She's absolutely fucking right, of course, but I don't tell her so, and I don't apologize, either. Instead, I say, "Don't pretend you didn't know what I am." She takes another cigarette from the half-empty pack on the dash, lights it, and at first I think she's staring at me, but really she's only staring at the place where the pale red light isn't. In the darkness, her face is like a painting on black velvet. "Don't you even feel anything?" she asks. "Anything at all?" Before I can reply, she says, "There's a little cemetery off over there, on the far side of that pasture. There's a dozen or so marble headstones, but the dates are mostly worn away. Acid rain, you know, it ruins the marble. Acid rain from pollution, makes the stone soft. Makes it rot." She pauses, takes a drag, holds in the smoke a moment, exhales. "I haven't ever killed anything, much less anyone." We pass a few houses lined up neatly on either side of Tuckertown Road, and the night is briefly interrupted by streetlights and porch lights and lamps still burning in windows, unsuspecting people asleep and dreaming in their beds or up late or maybe even already awake again and getting ready for tomorrow. Tidy rows of mailboxes. Tidy yards and tidy fences. "You knew," I say, and "Yeah, Chaz, I knew," she replies. "But knowing isn't the same thing as seeing, and it certainly isn't the same thing as being a party to it." And now the houses are behind us, along with whatever comfort might be found in the cold white electric glow of all those lights, whatever dim sanctuary. The night takes us back. The night is a jealous bitch, but she's also forgiving. I'm driving too fast again, my foot too heavy on the accelerator, and I'm trying to decide if the speed is worth the risk of cops and hitting deer when I smell sulfur. Before I can ask Easter if she smells it, she says, "Jesus, did you hear that?" and I see she's got both her hands clapped over her ears. "No," I tell her. "I didn't hear anything." And she asks, "Is that the car? Jesus, is it the *car* making that noise?" The stink of sulfur is suddenly overwhelming, and my stomach rolls like I'm getting seasick, like I'm stuck on the ferry from Galilee to Block Island. "Is it Morse code?" she wants to know. *I'm going to puke,* I think. *I'm seasick without even being near the sea, and I'm going to fucking puke right here on the steering wheel and in my lap if I don't get off the road right now.* I put my foot on the brake, slowing down and looking for some safe place to pull over. But there are steep shoulders on the left and on the right of us, steep shoulders and deep, weed-filled ditches. Then I finally hear whatever it is Easter's hearing, only it isn't loud at all, and certainly it's nothing that would ever make you want to cover your ears. In fact, it seems very far away, a muted, indistinct *beep-beep-beeping.* Maybe it does sound like Morse code. Maybe that's exactly what it sounds like, but I wouldn't know. I can tie forty different knots, every single one in the Boy Scout handbook, but I don't know shit about Morse code. "There's something wrong," Easter says, hands still over her ears, and if she sounded scared before, now she sounds terrified. "There's something wrong with the sky. Don't slow down. Don't stop. Please, don't stop." And back at the farm on Whisper Road, hardly even an hour and a half ago, she's watching me tie up the man and his wife with lengths of strong jute rope I bought that afternoon down in Wakefield. Easter asked me if duct tape wouldn't be easier and faster, and I told her easier and faster is sloppy, and sloppy is how people get caught. Sloppy is what the sheriffs and police detectives are always counting on. "Like this," I say, standing at an angle so she can see my hands. "Over and under and around." The man and woman are silent. I haven't gagged them, and I keep expecting him to make threats. I keep expecting her to beg or start crying. But they don't do either. I wish they would; it would be so much easier if they would, if I were angry. Anger takes the edge off everything. Anger is better than whiskey or cocaine when I need to steady my nerves. "Can't you talk, old lady?" I ask the woman, looping the rope about her skinny ankles, cinching it tightly. "Cat got your tongue?" Easter tells me to leave her alone. "We got what we came for, didn't we? There's no point being cruel." And I see then that the old woman is watching her, not me. So is the man, and I know they're both thinking how Easter's the weak one in this equation, how whatever slim hope they might have of seeing daylight and getting out of this alive resides there in her startling blue eyes. Hell, from where they're sitting right now, Easter probably looks as sweet as the Divine Baby Jesus wrapped up safe in Mother Mary's arms. It's her eyes. Her eyes have mercy in them. When we first met, I told her I'd never seen eyes that shade of blue, and that's when she told me it was called cornflower blue. "It's just a weed that grows wild in cornfields," she said. "Cornflowers, I mean. They bloom in June and flower all summer long." So, that's what I'm thinking, there in the farmhouse, in that that old couple's bedroom, looping rope round and round, that these two see God in my lover's cornflower eyes. "Did you hear that?" Easter wants to know, and when I ask "Did I hear what?" she shakes her pretty head and turns away. "Just hurry," she tells me. "Finish tying them up and let's get out of here." I reply, "Hurrying is just as bad as being sloppy. Hurrying *makes* you sloppy." Easter, she glances at the alarm clock ticking away the night on the little table beside the bed. The clock's face is washed with soft green light, like dashboard light, like the light on Easter's face when she reaches for a cigarette or opens the glove compartment or wanders the radio dial looking for a station that suits her fancy. "Sunrise is at 5:16," she says, "and we're expected in Hartford before noon. I'm not saying be sloppy, but we can't hang around here all night." And right *here* I feel the spark of anger I was hoping for, right fucking *here,* and I say, "Okay, fine. My bad. Let's get this the fuck over with and get back on the road." I reach down and pull the butterfly knife out of my right boot, flip it open, and Easter just stands there watching me while I cut their throats. I open their carotids and the arterial spray paints the floor and walls. Neither of them makes a sound. They don't beg. They don't whimper. They don't cry out in fear or pain. And I think that's fucking creepy, that's goddamn fucking eerie, and I can't help but wonder if this whole thing's gone south on us. I let go of the old woman's body, and it pitches forward, landing face down in its own blood. *Her* own blood. "You didn't have to do that," says Easter, just barely loud enough for me to hear. "You promised me no one was going to get hurt." Then she looks down at her hands, then back to the bodies, then back at her hands again. That's when she goes downstairs to the kitchen sink. I stand there in the bedroom a few minutes longer, staring at the dead woman and her dead husband, not really giving a shit that they're dead, but pissed off that Easter made me kill them. Pissed off that she's pissed at me, when it was her fault, when she's the one that threw that bright copper spark that set me on fire. I wipe the knife clean on the nubby white chenille bedspread, fold the blade closed, and stick it back into my boot. I go downstairs and find her at the sink. "I didn't mean to do that," I tell her. "I didn't come in here meaning to kill anyone." She doesn't look up, just squirts more soap from the green plastic bottle into her hands and says, "I never said you did. But they're still dead, regardless." I tell her that we need to go, and Easter says go on ahead, she's coming, she'll be right behind me, she just has to wash her hands first. And this is when the dogs in the pen out back start barking. I reach for the pistol tucked into the waistband of my jeans, but she stops me. "Why is it they call you Easter, anyway?" I asked her, the first night we met, and she told me, "When I was a little girl, I used to raise rabbits. My daddy, he started calling me Easter when I was a kid, and it just sorta stuck." And I said, "Rabbits? For what? For the skins? For the meat?" And she made a face and said no, just for pets. She never let anyone kill one of her rabbits. No one ever tried. And there in the farmhouse on Whisper Road she puts her hands on mine, her hands all wet and soapy, hands that have never been stained with the blood of rabbits or human beings. She tells me how I'm not going to shoot those dogs, because there's no need, because people out here are used to hearing dogs barking at night, and they'll just think it's because there's a skunk or a coyote or a raccoon poking about the garbage cans, getting them stirred up. "No more killing," she says, "not tonight. Not if you want me to stay." And then she looks back over her shoulder at the steam rising from the sink because she left the tap on, steam fogging the windowpane above the sink, and she says, "Chaz, did you hear that?" I ask her did I hear what, because all I heard is the damn dogs, and she says, "I don't know. I don't know what it was. Was it Morse code?" And she must have shut off the water before we left the house, but, if so, I can't remember her doing it. I can't remember walking back up the dirt road to where I'd left the car parked in the shade of two huge oak trees, either. And there must be a word for this, when you suddenly realize that you can't remember something you should, something that's just fucking happened. "Is that the *car* making that noise?" she wants to know. We were standing in the kitchen, and the dogs were barking, and everything smelled like dishwashing liquid and blood, and then we're driving down Tuckertown Road, and when I turn my head I see that pale red light skipping along above the treetops. "No," Easter insists, "there was something else, something in between there, after the kitchen, but before you asked me to look and tell you what I saw." And I say, "I don't think I'd know Morse code if I heard it." I can't remember getting back into the car or turning the key in the ignition. I can't remember stowing the box from the old couple's basement in the trunk of the car, but I know that's exactly where I put it. "Dots and dashes," says Easter. She's standing alone at the far end of the dock jutting out into Worden's Pond. I'm looking north, and on my right the sky's beginning to brighten. On my left, the night is as dark as night can be. There's a mist rising up off the water and from the tall grass and cattails growing all along the shore. There's a canoe tied up at the end of the dock, and Easter says, "A lot of people think the first time anyone used S.O.S. to call for help was when the *Titanic* sank, but that's a myth." I'm sitting on the hood of the car, watching her, trying to remember what happened after I smelled sulfur and she heard Morse code, how we got from there to the pond. That must be half a mile or more I've forgotten, and now the sun is coming up, even though the last time I checked the clock on the dash it was only a little past two thirty. I've forgotten half a mile and more than two and a half hours. "How's that even possible?" I ask her, and that's when I see the light, way out over the water, hovering just a few feet above the steaming surface of the pond. "Three dots," says Easter, "three dashes, then three more dots. Three short, three long, three short. Some people think it stands for something, like 'save our ship' or 'save our souls,' but the truth is it doesn't stand for anything at all." She's holding my pistol in her right hand, holding it down at her side, staring out across the water at the light that isn't skipping or skimming, but just hanging there like a fat butchered hog. "You should come back," I say. "You shouldn't get so close to that thing. We don't know what it wants." And I think then how the hood of the car is cold, how the engine block isn't popping and pinging the way it does when it's cooling off, and I tell Easter again that she should come back. "We don't even know what it is," I say. I'm amazed at how perfectly, utterly calm I sound. "Come back over here, and tell me more about the *Titanic* and Morse code. I don't know where you learn all this stuff." She shakes her head, and when she does I imagine that the pale red light sort of bobs along in unison. It isn't making any sound whatsoever. "No, Chaz," she says. "I think I'm exactly where I'm supposed to be. You promised me no one would get hurt tonight. You promised me, and then you killed them, anyway. You didn't need to do that." And it occurs to me that someone's standing there beside her, some-one or only the *shadow* of someone. *Get up,* I think. *Get the fuck up off your ass and go get her.* But I don't move. I'm not even sure I can move, my arms and legs feel so heavy, like lead weights, like marble headstones etched by years and years of acid rain. Out on the pond, the pale red light waits impa-tiently, and there on the dock, Easter raises the pistol and presses the barrel beneath her chin. *Get up. Get the fuck up and do something.* But then the shadow leans in close, and I imagine that it's whispering to Easter secret words that only she's supposed to hear, truths and revelations that I'll never know. She squeezes the trigger, and thunder blooms and rumbles and rolls away like sunrise, dashing the night apart upon the hateful shingle of the coming day.

WHISPER ROAD (MURDER BALLAD NO. 9)

As a kid I was terrified of lights in the night sky. All this time later, that hasn't changed. This story was written in July 2016, and was, in fact, the only story I managed to finish that summer.

Animals Pull the Night
Around Their Shoulders

1.

It's almost four o'clock on a Thursday afternoon when the Federal Express delivery truck deposits the big yellow box on my doorstep. This might be the last hot day of the short New England summer, and the driver looks annoyed at having to wrestle the box out of his truck and across the street to my front door. He rings the bell, but I don't go downstairs to answer. So, he'll either leave the box or he'll schlep it back across the street again and drive away. There are dark stains on his shirt, and his face is slick with sweat. I sit at my third-floor window, gazing down on the street, and the air conditioning wraps me in preternatural January and keeps me safe from the sun and the baking black asphalt and delivery men I have no desire to talk with. He rings the bell again, and I think, *Leave it. Just fucking leave it, and please go away,* as though I have some faith in telepathy. *Please, go away.* He frowns and stares up at all the windows of this old house staring out and down at him. Then the delivery man scribbles something on his pad, shakes his head, and goes back to his truck. He drives off down Parade Street, leaving the big yellow box behind as he vanishes into the broil of the afternoon. I close the curtain, not wanting to wait until the sun is down, wanting to go right this minute and retrieve the box. What is it people say, *Throw caution to the winds?* Couldn't I do that, just this once? It's the middle of the day, and everyone on Sycamore Street is still at their job or busy with housework or whatever, and no one's watching to see me come scrambling downstairs in broad daylight. And so what if they were? It's *mine,* isn't? Why should I have to sit here another three and a half hours, worrying that someone might come along and steal it? This isn't the worst neighborhood in Providence, but it certainly isn't the best, either, and people's mail gets stolen all the time. And there's this big yellow box like a flashing neon sign, flashing, flashing *C'mon, take me. No one will see. No one's watching.* But aren't they? Aren't they always? No, it's best if I wait. I can sit right here in my chair, at my table, and wait, and if anyone tries to steal the yellow box, I can be downstairs before they make off with it. I look away from the window, turning my attention back to the book that lies open in front of me, back to the full-color reproduction of John Charles Dollman's *The Unknown,* painted sometime around 1912. Night in some wasteland, and a woman, clothed only from the waist down, kneels before a small fire, her left hand held up and out towards the low flames and a thin tendril of white smoke rising up to the sky. She's not alone. There are thirteen chimpanzees with her. A topless woman and thirteen chimpanzees on what appears to be a snowy plain, so make what you will of that. I'm not entirely certain whether the artist intended snow or merely sand; the painting seems to me ambiguous on this point, and I can find nothing authoritative written anywhere that lays the matter to rest. But I think it *must* be snow. The woman's skin is as pale as the snow, or is pale as the sand, whichever. The chimpanzees are clearly all terrified of the fire – well, except for one, who sits apart from all the others, with its back to the whole strange scene. It's impossible to say what that chimp feels, as we cannot see its face. But the others, the artist has rendered their faces in various shades of terror, awe, dread, and so forth. Maybe they're afraid of the fire *and* the woman, and maybe that's simply because she isn't afraid of the fire. I turn away from the book on Victorian painters just long enough to peer out at the yellow box on the doorstep, just to be sure it's still there. It is, of course. I think again about going down for it right now, instead of waiting for twilight. I could do that. I could get up from this chair, go to the door of my apartment, walk downstairs to the front door of the old house, turn the deadbolt, open the front door, and bring it back upstairs with me. What possible difference does it make if anyone sees me? It's *mine,* isn't it, the box and anything that's inside the box, and what do I care if someone sees me bringing it in off the stoop? It's my name printed on the shipping label. It's addressed to me. I'm the one whom the delivery man was trying to get to answer her door. I'm the one who would have needed to *sign* for the box, if I hadn't already signed that slip of paper giving them permission to leave it. I let the curtain fall closed again and turn back to the book and John Charles Dollman's painting. Nothing good will come of my being impatient; nothing has, and nothing ever will. So, cut it out. Stick to the script, as they say. I count the chimpanzees again, because sometimes it seems there are only twelve of them, but no, I count thirteen, this time. The pale woman's long black hair hangs down below her breasts, almost to her waist. There are what appear to be beads or bangles of some sort woven into her hair, and there's a colorful bandana tied about her head. I feel as if I'm being shown the middle of a story, one scene taken out of context – a joke at my expense or the expense of anyone who's ever tried to make sense of *The Unknown*. There are no answers to be had for all the questions the painting poses, so where's the profit in my sitting here staring for hours, trying to *make* sense of it? I turn the page, and here's a photograph of two sculptures by a Frenchman named Emmanuel Frémiet. Each of the sculptures depicts a gorilla carrying off a woman. One woman is nude, one clothed. The nude woman is struggling, and the clothed woman appears to be dead. *Gorille enlevant une femme* is printed along the bottom of the page, and maybe that's the name of one of the sculptures or the name of them both. I can't tell. Also, there are two dates printed below the photos, 1887 and 1859, but there's no way to know which date is meant for which sculpture. I wonder if the man who thought up *King Kong*, decades later, had seen Frémiet's work; it seems to me very likely. There's a printed quote here from the sculptor: *At a time when a lot of noise was being made about mankind and apes being brothers, it was an audacious idea; and my work proved even more aggravating since, the gorilla being the ugliest of all the primates, the comparison was hardly flattering for humans. With great recklessness, this gorilla was dragging off a young woman.* I don't find the gorilla ugly at all. Frightening, yes, but not ugly. Maybe there are people who cannot tell the difference between what frightens them and what is ugly. Maybe to some people, it's all the same. I close the book. I've seen enough for now, women and apes and whatever it is those artists were suggesting, but didn't have the balls to come right out and say. I open the curtain again. The box is still there.

2.

Nora always talked to me like she was my therapist, instead of only my girlfriend. She doesn't live here anymore. She left me one winter four years ago, right after the first heavy snowfall. That must have been in December, before Christmas, but I'm no longer entirely certain. I *seem* to remember driving her through the snow to the train station, across the river and to the other side of town, and hearing Christmas music and seeing white electric

165

lights strung all up along Wickenden Street, so yes, I think it must have been not very long before Christmas, unless it only *seems* that way. She took the train back to Boston, and, so far as I know, that's where she is now. Maybe she's found another girlfriend or maybe she practices folk psychology on her cats. I'm not going to write about why she left. At least, I'm not going to write about that yet. Later, perhaps. Nora knew all about my bad dreams, and she also knew about what happened to my father when I was only eight years old, but neither of those things are the reason she went back to Boston. That's where we met, one afternoon at the museum of natural history at Harvard. I was making a sketch of the *Triceratops* skull, and she asked me to take a picture of her standing underneath the outstretched wings of the *Pteranodon* skeleton. Six months later, she came to stay with me in Providence, she and her two Siamese cats, and I have a cabinet full of charcoal sketches of her, because after Nora came to Providence, I didn't have to hire models to sit for me anymore. She's the first person I ever told about how my father died, how he was out walking one evening not far from the house where I grew up down in Cranston, and he was attacked and killed by dogs. No one saw the attack. No one ever was able to find the dogs that did it. But that's what went into the police and medical examiner's reports and whatever other paperwork we generate when we die violent, suspicious deaths. It was snowing that day, too, just like the day I drove Nora to catch her train, and my mother and father had been arguing, because he drank, and when he drank they argued. And when they argued, he went for long walks, no matter what the weather. And that day there was snow. "If it was snowing," Nora said to me, "then there must have been tracks. The dogs would have left tracks, so that's how the police would have known what happened to him." And I told her that no one ever said anything to me about there being tracks, but sure, that makes sense. It was a snowy day, and he was walking alone along Aqueduct Road towards Blackamore Pond, walking in the cold and the snow to let the anger bleed off and give my mother time to cool down, as well. They found him in the bushes and trees, right at the edge of the water. He was found half buried in dead leaves, and his throat had been torn out. He'd been so badly mauled that it was a closed casket funeral. And I became the kid whose dad had been attacked and half eaten by presumably wild dogs, which is probably as weird as junior high school celebrity can get. I told Nora that we had a dog at the time, a half golden retriever-half something else mix, and two days after my father's funeral, my mother poisoned it with lye. I know she did it, because she told me so. I think that's the only thing my mother ever killed. I never even saw her swat a fly or a mosquito. She'd always catch spiders and take them out of doors, instead of squashing them. We never had another pet of any sort, though, and I never did, either, until Nora showed up with her cats, whom she'd named Mulder and Scully after the FBI agents in that television show. I don't much watch television, but Nora does. When she asked me if I'd been upset by Mom poisoning the dog, I told her, honestly, that I honestly couldn't remember. I can't. "But it's not like *our* dog could have done it, could have been one of the dogs that killed him," I said, "because he was with us when it happened. I guess my mother just needed a scapegoat, so our poor dog, innocent and in the wrong place at the wrong time, became a martyr for *all* dogs everywhere, man-eaters and pacifists alike." Nora thought it was strange the way I could make jokes about something like that, never mind how thirty-two years had come and gone. I'm pretty sure me telling her about my dad's death and about Mom killing our dog was the beginning of the end for me and her. At least, that's how it seems in retrospect. "What did your mother do with the body?" Nora asked me, and I said how Mom had gotten a man who lived across the street from us to dispose of it for her. I told her that I don't know what the man, who drove an armored car for Wells Fargo, did with the dog's body. He might have wrapped it up in plastic garbage bags and then put rocks in the bags and sunk our dog in Blackamore Pond, not far from where they found my father; that's what a kid who lived one street over told me, but I never really believed him. I figured the corpse wound up in a landfill. That made the most sense. "And that's when your bad dreams started?" Nora wanted to know. "No," I replied. "Well, not right away. A few months later, maybe." But that was so long ago, I can't be sure. The way I remember it happening, they didn't start until after Mom found out about the little cairn I'd built on the bank of Blackamore Pond, right where they'd found my father. "I guess it was a sort of shrine," I said. "Seems like a normal enough thing for a kid to do, but it upset her, and she made me watch while she took it apart and tossed every one of the stones into the pond. She said it was morbid, doing something like that, and so I was careful never let her find out about the notebook I'd started keeping about animal attacks. If she thought a pile of rocks was morbid and pagan, she'd have probably shipped me off to the nuthouse if she'd seen my notebook." A couple of days after I told Nora what happened to my father, we were cooking dinner and she asked me about the notebook, about what I'd meant by "animal attacks." I told her that I still had it, and while she chopped basil and red bell pepper for spaghetti sauce, I went to the closet in the front hall and found it for her, the spiral-bound notebook I'd bought at Woolworth's not long before my ninth birthday. The cover is hot pink, Barbie pink. Pepto-Bismol pink. I brought the notebook back to the kitchen and finished dinner while Nora flipped through the pages, reading quietly to herself from the meticulously copied down accounts of fatal attacks on human beings by lions, crocodiles, wolves, tigers, sharks, pigs, dingoes, bears, hyenas, pumas, leopards, and even Komodo dragons. "Of course, that was back before the internet," I told her. "So, it's all stuff I copied out of books from school and the public library, mostly. I remember I found a whole book on the lions of Tsavo, and another one about the Beast of Gévaudan, but mostly it was a matter of finding a few lines here and a few lines there. I read a lot of old magazines and newspapers." Then Nora asked me, "And your mother never knew? She really never saw this?" And I said, "I told you already that she never did, didn't I?" After dinner, I put the notebook back where I'd found it, inside the box at the rear of the closet, and I covered the box up with an old coat I don't wear anymore. On two or three occasions, Nora asked if she could look at my pink man-eater notebook again, but each time I came up with an excuse not to get it for her. And I guess finally she got the idea and stopped asking.

3.

It's six fifteen p.m., and the yellow box is still waiting on the stairs. Across the street from the old house on Sycamore, across the street from my apartment, there are four teenagers – two boys and two girls – listening to loud music and all shouting at one another to be heard above the din of the loud music. Most of what they shout is in Spanish, and the music is also Spanish. I don't speak Spanish, and I dislike hearing conversations that I can't understand. Last year, that house sold to a family from the Dominican Republic, and they promptly painted it a garish shade of pink, almost exactly the same shade of pink as my man-eater notebook. I read somewhere that in very hot countries near the equator, where the sun is so much brighter than it is in New England, so much more intense, people paint their houses garish colors, trying to make up for the way the sunlight dulls everything. Maybe that shade of pink would seem reasonable in the Caribbean, with a Caribbean sun to take the edge off, but here it's an eyesore. Here, it feels like a threat. Like a challenge. An affront. I'm standing in the hallway outside my apartment door, out on the third floor landing, watching the four teenagers, and that awful music is pounding at the walls and at my ears and pounding in the spaces behind my eyes. I can't go out to get the box with the teenagers watching, and so I'm standing here trying to will them to turn off their music and go into the pink house or get back inside their car and drive away. But sometimes they sit out there all night long, drinking and smoking and yelling to be heard. I imagine they must all be half deaf, at this point. I should call the police, but I've never been that sort of person, the sort of person who complains about her neighbors. I don't want to start being that sort of person. The sun is getting low, and the yellow box is harder to see now, draped in growing shadows, almost as if it's fading from the world. Maybe that's exactly what's happening. Maybe, if I don't hurry up and get it, the box will simply dissolve, and there will be nothing left to show that it was ever there. Even the delivery man will forget having left it here, and probably that would serve me right, the way I've let it sit there for hours now. Maybe the twilight is a solvent. Down on the street, the four teenagers are shouting at one another while they stare at the glowing screens of their phones, while their thumbs dance a tarantella across those screens, as if in time to the music, having other, *electronic* conversations with other teenagers who are busy being noisy somewhere else. The window here in the hallway is open, and I can smell their cigarettes through the screen wire. And I have to piss, but I don't dare take my eyes off the package long enough to go to the toilet. Not the way the yellow box seems to be fading away, not when there might be nothing at all keeping it solid but the fact that I'm standing here looking at it. *If you want a thing badly enough,* my mother told me once, *that helps to make it happen.* A logical corollary would, I think, be that if you want a thing badly enough, that also helps to keep it from vanishing from the world. And also, it might be those kids who have been stealing mail, just for shits and giggles, because that's exactly the sort of stunt teenagers pull, and never mind if it means that someone doesn't get a disability check or maybe a bill goes unpaid and the power gets shut off. *Go inside,* I think. *Get back in your car and drive away.* One of them looks up, then, her eyes darting towards me, and I quickly step away from the window, feeling guilty, feeling like I've been caught in an indecent act, as if it's some sort of crime to watch the street from a window that I pay rent on every month. I take a deep breath, count to sixty, then count to sixty a second time. When I look out again, the girl's no longer looking my way. She's gone back to tapping at her phone while she shouts something at the other girl. Maybe she's shouting something about me. Maybe she's telling the others that the woman across the street is on to them, and so maybe they should stop taking mail from people's stoops and mail boxes. I glance at my wristwatch; it's six twenty-three. I turn my attention back to the yellow box. *Hurry,* I think. *Hurry,* and that's when I see the huge black dog watching me from the weedy yard of the house next door to the house painted the same shade of pink as my man-eater notebook.

4.

When we had sex, Nora always wanted me to be on top. She had a leather harness and a strap-on that she'd ordered from a catalog, from a sex shop in San Francisco, and she'd put it on me, and then I'd straddle her hips and fuck her. She'd make these very small, brittle sounds, the sorts of sounds I imagine a scared rabbit might make, or a faun, or any small animal that's trying very hard to be perfectly still in plain sight and blend into its surroundings and not be noticed by predators. But then it makes *that* sort of a sound, giving itself away, betraying itself, and whatever's hunting it sees it, anyway. I would slip that that silicone cock inside her, bearing down as she pushed upwards, and then our rhythms would synchronize, and she'd cover her face with both her hands and make those brittle sounds. The first time, I stopped and asked if I was hurting her, if I was doing something wrong, and she got angry and called me silly. So, I never asked again. I'd fuck her with the San Francisco mail-order dildo, and she'd hide her face and make the same noises I imagine frightened rabbits make when they try to hide from hungry coyotes or wolves or bobcats. The truth is, whether or not I never told her, that the small sounds she made got me wet. I would fuck her, and Nora would writhe beneath me, whimpering, and there was that flutter in my belly, that urgent, starving ache below my navel. She'd dig her nails into the mattress, and I'd lean over her, smelling sweat and her cunt and her breath and her lavender soap, smelling myself, too, and I'd lick at her throat. The first time, I expected her to tell me not to ever do that again. But she didn't. I'd lick her throat, and I'd get brave enough to nip at her earlobe or her shoulder with my incisors. I would *imagine* myself closing my jaws tightly around her larynx and only not *quite* biting down. I would imagine my teeth clamping shut, her pulse felt through my lips, my tongue, my gums. More than I wanted anything in all the world, I wanted to do that for real. But I never possessed even half the nerve and so had to settle for nipping her shoulder and only pretending I was doing something more. Except in my dreams. Time and again, I dreamed that I closed my jaws around her windpipe, and in the dreams there was nothing at all to hold me back – not compassion nor fear of the consequences nor even her struggles. I'd chomp down *hard,* and one hundred and twenty pounds per square inch is plenty enough bite force, even with my dull human teeth, and my mouth would fill with blood so hot it burned away even the stray dregs of my misgivings.

5.

I've never seen that dog before. I know all of the dogs that live along Sycamore Street – or that live somewhere else close by, but get walked here – and the huge black dog standing outside the house on the corner isn't one of them. After a moment, I realize that it's not *me* the dog is watching, but the teenagers. I wish I had my glasses, but I left them lying on the table with the book about Victorian painters. I wish that I could see the dog better, but at twilight my eyes are shit. I can't make out the breed, assuming that it's anything but a mongrel. It's big enough to be a Rottweiler, but I've never seen a Rottweiler around here. And, anyway, its legs are too long. And its ears and tail aren't right. This dog is a little too tall, a little too lightly built, to be a Rottweiler. It can't be much farther than twenty-five or thirty feet away from the kids now, but they don't appear to have seen it yet. As I watch, the dog crouches down and tenses, and its eyes flash an iridescent blue-green, that layer of cells just behind the retina, the *tapetum lucidum,* catching some stray scrap of light and reflecting it back. Did my father see that, I wonder. Was that one of the last things he saw on that snowy day thirty-two years ago, when a dog, or more dogs than one, tore out his throat on the muddy bank of Blackamore Pond? Did he even have that much warning? The black dog takes one step towards the teenagers, and then another, and I realize that it's stalking them. I shut my eyes, and maybe right then I say a prayer to the God of Dogs. After all, wasn't my father a blood sacrifice? Doesn't that mean I'm owed some stingy sort of boon, even after all these years? *Don't hurt them,* I might pray, maybe moving my lips, but making no sound whatsoever. *Just scare them off long enough that I can slip downstairs and open the door and get my package. You don't have to hurt them, but maybe they'll think twice about sitting out on the street, making so much noise and stealing people's mail.* And then, right then, I'm also remembering the night that Nora found the sketches I kept hidden on a top shelf in the room off the kitchen that I use as my studio.

171

That room gets the morning light. I should never have to hide anything, not from my own girlfriend and not here in my own house, and it *was* my name on the lease, even when she lived with me. But I knew what would happen if she ever saw them. I *thought* I knew, and that night she was rummaging around in my studio without even having asked my permission and found all those sketches bound up together in a stock portfolio as black as the dog out there on the street and tied shut with three black linen ribbons, *that* night she proved me right as rain, didn't she? I came home from the library, walking home in the snow, and Nora was sitting at the kitchen table, the portfolio lying open and the sketches spread out all helter-kelter. Some had fallen to the floor at her feet. "What are you doing?" I asked, feeling more surprised than anything else, confused because the pictures weren't on the shelf where they were supposed to be. Because I'd not meant for her ever to see them. Because this was something private that I knew perfectly she wouldn't understand, same as she wouldn't understand the urges I had when I fucked her with the strap-on from San Francisco. I asked again, "What are you doing?" And for an answer, Nora stared back at me and held up one of the drawings for me to see. It was the one I'd done of her lying naked and pinned beneath the claws of a lioness, Nora's belly torn open, the lion's paws and muzzle smeared dark with gore. "What the fuck is this?" she wanted to know, like she had any right to be asking. Then she motioned at all the others, and there were possibly a hundred or so all together by that point. I'd been working on them for months. She let the lioness slip from her fingers, and it seemed to take forever for it to drift back down to the tabletop. But by the time it had, she was already holding up another of the sketches, the one I'd done of a python – specifically, of a reticulated python, *Python reticulatus* – swallowing her alive. In the drawing, everything below her waist was already inside the snake, but you could plainly see the outlines of her legs beneath the interlacing diamond pattern made by the scales of the python's skin. "What sort of sick shit *is* this?" she asked, and then she tore the drawing into strips, and I just stood there and watched while she did it. I stood there and watched while she tore up another after that. And another. "They're only pretend," I said, I think. Maybe, though, that was only something I thought to myself, and I didn't actually *say* the words aloud. Nora picked up the sketch of her corpse being devoured by a pack of coyotes, and I stepped forward then and snatched that one from her before she could destroy it. And she slapped me. And, really, I don't remember much else about that night. We didn't talk about it, about the sketches and why I'd done them and why they were none of her goddamn business. She left the next day, and I was glad. Maybe I was also a little sorry that I'd be alone again, but the very next day was when I drove her to the train, and she and her two Siamese cats went back to Boston, and I was not sorry to see her go. Two male friends of Nora's came down to get her things, the week after she left. By then, I'd already packed everything up. They hardly even spoke to me, those two guys she sent, but I'm sure she'd told them I was some sort of lunatic pervert, some kind of sick fucking psychopath who gets her kicks fantasizing about women being eaten alive by wild animals. I could tell by the way her friends looked at me. They were polite, sure, but I could tell. And now I open my eyes, and it's almost dark out there on the street; I can hardly see the yellow box that the Federal Express delivery man left on my stoop so many hours ago, when it was still bright daylight. Maybe it's too late and the dusk has already absconded with the package. Maybe one of the kids dashed across the street when my eyes were shut and took it. But the big black dog is still right there, crouched low in the overgrown, weedy yard next door to the garish pink house, creeping along low on its belly, stalking the noisy teenagers. None of them has seen it yet. They're all too caught up in their music and phone texting and jokes that are probably being made at my expense. I could shout. I could warn them, and then no one would get hurt. But I've already said my silent prayer to the God of Dogs, and that would be a wicked, traitorous, fickle thing to do, shouting to the Dominican kids when I'm the one who has asked the God of Dogs to please frighten them away. Instead, I'll just wait and see, I think I won't have too wait long. I won't have to wait long at all.

ANIMALS PULL THE NIGHT AROUND THEIR SHOULDERS

The mysterious (and usually threatful) black dog pops up time and time again in my stories, beginning at least as far back as "The Road of Pins" (written in April 2001). The *why* of this is pretty much a mystery to me, as I have never owned or, to the best of my recollection, been menaced by a black dog. "Animals Pull the Night Around Their Shoulders" was written in September of 2016.

Untitled Psychiatrist #2

The hour begins as do almost all our hours together, with her asking how I've been doing, with me saying I've been okay, that I've certainly been worse, but really, what can you expect, given the state of the world. The hour begins with all the usual niceties and chit chat, an obligatory comment about the weather, for example, because last week it snowed, but today the high is supposed to reach seventy degrees Fahrenheit. The hour begins with me taking my place on the yellow checked gingham sofa, yellow like a banana popsicle, and then she leans back in her chair and crosses her legs and opens her laptop, balanced on her knees. I've been seeing shrinks a long time now, more than thirty years, and I remember when they made notes on college-ruled legal pads. I remember when they used pens for more than scribbling indecipherable ciphers on prescription slips, messages scrawled in a secret language meant to be read by no one but pharmacists. The hour begins with her glancing at the clock on the wall and with me turning off my iPhone. I remember when you didn't walk into your shrink's office carrying a telephone that's also a television and a camera and every other damn thing you can imagine holding in the palm of your hand. I was twenty-three the first time I saw a psychiatrist, and that was a very long time ago. The *Diagnostic and Statistical Manual of Mental Disorders* has gone through three or four new editions since then, so that a lot of the stuff I was diagnosed with back in the eighties is called something else now or is not classed as a mental disorder at all. I have lived long enough to have outlived any number of neuroses, psychoses, and disabilities. I have survived entire paradigm shifts.

"How has the writing been going?" she asks me, and I reply that it has hardly been going at all, and she says that she's very sorry to hear that. I suppose that, at least, in this instance, I have no cause to doubt her sincerity. If I don't work, I have to discontinue our sessions, and she loses a client.

Or a patient. Whichever. Over the years, I've had shrinks refer to me as both. But, then again, I also suppose that she sees quite a lot of people, and I seriously doubt that I'd be missed were I to stop coming. Indeed, sometimes, sitting here, I wonder to myself if she'd even remember our last conversation, were it not for whatever notes and figurative crib sheets she types up and keeps stored on the hard drive of her silver laptop, its anodized aluminum casing stylish and pressed thin as a razor blade. I talk, and her fingers dance over the keyboard.

"So," she says, "where would you like to begin?" We both glance at the clock again and see that the first ten minutes of the hour are mercifully behind us. "How have the nightmares been? Have they been any better? Have they gotten worse?"

"More of the same," I say, and she nods her head and looks attentive and concerned and a little surprised, despite the fact that she pretty much always asks this question and my answer is pretty much always the same. The nightmares are the main reason I started seeing her last year. I'd gone the better part of a decade without the services of a psychiatrist or psychotherapist, but bad shit happens, and bad shit sends our sleeping minds wandering back to places they ought not to go. Bad shit plays merry havoc, spinning monsters from the alloy of the present day and ancient fucking history. And I bring the monsters here, to this woman whose company I purchase in one-hour increments, and she writes me prescriptions for pills that never really do the trick, and sometimes we talk about this or that particular monster. She isn't actually a psychotherapist, so discussing dreams falls rather outside her area of expertise, but she's kind and listens, anyway. It apparently isn't in violation of any medical ethical code, listening, especially not when she's been very forthright about the fact that dream analysis isn't the sort of thing she's been trained to do. I suspect that, when you come right down to brass tacks, she's a magic-bullet sort of gal, more a disciple of Paul Ehrlich than of Freud and Jung. We've never had that conversation, though, so maybe I'm entirely in the wrong.

"The car wreck," she says, prompting me, prodding me, and I nod my head and look down at my hands folded together in my lap, then I look back up at the clock, and then I look at her, then down at my hands again.

"Mostly," I tell her. "Not exclusively, but mostly."

"How old were you again?"

"Seven," I reply. "Seven or maybe eight. I'm not altogether sure."

"So," she says, then hesitates, doing arithmetic in her head. "That would have been sometime around 1970 or 1971."

"I guess so, yeah. I'd have been in first or second grade. Something like that." And I start to say, *Lady, you hadn't even been born yet. You wouldn't be born for another ten or fifteen years,* extrapolating her age and an approximate birthdate from the dates on the framed diplomas displayed on her office walls. But I don't. I have been told on more than one occasion that I have an unpleasant tendency to use my age as a shield, to block that which makes me uncomfortable by wielding the default authority of time, and probably that's true. Instead, I say, "Nixon was president. We'd already walked on the moon. We were still fighting in Vietnam." She types something on her laptop, and I add, "I watched a lot of TV as a kid." I want to ask her if she even remembers Walter Cronkite, but I don't.

"This was in Alabama?" she asks, and I answer "Yeah, we'd moved back from Orlando by then, and we were living with my grandparents – my mother's mother and father – because Dad didn't have a job at the time. He'd lost his job in Florida, and he hadn't found a new one yet." I don't explain that he'd lost his job selling cars because he was a drunk, because she already knows that part. We did my childhood early on, the highlights, at least, the worst of the worst greatest hits, enough that she knows the broad strokes and how my father's alcoholism and the violence that followed from it are the ugly grit about which the black pearl of so many of my adult anxieties and neuroses were accreted. I cannot talk about the nightmares or the panic attacks, the arithmomania and other OCD symptoms or, really, any of the rest of it, without first trotting out my father having been a drunkard who liked to hit his wife and children, if only because I despise the absence of proper context establishing patterns from the chaos of memory and anecdote and latter-day symptoms, a framework for cause and effect.

"My father liked to drive," I say.

"You've mentioned that before," she replies, because I have.

"Sometimes, I think it was the only thing that he really ever enjoyed, besides getting drunk. But maybe I'm mistaken and he didn't enjoy either. My father was a singularly joyless man. Maybe the driving was nothing more than his version of pacing, getting in the car on a Saturday or a Sunday afternoon and just driving around with no destination in mind, except that, inevitably, the road always led him home again. He could sit behind the wheel for hours, go a hundred miles or more, but the trips always began and ended at our driveway." Then I almost draw a comparison with caged animals, and I'm thinking specifically about foxes and raccoons and coyotes I've seen jailed in pens much too small for them, and the animals pace from one corner of their cells to the next – back and forth and back and forth, ceaselessly – and I'm thinking, too, how their pacing is so reminiscent of my own retracing of steps I've only just taken during especially bad bouts of compulsive behavior. Counting my footsteps, then doing it all over again, and then again in the arithmomania's relentless, irrational waltz.

"You didn't like the drives?" she asks me.

"No, I didn't mind them, not usually. My sister and I would play games in the backseat, or I'd read books. You know, the shit kids do to keep themselves busy. Well, the shit kids used to do, before they were always glued to electronic devices and portable video games and what the hell ever. Anyway, sometimes I think that maybe he was trying to get somewhere else, trying to get away from us, from his life."

"If that were true, why did he take you and your mother and sister with him on those long drives? If that were true, why didn't he go alone?"

"So that he'd always have to come back," I reply and she nods as if there's some great significance in my answer. I know better.

"Do you want to talk about it this time? The wreck, I mean."

"I've talked about it before."

"No, you've mentioned it before. You've mentioned that you have nightmares about it, but you've never really talked about the wreck. All you've said is that when you were a child you saw a bad car crash and that it was very upsetting. Maybe you should talk about it."

I stop staring at my hands and look up, glancing her way, instead. The psychiatrist is rarely ever so direct or forceful. Most times, she seems perfectly content to sit there and listen and make her notes while I ramble along, my train of thought as aimless and circular as my father's weekend drives or the desperate pacing of caged animals. I think about saying no, that I shouldn't, and I think about changing the subject, and I think about getting up and leaving the office, paying the receptionist and going home. It feels like a sort of affront, her directness, this blunt attempt to coax more from me than I have said.

"Of course, that's entirely up to you," she says, and so maybe what I'm thinking and feeling shows plain as day on my face. I want a cigarette, and I remember the first psychiatrist I saw, all those years ago, how I was allowed to smoke in his office, how he smoked during our sessions. I look back down at my hands. There's a jagged old scar across the pad of my left thumb, a souvenir from a touch football game and a chunk of broken Coke bottle hiding in the tall grass of the field where we played, and I rub at the scar with my right thumb. Sometimes, it itches.

"Have you never discussed the wreck with anyone, not with any of your doctors before me?" she asks.

"Once," I tell her. "I talked about it once before. After that first time I was hospitalized. That would have been October 1990. I was still living in Birmingham."

"Did it help then, talking about it?"

"Not that I recollect," I tell her.

"Did you ever talk about it with your mother or with your sister?" she asks.

"I haven't spoken with either of them in years," I say, declining to actually answer her question. I force myself to stop rubbing at the itching scar, and I look at the clock again, and I see that we're twenty-five minutes into the hour. There's plenty enough time remaining to talk about the wreck and about the nightmares I have about the wreck. Or I can continue to hem and haw until my hour runs out. There are a few coins in the back pocket of my jeans, because there are parking meters out front of the building where the psychiatrist has her office. I fish out a quarter.

"Heads or tails?" I ask her.

She hesitates, then nods to me and calls tails.

I flip the coin, and it comes up tails. I put the quarter back into my pocket.

"They hit a deer," I say. "It was a car full of teenagers, a white 1969 Falcon sedan, and I don't know if they were all drunk, but the driver was. He's the only one who lived, and that was a miracle. I remember that's what my mother said when she found out the kid was alive, that it was a miracle. And she's the sort of woman who believes in miracles – water into wine, loaves and fishes, all that – so I suspect she meant it literally. Anyway, the car was coming around a hairpin curve, sometime after midnight, and they hit the deer. The highway patrol said the speedometer needle was suck at ninety-seven. Hell, going that fast, it probably wouldn't have made the curve if the deer hadn't been there. It was a big buck, one of the biggest I ever saw, a fourteen pointer." She asks what I mean, and I explain that its rack had fourteen points, seven on each antler. I explain that some people think you can tell how old a deer is by the size of its antlers and the number of points, but how that isn't really true.

"You hunted?" she wants to know. "When you were a kid?"

"Only a little, with my grandfather. But that was later on, when I was older. Except for air rifles, I wasn't allowed to handle a gun until after my tenth birthday. And we never brought down a buck that big. It must have been a goddamn magnificent animal, before the car hit it."

She types something into her laptop, then asks, "You aren't sure exactly when the wreck happened, but you can remember the make and model of the car, and that it was white, and how many points were on the antlers of the deer it hit?"

"Yeah," I say. "That's right."

"You actually saw the deer?"

"Yeah, we did. It was strapped across the hood of a pickup truck. I don't know who the truck belonged to, maybe one of the cops, maybe a friend of one of the cops or something, I don't know. The buck's neck was broken and its skull was caved in. The antlers were shattered in the crash, but someone had gathered up all the pieces, and they were laid out on the hood of the pickup with the dead deer. I remember Dad saying what a shame it was the rack got all busted up like that, what a fine trophy it would have made, hanging on someone's wall."

"Your dad was a hunter?"

"No, he wasn't. He didn't even fish."

"Oh," she says, "I see," then types something else on her laptop. I start rubbing at the scar again, and I don't say anything more for a minute or so, and it's quiet enough in the psychiatrist's office that you can actually hear the vaguely insectile ticking of the clock. I think how it's strange I've never before noticed that, the ticking of the clock on her office wall and how it sounds like an insect. Maybe all clocks sound like insects, and it has simply never occurred to me before.

Finally, I say, "Dad wasn't just the sort of man who slowed down for accidents. He was more the sort of man who pulled over and stopped for them. And, most times, Mom didn't tell him not to, even though she hated whenever he'd do that. Besides, it wouldn't have made any difference, and I suspect she knew it. If she'd told him not to stop, just to keep going, keep on driving, there would have been a fight, and he probably would have stopped anyway. But she'd never get out. Not ever. Not that I can recall. She'd always stay in the car with us, and sometimes, if it was a bad one, she'd tell us not to look. That day – and I think it was a Saturday because I don't recollect going to church that day – she told us not to look, but we did. And it was really something to see. Like I said, the car had come around that curve doing better than ninety, almost a hundred miles an hour, and it's hilly country through there, and mostly just woods, a narrow two-lane road winding along a ridge. The road was cut into the side of a steep hill, through solid chert and limestone, so there's a rock wall on your left – if you're heading north like the driver was – and there's hardly any shoulder on your right, just hickory and dogwood trees and a drop, straight down a good fifty feet or so. There's a marshy little creek at the bottom. The Falcon left the road with enough force it sheared some of those trees in half on its way down."

"Jesus," the psychiatrist says, and she folds her laptop shut and sets it on her cluttered desk and brushes at a bit of lint on the sleeve of her sweater.

And I continue.

"We couldn't actually see the car, me and my sister and mother, because it was still way down there in the creek. They hadn't towed it out yet. Did I mention that it was winter?"

"I don't think so."

"Well, it was. So, all the trees were bare, standing out stark against the blue winter sky. I can remember that. And I can also remember how fast the car got cold after Dad cut the engine and got out and so the heater wasn't blowing anymore. I can remember how cold the air was, rushing into the car when he opened the door. It was very cold that day, and it was windy, too. Well you know, cold for Alabama. My sister had a blue fake fur coat that one of my aunts had bought for her. We used to call it her Cookie Monster coat, because it looked like someone had skinned the Cookie Monster to make it. Or Grover or some other blue Muppet. She was wearing it that day. And she was standing up in the backseat, trying to get a better view, and my mother made her sit down. She was like that, my sister, so maybe she inherited his morbid curiosity, his natural inclination for gawking at other people's misfortune. She's about a year and a half my junior, so she couldn't have been more than five or six years old. Anyway, there were a couple of highway patrolmen standing at the edge of the drop off, and my father walked over and talked with them. I didn't hear much of what was said. They seemed sort of annoyed that he'd stopped and gotten out, and they kept looking over at us, at our car."

"They didn't tell him to get back in his car?"

"No," I say. "They didn't. All the times Dad stopped for wrecks, I don't remember that every happening. Or, if it did, he never told us."

The psychiatrist nods, and I continue.

"Dad had taken the keys with him, so Mom couldn't switch on the radio. But I remember she was messing around with the dials, anyhow, just to have something besides the wreck and those two highway patrolmen to occupy her attention. And then one of them pointed, sort of like he was pointing at the sky or something in the sky, like you'd point at an airplane or a cloud or bird going by overhead. But he wasn't pointing at the sky, he was pointing at those torn-up trees that the white Ford Falcon had plowed into on its way down to the creek bed. I realized there was stuff caught up in the branches, just hanging there. I followed the patrolman's finger, and I saw there were clothes hanging in the trees, and how in places all the bark was stripped off, and I saw there was something else, too. At first, I wasn't sure what I was seeing. I thought maybe it was a clump of some sort of moss or something growing on a branch. But then I realized that it was hair. Human hair. It was a woman's long hair, sort of light brown or dirty blonde, and there was also a smear of something dark along the trunk of the tree where the bark had all been torn away, just below the branch that had the hair knotted around it. And after a few seconds I knew that I was seeing blood. The highway patrolman who was pointing shook his head, and my dad shook his head, and I told my mother to look, that someone's hair was caught in the tree."

"Did she look?" the psychiatrist asks.

"No. No, she didn't. She just kept fiddling with the radio knobs, like she could make it play by sheer force of will, and she told me to be quiet, that I was going to upset my sister if I kept on like that. She said whatever it was that I was seeing, it wasn't what I thought I was seeing, and to stop staring and mind my own business."

"Did you?"

"Did I what?"

"Did you stop staring?"

I only hesitate a moment or two before answering her. "I might have wanted to. I'd like to think that I wanted to. But no, I didn't. And Mom didn't tell me again. She was too busy with those radio dials, fine tuning the silence and all. One of the highway patrolmen lit a cigarette, and then my dad lit a cigarette, and the three of them stood there talking and gazing down towards the wreck. And after a little while more, Dad walked back over to the car and got in. He didn't say anything right off, just put the key back into the ignition and the radio roared to life. It was just static, because he'd caught my mother in between stations. A *roar* of static, and me and my sister had to cover our ears. I realized then, I think, that Mom was angry, and when I looked at my father's face in the rearview mirror, he looked sort of sick. I mean, he'd stopped for god only knows how many wrecks over the years, but I could tell there was something different about this one, that it had really messed with him."

"Are you sure you remember these details," the psychiatrist asks me. "Like your father's demeanor after he came back to the car, and you and your sister putting your hands over your ears. Your mother and the radio. That sort of thing. This was almost fifty years ago, after all."

I consider lying to her, and I also consider telling her the truth, and then, instead of doing either one, I continue with my story. But if I am to be honest with myself, since I was not necessarily honest with her, I would have to say that she has a point: these memories are so old and threadbare and have been played over so many times in my mind's eye that I can no longer be sure what part of them is real and what is embellishment, what is nothing more authentic or factual than me filling in blank spaces to make a better tale. That's what I do, after all. At least, that's what I do when the nightmares don't make the insomnia so bad that I'm unable to sleep. If I can't sleep, I can't work.

"Mom switched off the radio. Or maybe she just found a station. Dad started the car and pulled away, and I watched out the back window and saw that the two highway patrolmen were watching us leave. I imagine they were relieved, glad to be rid of him. Mom said, 'I wish you wouldn't do that,' and Dad, he asked her what it was she wished he wouldn't do. She didn't tell him. She took his cigarette from him and sat there smoking and pretending to fuss with her hair in the little mirror on the sun visor."

"Do you remember her reflection, too? The way you remember your father's?"

I just shrug, because I suspect I don't remember either, and I think, *She's on to you,* and I look up at the clock and am surprised to see that we only have fifteen minutes until the top of the hour, which means there's only ten minutes of actual session left to go. A psychiatrist's hour is never more than fifty-five minutes long.

"And that's the dream?" she asks.

"No," I tell her. "No, that's not the dream. I mean, yeah, sometimes the wreck is in the dream, sure. Sometimes, I dream about my sister's blue Muppet coat and Dad standing there talking with the cops and me seeing a dead girl's hair hanging from the trees. I've even dreamt about the wreck itself, that I'm standing in the road when that drunk driver comes barreling around that hairpin curve, and it's me he sees, not a fourteen-point buck, and he swerves to miss me, and that's why he runs off the road. But that's only happened a couple of times. Mostly, none of that's the dream."

"Then what is?"

I stop looking at the clock, and I look at her again. The psychiatrist has a fondness for pastels, or so it seems from the way that she usually dresses. But today she's wearing a dark red turtleneck sweater. Maybe the color is actually burgundy or claret, but I'll call it dark red. A dark, deep red with just the faintest hint of brown to it, and it strikes me how odd that is, that on this day when I'm telling her the awful tale of the car crash, she's not wearing pink or baby blue, but this dark shade of red, and how in my memory, that's the same color as the smear down the trunk of a hickory tree.

"In the dream," I reply, "in the actual dream, the way it usually happens, the way it happens frequently enough I can call it a proper recurring dream, is that I'm walking along that stretch of road at night. It's freezing cold, and I'm walking along and hugging myself and wishing I were somewhere warm, home in bed or anywhere else at all but there. I never know why I'm there, out on that road. But I come to that curve, and standing right in the middle of the road is a naked woman. Well, a naked girl. She can't be more than seventeen, maybe not more than sixteen. And her hair is long and blonde, and it's matted and snarled, and there are twigs and dead leaves caught in the strands of it. And she has antlers. She has enormous antlers, seven points on each one, and she's standing there staring into the darkness where the shoulder drops away to that creek. She's the most beautiful thing that I've ever seen, until she turns and looks at me, and then I realize that no, she's the most terrible thing I've ever seen. And then it occurs to me that maybe those are one and the same, and there really is no distinction between beauty and terror. She turns and looks at me, and her eyes are the eyes of a buck, and her nose is bleeding and some of her teeth are broken and others are missing. And then, when I'm about to look over the edge to see what it is she's staring at – because in the dream, I never remember about the car wreck, not when the dream is *this* dream – she tells me not to look, that I don't want to see. No, that's not right. She *warns* me not to look. She says, 'Kid, if you look, you're never going to be able to stop seeing what you'll see down there.' And she sounds tired and sad and cold. 'Take my word for it,' she says. 'You don't need that shit in your head. You don't want to go carrying that around your whole life.' But, all the same, I look. And the little ravine between that ridge and the next is full of shattered cars and bones, and even though it's night and I don't think the moon is out, I can see that the creek is frozen over and the ice is red. 'I'm sorry,' the girl with antlers tell me. 'I wish you hadn't had to see that.' And I turn then to ask her – I don't know. I never actually get to ask her anything, and I don't know what it is I intend to ask her, just that there's a question in my mind that needs to be spoken, that needs answering. But when I turn back to her, she's only a buck, and before I can say anything, she darts away into the darkness, and I can hear owls in the trees, and the wind blowing along the ridge is sharp as broken glass. Usually, that's when I wake up, after the girl who's become a buck runs off, after I hear the owls."

And then we sit staring at one another, the psychiatrist and I, me on the banana-yellow couch and her in her chair, and for a long moment filled up with nothing but the insectile ticking of the clock neither of us says a word. I realize that I'm rubbing at the scar again, and, again, I make myself stop. Then she opens her shiny silver laptop back up and says, "Wow. Okay," and I don't know what I'm supposed to say next, so I wait while she stares at the computer's screen. In seven minutes, it'll be time to see her next patient. Or client. If she were to ask what I'm feeling, I'd say I feel as if there's some sort of thread pulled tightly between us, a length of baling wire or nylon fishing line, something that doesn't break, something that has to be cut if you want to get free. I feel as if something needs to be *said* to break it, but I don't want to be the one to speak.

So, she does it for me.

"Look at the time," she says. "We've let it get away from us, haven't we? Anyway, next month I'm going to be on vacation. I'm going to Mexico for a few days, so we'll need to move your appointment until the last week. Is Friday, okay? Friday the thirty-first?"

I don't mind the awkwardness. It doesn't disappoint me. I wasn't sitting there expecting pearls of wisdom to come tumbling from her lips and save me from my inconvenient psyche. Like I said, I suspect she's a magic-bullet gal at heart. Whatever it is she signed on for when she accepted those diplomas, it wasn't listening to nightmares. I tell her that Friday the thirty-first will be fine, and she enters the appointment into her computer, and then she writes the date and time on a small off-white card and hands it to me. She also hands me the three slips of paper with her indecipherable writing that I'll carry to the pharmacy to exchange for the pills that help me sleep and help me keep the anger at bay and that help me distinguish what is real from what isn't. She tells me to call her if I need anything, anything at all. I say that I will. She tells me that while she's away there will be someone else at the clinic on call to handle her cases, if there's an emergency. I assure her I'll be fine. I tell her to enjoy the trip, and that I've never been to Mexico.

"Neither have I," she says, and she opens the office door for me, and I walk out into the hallway bathed in starkly antiseptic fluorescent light, and, only a few seconds later, the door clicks shut behind me.

UNTITLED PSYCHIATRIST #2

Written in in late February and early March 2017, this is one of my more straightforwardly autobiographical stories, though I have never recounted this episode from my childhood to a psychiatrist. Probably I ought to have. It's undoubtedly one of those reasons I write such unpleasant things. The actual wreck described in the story occurred a few miles west of Leeds, Alabama, on State Route 119 at Lake Purdy, probably sometime around 1973. But – and I'm not sure why – for "Untitled Psychiatrist #2" I moved that accident to the site of another wreck that my father stopped for, a year or two later, somewhere off US Highway 78, between Leeds and Birmingham. Both involved a lot of dead teenagers.

Excerpts from *An Eschatology Quadrille*

1.

June 1969, West Hollywood

It would be a gross understatement to say that Maxie Honeycutt is a nervous man. Cat gets out of bed every morning, he checks his shoes for bugs, and not the creepy-crawly sort, but the sort he imagines the DOD and CIA and the goddamn LAPD leave there while he sleeps. Cat sits down to breakfast, he's digging in his box of Post Toasties to be sure no one's planted a microphone at the bottom. One day or another, he'll be walking down Sunset Boulevard or Ventura and a car's gonna backfire and Mr. Maxie Honeycutt's gonna shit himself, then drop dead from a coronary. This will happen, sure as pigs make little baby pigs, this or some other equally histrionic ending for the skinny little man his friends – such as they are – call Paranoid Jack. No one quite remembers why people started in calling him Jack, though the paranoid part is obvious to anybody who's spent fifteen straight minutes in this cat's company. So, you'd think he'd do his best to steer clear of weird shit and questionable business ventures with nefarious individuals. You would, however, be wrong. For example, tonight, Maxie's in a booth at the Whiskey a Go Go, trying to be heard over shitty acid rock and a hundred stoned motherfuckers talking all at once. Across from him, Charlie Six Pack is rolling a joint, some primo shit just come in from Panama. Charlie Six Pack is a good example of the company Maxie Honeycutt keeps. Cat spent seven years up at Folsom for robbery and a concealed weapons charge. Says he didn't do it, but what the fuck else would he say?

Maxie leans way across the table, not quite shouting, but it's not like he can hear himself think over the noise. And he says, "I don't give two shits and a crap what the damn thing's worth, man, cause I ain't gonna hold it, not for love nor money."

"Man, don't be like that," says Charlie Six Pack. "I thought you were my go-to guy, right? I thought we was tight, man, and you were the guy I could go to when I can't go to anyone else, right?"

"Well, no," replies Maxie. "No, not this time. This time, you'll just have to find someone else. I ain't holding that thing. I don't even like to look at it."

Now, what he's talking about is the little jade figurine that Charlie Six Pack came back from Nevada with last week. There's a brown paper bag on the table between them, and inside the bag is the figurine. The bag's rolled closed, and there are what appear to be grease stains on it, like maybe it held fried chicken or churros before it held the jade figurine. Charlie, he calls it an idol, claims it was carved by the Apaches or the Incans or some shit like that. For all Maxie knows, it was made last month in Tijuana or by some Buddha Head down on Magdalena Street. Whoever made the thing, that cat must have been having just about the nastiest magic carpet ride since Albert Hofmann accidentally dosed himself back in 1943. It's almost big as Maxie's fist, the thing in the bag, and when Charlie pulled it out and showed it to him, Maxie got this queasy tight feeling in his gut and goose bumps running up and down his arms.

"Yo, man, don't be like that," says Charlie Six Pack says again, and he scowls fit for a Greek tragedy and lights the doobie. "Forty-eight hours, right? Hell, probably not even that long. Just until the Turk comes back from that thing in Catalina and I don't gotta worry about my place getting tossed before I can make the handoff, okay? Pigs toss the place and find this, then nobody gets a payday."

"What the hell the pigs gonna want with it?" Maxie asks, eyeing the greasy paper bag even more warily than before. "You steal it?"

"Man, if I'd have stolen it, I'd have told you up front."

"Then what do the pigs want with it?"

Charlie Six Pack sucks in a lungful of Panama red, and he squints at Maxie through the haze. "Pigs don't want shit with it," says Charlie, and he blows smoke from his nostrils like a Chinese dragon. "I'm just saying, is all. Why take chances?"

"Well, I don't like it," Maxie Honeycutt tells him.

"I ain't asking you to like, man."

"What's the Turk even want with something like that?"

"Jesus, Jack, what the Turk does and does not want ain't none of my business, and it sure as hell ain't none of *your* business. One night, maybe two at the outside, you get five percent of my cut, just for babysitting a paper bag. And don't tell me you can't use the bread. I know you, and I know better."

"Ain't the bag that bothers me," says Maxie, Mr. Paranoid Jack himself, he who swears it was aliens working with the Mafia, the Bilderberg Group, and the RAND Corporation had Jack and Bobby Kennedy killed. Same cat will talk for hours about how fluoridated water, filtered cigarettes, and artificial sweeteners are an Illuminati plot aimed at pacifying the masses. Point being, the cat is given to flights of fancy.

"Man, you're one for the books," says Charlie Six Pack. "Why don't you just simmer down and stop freaking out on me." He takes another toke, shakes his head, then offers the joint to Maxie. Now, normally Maxie's fine getting high with the likes of Charlie Six Pack, but right at this particular moment, well, he's thinking he's better off trying to keep a clear head. So he says no thank you, and he asks again where the thing in the bag came from. Not that he actually wants to know, mind you, or thinks he'll get any sort of an honest answer, but Maxie figures he keeps this up long enough, Charlie's bound to grow discouraged and go looking for someone else to hassle.

"I told you," says Charlie, "some Indians made it. You ever heard of the Donner Party, those folks got lost in the mountains and had to eat each other to keep from freezing to death?"

"Yeah, man," Maxie replies, "I've heard of the freaking Donner Party. Who the fuck hasn't heard of the freaking Donner Party?" And he sits back in the booth and takes an unfiltered Pall Mall from the half-empty pack in his shirt pocket.

"Okay, well, so the dude from whom I acquired this little objet d'art," and Charlie nods at the paper bag, "this dude's a professor out in Salt Lake City, this Mormon dude from – what's the name of that Mormon college? Brigham-Young? Yeah, that's it, right? Anyway, man, he claims the doodad there belonged to one of the survivors of the Donner Party, one of those didn't get eaten, but did some of the cannibalizing. Professor, he tells me that this guy –"

"What was his name?"

"What was whose name? You mean the Mormon dude?"

"No, man. The Donner Party cat."

"Fuck if I know," says Charlie Six Pack, and he takes another hit. "Who cares what the guy's name was, man? Do you want to hear this or not?"

Maxie Honeycutt, he taps his Pall Mall on the back of his left hand, then lights it. He shrugs and stares at this chick at the bar, because he thinks she looks a lot like Grace Slick, and he's got a serious hard-on for Grace Slick, even if he can't stand fucking hippie music.

"I wouldn't have asked if I didn't," he says.

Right then, Charlie Six Pack snaps his fingers real loud and Maxie jumps. "Now I remember, man. His name was Breen. Patrick Breen."

"Whose name was Patrick Breen? The professor?"

"No, man, the cannibal. Way that guy at Brigham-Young told it, Breen said he found the thing –" and Charlie nods at the greasy paper bag again – "up there in the mountains, and it was the doodad here told Breen that if they ate the dead people, if they could get over being all squeamish and shit, maybe they wouldn't all starve and freeze to death hundreds of miles from civilization with no hope of rescue till spring. Some kind of Indian fetish or heathen idol or some shit, I don't know, right, and desperate people, well, you figure they were all just looking for some excuse not to let that meat go to waste. So, great, fine, blame it on voices from this doodad. Rationalization, man," and Charlie Six Pack taps at his forehead.

"How'd this professor get his hands on it?"

"No idea, man. He didn't say, and I didn't ask."

"And what's the Turk want with something like that?" Maxie asks again.

"Look, ain't the Turk who wants it. It's this cat way the hell off in Australia, right? So, you gonna hold onto it for me or what? You do it, I'll cut you in for *seven* percent."

"I don't want to go getting messed up in some sort of heavy Apache hoodoo horseshit," Maxie Honeycutt tells him, and he takes a long drag on his Pall Mall, then checks his watch like maybe he's got somewhere better to be when he most certainly does not. "I don't like the look of the thing."

"Oh, for pity's sake," sighs an exasperated Charlie Six Pack. He licks a thumb and forefinger and pinches out the joint, then stashes it in a snuff tin. "I always knew you was crazy, man, crazy fucking Paranoid Jack, loonier than a run-over dog, but I didn't ever take you for the superstitious sort. Didn't finger you for the sorta guy's gonna let a spook story get in between him and easy money, leaving me fucking hanging in the wind like this."

"It ain't nothing personal, Charlie."

"Sure it ain't," Charlie tells Maxie, and the cat makes no effort whatsoever to hide his displeasure. "But don't think word ain't gonna get back to the Turk how you had a chance to lend a hand and didn't do squat, all right?"

"Sounds fair," says Maxie Honeycutt, though he doesn't think it sounds fair at all, the off chance he might find himself in Dutch with the Turk just because he doesn't want to play nursemaid to Charlie Six Pack's little green gargoyle.

"What time you got?" Charlie wants to know. "I have to make some calls, man, try to find someone ain't such a goddamn pussy."

"My watch says it's seven fifteen," Maxie tells him, "but it's running a little slow, because of all NASA's excess electromagnetism or something."

"You and your fucking watch," snorts Charlie Six Pack, and he takes his greasy brown paper bag and leaves Maxie Honeycutt alone in the booth. And Maxie, he tries hard to feel relieved. He sits there chain smoking Pall Malls and staring at that girl who doesn't look even half as much like Grace Slick as he at first glance thought she did. He'll have a few beers, stick around for the band, then head back to Silver Lake and the two-room rat-trap he calls home. And round about dawn, cat's gonna wake up from the worst bad dream he's had since he was a kid. He's gonna wake up and find he's pissed the sheets. He'll turn on the radio real damn loud and sit by the kitchenette window, smoking and drinking from a warm bottle of Wild Irish Rose while he watches the sun come up. He'll sit there trying hard not to think about Charlie Six Pack's ugly fucking doodad or blizzards or a raw January wind howling through high mountain passes.

2.

January 2007, Atlanta

The way I heard it, Ms. Esmé Symes was born Esther Simon, the youngest daughter of an evangelical minister who spoke in tongues, handled rattlesnakes, and drank strychnine from Ball Mason jars. There are two or three different stories floating around about why she up and left that pissant backwater Florida town, but they all come back around to her daddy not keeping his hands to himself. Might be she killed him. Might be her momma killed him. Might be the man only lost his ministry to the scandal and slunk off into the Everglades to drink away whatever was left of his miserable, sorry life. Whichever, Esther became Esmé and spent some time with a traveling show, reading palms and Tarot cards, telling rubes what they'd want to hear about their futures, instead of telling them what she really saw. Oh, I'm not saying I believe she was a bona-fide psychic or clairvoyant or whatever. But that lady, she most definitely made a living convincing people she *was,* and, to tell the God's honest truth, if I'm gonna deny there's anything to all this sixth-sense folderol, well, then I'm left with the mystery of how exactly it was she led two detectives from APD Homicide to that empty warehouse between Spring Street and West Peachtree.

It wasn't the first time she'd helped the police. There was that kid who'd gone missing out in Stone Mountain, two years earlier, and there was the Decatur woman who'd been raped, murdered, dismembered, and buried in her own backyard. Remember her? Well, Esmé found both of them, so when she made the call about the warehouse, we sat up and listened. Now, if she'd been up front and warned us what she thought we were going to find in there, I like to think someone would have had the good sense to hang up on her. To tell her to go fuck herself. But she didn't. And looking back, that whole day seems sorta like walking into an ambush, climbing the three flights of stairs up to that long fucking hall, and then, she'd told us, go all the way down to the end. That's where we'd find what we were looking for. Down at the end of the hall.

Franklin Babineaux, that skinny kid from New Orleans, he's first into the room, and then me, and then Audrey. Yeah, she was still my partner, right. This was still six months or so before her accident. Anyway, so, by the time I make it through the door, Babineaux, he's already gotten an eyeful, and he's just sorta standing off to the side, fucking dumbstruck, gawking. And there before us was the nightmare that Esmé Symes had neglected to elaborate on. My first thought – I shit you not – my very first thought was how it all had to be some sort of sick-ass practical joke. Something like that, your brain doesn't want to admit you're really seeing what you *think* you're seeing, and if you *are* seeing it, well, then it can't possibly be what it *looks* like. Oh, you've seen the photos, I know, but the photos, let me assure you, they don't convey one one-hundredth the sheer surreal fucked-upness. The photos, they're like a fading memory of the real thing, like, let's say, a copy of a copy. For one, you look at them and you don't get the smell. Like a fish market or a salt marsh at low tide, and just beneath the oily, fishy, ocean smell, there was the sharp metallic stink of all that blood. See, you take away the smell and you take away that punch to the gut. Thank sweet damn Jesus it was winter. I don't even want to imagine what it would have been like walking into that shitstorm in July, instead of January.

But, like I said, first thing through my head was that someone had set it all up just to fuck with us. Because right there in front of me, hanging from the ceiling was this goddamn fourteen-foot great white shark. The tip of its nose was just barely touching the concrete floor. I knew straight off what kind of shark it was, because when I was a kid, my dad and me, we used to deep-sea fish down in Destin, and once one of his buddies landed a great white. Only, the one in the warehouse was bigger, a lot bigger. Probably, right then, it looked like just about the biggest goddamn fish ever was. Later, I heard it weighed in at something like fifteen hundred pounds. Anyway, the shark had been suspended from a hook, from a block and tackle rig that had been set into the ceiling of that place, a rope looped about the shark's tail. Its jaws were bulging out of its mouth, just because of gravity, I guess, because of its own weight. There were rows and rows of glistening triangular teeth big as my damn thumb, serrated like a steak knife. And its eyes were bugging out, too, those horrible black fucking eyes. Even when a shark's alive, its eyes look dead.

Of course, you know that's not the worst of it. Not even close. That fish was just the opening act, right?

So, there we are, and the initial shock's beginning to fade. Audrey, I remember she started in laughing. At the time, it pissed me off, but now I get it. I mean, it really is like the setup for a bad joke, right? Three cops walk into an empty warehouse in downtown Atlanta. There's a fucking dead shark hanging from the ceiling. One cop says to the other cop, et cetera. Real funny. Anyway, I remember Babineaux looking over at me like he was thinking, *Hey man, you know what happening here, right? You've seen this shit before, right?* Me, I'm just trying to let it all sink in, okay. Because it's not just the shark. There's this enormous design drawn on the concrete floor, sorta painted on the floor in red sand. You know, like those Tibetan monks do. Later, one of the specialists that the department called in – an anthropologist from Georgia Tech – he said the design was supposed to be a mandala, like in Hindu religion. But what it put me in mind of was a maze. And right at the center of all those parallel lines, all those circles inside circles, was the shark.

"Call it in," I say to Babineaux, and Audrey, she says to me, "What the fuck is he supposed to call it in as?"

I was the one who found the body. But you know that, too. Those lines of sand on the floor, they were spaced just far enough apart from each other that you could walk without stepping on them. Straight off, I felt this instinctual sorta revulsion at the thought of doing that, putting a foot down on one of those lines. Step on a crack, break your momma's back, right? So, while Babineaux is making the call, I go and ignore that little nagging voice in the back of my head that's telling me just to get the fuck out and let someone else deal with this crazy shit. Audrey, she tells me we should wait for the ME, and when she says that, I swear she sounds scared. And that also pisses me off. "Christ," I tell her, "it's just a goddamn *fish*. What the fuck." All the same, crossing that space between the doorway and the shark – and it couldn't have been more than ten feet – I am perfectly cognizant how I'm being so careful not to step on even one of those lines, acting like some superstitious seven-year-old, and, hey, that's something *else* pissing me. That's the thing pissing me off the *worst*.

I get up close, and I see how the shark's belly is split open, right down the middle. Well, not just its belly. The fish has been sliced open from the underside of its head most of the way back to the tail. And here and there, it's been sewn shut again with nylon fishing line. We couldn't see that when we first came in, because of the angle it was hanging at. Anyway, this doesn't come as a surprise. No reason it should. You catch a fish, you gut it. And who the hell ever had gone to the trouble to drag a fourteen-foot great white shark up three flights of stairs, surely they'd have done themselves the favor of not hauling along the extra weight of its innards. That's just plain common sense.

"They're on their way," says Babineaux.

I reach into a pocket and pull out a pair of latex gloves, and that's when I see three fingers poking through between a gap in those nylon stitches. A thumb, an index finger, the middle fucking finger – a *woman's* fingers with this deep red nail polish, some shade of red so dark it was almost black. And the fingers, they're fucking moving, okay. I yell "We need an ambulance, we need a fucking ambulance right fucking now," or some shit like that, and I'm digging around in my coat, trying to find my pocket knife. Next thing I know, Audrey's standing there beside me, and Jesus God, the look on her face. I could talk all day, and I wouldn't ever come up with words to convey that expression. She starts in tugging at the fishing line with her hands, but it's slippery with blood and oil and shit, and the line's like, you know, hundred-pound monofilament test. Finally, I get my knife out and start in cutting, and – whenever I come to this part of the story, it's always like, looking back, like right here a flashbulb goes off in my head or something. Suddenly, everything is so clear, so stark, more real than real – and yeah, I know that doesn't make sense. I get that, see, but I don't know what would. If you've ever been in a car crash, it's kinda like that.

That exact instant when two cars collide, a moment that seems so perfectly defined, but that also seems smeared.

Anyway…

It doesn't take me all that long to get the fish's belly open again. I nick myself once or twice in the process, but I don't even realize that until later, when the EMTs arrive. I have a scar on my left palm from that day. Souvenirs, right?

She was still alive, the woman they'd stitched up inside the dead fish. Only barely, but, well, you've read the files. You probably read the book that cocksucker from New York City wrote about the whole thing. So, you know how it was. We're standing there, and Audrey, she's saying, "Oh God, oh dear God, oh God," over and over, and back behind us, Babineaux is praying the fucking rosary or some other sorta Catholic mumbo jumbo. The woman in the shark, she's completely naked, and she looks maybe twenty-five, probably younger, but it's hard to tell much because she's covered in blood and gore and rotting shark, head to toe. "We have to get her out of there," says Audrey, and I'm holding the sides of the fish's belly open, and Audrey, she's leaning in and putting her arms around the woman. Thank fuck she wasn't conscious. I think that's the one small piece of mercy we got handed that day, that she wasn't conscious. Audrey's in up to her shoulders, and I'm starting to gag from the stink. I just know I have maybe ten seconds before I spew coffee and Krispy Kreme donuts, and that's when Audrey says, "Oh Jesus, Mike, they've been sewn together."

"What?" I ask her. "What's been sewn together?"

"She's *sewn* in here," Audrey replies, "sewn *to* the fucking fish," and there's this terrible, brittle tone in her voice, like eggshells. I'm never gonna forget the way she sounded. And that's when I saw what the woman inside the shark was holding. The sons of bitches who'd done it to her, they'd arranged her hands – sewn *them* together, too – so that she was cradling the damned thing in her palms. She seemed to be holding it out to us, like an offering. Only, I knew it wasn't three cops that offering was meant for. I don't know what the fuck I was thinking – hell, I wasn't thinking, not by then. I was running on shock and instinct and adrenaline, shit like that. I took it from her hands, the jade idol, what the fuck ever it was, and I just stood there, holding it, staring at it. You spend fifteen years on the force and you think maybe you've seen evil, maybe you've stared it in the face enough times that you and evil are chummy old acquaintances. But I knew that day how wrong I was. That chunk of rock, not much bigger than an orange, *that* was evil, true and absolute, indescribable, and I wanted to put it down. More than anything, I just wanted to set it down on the floor with the lines of red sand. But I couldn't. It sounds hokey as hell, but it's like that Nietzsche quote, about staring into the abyss and it staring back into you. I was still standing there holding that thing when backup arrived. I'm told they had to pry it out of my hands.

As for Esmé Symes, one week later she hung herself with an extension cord. She'd already been brought in twice for questioning, so I think she knew she was the closest thing we had to a suspect, that she was in the department's sights. The DA was screaming for blood. And her apartment, it was fucking wallpapered with sketches of that goddamned jade atrocity, right? Dozens and dozens of sketches, from all different angles. But she didn't leave a note, not unless you're gonna call all those drawings a suicide note. You ask me – and I know you didn't – but you ask me whether she was involved or not, and all I got to say is Miss Esmé Symes got off easy. She got off scot-fucking-free.

3.

December 1956, West of Denver
My Dearest Ruth,
I'm beginning this as the train pulls out of Union Station. The day is bright and sunny, though it snowed here last night, and I imagine it's as fine a way to spend a Christmas Eve as any, being ferried on steel rails through the Front Range of the Rocky Mountains. I'll post the letter when we reach Grand Junction, and then I'll be traveling on to Sacramento. I have quite a lot of work to do before the semester begins. I hope that you're well, and I hope this holiday season finds you in all ways better than did the last.

When I spoke with Sarah Beringer in Chicago last week, she was emphatic that I write and tell you of my encounter with Marquardt and her woman, though I can't imagine I have anything to say that will prove useful to anyone who's had as much first hand experience with those two as have you. I'm also not especially keen to revisit that autumn evening in Providence. It still, on occasion, gives me nightmares. I've awakened in a cold sweat from dreams of the gathering on Benefit Street. Regardless, I promised Sarah that I would write, and I do hope that I may be of some help to you, no matter how small. I trust, of course, your discretion in this matter, and I trust that what I write here will be kept strictly between the two of us.

As you know already, as Sarah has told you, I met Marquardt through an acquaintance, an anthropologist formerly on faculty in the Dept. of Archeology at Brown. He has asked that I please omit his name from any and all accounts I may write on the subject of Dr. Adelie Marquardt, and I am bound by our friendship to oblige him. It only matters that he knew of my interest in Dagon and in Semitic Mesopotamian fertility gods in general and that, through him, the fateful introduction was made, following a lecture at Manning Hall. That was on the afternoon of October 12th of last year, and it was there that I was invited to the gathering on Benefit Street. I admit that I found Marquardt personable enough on our initial meeting. Certainly, she's striking, just shy of six feet tall; the sort of woman I do not hesitate to term handsome. I don't mean in any way *mannish,* but handsome. The sort of woman for whom I've always had a weakness. From what I've gathered, she excels at making good first impressions, the same way, I think, that a pitcher plant excels at seducing hungry insects. Aggressive mimicry, as the evolutionists say. Her grey eyes, her easy smile, her immediate interest in whomever she's speaking to, the authority in her voice, and yet, I also confess to feeling the faintest inkling of apprehension when we shook hands. I can't say why. I mean, I don't *know* why. The vestige of some primal survival instinct, perhaps, something meant to keep us safe that human beings have, to our detriment, forgotten how to recognize for what it is.

Her companion was not with her that day, and I gather that's fairly unusual, seeing the two of them apart. I wouldn't meet her until the evening of the gathering.

"I know your work," Dr. Marquardt told me. "Your article in *Acta Archaeologica* on the Septuagint's account of the destruction of the idol in the temple of Dagon in Ashdod. I read that. Fascinating stuff."

Now, if you wish to flatter me, Ruth, and gain some measure of my trust, you have only to claim a passing familiarity with my research. I'm easy that way, as, I suspect, are most academics laboring in obscure and esoteric fields of study.

"I have something I'd very much like you to see," she continued. "A piece I'm told was recovered from the ruins at Ras Shamra during Claude Schaeffer's excavations there 1929. It's been hidden away in a private collection for decades, so you won't find it in the literature anywhere." She told me that no one seemed to know why the artifact in question hadn't gone to Strasbourg with the rest of Schaeffer's material.

"If it's genuine," said Marquardt, "it's very important, indeed."

I told her I looked forward to seeing it, thanked her for the invitation, and we parted ways. I spent most of the next week up at Harvard, at both the Semitic Museum and the Peabody. My department's endowment is modest (some would say meager), and it isn't often I have the opportunity to visit institutions back East. As is always the case when I can travel, I was determined to make my stay as productive as possible, wringing the most from every waking hour, even if it meant wearing myself down to a frazzle. Which I promptly did. By the evening of Dr. Marquardt's gathering, which was Friday the 29th, I was exhausted, and I very nearly begged off. Of course, in hindsight, heeding the wishes of my exhausted mind and body would have proven the most fortunate course. I'd not now be writing you this letter, and my sleep would not be so frequently interrupted by bad dreams. My nerves would not be always on edge. Hindsight, though, is rarely more than a cruel voice, taunting us from the shadows.

I showered, got dressed, and walked from my room at Miller Hall to an old slatboard house at 135 Benefit. It's built partway into the steep hill, with the basement opening out onto the street, and has been painted a ghastly shade of yellow. I've read it was constructed in 1763 by a Providence merchant named Stephen Harris, who fell on hard times almost as soon as the house was completed. Therefore, naturally, it has a reputation as a cursed house. I'd been told to arrive at 6 p.m. sharp, so the sun was well down by the time I reached the address. A housemaid greeted me at the door, and I found to my surprise that the gathering was already in full swing.

The maid took my coat and ushered me from the foyer down a narrow hallway to a spacious drawing room. The air was smoky and redolent with the commingled odors of cigarettes, cologne, and perfume. Adelie Marquardt spotted me almost at once, and I was immediately introduced to her companion, Ecaterina, for whom I never got more than a first name. She was a very pretty woman, dark eyed and her hair black as coal, and I must confess that she and Marquardt made quite a dashing couple. She's from Bucharest, the companion, and she spoke with a heavy Romanian accent.

"I trust you had no trouble finding the house?" asked Marquardt, and I assured her that I'd had no trouble whatsoever. "Good," she said, "good. I don't yet know Providence well myself, and I confess I still get turned about from time to time."

"Am I late?" I asked, looking about the crowded room.

"No, no. You're right on time," she said. "You're fine, my dear."

Another servant arrived, this one with a silver tray of fluted glasses, and she offered me champagne. I took a glass, though I've never much cared for the taste. Marquardt had begun explaining how she and Ecaterina had met in Paris, four years earlier, but I was, at best, only half listening. My attention had been drawn to the other guests, of whom there were at least fifteen or so. And Ruth, when I say that they were an odd lot, I am not exaggerating. I know that I have a reputation for being something of a prude. I've never kept company with Beatniks and Bohemians and whatnot, but I think even your beloved Kerouac and Ginsberg would have been taken aback by this outré bunch. Most were women, and there was a definite effeminacy about the few men in attendance, both in manner and appearance. I would say there was a conscious, purposeful outrageousness to the way these people dressed and carried themselves. They reminded me of a flock of some peculiar species of songbird, birds whose feathers are far too gaudy to be beautiful and whose bodies are so ungainly that one wonders how it is they manage ever to fly.

"Well, would you like to see it now?" asked Dr. Marquardt. "The artifact from Ras Shamra?"

I might have said yes. Or I might only have nodded. I can't remember. But I do recall that, just then, I noticed a young man on his knees before the fireplace. He was entirely naked, save a crown of ivy on his head and a red cloth tied about his face for a blindfold. His lips and cheeks had been rouged, and his head was bowed slightly, so that I couldn't clearly see his face. A woman stood on either side of him, each dressed in gold and garish shades of red. Each held a silver chalice. I started to say something, to ask for some explanation of this bizarre tableau, when Marquardt said, "Oh, don't be shocked, my dear. It's only a bit of sport. We like our games, you know."

All this time later, little details still keep coming back to me. For example, it was just a few weeks ago that I remembered the huge old Victrola in the drawing room, and that the record on the turntable was Hoagy Carmicheal's "Star Dust." That was a favorite of my mother's, and it was also one of the first songs I learned to play on the piano (I gave up music after high school). Oh, and the roses. I've not mentioned them. There were bouquets of rose buds placed all about the room, arranged in reproductions of Ming vases. There must have been a hundred roses that night, but not even a single one of them had opened. Their petals had been dyed blue, *Mohammedan* blue to match the blue of the porcelain vases. I'm digressing. But all of these details, and so many others that I don't have time to include here, somehow they added up to a singular wrongness, as if the room in that yellow house at 135 Benefit Street had been carefully decorated so as to achieve a very specific and disorienting effect.

There were pocket doors separating the drawing room from a small book-lined study, and Marquardt slid the doors open and ushered me inside. Ecaterina followed, and then Marquardt pulled the doors shut again, muffling the music and the voices of the other guests. In the center of the room was a small table, a scallop-topped tea table, and the thing that she'd invited me to that house to see sat alone at its center. When I saw it, I think I actually gasped. Were I writing to almost anyone else, Ruth, instead of to you, instead of to someone who has had firsthand experience with these people, I think that might sound hysterical. But yes, I must certainly have gasped. And my reaction seemed to please both Marquardt and her companion. They exchanged a smile, and I had the distinct impression that they were sharing some secret between them, like the punch line of a joke to which I'd not been privy.

"Remarkable, isn't it?" said Marquardt. "The craftsmanship is exquisite. And obviously it isn't actually Ugaritic, despite its provenance. Likely, it came to Ras Shamra from Egypt, possibly during the reign of Amenemhat III, sometime after 1814 BC. According to Schaeffer's field notes, this piece was found in association with a stela depicting the pharaoh."

For a few moments, then, I forgot Marquardt and her companion and their strange guests. I forgot about the blue roses and the naked boy kneeling at the hearth. For those few moments, the statuette on the table completely consumed my attention. Yes, the craftsmanship was exquisite, but there was nothing of beauty about the object. It was in all ways hideous. If I say it was wicked, would you understand my meaning? I think you might, knowing what you know and having seen what you've seen. The jade statuette was a wicked thing. And vile. And yet I found myself unable to look away from it.

"It isn't Dagon," I said, finally. "Whatever else it's meant to be, it clearly isn't an image of Dagon."

"I agree," said Marquardt. "Obviously. Are you familiar with the early Sumerian and the later Assyro-Babylonian texts that suggest Dagon, or Dagan, had a wife? And that the wife may have been the goddess –"

"Of course," I said, interrupting her. That isn't like me, interrupting anyone. But suddenly I was dizzy and my mouth had gone cottony. I took a sip of champagne and stared at the hideous statuette. "But this isn't Ishara."

"No, it isn't. But in Schaeffer's notes, there's a description of something he calls 'Mother Hydra,' and it's accompanied by a sketch of this artifact. He says that when one of his workers uncovered the figurine, all the men fled in terror, and that only after it had been removed from the site would they return to the diggings."

"So, if it didn't go to Strasbourg, where did it end up?" I asked.

"As I said, a private collection. It appears that Schaeffer sold it to a Frenchman, Absolon Thibault Moreau, who'd been a student of Helena Blavatsky's when he was hardly more than a boy. Moreau was obsessed with the various myths and traditions concerning sunken continents – Atlantis, Lemuria, Mu, and so forth – and he believed that the Phoenicians knew of a submerged land in the South Pacific called R'lyeh. He also believed that the god Dagon had originated in R'lyeh, and that the god's consort, this –" and Marquardt waved a hand at the statuette, "still dwelt there, waiting for a coming apocalypse – a great flood, to be precise, that would herald the resurrection of a still mightier being than either Dagon or his wife."

There was a sharp knock at the doors, then, and Ecaterina slid them open just enough to whisper with whoever was on the other side.

"So, if it went to this Moreau fellow," I said, "how did it come into your possession?" I'd taken a step nearer to the table and the statuette, and as much as I wanted to be away from the thing, I also wanted to pick it up, to hold it, to know the weight of it in my hands. I imagined it would feel oily.

"He was arrested for murder," she said. "Eight murders, to be precise. The bodies were found buried on his estate, just outside Avignon. There were allegations of cannibalism, but nothing was ever –"

Just then there was a terrific commotion from the drawing room. Someone cried out – an awful sound, like a cornered, hurting animal – and my mind returned at once to the blindfolded boy at the fireplace. Ecaterina quickly pulled the pocket doors shut again. She glanced over her shoulder and muttered something in Romanian. At least, I assumed it was Romanian. And I saw, or more likely I only imagined that I saw, a reddish iridescent shimmer in the woman's eyes, like the eyeshine from a wild animal. And I thought to myself, *I do not believe in werewolves, but if I did, then I would believe without hesitation that's exactly what this woman is.*

Then Adelie Marquardt took my elbow, and she said, "You must leave now. I do apologize, but there's an urgent matter that requires my attention. I regret the inconvenience." The way she said this, it seemed exactly as if she were reading a prepared and carefully worded statement. She nodded to a small door opposite the tea table, a door I hadn't noticed. "That will lead you back out to the street. It's best you hurry."

And I did hurry. I found that I wanted – more than I'd ever wanted anything, I think – to be out of that house and away from those strange people and that wicked statuette. Somewhere above us, bells had begun to chime; they sounded very much like buoy bells. I exited the study, followed a narrow, musty hallway, and was soon outside on Benefit, once again looking back from the safety of a flickering pool of gaslight. I'm not sure how long I stood there by the lamppost, my heart racing, regarding Stephen Harris' unlucky yellow house. Five minutes? Ten? And then I went back to Miller Hall. I left the lights burning until dawn, and I didn't sleep. I left Providence the next day, three days earlier than I'd planned, and was grateful to be on my way back to California.

I will add one last thing, and then I'll close. Two weeks or so after that night, I received by mail an envelope containing a clipping from *The Providence Journal*. There was no return address, and I have no idea who sent it, but there was a Boston postmark. On November 5th, a week after Marquardt's gathering, a body was found floating in the Seekonk River, not so far from the yellow house. The nude body of a young man. His eyes and tongue had been cut out.

As I said, I'll post this from Grand Junction. Be safe, dear Ruth. Please stay away from that woman.

Yours Truly,
Ysabeau

4.

April 2151, Isle of Brooklyn Proper

A light wind is blowing from the northeast, and the morning smells like oil. The sky is filled with hungry, noisy gulls.

From her perch on the roof, Inamorata is using Old Duarte's spyglass, trying to spot the slick she's been told rose up in the night, a great black bubble freed by a breach in one of the ancient concrete storage tanks. It only takes her a moment to pin it down, a muddy, iridescent smudge marring the blue-green shimmer of Queens Bar, less than half a mile out from Prospect Beach. A slick that long, that wide, it could easily yield fifteen, maybe twenty thousand gallons. She's seen bigger, but not for several years now, and not since the Hud extended its reach down to the barrier islands. It's surprising there's not already a company team on the scene, siphoning it off. There will be soon enough, surely by noon, noon at the latest. One of the big sweeper skiffs docked at Carnegie Island and a host of support vessels will slip smooth and silent through the heat haze, set up shop, and get to it. And any jackals caught trying to nip a tub or three will be sunk on sight, with the governor's blessings. But for now, the slick is a pristine blemish on the sea. In this light and at this hour, it's almost beautiful, the way that so many poisonous things are beautiful.

Inamorata puts down the spyglass just as Geli comes up from below. She's a sanderling girl, is Geli Núñez, stalking the drift lines for whatever refuse the tides fetch up. She's nineteen, and most of her life she's spent on the Row, with the other beachcombers and the crabbers and the bums. Before she met Inamorata, before they became lovers and Geli came to live with her in Old Duarte's house on Cemetery Hill, she worked for one of the black-market agents. Now, Inamorata has her registered with a legal pickers syndicate, and Geli gets top dollar and doesn't have to worry quite so much about the law.

"You seen it, then?" she asks Inamorata.

"I've seen it," Inamorata replies.

"It's a gulper," says Geli, and she sits down near Inamorata's perch and begins emptying her morning's haul of plastic out onto the roof to dry and be sorted. In the sunlight, Geli's auburn hair shines like a new copper pot.

"It's big," Inamorata tells her, "but it's not as big as all that."

Geli shrugs and pulls a fat wad of green nylon fishing line from her gunny sack, all tangled with wire weed and kelp. "Well, Joe Sugar, he says it's a gulper."

"Joe Sugar lets on, and you know he hasn't seen it for himself. Good take?"

"Oh, just you see this," Geli grins, and she looks up, squinting at the bright morning sky, cloudless and a shade of blue so pale it might as well be alabaster. "Down at the pilings, right in close to Fincher's docks, there was a stranding. All of it starfish and urchins, hundreds upon hundreds of them – thousands even, maybe. Starfish and urchins big about as my hand. I think they might'a washed upcurrent from Park Sloop or the Slaughter."

Inamorata looks back to sea again, staring out across the water towards the oil. "Could have been poisoned by the slick," she says, half to herself.

"Maybe. There was some sheen on the sand, so might have been the slick got them. But, anyway, that ain't the point of it," and then Geli reaches deep into her sack and pulls something out from the very bottom. "This," she says and holds it up for Inamorata to see. "Found it at the stranding, mixed in with the dead starfish. It's jade, I think. Real jade, not poly or resin. It doesn't float. Gasper already offered me an even twenty for it, before I could get back here, which means it's worth eighty, easy and sure."

Inamorata is island born and island raised, not so much more than a sanderling herself, and in her twenty-seven years she's seen her share of ugliness and misbegotten dragged in by the tides. There's a whole drowned world out there, always puking up its secrets and mistakes, the shameful ghosts of a wasted, shining petrol city that went under before her grandmother's mother was born. But this, this is something rare, indeed, the milky green lump in Geli's hand, and it catches her off guard.

"Looks Japanese," says Geli. "Doesn't it look Japanese? I think maybe it's an oni. An oni or a dragon."

To Inamorata, it doesn't look much like either. Geli holds it out to her, and Inamorata leans forward and takes the thing from her hand. It's about as big around as her balled up fist and heavy – definitely stone – though she's hardly qualified to say whether it's actually jade or not. She holds it up to the sun, and finds that it's translucent. Whoever carved this stone, whenever and whyever it was carved, however many decades or centuries ago, they'd clearly meant to convey something terrible, and Inamorata would have to admit that they succeeded in spades. The word that comes first to her mind is troll, because when she was little her mother told her a fairy story about three nanny goats trying to cross the ruins of the Williamsburg Bridge. But there was an enormous sea troll nesting below the span, a monstrous, malformed creature of slime and muck and rusted steel, and whenever the goats tried to cross, the troll would rise up and threaten to eat them. This thing that Geli's found on the beach, it could be the graven likeness of her mother's bridge troll, a refugee from Inamorata's childhood nightmares. Except, she always imagined the troll to be male, though she can't recall whether her mother ever explicitly stated that it was. The maybe-jade thing, it's unmistakably female, an obscene caricature of the feminine form, from the exaggerated fullness of its breasts, hips, and buttocks to the gape of its vulva. But its bulging eyes, those make her think of the fishmongers' stalls down on the Row, and the mass of finger-like tendrils sprouting from its belly remind her of a sea anemone.

"It's not the bridge troll," Geli says, and Inamorata frowns and looks at her, then looks back at the ugly lump of green stone she's holding. Emil Duarte, who's seventy-three and went to school in some faraway dry place, has referred to Geli as an "innate twelfth-hierarchy intuitive," and he has explained to Inamorata how people like Geli are used by the military and the multicorps. Down on the Row, there are superstitious folks who call her a witch, who think possibly she's possessed by demons, because of the way she reads minds and often knows things that she shouldn't know, that she has no way of knowing, and that she can never explain how she knows. Inamorata hasn't ever told Geli Núñez about her mother's bridge troll story.

"And Gasper offered you twenty?" she asks, passing the thing back to Geli. The stone has a slippery feel to it, oily, and when she looks at her fingers and palms, they glisten like she's been handling slugs. She wipes her hands on her skirt.

"I can do better," Geli replies.

"Probably," Inamorata agrees. "Have Sully post it for you, full span. I'll cover the tab. You want more than forty, then the buyer's gonna have to come from somewhere besides the island."

"Will do," says Geli, turning the thing over and over, examining the object from every angle.

Admiring it, Inamorata thinks, and the thought gives her an unpleasant little shiver. *To Geli, it isn't horrible at all.*

"I wish you could have seen all those starfish and urchins," Geli says, and she returns the green thing to her gunny. "Heaps of them, thousands and thousands, like maybe the sea's gotten bored with starfish and urchins and sent them all packing."

And just then, far out across the water, a siren starts to wail; a few seconds later, another pipes up, and shortly after that, a third joins the chorus, the shrill cry of the Hudson Authority's hurricane warning towers. Inamorata picks up the spyglass again and scans the low waves, but there's still no sign of a company crew, only a few ragged fishing boats, bobbing and rolling and going about their day-to-day business. The waves, the boats, and the slick. Nothing she can see to warrant an alarm.

"What's happening?" asks Geli, sounding more curious than concerned. "Why would they wind up the screamers on a day like today? There's not a cloud in the sky."

"I don't know," Inamorata tells her, and then she focuses on the slick, which seems bigger than it did only five or ten minutes before. An enormous flock of gulls has gathered above it, and she watches as the birds dive, one by one, from the sky and plummet headfirst into the oil. There's no splash when they hit. Not even a sludgy ripple. They're just gone. But odder still, the slick seems to be drifting nearer Prospect Beach, moving south and east, even though the current from the sound should be pushing it west, off towards Liberty Bay.

"You go find Emil," she says, and the way she says it, Geli doesn't hesitate, and she doesn't ask why. She just gets up and heads quickly back downstairs, shouting for the old man. Inamorata doesn't take her eye from the spyglass, not looking away from the falling birds or the shimmering oily patch, hardly half a mile from shore now and creeping slowly closer. But she's thinking of that ugly chunk of stone from Geli's sack, and she's thinking of dead starfish and sea urchins, and she's remembering the way her mother did the voice of the bridge troll.

And the sirens scream.

EXCERPTS FROM *AN ESCHATOLOGY QUADRILLE*

Ellen Datlow needed a Lovecraft story, and I was tired of writing Lovecraft stories, and I thought I was going to have to bow out of the anthology. But at the last minute, *voila,* I wrote this. Or at least that's how I remember the whole affair. But it might have happened differently so don't quote me. Someday, I'd like to do another story about Maxie Honeycutt. "Excerpts from *An Eschatology Quadrille*" was written in December 2015. Note that the geography and place names of the story's fourth and final section are borrowed from the speculative cartography of Jeffrey Linn, imagining a one-hundred foot sea-level rise and the creation of a "Sea of New York," following from the melting of roughly half the world's ice caps.

Ballad of a Catamite Revolver

As a practical sort of rule of thumb, babylon never bothers with any-thing below West 14th. Shit, not even the meter maids come down this far. Past Gramercy, it's the Wild and Woolly West all over again, noth-ing but cowboys and hindus, feral dogs and starving children who will shoot you in the face for the clothes on your back and whatever spare change they can siphon off your corneas. Rule of law does not apply down here in the sinking lands, and yet and still when the raggedy velvet curtains part to reveal the stage laid out before me and all those players assembled thereon, I see how the actors have gone to some not inconsiderable trouble to disguise themselves against the eyes of patter drones and wires and offi-cers of the Inquisition. In a sorry kind of way, I find it funny, their caution, but in another way entirely I can't fault no one for the consequences of their paranoia, whether it be founded in hardcore actuality or not. Before Manhattan, I did a stint in Philly, and before Philly I drove a mariah in a place ain't even got a name worth mentioning no more. One of those glow-stick cities the Feds are still so busy trying to scrub from off the charts, and in all these former and more or less misbegotten lives of mine I handled grey commodities and contraband of the sort you don't get the luxury of jail for relaying and profiting from. I've had babylon hot on my heels on more occasions than I care to cognitate. So, yeah, paranoia I get, even when it's foolish, groundless paranoia. Better safe and considered pollo poco by them in the know than to wake up one night and find yourself the object of a comeuppance so brutal it leaves everything all the way back to your Great Aunt Luella bleeding out and begging for mercy that ain't never bound to be delivered. I lean back in my seat, and I roll a cigarette and watch the tableau spread out before me and the handful of others who have ponied up the price of admission to pass a couple of hours being occupied by something less concrete than their streaming day to days, by something happening before their very actual eyes, unfurling likewise in the here and now, pixel free and genuine. Something that has not seen fit to submit and pass itself through the sanitizing, pick-apart filters of dear ol' hanging babylon, in which gods we trust. The actors are nude, and they have all been painted and prettied up to skillfully mimic jip-market junker droids to any casual observation – which is about the most those get ups could ever hope to fool. A sideline scan askance, maybe, and maybe a carbon que, but not anything with a partways decent concordance and a sniffer on it. I light my charch, and the musicians in the orchestra pit play what I will let stand as an overture. It's not an unpleasant sort of noise, not if your idea of music is cats caught in a screwjack. I had a off-again girlfriend I left back in Philly who fancied herself a DJ, and she would have been able to explain to me precisely which sub-lineage of Eurasian pop symphonics is to best be blamed for this racket assaulting my malleus, incus, and stapes, bless her lying soul. I breathe out smoke, and I follow the paths the spotlights are slicing through the stagnant, smoky theater air, and I do not fail to notice how I am now being kept waiting by the lousy yegg who was supposed to be waiting here for me. Speaking of paranoia, as we were, if mine own had not long ago been marshaled so that it serves me and not the other way round, I'd be skedaddling right about now. I'd be surfing cross streets and alleyways and catching a skipcar back up past the line, then laying myself low for a week or so. But, see, that's why Dimitriadis pays me what I ask, plus perks, because I'm not the type who goes rabbit just because some no account layabout nogoodnik can't tell time or simply has no decent regard for punctuality. I try not to dwell on it, I do, and I try not to ponder the inconvenient possibility that the yegg will be a no-show, and I watch the stage. A circle of plastic cargo hauls of various shapes and sizes have been painted so that they just about almost pass for a weathered ring of stones, granite or slate or whatnot, and at their center is a sheet of mirrored fabric that I've guessed already is meant to be mistaken for a pool. And behind the stone-encircled pool there stands a forest of acrylic trees and shrubbery passably rendered on what is likely no more than castaway bed linens all stitched together so that the phony weald stretches from one side of the stage to the other. To my right, an actor sits alone, kneeling on one of the counterfeit stones and gazing down at his ownself gazing back up from his own reflection, and another actor, well, she sits more to my left, and she is staring across at the man who is staring down into the pool. The man, he reaches out and does not quite touch the surface of the waters. Possibly, I reckon, this is merely because to do so would sour the illusion for his audience, when his touch failed to send concentric bands of ripples spreading out across the pool. His fingertips hover at best an inch above that silky membrane of pretending surface tension and woven polyethylene, and by Jim and by Allah, I'm bored shitless already, and I just want this lazy fucker to show up and sit down next to me so as I can make the handoff and be gone. The air trapped in this place is redolent with that perfume I learned oh so long back to associate with flood zones, the funk of estuary mud, of chemicals and saltwater and dying fish, of rotting wood and rust and crumbling cement. The smell of drowning, some would say, but I am myself not so inclined to poetry and fancy. It'll be days before I get that stink out of my nostrils and longer still before I can fully chase it from my clothes. Uptown and dryside, you hear the swells and straphangers, the bureaucrats and all them ducky shincrackers opine how One Day Real Soon like, the hallowed borough of Manhattan is gonna say enough is enough and flush this goddamn toilet, hit that big ol' red button marked PURGE, and the folks who live down here will all go swirling away down with their sinking ship or they will all of them fuck off to Port Elizabeth or Newark or the Brooklyn archipelago or some other swamp sump where water rats have not yet been made entirely unwelcome. It's not so much one way or the something else to me. It ain't so often I get sent to the flood zones, so this ain't nothing personal, but I can see how a program of systematic demolition and deportation could only improve the city's flagging reputation and sagging gene pool. I put my feet up on the back of the seat in front of me, and I watch the painted actors, neither of them speaking a word as of yet, and so maybe this is some manner of a pantomime. To try and take my mind off how pissed I'm getting at being kept waiting, I squint through the smoke and gloom and glare at the unclothed performers, their airbrushed skin glinting like the chrome it ain't – him in highlights of blue and she in highlights of the palest pink, just like those Korean plastic pals from a few years ago, most of what wound up on the scrap heap because of problems with hazardous motion, something about force feedback and faulty inductive sensors. In that former aforementioned shithole not worth mentioning the name of, back then after my stint in Philly, among my favored merch was boppers, so I know a bit about robotics. I think they're both wearing contact lenses, the actors, not only to complete the general intended subterfuge but to hopefully in particular foil the efforts of any c-swats might be lurking about. The noise from the orchestra pit swells, stumbling up a few octaves, then tumbling back down – violins and clarinets and washtubs – and for a moment I actually put my hands over my ears. I think, this yegg who can't be bothered, he can damn well pay for new auditories, if this commotion starts in shorting mine out. He can pay with creds or he can pay with blood, ain't making me no never mind. Anyway, as the music dies down to a dull screech, the man on the rocks, he says, "Oh, you beautiful boy. Oh, you beautiful, marvelous boy. I will have you, or never will I have another touch me." And the woman, she says, "Touch *me*." But he does not even look up to acknowledge her existence. "If I let down my arm as a ladder between the worlds," says the man, "would you take my hand and join me?" And then the woman, she says, "Join me?" I yawn and the time scrolling past my eyes says I have been sitting here almost half an hour now. If it were a surprise party awaiting me or some other manner of snare, well, it would have sure been sprung by now. Unless, I suppose, the architects of my undoing are too busy enjoying the show to get the job done. But still and all, I'm about to get up and head for the neon sign glowing E_IT when this yegg I been waiting on finally deigns to make an appearance, and I'm somewhat tossed a curveball that she's a she and not one of Shiloh's usual cock apes. But hey, whatever, don't look a gift horse in the mouth, and she sits down, and she says, "Ohayo gozaimsu," even though ain't the neither one of us Japanner and even though it's almost goddamn nine o'clock in the p.m. "You might want to have someone look under the hood," I tell her, "if you actually think it's morning. Or you could buy a watch. I know a man." She does not immediately reply, but looks down at the stage. She leans back and crosses her legs, getting comfortable, making herself to home like she's come for the duration. I say, "Whatever to the contrary you may have heard hereabouts, baby doll, I don't especially like to be kept waiting, and most especially do I not like to be kept waiting in the sump." And she, without turning her pretty head my way, she smirks half a smile and replies, "I imagine that you'll live. I don't suspect I've done you any permanent harm." And I say back, "You ain't who I expected," and she asks, "Who did you expect?" and I say, "Not you." And then she laughs. "Relax," she says to me. "And stop worrying about what I do and do not have between my legs." Me, I reply, "I never said –" and she cuts me right off short with, "You didn't have to, mook. It's written all over your damn face." So, I look back at the stage then, and the pink lady is hugging herself and looking all kinds of forlorn. "You go in for this melodrama claptrap?" I ask, just to change the subject. And then, before she can answer the question, I realize just to whom it is I am speaking and that she ain't just another of Shiloh's goons. And I don't see no gain in claiming I didn't feel a shiver run down my spine and frost in my bowels. "Echo and Narcissus," she says, and for a second I'm sitting there trying to decide if that's some scrap of cipher ain't no one on Dimitriadis' end seen fit to fill me in upon, until I realize she's talking about the show. "I thought you was in prison," I say. "After that shitstorm in Nebraska, I thought they'd have tossed you in Hades and thrown away the key." And she says, "Well, then I guess that's about what you get for thinking." Now, let me pause in this narration to explain what I knew back then about the lady sitting next to me. Sure, she was in Shiloh Dozer's employ. No doubt about that. So at least I could stop worrying if maybe she was an intercede from the Organitskaya or the Mafia Mexicana or even just a Fed meat puppet flying under my radar. This karena, she's got a pedigree long as my dick, and one what every handover and under-grifter from Dubai to Kingdom Come has at least heard rumored about. She's a bit of macaroni in old Shiloh's hatband, that one, who is known to babylon as Belev Andler, being that is the name of her birth, daughter of a Trumpland organ grinder name of Hadrain Kennett, though she was given the matronymic sobriquet and not her daddy's name for reasons unbeknownst to me. And maybe to everyone else, as well. During the war, she made her reputation running ammo and wetware up to the Maritime Canadians, and in the several years that have followed after, Dame Andler has had her fingers in just about every filthy little racket what turns a pretty penny. So, I know that if Shiloh put her on this exchange, then he means it go down like eggs in coffee. Whatever I am holding, he values even more than I was under the impression he does. This ain't routine. This ain't skittles. I watch Belev Andler for a moment, taking her in – her shiny white hair slicked back razor sharp and astroglide smooth, her aquiline nose that might not sit so very fine on the face of a lesser woman, her lips tattooed the color of graphite. She's got on sunglasses, so I can't see her eyes, but I have heard tales, I have, of the prototypes of Berliner micro-optics plugged into her skull. I sit there in my seat, and I get myself an eyeful, and then I go back to watching the nonsense on stage. What I know of her exploits would fill a list long as my arm, even keeping in mind how you can't put stock in every little goddamn scrap of gossip you hear come over the fence, not even from them what tends to be trustworthy, go-to sources of intel, not when one has plainly entered the province of gangland demigods. But I know some stuff for an actual, like how she's dealt in everything from nickel nukes to

Chinese adonasysphoricyacane, from retroviral harmonics to unregistered human breeding stock. The world is well and truly your oyster, yegg, if that what you consider verboten amounts to a null set. When the Atlanta riots were in full bloom, she controlled all the berserkide and freon flowing south from the best yankee chemists. She's the cat who creased the Duke of Illinois after Chicago went dark, back in '92, and I don't mean she brokered the hit. I mean she pulled the trigger. Belev Andler, she plays all the puppet gangs and netrunners and panther cozies. Why, I even have it on reliable authority that it was she herself and none other who hand delivered the Sycorax chip to – but wait. I'm going on, ain't I? These are things you know or you don't know them, and it ain't my place to play wikishines and fill you in. Point is, suddenly nothing about this meet-up was ordinary, and that put me on my toes, even if I'm sitting there bumping gums at Andler like it hasn't. "Echo and Narcissus," says she, and when I ask what was that, she hooks a gloved thumb at the illicit pageantry playing out on the boards below. And she says to me, "I take it Greek mythology isn't your sip of tea, Mr. Harlow." I answer, "I'm afraid I am naught but lowbrow as they come," and that makes her smile again. Then I add, "But also I am not entirely adverse to new experiences." She says, "Always good to hear," and on stage the blue boy staring into the artificial pool runs his fingers through the hair of the cheap wig on his head and says, "I will hold you in my arms, or there will never be anyone else for me." And then the pink lady, she whispers in turn, "Never be anyone else for me." I think how well sound carries from the stage to where we're sitting so many rows back and how that must have lots more to do with the actors wearing mikes than the acoustics of this dilapidated auditorium. I wonder what this space might have been before being repurposed for a theater of the banned and frowned upon, pondering all the ages the building has stood and all the many roles it has played, and how, in that regard, it ain't so very different from a thespian itself. "Echo," I say, "yeah, okay. I get it. So that's why she can only repeat the shit he's saying, instead of speaking for herself." Andler nods and says, "You really don't know the story, do you?" and she sounds amused at my ignorance, and I admit that I do not know the story. So, she explains how the pink lady is meant to be a mountain nymph named Echo and how the nymph conspired to help Zeus hide his multitudinous infidelities and indiscretions from his wife, the goddess Hera, whom the Romans named Juno, as in Alaska. Whenever Hera would get suspicious and start in prying and asking questions, Echo would distract her. Echo was a talker, a regular chattertrap, and she'd keep it up for hours on end, but eventually, says Belev Andler, eventually Hera copped wise to Echo's conspiracy, and she cursed the nymph so that she could only ever repeat the most recently spoken words of other people and never her own mind. Then Echo fell in love with Narcissus, the actor in blue paint, but Narcissus loved no one but Narcissus, pining over his own prettiness in an alpine pool, and, well, that's the gist of it. "So, she can't tell him how she feels," says Shiloh's agent, to which I reply, "And even if she might, it wouldn't do her any good, what with his given preoccupation. I get it. Hence, narcissism. Okay, so, tell me this, then. Why the hell have the censors shut this one down? Where's the subversion I'm not seeing?" Belev Andler takes from her sharkskin jacket a shiny silver case, and from the case she produces a cigarette rolled in paper the bloody color of a pomegranate. She asks me for a light, so I politely oblige. She blows a smoke ring, then points towards the stage with the smoldering tip of her charch. She says, "Well, it doesn't actually have much to do with the story of Echo and Narcissus, why the story of Echo and Narcissus wound up on the blacklist." I ask, "Then what *does* it have to do with?" She takes another drag, blows another smoke ring, and she says to me, "A few years back, there was a genejack up in – I think it was Montreal, but don't quote me on that. This slicer got himself mixed up in the affairs of some mid-level minister's wife or another, some dyke twist who'd fallen in love with the daughter of an elected official considerably higher up the food chain than herself. Problem for her was, more than anything else, the daughter in question wasn't in love with her and was, in fact, engaged to marry a wealthy young businessman from Brazil who was doing consultant work with her father. Brazil or Argentina, I'm not sure which, but I think it was Brazil. So, the mid-level minister's wife – and she's a total gold-seal loon, by the way, name of Margaux Margosian – she hired the slicer to rip the guy's DNA profile and do what he does, at twice or three time his normal fee, as the risk to himself was pretty damn obvious, so that she could have the kid from Brazil killed and take the guy's place. If it worked, she'd have her beloved and no one would be the wiser. But everything that could go wrong did, pretty much, including Margosian dying on the operating table, right in the middle of the procedure, and at the trial of the genejack he let slip that his client had been inspired by a variation on the myth of Echo and Narcissus in which Echo wears a copy of Narcissus' face in order to finally win his affections. Some Spanish writer, I don't remember his name. One of the Castilians, I think. But it turns out that the father of the girl the slicer had been employed to sucker, he had the ear of the censorship and decency board, and as far as he was concerned, this was all because of the tale of Echo and Narcissus. To wit, the moral of our story," and again she points at the stage with her cigarette. Me, I say, "Sooner or later, love makes mooks of us all," and Belev Andler responds you better fucking believe it. So, alright then, I'm thinking, we come this far, and she's chatting me up like our masters ain't always a cunt hair's breadth from open war, so maybe this deal's gonna go down by the book and everything is jake. Sure, so maybe her turning up to what was supposed to be nothing but a garden-variety swap of goods for currency don't mean nothing more sinister than Shiloh wants this package coddled in the best of hands. Or maybe she just got bored and volunteered. It happens. The best and most celebrated crook has days when they just wanna be down among the common folk, turning the common grift, playing their part in the common hustle, doing a spot of grunt work and reminiscing about the simpler days when they were not yet such a much. We all get homesick. But still I'm left uneasy, you understand, waiting on the fall of the second shoe, as it were. And then, right on cue, she says to me, she says, "You got questions you're not asking," and there ain't no point in my being insincere, so I nod my head and tell her, sure, I got questions, but the answers ain't of a necessity any more my business than what side of the bread she butters her toast on. And now I see that maybe her being here isn't at all about gods walking among the lowly plebes and mistaken as one of their own, that it's maybe more her being the sorta sick twist gets her jollies in watching the plebes cower and curtsy and shit themselves as she passes, leaving despair and hasty prayers in her wake. "Then you should ask them. Or at least one," she tells me, smoking her charch and keeping her eyes on the stage. "You should choose one and at least ask it." My own smoke has burned down almost to my fingers, and I drop it to the theater floor and crush it out with my left heel. "Maybe," says I, "this is Shiloh Dozer looking to pick a rumpus, looking for an excuse to throwdown on Mr. Dimitriadis," and she says aw, that's so cute, how I call him mister, even when he ain't around. Then she says, "No, it isn't like that. If Dozer wanted a fight, he'd start one himself, not send a lieutenant round to do the honors. This is nothing but friendly conversation among the rank and file, teamster to teamster. I'm politely offering to satisfy some miniscule fraction of your curiosity, that's all. I know how people talk. Sometimes, I like to set the record straight is all." And on the one hand, I'm cogitating, she sounds reasonable as jam, almost matter of factly, so maybe if I just nod and go along, I ain't gonna be pulling a gumby, but only rubbing the belly of the beast, indulging this kink she's decided to inflict upon me. But I have never trusted calm, and I do not trust the calm in her voice, this purring Olly climbed down off her marble pedestal to play Katz und Maus with the yono. "Ain't enough we just make the trade and go about our way?" I ask, and she says no, it ain't enough. She's come all the way down to the sump, and she's too ponied up the ticket price to watch these faux-bot players, and what she wants is me to ask. And she don't have to say how I know the sorta insulted she'll be should I decline her generosity. Some of us stay playground bullies and don't just start off that way. "Fine," I say, because what the fuck else am I gonna say, yegg? She takes out that silver case again, takes out another pomegranate charch and lights the second off the first, then flicks the spent butt away into the darkness, sparks spinning ass over sparks. "And don't play patty-cake," she warns. "You won't have this chance again, Mr. Harlow. Make it count." And I ask if whatever I might learn from this inquiry is to be considered privileged knowledge or if she maybe expects me to turn it about all loaves and fishes among the multitudes. "I shall leave that to your discretion, which must be considerable, seeing how high you've risen in such an esteemed corporation." And now she's just being shitty, giving off the high hat, but I am not about to call her on it. Ten will get you twenty she's studded back to Shiloh in his tower by the sea and he is laughing his backside off, waiting on some proper donnybrook to unfold for his hallowed fucking amusement. "It isn't a trap," she says, and I say I sure would feel a lot better if I could see her eyes when she says that, and she tells me that people in Hell want ice water and cold beer. "Yeah, okay," I say, just finally sick of jousting, "yeah, fine, I gotta question, something I been hearing bandied since before you handled the Sycorax installation. I have assumed it to be naught but idle chatter, and I never would have dignified it with any sort of serious investigation, only here you say you want the hard question, and maybe this is the hardest I got." And by now I'm wondering if I can quickdraw this bitch, if I can show her mine before she shows me hers, bang-bang, because that's just how fast shit goes to shit down in the sinking lands where we ain't got no elsur babylon intrusions to keep us playing nice. "Let's hear it," she says, and on the stage, the pink lady is holding up a machete, and I wonder where the fuck she got that from and when the fuck she got it. "Before I'd hold you to my breast, lovely Echo," says Narcissus on his rock, not bothering to look away from his own reflection, "I would draw my final breath and be laid to rest, food for the worms." And Missus Echo, she says, "*Food* for the *worms*." So, then and there, I give Belev Andler my best shot, being as how that's what she's asked for, while she watches the show. I say, "Here's what I heard one night in a teamster saloon over to the Jersey Isle. Well, not teamster proper, more hardly a step up from thrash and thriller gang, more like. The sorta joint where the entertainment bleeds, you dig, and I'm just telling you this for context. Sense of place stuff, as the Longfellows in their powdery wigs might say. I was staying sober, as I was there on business, and as yeggs get expired in there just for walking through the door." Belev Andler, she says, "The company we keep," and she shakes her head in a pretense of dismay. "Not me, sister. Not by habit. I was there on orders. But I digress. Point of it is, here was this yakking slitch – I never got her name, nor would I likely recollect it if I had. She'd heard about Sycorax, just like the rest of us, and she was on about it, and then she drifted into more personal waters as regards your reputation, and, natural, we was all ears. You could'a heard a pin drop." And Andler, she grins and nods and says, "I betcha could." She takes a drag and blows smoke from the nostrils of that finely chiseled aquiline snout of hers. "What was it she told you?" and I hold up a hand like a traffic dick and tell her, "I'm coming to that. Keep your trousers on." And she laughs, and I think again about the reconditioned Walther P4 9mm sitting useless in my shoulder holster, but ain't no way I'd get a shot off before she did me whatever mischief would be her preference. "She was a professional drunk," I say, "among other more lucrative trades, and I always set only so much stock in the words of rummies. But what she said, holding court that night while some betty was being filleted alive for the entertainment of lesser men than myself, what she said was how she'd heard how Belev Andler was the sorta swag got her rocks off fucking corpses." The words spill from my lips, and my mouth is gone dry as grandma's twat, and my heart's a step away from code. But on I slog. "This slitch, she said before Shiloh scooped you up and made of you a respectable piranha you were a recycling ghoul off in deepest, darkest Trumpland, dealing spare bits and pieces to vat jobs in Detroit and Cleveland, Pittsburgh and all them other rustbowl shints. Me, I'm just a dumb yegg and I don't know from Adam, but here's what she was saying, as here's what you was asking me to relate." And now I look over at Andler, and she's all eyes forward, and I note how the line of her jaw seems just a little firmer than it did a moment ago. She's not *not* smiling. I don't know what you'd call that expression. I've seen it plastered on the mugs of hyenas. I continue: "Way she told it, you took a

cut from your percentage in the cooler and nothing got you harder or wet-
ter than a whiff of embalming fluid. She said she'd heard it you had an
especial bruise for candy boys what still got their peckers, what ain't yet
gone knifeside for their shiny new piss fenders." In my head, you know I'm
thinking at myself, *Shut the fuck up, fella, because you done said more than
enough to bury you six feet deep and six times over.* But I'll own the truth, and
the truth is I found myself all at once daffy on the adrenaline rush of all
that tension and misgiving. Now, I been sober mostly since the last five
years, going on seven, and any rush I can cadge without technically falling
off the wagon, that's a blessing and I go for it. "What else?" asks the Lady
Belev Andler, and I ask right back, "Jesus, ain't that enough?" She takes a
long drag on her charch and the cherry glows bright there in the theater
gloaming. She repeats herself – "What else?" – and I curse silent to myself
and I spit on the floor between my legs. "This slitch on Jersey Isle," I say,
then pause as it occurs to me that the adrenaline edge is beginning to fade
away, here and gone, quick as a bunny, and fuck my fickle endocrine pumps.
"She said," prompts Andler, and so I continue. "She *said,*" says I, "that it
was from a cadaver that you eventually acquired a fairly unpleasant bug,
the lingering chronical sort that won't kill you off, but for which there is
not exactly yet a cure. She didn't know what species for sure, and I ain't
gonna repeat all her colorful speculations, so don't you ask me to. And she
said the tainted dead shehe what infected you was born your own brother,
and that's the how of you getting this thing for candy boys. She did not
hazard to hypothesize how it came to be you preferred them dead, and now
that's all I'm gonna say on the subject, and if that don't suit you, take it up
with Dimitriadis." I can hear the snip of rattle in my voice. If she was trying
to intimidate me and put me off my balance, well, it should be plain to her
that she has succeeded. I think about the Walther again, and I think about
the hole it would make going into her face and the bigger hole it would
make when the slug came out the other side. "Are you enjoying this, Mr.
Harlow?" asks Andler, and I sorta laugh a sickly laugh and reply, "Was I
supposed to not? You tell me, sister, so I know the correct answer, 'cause I'm
sick of guessing. I just want to make the drop and dangle." Then I look back
down at the stage, which, in my distress I admit I had at this point half
forgot, and I look again just in time to see fair Echo painted in shades of
pink chrome to mimic a Korean sex droid, machete held high, I see her step
across that phony mountain pool. She walks on the water sure as Jesus
Harold Christ, and the blue boy he finally looks up from his reverie of

self-infatuation, and I'm supposing that's only because she's muddled his beloved reflected countenance. I know right then what's coming, and I'm thinking how nobody warned me this was a goddamn guro joint, and I hear myself as if from faraway muttering to no one in particular, "Ah, shit on me," and then I see that Belev Andler is on her feet, though I have no recollection of her having got that way. She's cradling this goddamn gargantuan Bison-2 Russian submachine hand cannon, like Jehovah's own Doctor Johnson, like the belated revenge of Vladimir Vladimirovich Putin, and to this day I have no idea where might she have been hiding the thing up and until that moment. She squeezes the trigger before I can cover my ears and pops off a few of those 9x19 parabellum rounds. Down on the boards, the pink lady's head explodes, and she drops limp and sprawling in a spray of her own juice and scrapple. From the balcony above, someone screams, which is, mind you, all kinds of ironic, and then there are people shouting, and Mr. Narcissus is just sitting there looking lost and thick as pig shit, spattered in the pink lady's gore. "Motherfucker!" howls someone somewhere in the joint, "Motherfucker! Motherfucker!" and I look up at Belev Andler and say, "For the love of Mike, no one ever mentioned you being loony in the bargain," but I can only half hear what I'm saying, from the ringing in my ears. She lowers the barrel of the gun and sits back down in her seat. "You got the package?" she asks, all at once the perfect semblance of businesslike. "Yeah," says I, "I got the goddamn package. It's right here. I wouldn't be fucking sitting in this shithole if I didn't have the goddamn package, do you think?" I don't bother to not sound as pissed as I am, because I have had it there and back again with this twist's games. On stage, well, all sorts of chaos and confusion and perplexity unfurls, which I can admit in a different context I might have found amusing, given what the proprietors of the place and the director of the show had laid in store for us. Narcissus, he's wiping brains and blood off his face, and I figure, from what I know of guro theatralik, blue boy is doped to the gills with coby and metazine, feeling no pain nor remembrance of pain nor fear for his imperiled mortality. And, from what I know, likewise the pink lady was probably stringing on a cocktail of coke and spice. It's in the contract, how the players get their sweets, lest anyone get cold feet when the moment comes. "No one told me this place was guro," I mutter through the ringing in my skull, and Andler says how we need to conclude the transaction because she has to piss and dangle, how she has places to be dryside. Some of our fellow audience members have commenced to boo and give voice to their disappointment. "Gladly," says I, and I reach for the shiny green and orange cylinder of anodized aluminum in the seat next to me, and I hand it out to her. "You have the sum?" she asks. "Dozer said I should see it before I pay you." And I tell her yeah, I got the sum, hold your horses, and I punch in the seven digits and the cylinder slides open, disgorging the eight inches of borosilicate Pyrex glass tubing that has been until that moment protected safe inside. "Just like was agreed," I tell her, and she takes the cylinder and the tube from me and looks more closely, holding it up so what little light there is shines through the translucent amber contents of the tube. "Just like was promised," I tell her, nodding at the package. "One hundred and twenty-five milliliters, raw and straight from the hives of the Upper Machakheli Valley, regurgitated from bellies of the finest Turkish bees. Ain't nowhere gonna get you nothing purer." Down on the stage, a fat man and a tall skinny man – a regular L&H – are leading the blue boy away, and I fancy if his unexpected and undesired survival means his contract is cleared or if they'll put him straight back in the chute, slotted for the next performance and the lusting eyes of them what get stiff and soggy watching snuff. Andler, she presses her thumb to the pound sign printed on the orange and green cylinder, so the tube slides back inside and the treasure is sealed safe away. "I never screwed my own brother, neither dead nor alive," says Belev Andler, watching at the stage from behind the inscrutable windows of her sunglasses. "That part is a damned lie." And I nod and say, "I ain't got no reason to believe otherwise to the contrary." She stows the cylinder inside her raincoat, and I'm just about wondering to myself if that coat of hers was tailored by black-ops spooks with some sort of dimensional transcendentalism hypercube mojo going for it, cause now I don't see the Bison-2 anywhere, so where the fuck is she hiding the thing, right? Well, no, I don't ask. The handoff has been made. The customer's agent is in possession of the goods. My duty is done, and I can catch the next skip back north of the line and not set foot in the sinking lands again until Dimitriadis takes a notion that's what I gotta do. Huzzah. Andler takes her leave, and I sit in my seat, giving her the standard fifteen until I also take my leave. The house lights come up, and the unsatisfied crowd, struck with blue balls over the carnage what they have this night been denied, are filing by ones and twos and thrice out of the auditorium. The musicians in the pit are putting away their horns and fiddles. On stage, some yegg is mopping away the mess Andler's bullets made of Echo's head, and some other yegg shows up from the wings with a white cadaver pouch to receive her mortal remains.

And I think how maybe it's time I ask my keepers for a few weeks down-time, and how I'd use it to go inland – Kansas or Oklahoma, Denver or Cheyenne, I don't know – where I ain't got to smell the sea even when I'm dryside, and where maybe I can toss my sobriety and stay drunk long enough to put the thought of Belev Andler and the painted actors in back of me, them and all the months worth of bushwa just as bad or worse. And then I gather myself up and head for the sign glowing E_IT, and as I go, one of the mooks in the cleanup crew shouts at me how the next show's at twelve midnight and how I should stick around, 'cause, boy howdy, it's gonna be a doozy. I do not reply, and I do not even look back over my shoulder, and I do not slow down until I am out on the rainy street.

BALLAD OF A CATAMITE REVOLVER

I see this as a scene from a film directed by John Hillcoat, with music by Nick Cave and Warren Ellis, from a screenplay by Quentin Tarantino (though Tarantino wants nothing to do with the final cut and the credit goes to Alan Smithee or Cordwainer Bird or – well, you get the picture). The part of the narrator is played by an older Douglas Booth (or a younger Jude Law), and the part of Belev Andler is played by Charlize Theron. The story was written in March 2017.

Untitled Psychiatrist #3

There is something almost archetypal about this office. It might be a movie set or a theater stage, carefully constructed from blueprint schematics set forth as the Platonic ideal for the space where a psychiatrist should hold court and ply their trade and do as little damage as they may. The furnishings are uniformly Victorian and artfully mismatched, a gathering of slightly battered antiques that work together in ways the craftsmen who made them never could have foreseen, much less intended. The wood is carved cherry and mahogany and is upholstered with threadbare silk brocade in shades of red and orange and gold, brown and butterscotch, an easy, autumnal assemblage perhaps conceived as an anodyne to melancholy and anxiety and dread. There is a desk and a chair behind the desk and another chair. There is a chaise lounge draped with paisley batik, possibly to conceal breaches in the fabric where cotton padding shows through. There is a tall floor lamp with a fringed shade, and there are two walls lined with bookcases, the shelves stuffed with leather-bound and cloth-bound volumes. There's a fireplace fashioned of bricks glazed green as moss and the grey slate mantel shelf sports several natural curiosities that might have been pilfered from the cabinet of a John James Audubon or a Charles Darwin – a large fossil trilobite, a small taxidermied bird beneath a bell jar, a framed assortment of butterflies. Except about the periphery of the room, the floorboards are concealed beneath a worn Persian carpet woven in colors that complement the upholstery, a stately labyrinth of interlacing arabesque. Hung above it all, a ceiling of tin-plated galvanized steel medallions painted to mimic verdigris. There is a wide bay window on the east-facing wall, hidden now behind a heavy curtain of apricot velvet to avoid unwanted distractions, but whenever the curtain is pulled back there is a splendid view of Central Park and the Sheep Meadow and the wide sky above Manhattan.

I cannot myself afford these stately accommodations. I am here because someone else foots the bill, someone to whom I was married for a time, though I would hesitate to say the man was ever truly my husband. He was only the man to whom I was married by law and with whom for the space of five years I shared a stingy, halting sort of existence. Together, we suffered a stately limbo, you might say. Part of the divorce settlement decreed that he would see to such expenses as these whenever and for however long I deemed them necessary, no questions asked. And to his credit he has never yet protested that I might seek a more affordable class of therapist, for the sake of his not bottomless pocketbook. Perhaps I would, if it didn't suit me to see him inconvenienced. It's not as if I have any particular faith in this particular woman. For that matter, it's not as if I have any faith in her science, or what she and all other alienists would have me *believe* is science and not merely a freshly cobbled together class of superstition and flim-flam disguised with statistics and pharmaceuticals as something more exact and efficacious than witchcraft or a confessional booth. Truthfully, on the subject of psychotherapy, I suppose I'm rather like an atheist who perversely insists that she must pray, regardless of her absence of faith, and that furthermore only the most ostentatious of cathedrals are suitable to her infidel's worship. I will have the Cathedral of St. Patrick or I will have nothing at all. It's like that, I suppose.

As for Dr. Amelia Novas, she was born in Buenos Aires and earned her doctorate at Yale. The former I know because she told me and the latter because of the framed diploma hanging on her office wall. She's a handsome woman stranded somewhere in late middle age – latest fifties, earliest sixties – her hair a perfect balance of salt and pepper. There's a nervousness about her eyes that seems ill-fitted to her chosen profession, and she has a habit of tapping the eraser end of a yellow No. 2 Ticonderoga pencil against the underside of her chin while she listens. If I found it annoying, I would ask her to stop. She has a fondness for plaid skirts and cardigan sweaters and sensible shoes, and every time I have seen her she's been wearing the same pair of diamond stud earrings, but no other jewelry. There's something about her accent that I find soothing, which is likely the only reason I have seen her three times now, if you count today.

I'm sitting on the chaise lounge with my eyes on the curtains hiding the view of the park. She asks me how I've been, and I cross and then uncross my ankles. I tell her I've been well, which isn't exactly the truth. Every time I have seen Dr. Novas she has offered me my choice of the chair or the chaise, and every time I have chosen the chaise. She always asks if I would be more comfortable lying down, and I always tell her that I would rather sit up.

The first time I came here was two weeks ago, on a rainy Monday evening, and we talked about nothing in particular for a full fifty minutes. The second time was last Thursday morning, and I talked to her about my childhood in rural Georgia, about my alcoholic father and both my alcoholic grandfathers and an alcoholic aunt who overdosed on barbiturates when I was still in grammar school. I described the aunt's funeral, and how I was expected to kiss the corpse before the casket was closed. I explained that I suffer from very bad dreams and possibly some vague brand of post-traumatic stress. I suspect that Dr. Novas understood that I was stalling, cobbling together my resolve piecemeal. I imagine she's seen that sort of thing plenty enough times before. I don't imagine it much matters to her what we talk about, not so long as the checks clear. Anyway, today I have resolved to finally get to the point, before I lose my nerve and thank her for her time and stand up and leave this office and this building and never look back. I am all too keenly aware that things could go that way.

"What would you like to talk about this week?" she asks me, after the customary pleasantries have been exchanged, the requisite chit-chat that eats up the first ten minutes of the session. I reach for the slender black padded nylon case at my feet, which holds my laptop and a single manila folder and nothing else. I unzip the case and take out the folder, then zip the case shut again and set it back down on the floor, carefully propped against one corner of the chaise. I open the folder and take out its contents – an article that I've photocopied from a 2012 issue of the *Journal of Psychiatric Practice*, five pages held together with a single staple.

"You wrote this," I say, stating the obvious, and when I offer her the article, she takes it and sits reading over the first page. She turns to the second, nods, then lays the photocopy down on her desk and looks back at me. I glance towards the velvet curtain hiding the New York City skyline. There's a slender rind of bright sunlight where the two halves of the draperies meet imperfectly, and it makes me squint.

The title of the article is "Lycanthropy as a Culture-Bound Syndrome: A Case Report and a Review of the Literature." I've read it all the way through seven times.

"Yes," she says. "Yes, I did. Is this why you're here, why you've come to see me, because I published this paper?"

"I found that last April," I say, not answering the question.

"It took you over a year to decide to come see me?" she asks.

"It took me a year to get up the nerve," I reply.

"And why is that?"

I laugh a small, dry laugh that might easily be mistaken for a cough, and I ask her, "Is that something they taught you at Yale?"

"What do you mean?"

"I mean, did they teach you that it's disarming, to pretend not to be fazed by the weird shit people tell you? That it puts lunatics at ease?" I glance at her, then right back at the curtain and the sliver of sunlight.

"It's just that I don't want to jump to any conclusions," she tells me. "You've presented me with an article that I wrote five years ago. Now, I can imagine any number of reasons why you're here, why this article has brought you here, but until you tell me, I won't know which one is the correct one. And until I know that, I'm not at all sure how I should react. Does that seem fair?"

I look away from the curtain to the office door, and her eyes follow mine.

"Are you thinking about leaving?" she asks.

"No. But I am wondering why I ever thought this was a good idea," and I cross my ankles again, and I go back to staring at the curtains. I want a cigarette. I envy all those people who went through analysis in the years before smoking became as frowned upon as drowning kittens. I imagine bygone days when patients and their doctors conversed amid peaceful grey clouds of nicotine and no one gave it a second thought. Downstairs, in the lobby, there's a big sign warning everyone who comes through the door that the building is a "tobacco-free facility" and woe betide all transgressors.

"Would it help," she says, "if I tell you that you're not the first person who's come here because of this article?"

"Not especially," I reply. "I've never understood people who find comfort in knowing that they're not alone in their suffering."

"Are you suffering?"

I take my eyes off the door and stare at my feet and the carpet, instead. I'm wearing sneakers, and I see that the left one is coming untied.

"Can we slow down?" I ask her.

"Absolutely," she replies. "Would you rather we change the subject and come back to this later on?"

"No, I'd just like to slow down a little, that's all." And then I almost tell her how I've tried to work this conversation out in my head, how I have tried to anticipate the course of it – how it is I'm going to try and explain myself to her – and how, despite all that, everything's coming out wrong. I almost tell her about sitting in front of a vanity mirror in my bedroom, rehearsing my lines, speaking the words aloud to no one but my reflection. But then I decide it's better that I keep all that to myself.

"It isn't what you think," I say. "It isn't that." I want to lean over and retie my shoelace, but I don't. Instead, I look up at her, and she's watching me.

"What I told you about not jumping to any conclusions," she says, "I meant that."

"I think everyone jumps to conclusions. No offense. It's just what people do. We can't help it. It's just the way our brains are wired. Sure, maybe we want to be objective and methodical and reserve judgment until all the facts are in, but that's not how we work, not in the real world. Human beings, I mean. That's not how our brains work. Listen to me, lecturing you on psychology."

"Maybe I should be paying you," says Dr. Novas, and then she smiles to show me that she meant it as a joke.

"I don't have the patience for it," I tell her.

"The patience for what?" she asks.

"The patience required to do your job, to sit there and listen to people. I don't have the patience to pretend that I care about their problems. To be honest, I hardly even care about my own."

She taps at her chin with her pencil.

"Is that what you think I do, only pretend to be concerned?"

I nod and say, "I believe so, yes. Otherwise, without that distance, without the remove afforded by emotional detachment, it would quickly become unbearable, the weight of your concern for them all, the need to make them better, to relieve their suffering. I think maybe that's why so many saints are mad."

"Are you Catholic?" she asks.

"I was raised Catholic."

"But now?"

I shrug and say, "I still keep a rosary on my nightstand. I still wear a St. Christopher medal. A priest might only say that I'm lapsed."

"And what would you say?"

I look back down at my shoes and at the autumn-colored carpet. I wonder how many people sit where I'm sitting on any given day. I wonder how many people a week sit (or lie) here on the chaise and talk to Dr. Novas,

fervently hoping that she has whatever answers they need, that she will dis-
pense a solution, the psychoactive equivalent of Ehrlich's magic bullet to
make them all better. Of course, when offered their choice of the chaise
lounge or the chair, some percentage surely choose the chair. But still. If she
only sees five or six people a day, and if she only works five days a week, that's
twenty-five or thirty people a week. How many must she see in a month?

"I would say that I don't spend all that much time thinking about
religion," I tell her. Add that to the laundry list of lies I've told here in this
room. "What about you?"

"I too was raised Catholic," she says, and she stops tapping her chin
with the pencil and sets it down on top of the photocopy on her desk. "But
I have not been to mass or taken confession in a very long time now. So, we
have that in common."

"Did you lose faith?" I ask her.

"I would say that it's more complicated than that. Did you?"

"Not exactly," I reply, and then my eyes go to the objects lined up neatly
on the slate mantel above the green-glazed bricks. And my mind seizes on
those objects – the bird, the butterflies, the trilobite – casting about for a way
to maybe purchase a little more time before we have to return to the reason
that I've come here for three consecutive weeks, before we return to the rel-
evance of the article on lycanthropy. "Do those things have any particular
significance?" I ask Dr. Novas, and I point at them. "To you, I mean."

She looks at the mantel, seems to consider my question for a moment,
and then she looks back at me.

"Before I began studying psychiatry," she says, "I wanted to be a zoologist."

"But something happened to change your mind?"

"Not only one thing, but many different things, I think. Did you know,
Sigmund Freud also considered becoming a zoologist before he turned to
medicine. Well, originally he'd intended to study law, but after that. He
once spent a month at a research station in Trieste dissecting eels, trying to
locate the male sex organs, but was unsuccessful."

"No," I say, "I didn't know that. Where's Trieste?"

"Italy. Northeastern Italy, on the Adriatic Sea, near the border with
Slovenia. A century and a half later, we still have not solved the mystery of
the life cycle of eels."

"I didn't know that, either." I glance at the clock and see that it's now
twenty minutes after the hour. I say, "I suppose it's pretty obvious that I'm
stalling."

"It is, but you asked that we slow down."

"I did. But there's a difference between slowing down and avoiding the subject altogether." I point at the mantel again. "When I was a kid, down in Georgia, there was an abandoned limestone quarry near our house where I used to find trilobites. They weren't anywhere near as big as that one, though. They were all very small, not much larger than the nail on my pinky finger," and I hold up my left hand and extend my left little finger so that she can see what I mean. "There were other fossils in the quarry – snail shells and bits of coral – but I was always looking for the trilobites. Sometimes they were stretched out flat and other times they were curled up the way pill bugs and armadillos roll themselves up when they're in danger. At one point, I had a whole cigar box full of them that I took to school a couple of times for show and tell. But I don't know whatever became of it, the box or all the trilobites. You grow up and lose things, things that once had meaning to you. That once were precious. You just forget about them one day, and by the time you finally remember them again, they're gone."

"Like memories," she says, and I shake my head and very quietly mutter, "No, not like memories," even though I probably agree with her. Suddenly, I'm not in the mood to be agreeable. And I'm even more not in the mood to think about my childhood in the mountains of Dade County, Georgia, more than four decades past, and never mind if that's exactly where and when the ghosts that have dragged me here were born.

"You grew up near Chattanooga?" she asks. "Am I remembering that correctly?"

"Just a little way south of Chattanooga," I reply. "A place called Rising Fawn."

"That's a very unusual name. Is there a story behind it?"

I almost say no, not that I'm aware of. But only almost. Instead, I tell her, "Yeah, I'm not sure that it's a true story. But there's a story, all the same. They taught it to us in school as if it were a historical fact. Supposedly it's named for a Cherokee Indian chief who was born there back in the late eighteenth century. Supposedly, the Cherokees named their children for the first thing the father sees after the child is born, and this chief's father saw a fawn rising up from the place where it had been sleeping, and so he named his son Rising Fawn. Like I said, I don't know that it's a true story. It smacks of anecdote to me. I suspect that it isn't true. The mountains down there are full of stories like that. I think one reason that the white settlers were so quick to murder and drive out the Indians was so there'd be no one to contradict all the tall tales."

"Why you are here, it has something to do with Rising Fawn? It has something to do with your childhood there?" And then she points at the photocopy on her desk. "It has something to do with this paper that I published five years ago?"

"Yeah," I say, because I'm tired of these digressions and quotidian bullshit. I look at the clock again. It's almost thirty minutes past the hour, thirty minutes left to go until the next hour. And I think, what I have come here to say, it's like jumping in cold water or pulling off a Band-Aid. Do it fast. Get it over with.

"Take your time," says Dr. Novas. "You're fine."

"Am I?" I ask. "Am I fine?" But before she can answer me, I hold up a hand to stop her. It wasn't the sort of question that wants an answer. It was the sort of question whose answer I already know. "I was ten," I say. "I was ten years old, in 1975. I was in fifth grade. It wasn't too long after Christmas, but it was sometime after New Years. We still had our Christmas lights up, though, because my father was bad to leave them up until February, sometimes. It gets cold back up in those mountains, and it snowed a few times that winter. We were living in an old farmhouse out on Hanna Cemetery Road, and that place was drafty as hell. We probably weren't the poorest family in town, probably not by a long shot. But we were plenty poor enough."

"You've come a long way from there," Dr. Novas says.

"Not so far as you might think," I reply, and she kindly doesn't disagree.

"What was your father's work?" she asks.

"That isn't really relevant."

"No? All right, then. I was only curious."

I stare down at my shoelace, which seems even nearer to being untied than it was just a moment ago, even though I've hardly moved a muscle.

"He had a job up in Trenton, fifteen or twenty miles away, working in a machine shop. I think he made tractor parts, mostly, tractors and things like that, heavy farm equipment. Well, when he wasn't too drunk to work. An uncle of his owned the place, which is the only reason he never got fired."

"And your mother stayed at home?"

I nod. "Yeah, she did. There was me and my sister, and she stayed at home."

"Did she drink, as well?"

"No, she had Jesus and the Virgin Mary and the Pope and all that. But I think it worked for her just about the same as whiskey and beer worked for my dad."

"Were there many Catholics there, in Rising Fawn?"

"No. Just Baptists and Methodists and Pentecostals. When we went to church, which really wasn't all that often, we went to St. Katharine Drexel, which was also up in Trenton. We went to school in Trenton, too."

"Why didn't you just live there?"

"The farmhouse, it belonged to an aunt, and we didn't have to pay rent. Or maybe we were supposed to pay rent, but she wouldn't kick us out when my father couldn't be bothered. Anyway, I liked it there. It was a good house, even if the winters could be sort of miserable. I never wanted to live in town. In Trenton, I mean. Back then, I never could have pictured myself living in Manhattan. Hell, back then I couldn't have pictured myself ever living in Chattanooga."

"And yet here you are. Did you come to New York for school?"

"It's a long story how I came here, why I'm still here," I tell her, "and it's not this story."

"Okay," she says. "Okay. I understand. Do you ever go back home to visit?"

"No. There's nothing there to go back to. My parents are both dead and my sister married her high-school sweetheart and moved away to Florida. I still have family in Rising Fawn, but no one I'm close to, no one I ever want to see again and probably no one who'd ever want to see me. I left in 1982, and I've never looked back."

That last bit is a lie, of course, and, of course, Dr. Novas knows it's a lie.

"I see," she says. "But *this* story, the story that has brought you here and that you want to tell me," and then she trails off, leaving the sentence unfinished, leaving me an opening.

Last chance, I think, calculating how few footsteps separate me from the office door, how easy it would be to cross that distance. It's not like she would try to stop me. But I stay right where I am. I reach down and untie my sneaker and tie it back tightly. And then I sit up straight again and tell Dr. Novas a ghost story. I call it a ghost story because I don't know what else I'd call it. I call it a ghost story because it is the beginning of a haunting.

"Like I said, it was winter, not long after Christmas. And there was snow. It had snowed on and off for two days. Just three or four inches, really, but the roads were icy and the buses from Trenton couldn't get out to us, so we got to stay home. I was never crazy about school."

"Were you a good student?" the psychiatrist asks me.

"Yeah, I was a good student. Well, good enough. I just didn't care much for school. I never had many friends, because I never really wanted many friends. I was that kid, you know. I was happier in my bedroom with a book or off in the woods alone somewhere than spending time in the company of other kids my age. I wasn't exactly anti-social, I don't think. I just liked being alone."

"Were you close to your sister?"

"Sure, yeah. She was my kid sister, two years my junior."

And then Dr. Novas apologizes for interrupting me, and I tell her no, that's fine, and then I continue.

"So, like I said, it snowed and we had to stay home. And that first night after the snow, I woke up about twelve, not long after. I remember the time because I had an AM-FM clock radio that I'd gotten for Christmas that year. Anyway, I woke up. Or, rather, something woke me. Something I'd heard in my dreams, a sort of animal sound, and I really can't describe it any better than that. I lay there listening to the darkness, for whatever it was I'd heard. I didn't have a nightlight or anything, and there weren't any streetlights out that far, so at night it was so dark I could hold up my hand in front of my face and not see it. The sort of dark your eyes never really adjust to. What people mean when they say *pitch* dark. And lying there, I heard what sounded like something moving around outside below my bedroom window. But I really wasn't scared. I just figured it was a stray dog or a raccoon or a fox, something that wasn't hibernating, come down out of the woods and looking for something to eat. And after a while I fell back to sleep. But the next morning, there were footprints all around the house. Human footprints, made by bare feet, someone who'd been walking barefoot in the snow. They circled two or three times around the house. They were small, not like a child's feet, but small and slender, like maybe it had been a woman. At least, that's what my mother thought. She wanted to call the sheriff, thought that maybe someone was lost and needed help. But my father said no, there wasn't any reason to get the cops involved. He was adamant about not involving the police. Dad had a way of putting an end to a discussion, if it was something he didn't want to happen or something he didn't want to hear anything else about. My mother took some Polaroid pictures of the footprints, but I have no idea whatever became of them. And it was strange, you know. It sort of freaked me and my sister out a little, but Dad assured us we didn't have anything to be afraid of, that whoever it was wouldn't be coming back, and even if they did we had good locks on the doors and windows and they couldn't get in. Still, Dad didn't go to work that day. Maybe Mom asked him not to. I don't know. But he started drinking that afternoon and was good and drunk by dark. When he was drinking, it was best to just stay out of his way. We'd all gotten good at that."

I sit here on the chaise in Dr. Novas' well-appointed office, comfortable and safe on the paisley batik throw covering the chaise, and I stare at that uneven bright streak where the draperies do not quite meet, where the sun gets in, and I repeat the events of a freezing January morning forty-two years ago. I talk about things I've never told anyone. I talk about them like they have no power over me.

"I woke up again the next night. Just about the same time as the night before, maybe a little later. And again I lay there listening, but this time I didn't hear anything. I had to piss, though, so I got up and went out and down the hall to the bathroom, which was nearer my parents' room and my sister's than to mine. But once I was in the hallway, I saw there was light coming from the living room, like Mom and Dad were up late watching television. Sometimes they'd stay up late for Johnny Carson and old movies. I went to the end of the hall to see what they were watching. There wasn't going to be school again the next day, so I figured maybe they'd let me sit up and watch TV with them for a while. But it was just my father, and he wasn't watching the television. It wasn't even on."

"He wasn't?" asks Dr. Novas, and I shake my head.

"No. See, Dad had an old Super 8 camera that he'd had as long as I could remember. Every now and then he'd pull it out and make home movies of a birthday or a holiday or whatever. That night, he had his projector set up on the coffee table and his screen set up on the other side of the room. He was sitting on the sofa, running the projector, and I could tell he was so drunk it was a wonder he was still conscious. I remember I could smell the whiskey. I also remember there was a bottle open on the table by the projector. When I looked at the screen I saw what he was watching."

I sit there on the chaise, my ankles crossed, the autumn-colored carpet spread out before me. The clock on Dr. Novas' wall sounds very loud, ticking off my heartbeats. I let almost a full minute slip by without saying anything more, and finally she asks me, "Do you want to continue? Do you want to tell me what he was watching that night?"

I nod yes, even though finishing the story I've begun is probably the last thing I want to do.

"It was in color. Most of the movies he made were black and white, because the film was cheaper, and cheaper to have developed, but that one was in color. I saw right away that it had been taken from the vantage point of our front porch, looking out towards the road and the trees on the other side of the road. There likely wasn't more than thirty feet from our front door to the road. The film had been taken in the fall, and the trees on the screen seemed unnaturally bright. Garish, really. Almost obscene. I stood there in the doorway, and he had no idea I was watching. He hadn't noticed me. I stood there listening to the click-click-click of the projector, watching those garish trees, and he struck a match and lit a cigarette. And that's when I realized that it wasn't the trees he'd been filming. There was something standing beneath the trees at the edge of the road. For just a second, I thought maybe it was a black bear. There are still black bears in that part of the state, or at least there were back then. But then the thing beneath the trees moved, and I saw it wasn't a bear, that it wasn't any sort of an animal. It was a naked woman, filthy, muddy, and she was carrying something, something that hung limp in her arms."

Dr. Novas shifts in her seat, watching me. She seems very alert now.

"She had long red hair, and she stepped out from beneath the trees, out into the road, and I saw that what she was holding was a dead dog. A pretty big dog, though I couldn't make out the breed. But as big as beagle. My granddad kept beagles for hunting, and that's the first thing I thought of. That the dog she had was about the same size as a beagle. I think its neck was broken, the way its head lolled to one side. And right after I saw that what she was holding was a dog, I realized that it wasn't just mud she was covered with. There was blood, too, and it seemed as vivid and garish as the leaves on the trees. She stepped out into the road, and then she turned her head and saw my father – I assume it was him filming her – and for a few seconds she just stood there, still as a stone, staring straight at the camera. Then she turned around and walked back into the trees. She didn't run. She just calmly, casually walked back the way she'd come. And right then, I must have made some little sound or another, because Dad looked up and saw me watching. He yelled at me to go the hell back to bed right that instant. That's when I saw he had his shotgun out, propped up against the couch. I started crying. I'm not even sure why, whether it was because the movie had scared me, because

232

I had connected the dots between it and the footprints in the snow, or if it was because he was yelling at me, or both. But Mom, she came out of their bedroom right then, and she told him to shut up, and she took me back to bed. She stayed in the room with me all night after that, even after I'd stopped crying. She just sat there in her house coat at the foot of the bed, smoking and holding her rosary, fingering the beads. I distinctly remember that she had her rosary. I woke again for a little bit near sunrise, and she was still sitting there, watching my bedroom door. And I felt safe. Like your parents can make you feel when you're a kid. Like they really do have the power to protect you from pretty much anything."

Dr. Novas takes a deep breath and lets it out very slowly.

"I never asked about the movie, and neither of my parents ever said a word about it. Sometimes, I'm fairly certain I just dreamed the whole thing. Or dreamed part of it. Maybe I really did get up to pee, but I was only half awake and dreamed the part about him watching the movie. After I moved away and went to college in Chapel Hill, I told myself that was exactly what had happened, whenever I recalled that night."

"Is that what you believe now?" Dr. Novas asks. "That it was only a dream?"

"Do you think I would be here if I did?"

"I think that's a good question and a good place to stop for today," she says, and I look at the clock and see that the hour's almost up. "I think that's a good place to pick up again next week. That is, assuming you want to continue seeing me."

"Maybe," I tell her. "Probably," and Dr. Amelia Novas, who was born in Argentina and almost became a zoologist and has published a paper on lycanthropy, she writes out a date and a time on a lavender appointment card and hands it to me. I slip it into a side pocket of the slender case that holds my laptop. I thank her for listening, and she tells me to call if I need her before our next session. She asks if I need a refill on my Ativan script, and I tell her no, that I'm still fine. And then I go on my way, feeling no lighter for having passed the story on to her, feeling not the least bit unburdened, having no more faith in the power of psychiatry than I did an hour before. When I reach the elevator, I hold the door until someone else comes along, because I don't like the thought of being shut up inside that tiny space, with only my memories for company.

—————— ⟺ ——————

UNTITLED PSYCHIATRIST NO. 3

You can only write so many stories about lycanthropy before you have to admit it's a full-fledged obsession. I probably passed that point a long, long time ago. This story was written in May and June 2017.

Albatross (1994)

I open my eyes, and above me is the cloudless blue sky, the blue sky so wide and vast and unmarred by anything at all save a couple of herring gulls drifting far above me. I float on the sea, face skyward, and the waves buoy me up, and the wind, in turn, lifts the gulls a little higher, as if there may be some necessary distance between us, some measure of space to be maintained. The water rolls and drops me into a trough between waves, and I imagine invisible lines connecting my heart to the twin hearts of those birds, and when I sink, they also are drawn nearer to the earth. I float in the sea out beyond Moonstone Beach, not very far offshore at all, fifty yards at most. But already the drowned edge of the continent is falling away and the sea is getting deep beneath me. I rise, and I fall, and rise again, as weightless it seems as when I drifted those nine long months in the inner sea of my mother's womb, weightless as the feather of a gull or a cormorant or a tiny flitting plover. I am held perfectly in this moment at the intersection between two worlds – the sky and the sea – held here by laws of biology and chemistry and physics, by affairs of density and composition, salt and water and weight. There is an almost perfect balance, unlike any peace I have ever yet felt on land, the land that I was born to when my mother's body finally grew tired of carrying me and pushed me out into the dry, air-bound world of men who walk and hardly ever float again. How far up to those soaring gulls? A hundred feet? Two hundred? How far down to the seafloor below me? Eight feet? Nine? Ten? Take a deep breath, rise and fall and rise again, and soon enough it will be twenty. I close my eyes, hiding the birds from my mind, and I wonder how long it might take me to drift all the way, currents willing, from Moonstone across the sound to the shores of Block Island, almost ten miles if one is a gull or if we draw a straight line, north to south, on a nautical chart. More likely, the water would carry me south and west towards Watch Hill and Fisher's Sound and

Long Island Sound and a hundred tiny specks of sand and stone that hardly even manage to rise above the high-tide mark. The sea inhales, and I rise towards the gulls and the blue. The sea exhales and I fall. It is very much a breathing being, the sea, girding dead, dry land all about the circumference of the world, where human beings are born from the uterine brine of a woman's body and might never again go back to the sea. We may try, but we will never again *belong,* cursed with lungs, our gills traded for the promise of something better that has never yet materialized, even down all the long eras of geologic time. We – the great collective hominid *we* – can never go home again. At best, we can only be infrequent visitors. We can dare to skate across the face of the waters, and we can drift and swim, and we can even dive for short and perilous visits into the depths, but always will we be interlopers. And now I am no longer floating on the waves, but standing, instead, on the sand looking at the broken thing that washed up in the night. At my back are low dunes crowned with green tangles of poison ivy and beach roses blooming pink and white, low dunes dividing the narrow beach from the muck of salt-marsh lagoons beyond, from tea-colored Trustom Pond, specked with swans and geese. It's early morning still, the summer sun riding low in the eastern sky, a stubborn chill clinging to the June wind whipping over the shore and the sea. And here is me and here, too, is the kid, and no one else is in sight. The kid is barefoot, and her dirty blonde hair is almost the same color as the sand. She might easily be the sand's daughter.

"I don't think that's a whale," says the kid.

"I think you're right," I reply.

"Then what do you think it is?" asks the kid.

And I start to say that I have no idea whatsoever, but then I stop myself. The truth is, I have far too many ideas, and none of them are very sensible. None of them are anything I'd like to say aloud.

"Well, it's not a whale," the kid says.

"No," I agree, "it's definitely something else."

"This one time," says the kid, "I saw a dead humpback whale that washed up on the rocks below the Beavertail Lighthouse. It didn't look anything like this. And this other time I saw a dead basking shark, and this *other* time, my mom and I, we saw a dead sea turtle, a big ol' leatherback, and none of those things looked anything like this."

"Yes," I agree, "it doesn't look like any of those animals."

"What do you think could have killed it?" she asks.

"Hard to say. I think it's been dead a long time. It's pretty far gone, so it's hard to say how it died."

The sky is filled with the raucous screams of impatient, hungry gulls, and I look up and shade my eyes to see them soaring overhead, wheeling above us – herring gulls and laughing ring-billed gulls and a few huge black-backed gulls, all gathering for a feast of carrion, and not one among them concerned with the identity of this thing the tide has dragged up onto the shore. Gulls have no use for taxonomy, but care only that a meal won't fight back when they tear it apart with their sharp, hooked beaks. I look down again, and the fluids draining from the carcass make an oily, iridescent sheen on the sand.

"Strange how it doesn't smell bad," says the kid, and this is the first time I realize that there's no smell – or *almost* no smell. The stench should be so awful that the kid and I are only managing to stand this close and not gag by speaking and breathing through cupped hands and T-shirts pulled up over our mouths and noses for impromptu and entirely insufficient gas masks.

"Maybe it's the direction the wind's blowing," I suggest, knowing that it's nothing of the sort. "Maybe the wind is carrying the smell away from us, blowing it back out to sea."

And now the kid looks at me with that skeptical eye reserved for instances when adults have revealed themselves to be not even half so wise and sensible as they'd have children believe. Then she frowns and with her bare right foot kicks dirt at the dead, stranded thing sprawling before us.

"I don't know why it doesn't stink," I admit, but I can tell the damage has been done. She shrugs her thin shoulders and looks east, back towards Galilee and Point Judith. I almost ask some very grown-up question or another: Where are your parents? Where do you live? What are you doing out here alone, so early in the day? Instead, I say that maybe I should call Mystic Aquarium, and the kid wants to know why, so I tell her that there are people there trained to deal with strandings, with rescuing beached whales and turtles and the like.

"It's not a whale or a turtle," she says. "And I think it's long past rescuing."

"They send people out to look at corpses," I tell her. "They also do that."

"What kind of people?" she asks.

"Mostly they're scientists, I think. Marine biologists, zoologists, oceanographers – people like that. Conservationists who keep a record of what dies and what washes ashore, people whose job it is to find out what's killing animals, if it's pollution or the propellers of boats or fishing nets or…whatever."

"Would they haul it away?" she asks.

I tell her that I don't know. Maybe, but I'm not sure. She asks how I know so much about this sort of thing, if I'm a school teacher or something, and I tell her no, I just read a lot. The sea lifts me up, and I open my eyes, and I watch the two gulls wheeling above me, and we are tied, heart to heart, with invisible kite string. The sea lifts me up and drops me down and then lifts me up again.

"I'd sure like to know what it is," says the kid, kicking more sand at the corpse. "But I can't hang around here all day."

The sea lifts me up, and the birds rise.

"You and your parents live near here?" I ask, asking one of those grown-up questions I'd tried to avoid. It earns me another suspicious look.

"It's just me and my mom," says the kid. "We come here every summer. We come here from Connecticut." I don't ask from where in Connecticut. "Maybe it's a sea monster," she suggests, and I smile.

"You believe in those?" I ask her. "You believe in sea monsters?"

"They're in the Bible," she replies.

"Are they?"

"Sure," she says. "Leviathan, in the Book of Job. But I should be going." She looks at the gulls and the sky and the sun, and she adds, "It's getting late."

The sea lifts me up and up and up, so high that I almost think if I stretch out my arm, my fingertips will brush against the feathered ivory bellies of the wheeling birds. How soft they would be to touch, softer even than the sea, lighter even than the weight of my soul negated by the rise and fall of the waves. I would feel their hearts beat.

The kid says goodbye and that she hopes I can figure out what the dead thing is, and then I watch as she walks away towards home. I watch as she grows small and smaller and smaller still, growing indistinct in the distance until I can't see her anymore and I'm left alone with the stranding and the hungry, screeching gulls. I linger there maybe ten minutes more, and then I turn and walk back to my car parked on the road beyond the dunes. I look back once, and the birds are all descending on the carcass en masse, falling viciously, greedily, upon it, squabbling among themselves, jostling for the best bits, I suppose.

I float, and the sleek, dark silhouette of a cormorant streaks by above me. I close my eyes again, and the next trough takes me back down, and

I am sitting at a table in the Peace Dale Library, two days later, only seven miles inland if one is a gull, turning the glossy pages of a book on sea monsters and sea serpents. There's a chapter midway through about mysterious carcasses that have been found washed up on beaches all around the world. With a yellow pencil I am making notes on a yellow legal pad, though I'm not entirely sure why. I could simply check the book out and take it home with me, read it at my leisure and in the privacy of my apartment, but I'm making notes, instead, a neatly annotated list, flush left – 1808, the Stronsay Beast in the Scottish Orkney Islands; 1896, Florida's St. Augustine Monster, for a time believed to be a gigantic octopus; a glob of flesh that washed up in Margate, South Africa in 1924, nicknamed "Trunko" by the press; other carcasses in Tasmania in 1960 and 1970; something on a beach in New Zealand in 1968; the Japanese trawler *Zuiyo-maru* in 1977, and this time there are grisly color photographs of whatever it was the ship had snagged, and maybe it was a latter-day plesiosaur, but more likely a very badly decomposed basking shark; Bungalow Beach in the Republic of The Gambia, western Africa, June 1983, something with a long snout and four stout flippers, possibly only a small whale, but the cryptozoologists all want to believe it was a prehistoric reptile, an ichthyosaur or mosasaur tardy for its own extinction. And on and on and on. Giants die in the sea, and they drift and rot, are nibbled and gnawed and pulled apart by the jaws of scavengers until familiar shapes become grotesque and unfamiliar. Until the world's tides leave them on all the world's beaches, like a cat thoughtfully depositing last night's mangled kill on the welcome mat. In the margins of my list, I scribble from memory notes regarding pareidolia and Rorschach inkblots, Fata Morgana mirages and molybdomancy. I finish with the book on sea serpents and return it to the shelves (ignoring a sign imploring me not to do that very thing), exchanging it for a King James Bible. It doesn't take me long to find what the kid was talking about, Job 41: 1-34, *"Behold, the hope of him is in vain; shall not one be cast down even at the sight of him?"* The sea lifts me, and far above the gulls I spot the misty white contrail of a jet plane. I cannot help but wonder where it's bound in such a hurry. The gulls and I take our time. The sea takes its time, as it has been doing now for more than four billion years. The jet races on towards wherever it's going, filled up inside with a human cargo, like Jonah in the belly of that great fish. I turn my head to the left, back towards shore, and as I gain the crest of a wave I catch sight of the beach. It seems far away and of very little consequence whatsoever. The sea pulls me down once more, and once more I lose sight of land and again turn my face skyward. I shut my eyes, knowing that the gulls won't mind, and now three days later – three nights later – and I am only dreaming. Later, I'll write down what I can recall of the dream, as I almost always do, a habit I got into many years ago, when I was still in college in North Carolina. I have many volumes of my dreams carefully written down and kept on shelves and in desk drawers, as if I'm going to need them some day, as if I'm stockpiling dreams and nightmares against some future, expected calamity. In this dream, I'm standing on Moonstone Beach with a blonde-haired kid, and she's asking me if the scientists who come from Mystic Aquarium will steal away the dead thing lying on the sand before us. Sleeping, I answer the same as I answered her question awake, that I really don't know, but possibly.

"They may want to study it," I tell her. "It might be something important, a new species, a kind of creature they've never seen before."

"Well, be sure to tell them it was me who found it, that it was me who saw it first, that I was already standing here when you showed up. Don't steal the credit and glory that should rightfully be mine."

"I wouldn't, but why don't you tell them yourself?" I ask.

"I won't be here, that's why. I should be getting back. My mother is an old conjure eel, and she'll be worried if I'm late for lunch."

"Isn't it a little early for lunch?"

"It's sort of a long walk back home," she tells me. "It's a long way back to the bottom from here." And then the kid says, "All that white hair on it, maybe it's a sort of polar bear," and she points at the carcass.

"I don't actually think that's hair," I tell her. "I was reading in a book how when whales decompose, when their blubber rots away or is eaten away by scavengers, the collagenous matrix of the blubber is often left behind and how those collagen fibers can resemble white hair."

"It doesn't look like a whale to me," says the kid, tenacious as a Greek chorus.

I agree, but then I add, "It doesn't look like a polar bear, either. And what would a polar bear be doing in Rhode Island?"

"I should ask the Drawling-master," says the kid. "She's an old conjure eel, and she knows things you'd never have guessed at. Maybe because of global warning."

I nod a noncommittal nod, and I stare at the thing on the sand, and I try to figure out which is its front end and which is its rear. I should be able to discern at least that much. But nothing even vaguely resembling a skull remains and neither anything that resembles a neck any more than it might also resemble a tail. I say to the kid, "She teaches you drawling, stretching, and fainting in coils, doesn't she?"

The kid looks surprised. "How did you know that?" she asks.

"I read a lot," I reply.

"Like how dead things don't always look the way they did when they were alive?"

"Like that," I tell her. "And other things besides."

She points at the decayed, seeping, seemingly odorless mass on the sand, and she says, "It makes me never want to swim in the sea again, knowing there are things like that lurking about in the water. It makes me think I ought to tell my parents we should find somewhere else to spend our summer vacations, somewhere far from the shore." And then she takes a cautious couple steps back from the carcass.

"I don't think it can hurt you now," I say.

"But you don't know that, not for sure."

"No," I admit. "Not for sure."

"Then I'll keep my distance, thank you very much. For all we know, it might be a shoggoth." I tell her that I have no idea what that is, and the kid says, "Next, you'll expect me to believe that you've never heard of a bandersnatch or a snark or a hippocrump."

Dreaming this dream, I'm in no mood to argue with a child, not even one who could pass for the daughter of the sand, and so I let the matter drop. I look away from the dead thing, gazing out to sea, instead, where a swimmer bobs on the waves, rising and falling, and I wonder if the kid is right and if I ought to try and warn him or her that it might not be safe to swim here. After all, in a book in the Peace Dale Library, I read all about the tradition of sea monsters off the shores of New England, about the famous sightings in the summer of 1817 of a giant serpent in Gloucester Harbor and of another monster seen in a salt marsh at Eastport, Maine in 1868. In that same book, I saw a photograph supposedly taken in 1910 at Little Neck, Ipswich, Massachusetts, of a huge serpent with a child's legs dangling from its toothy jaws. But the photographer, a local man named George Dexter, was known for his clever hoaxes, including a wagon towing an enormous clam to market, as clam the size of a milk cow. I almost mention the fake sea serpent photograph to the kid, but only almost.

"Our waters are as haunted as any," she says. "More haunted than some," and I raise my left arm and wave at the swimmer floating on the waves. But if they see me, they make no sign that they've seen me and they do not head back to shore. Dreaming, I close my eyes, and I can hear the surf and the wind through the dunes and the birds circling the carcass, and I can hear the blonde kid talking about monsters in the water. I open my eyes, and I'm only lying in my bed in the house where I live in Providence, and I can (still) hear the wind, and I can hear a radio playing too loudly down on the street, and I can hear my own heart beating like the kettle drum in the breast of a wheeling gull. My sheets are damp with sweat, despite cool night air getting in through the window I left open. My mouth tastes like foil or pennies or a newly filled tooth. *Is that the taste of adrenaline?* I wonder. *It isn't the taste of the sea.* I get up and find my robe. I go to the kitchen and put on a kettle to make a cup of tea. The sea lifts me up, and then it falls away beneath me. In my dream, just before I woke, the kid had said, "The sea is Poseidon's own bellows, fanning the cold blue flames of the deep." I make my tea, and then I sit down and write out the dream before it fades away and is forgotten. The air in the kitchen smells of chamomile, spearmint, and lemongrass, and more faintly of mildew and old grease. On a yellow legal pad half filled with notes on sea serpents, I write *My mother is an old conjure eel...*

The sea raises me. The sea drags me down.

And here now, four days later, one day after my visit to the Peace Dale Library, the day after the dream of the kid and Moonstone Beach, I sit in a coffeehouse on Wickenden Street, and it's raining on the other side of the plate-glass windows, and I'm sipping hot black coffee. I have never yet gotten used to these cool Rhode Island summers. To my Southern-born eyes, it could be March or April out there, this chilly rain a downpour to bring about May flowers. I'm not alone. Rachel sits across from me, with her own steaming cup of coffee. We've been dating, on and off, off and on, for more than a year, but for the last two months she's been away in Italy and Spain doing research for a book that she's writing on the Crusades and Islamic contributions to the culture of Medieval Europe. She takes her work more seriously than she takes our relationship, but I've never faulted her for that. Unlike me, she has ambition. Unlike me, she has the drive and desire to amount to something more than the mere sum of her days. Or maybe it's just that the sum of her days will add up to more than will mine. She lights a cigarette and blows smoke towards the ceiling of the coffeehouse. She's just finished telling me about her visit to the ruins of the Phoenician port of Motya and of a marble sculpture of a charioteer that was discovered there in 1979, on display now at a museum in Sicily. I've only half been listening to her, my mind wandering as it too often does, distracted by whatever music is playing in the coffeehouse, distracted by the sound of tires out on the wet streets, distracted by the dream I had the night before. And we've spent enough time together now that she can tell when I'm not paying attention. She knows me well enough to know that I'm only rarely especially interested in those things that she's passionate about and to know I'm no good at feigning interest that isn't there – which, likely, is one reason that we've been off again-on again.

"A penny for your thoughts," she says.

I light a cigarette of my own, drop the spent match into the black Bakelite ashtray on the table, and reply, "Nothing really. Just…I should have gotten more sleep last night, that's all." And for a few minutes we talk about my insomnia, instead of her trip to a tiny island off the west coast of Sicily.

"Oh, I almost forgot," she says. "On the ferry back from San Pantaleo, I heard the strangest thing," and then Rachel tells me a story that she was told by an old man, a story about a child who was swimming in the sea not far from the ruins of Motya and was savagely attacked and killed by something in the water.

"A shark," I say.

"He insisted that it wasn't a shark," she replies. "He said that the little girl lived just long enough to tell the fishermen who pulled her from the sea and tried to save her life that what had attacked her wasn't any sort of fish. Whatever it was, it had bitten off one of her legs below the knee, and she bled to death before the fisherman could get her back to shore and a doctor."

"It certainly sounds like a shark attack," I say.

"I know," says Rachel. "But the old man was adamant that it wasn't."

"He was adamant that a *dying child* said that it wasn't. You can't consider a dying, terrified child to be the best and most reliable of witnesses."

"I'm only telling you what I heard," Rachel says, more than a hint of annoyance creeping into her voice, and she turns away from me and sits smoking and watching the rainy street and the cars rushing past and the people on the sidewalk with their umbrellas and galoshes, passing by the coffeehouse windows.

I wait a few moments, then ask, "Did she say what it was instead of a shark?"

"She said it was a demon," Rachel tells me.

"A demon," I say.

"Yes, that's what the child said, that she was attacked by a demon in the water, that it was a demon that chewed off her leg."

"Well, you mean that's what the old man *told* you she said."

Rachel shakes her head and laughs a dry, humorless laugh. She takes a drag on her cigarette and says, "Yeah, that's what I said. That's what he *said* she said. Jesus, I hate when you get like this."

"Like what?" I ask her, knowing that I shouldn't have.

"Pedantic," she replies. "I hate when you get so goddamn pedantic, that's what."

The sea rolls, and I roll with the sea, and in the wide blue sky above me, two gulls bob and dip and soar on the wind. I think that, by now, it must be at least twenty or thirty feet down to the bottom. I wonder what the birds think of the sight of me, floating with my legs straight and my arms out wide as if I have been crucified upon the water.

"That's all the dying girl said, that it was a demon?" I ask.

"That's all she said," replies Rachel, and then she corrects herself. "No, that's all the old man *said* that she said. That's what he told me that evening, on the ferry back from San Pantaleo."

"Maybe the girl had never seen a shark," I suggest. "I mean, you know, not up close like that. It would be horrifying, and she was only a child, after all."

"Or maybe what attacked her was something besides a shark," says Rachel, and then she stubs out her cigarette and tells me that she needs to take a piss. She goes to the restroom, and I sit and watch the windows and the rain and the cars until she comes back.

I start to tell her about the thing on the sand and the blonde-haired girl, but then I change my mind. I'm not sure why. We go back to my place, and I cook dinner, and afterwards we fuck. Rachel doesn't stay the night, but then she rarely ever does. She says I talk in my sleep, when I sleep, and it keeps her awake, and when I can't sleep that keeps her awake, too.

I am lifted up by an especially high wave, and as I slide down the other side I am turned about some forty-five degrees or so, and now my head is pointing out to sea (or towards Block Island) and my feet are pointing back towards the shore. I watch the gulls watching me. I shut my eyes, and I think about all the creatures that might be gliding or wriggling by just beneath me, only inches away, the menagerie of scales and fins, sharp teeth and sleek bodies, that might, at this very moment, be so near that I only need to reach out my hand and touch them. Besides the eyes of the two birds, how many pairs of eyes are watching me? How many dim alien minds are wondering what I am and how it is that so strange a beast, so utterly helpless and unsuited to the water, has come to be among them? How many are wondering if I'm dangerous and how I might taste? As I've said, I am an interloper here. I don't belong, no matter how much I have always loved the sea, no matter how strong a swimmer I might be. My ancestors showed it their backs hundreds of millions of years ago, and sometimes I imagine that the sea must hold a grudge against all those who have deserted her. What manner of dark bargains have been struck between the waters and those few vertebrate lineages that have seen the error of their progenitors' ways and gone *back* to the sea? What promises made possible the evolutionary alchemy that has changed legs back to flippers time and time again? What was sacrificed by the whales so that paradise could be finally regained? What does it take to show the oceans you've well and truly repented your wicked, unfaithful ways?

I am as good as a compass rose. My feet point north, articwards, my head towards the far away equator. I rise, and I fall, and my restless mind is filled with questions.

What pain comes along with drowning?

And now it is Friday afternoon, so almost a week come and gone since I sat and made notes in the Peace Dale Library, two days since the coffeehouse and Rachel's tales of Motya, and when I'm done with work I drive back down to Moonstone Beach. I park my car behind the dunes, in the gravel turnaround beside Trustom Pond, and I follow the trail that leads between the tangles of poison ivy and beach roses, bayberry and goldenrod, and out onto the cobble-strewn shoreline. I'm not surprised to find the girl there. I know that I should be, but I'm not. I'm more surprised to see that the stranded carcass is still lying where I left it a week ago. I never made the call to the Mystic Aquarium, but I thought surely someone else would have. And, regardless, the tide should have towed the thing back out to sea days ago. It might well have washed up somewhere else, but not here again, not in the exact same spot as before. Its bulk has only shifted slightly. It might be buried a little deeper in the sand, but nothing else has changed. And there's still no stench. The kid is poking at the carcass with what appears to be a wooden broom or mop handle, and when I approach she looks up, brushes the hair back from her eyes and smiles. She has an easy sort of smile. She's wearing a Nirvana T-shirt and cutoffs and sunglasses with frames molded from glittering gold plastic.

"It's still here," she says.

"I see that," I reply.

She says, "It's almost like the sea doesn't want it back." Which is exactly what I'd been thinking.

"Have you shown it to anyone else?" I ask her.

"We had to go to Boston for a few days," she tells me, instead of answering yes or no. "I have an aunt and uncle who live there, and we had to go visit them, same as every summer." And then she says that she doesn't much like Boston, and that she likes her cousins even less. I ask her again if she's shown the carcass to anyone else, and this time she says no, that she hasn't. The warm late afternoon breeze blows her hair back over her eyes, and she brushes it away again.

"I'm not especially fond of Boston, either," I admit.

"Did you find out what it is?" she asks. "Did you talk to the people at the aquarium like you said you were going to do?" I tell her no, I don't and no, I haven't. She looks disappointed and sits down in the sand, three or four feet back from the dead thing. She offers me the broom (or mop) handle, but I tell her to keep it.

"Suit yourself," the kid says, and she takes off her sunglasses. I notice for the first time that her eyes are Coke-bottle green. She's made a tiny cairn of rounded white stones, the moonstones that give the beach its name. In a circle around the cairn, she's arranged an assortment of crab and lobster claws and a few periwinkle shells.

"What's that?" I ask her. "What are you making there?" And I point at the cairn, but she only shrugs, and so I don't ask again. Instead, I stand staring at the carcass in the sand. Either it's more bloated than before or just bigger than I remember, a good eight feet from one end to the other, and three or four feet high. It's still leaking whatever oily, iridescent substance it was leaking before. The thought occurs to me that this time there's no noisy flock of seagulls waiting for us to go away so that they can pick at the carcass. There are no flies or maggots, either, and not even any tiny, scavenging crabs. I wonder if the thing might be toxic. I wonder if the gulls who dined on it a week ago are lying dead in the marshes somewhere.

"I was thinking I might go for a swim," I tell the kid. "That's usually why I come here, to swim."

"My father says it isn't safe. He says there's an undertow and rip tides. I'm not supposed to swim here. I'm only supposed to swim back there, at Matunuck," and she waves a hand at the east. And I tell her yes, there are undertows here and that you have to be careful and that she should follow her father's advice. She adds another white moonstone to her cairn.

"But you're going in anyway?" she asks.

"Yeah, I swim here a lot. Don't worry, I'm careful. And I'm a good swimmer."

"I might not be here when you're done," she tells me.

"Then maybe we'll see each other another time, sometime soon. I come here a lot. I live in the city, but I don't like it very much." I start to tell her that I dreamed of her, of her and the dead thing, but then I don't.

"We're leaving tomorrow," the kid tells me, "so probably not."

"Well, then it's been good to meet you," I say.

"Do you swim naked?" she asks, and I tell her no, that I'm wearing my bathing suit under my clothes. And she says that she only asked because her parents said that, back when they were kids in the seventies, this had been a nude beach, and I tell her I didn't know that.

The sea lifts me up, and it drags me down, and the child draws a circle in the sand, enclosing the moonstone cairn and the sharp bits of crustacean claw. Then she draws another circle around that.

"I don't suppose we ever will know what it is," she says, and then she pokes at the carcass again with her mop (or broom) handle.

"Maybe that's for the best," I tell her.

"It isn't a whale," she says again, and once again I agree. We say our goodbyes, and I leave her there on the sand with the dead thing. The water is colder than I'd expected, but then it always is. I've still not grown accustomed to swimming in a sea that's never warm. I swim out, and when my feet can no longer touch the bottom, I float.

ALBATROSS (1994)

Written in October 2017, you can file this one in the same drawer with "The Bone's Prayer" and "Sanderlings" and my various other tales of peculiar things found washed up on the shores of Rhode Island. I would also point to a scene from Peter Straub's *Julia* (1975), involving a child and a mutilated turtle. It's one of those scenes that, though I can't say why, really struck a nerve, and I also pay homage to it near the beginning of my novel *The Red Tree*. As for why "Albatross (1994)" is set in 1994, as I explained in my blog, it's "…because I wanted someone to be able to smoke in a coffeehouse, and nothing had occurred in the story to prevent the year being 1994. We were allowed to do that when I was young, smoke in public places." Also, I did not invent either George Dexter or his sea-serpent photo.

Fairy Tale of Wood Street

1.

I'm lying in bed, forgetting a dream of some forested place, a dream that is already coming apart behind my waking eyes like wet tissue between my fingers, and Hana gets up and walks across the bedroom to stand before the tall vanity mirror. The late morning sun is bright in the room, bright summer sun, July sun, and I know by the breeze through the open window that the coming afternoon will be cool. I can smell the flowers on the table by the bed, and I can smell the bay, too, riding the breeze, that faintly muddy, faintly salty, very faintly fishy smell that never ceases to make me think of the smell of sex. I watch Hana for a moment, standing there nude before the looking glass, her skin like porcelain, her eyes like moss on weathered slabs of shale, her hair the same pale shade of yellow as corn meal. And I'm thinking, *Roll over and shut your eyes, because if you keep on watching you'll only get horny again, and you'll call her back to bed, and she'll come, and neither of us will get anything at all done today. And you have that meeting at two, and she has shopping and a trip to the post office and the library to return overdue books, so just roll over and don't see her. Think about the fading wet tissue shreds of the dream, instead.* And that's exactly what I mean to do, to lie there with my eyes shut, pretending to doze while she gets dressed. But then I see her tail.

"Look at us," she says, "sleeping half the day away. It's almost noon. You should get up and get dressed. I need a shower."

Her tail looks very much like the tail of a cow. At least, that is the first thing that comes to mind, the Holstein and Ayrshire cows my grandfather raised when I was a girl and my family lived way off in western Massachusetts, almost to the New York state line, the cattle he raised for milk for the cheese he made. Hana's tail hangs down a little past the bend of her knees, and there's a tuft of hair on the end of it that is almost the exact same blonde as the hair on her head. Maybe a little darker, but not by much. It occurs to me, dimly, that I ought to be shocked or maybe even afraid. That I ought, at the very least, be surprised, but the truth is that I'm not any of those things. Mostly, I'm trying to figure out why I never noticed it in all the months since we met and she moved into my apartment here in the old house on the east end of Wood Street.

"I smell like sex," Hana says, and she sniffs at her unshaved armpits. Her tail twitches, sways side to side a moment, and then is still again.

"Maybe you should just forget about the shower and come back to bed," I say, and while the sight of her tail didn't come as a surprise, that does, those words from my mouth, when what I was just thinking – before I saw the tail – was how we both have entirely too much to do today to have spent the whole morning fucking. I realize that my hand is between my legs, that I'm touching myself, and I force myself to stop. But my fingers are damp, and there's a flutter in my belly, just below my navel.

"You don't really want me to do that," she says, glancing back over her shoulder. And I think, *No I don't. I want to get up and have a bath and get dressed, and I want to forget that I ever saw that she has a tail. If I can forget I saw it, maybe it won't be there the next time I see her naked. Maybe it's only a temporary, transitory sort of thing, like a bad cold or a wart.*

"I was thinking we could go to the movies tonight," she says, turning to face the mirror again.

"Were you?" I ask her.

"I was. There's something showing at the Avon that I'd like to see, and I think tonight is the last night. This is Wednesday, right?"

"I believe so," I reply, but I have to think for a moment to be sure, to make it past the sight of her tail and the wetness between my thighs and the dregs of the dream and the smell of Narragansett Bay getting in through the open bedroom window. "Yes," I say. "Today is Wednesday."

"We don't have to go," she says. "Not if you don't want to. But I was thinking we could maybe get a bite to eat, maybe sushi, and make the early show. If your meeting doesn't run too long. If there isn't something after-wards that you have to do."

"No," I say. "I don't think so. I should be done by five. By five-thirty at the latest."

Her tail twitches again, and then it swings from side to side several times, and once more I'm reminded of my grandfather's milk cows. It doesn't seem at all like a flattering comparison, and so I try to remember what other sort of animals have tails like that, long tails with a tuft right at the end. But I'm unable to think of any others except cows.

"Are you feeling well?" she asks, watching me from the mirror, and I catch the faintest glimmer of worry in her green-grey eyes.

"I'm fine," I reply. "I had a strange dream, that's all. One I'm having a little trouble shaking off." And I almost add, *I had a dream that you were a woman who didn't have a tail, and that I lived in a world where women don't, as a rule, have tails.*

"My mother used to call that being dreamsick," says Hana, "when you wake up from a dream, but it stays with you for a long time afterwards, and you have trouble thinking about anything else, almost like you're still asleep and dreaming."

"I'm fine," I tell her again.

"You look a little pale, that's all."

"I never get any sun. You know, I read somewhere online that ninety percent of Americans suffer from vitamin D deficiency because they don't get enough sun, because they spend too little time out of doors."

"We should go to the shore this weekend," she says. "I know you hate the summer people, but we should go, anyway."

"Maybe we'll do that," I tell her, and then Hana smiles, and she leaves me alone in the bedroom and goes to take her shower.

2.

As it happens, we don't go for sushi, because by the time I'm done with work and make it back to our apartment on Wood Street, Hana has read something somewhere about people in the Mekong Delta dying at an alarming rate from ingesting liver flukes from raw fish. I can't really blame her for losing interest in sushi after that. Instead, we go to an Indian place on Thayer, only a block from the theater, and we share curried goat and saag paneer with ice water and icy bottles of Kingfisher lager. While we're eating, it begins to rain, and neither one of us has brought an umbrella. We each make do with half the *Providence Journal*. The newsprint runs and stains our fingers and stains our clothes and leaves a lead-blue streak on the left side of Hana's face that I wipe away with spit and the pad of my left index finger. The theater lobby is bright and warm and smells pleasantly of popcorn, and standing there while Hana buys our tickets it occurs to me that most of the day and part of the evening has gone by without me thinking about Hana's tail.

"Would you like something?" she asks, looking back at me, then pointing at the rows of overpriced candy behind glass.

"No," I say. "I'm fine. I think I ate too much back at the restaurant."

"Suit yourself," she says, and then she asks the boy working the concessions for a box of Good & Plenty and a large Dr. Pepper.

For just a moment, it seems that I must only have imagined that business with Hana's tail. It seems I must surely have awakened from an uneasy dream, which I have since almost entirely forgotten, and being only half awake – half awake at best, my head still mired half in the dream – I saw a tail where there was not actually a tail to see. And here in the theater lobby, my belly full and my hair damp from a summer rain, it seems a far more reasonable explanation than the alternative, that my girlfriend has a tail. I look at her tight jeans, and there's plainly no room in there for the tail that I thought I saw, the tail that reminded me so much of the tails of my grandfather's cows.

Hana pays for her soft drink and for the candy, and I follow her out of the bright lobby and into the dimly lit auditorium. The Avon is an old theater, and it has the smell of an old theater, that peculiar, distinctive blend of sweet and musty and very faintly sour that I can't recall ever having smelled anywhere else *but* old movie theaters. It's a smell of dust and fermentation, an odor that simultaneously comforts me and makes me think someone could probably do a better job of keeping the floors and the seats clean. But when a theater has been in continuous operation since 1936, like this one has, well, that's more than eighty years of spilled cola and fingers greasy from popcorn and Milk Duds getting dropped and ground into the carpet in the darkness when no one can clearly see where they're putting their feet. We take our seats, not too near the screen and not too far away, and it occurs to me for the first time that I don't actually know what we've come to see.

"I think you'll like it," Hana says, peeling the cellophane off her box of Good & Plenty. She drops the plastic wrap onto the floor. In the past, I've asked her please not to do that, but she only pointed out that someone gets paid to pick it back up again and then she did it, anyway.

"I don't even know the title," I say, wondering if she told me, and I just can't remember that she told me. "I don't know the director."

"It's German," Hana says. "Well, I mean the director is German, and I think some of the funding came from Deutscher Filmförderfonds, and it's set in the Black Mountains, but it's actually an English language film. I think you'll like it. I think it did well at Cannes and Sundance." But she doesn't tell me the title. She doesn't tell me the name of the director. I try to recall walking towards the theater from the Indian restaurant and looking up to see what was on the theater's marquee, but I can't. Not clearly, anyway. I rub at my eyes a moment, and Hana asks me if I'm getting a headache.

"No," I tell her. "I'm just trying to remember something. My memory's for shit today." I don't tell her that I'm wondering if forty-four is too young to be displaying symptoms of early onset Alzheimer's.

There are a few other people in the theater with us. Not many, but a few. I hadn't expected a crowd. After all, it's a rainy Wednesday night. No one is sitting very near us. Some of the people are staring at their phones, their faces underlit by liquid-crystal touchscreen glow. Here and there, others whisper to one another in the way that people whisper in theaters and libraries and meeting halls and other places where you've been taught since childhood to keep your voice down. I stare across the tops of the rows of seats dividing us from the small stage and the tall red curtain concealing the screen. Hana takes a pink Good & Plenty from the box, and she offers it to me.

"No, I'm fine," I say.

"Woolgathering," she says, and I say, "A penny for your thoughts," and she says, "No, I asked first." Then she puts the candy-coated licorice into her mouth and chews and waits for whatever it is she thinks that I'm supposed to say.

"It's nothing," I say.

"It's something," she replies. "I can tell by the lines at the corners of your eyes and that little wrinkle on your forehead."

I'm trying to come up with something to tell her that isn't *This morning, I saw your tail, or at least I think I saw your tail,* when I'm rescued by the curtains parting and the screen flickering to life, by giant boxes of cartoon popcorn and cartoon chocolate bars and a cartoon hot dog marching by and singing "Let's All Go To the Lobby."

"Isn't there a word for that?" Hana asks me, shaking a couple more Good & Plenty out into her palm.

"A word for what?"

"For anthropomorphized food that wants you to eat it. Like there's a word for buildings in the shape of whatever's being sold there."

"I didn't know there was a word for that," I reply.

"Mimetic architecture," she says. "I remember that from an advertising and mass media class I had in college. And I thought there was also a word for food that wants you to eat it. You know, like Charlie the Tuna. Like that," she says and points at the screen.

"If there is, I don't think that I've ever heard it."

And then the ad for the concessions stand ends and the first trailer starts, and it occurs to me that I have to piss rather urgently. I should have done it before I sat down, but I was probably too busy trying to decide whether or not I truly did see Hana's tail that morning. The first trailer is for some sort of science-fiction comedy about a grumpy old man and a wise-cracking robot driving across America, and I tell Hana that I'll be right back.

"You should have gone before we got our seats," she says. "Hurry, or you'll miss the beginning. I hate when you miss the beginnings of things."

"I'll be right back," I tell her again. "I won't miss the beginning. I promise."

"You say that," and she reminds me how, last spring, I missed the first ten minutes of *Auntie Mame* when it was screened at RISD, and how I missed even more of the start of the last Quentin Tarantino film, even though we'd gotten tickets to a special 70mm screening. And then she tells me to go on, but not to dawdle and not to decide I need to go outside for a cigarette. I assure her that I won't do either, and I get up and leave her sitting there.

<h1 style="text-align:center">3.</h1>

At the back of the auditorium, there's a very narrow flight of stairs that leads up to a tiny landing and to an antique candy machine and two restroom doors, Gents and Ladies, and to the door of the projection booth. The candy machine is the sort that was already becoming uncommon when I was a little kid, the sort that takes a quarter or two and you pull a knob and out comes your Hershey Bar or whatever you've selected. The machine is now undoubtedly a museum piece, and even though there's no "out of order" sign on it and the coin slot hasn't been taped over, I can't believe the thing actually works. I've never tested it to find out. The candy wrappers lined up neatly inside look dusty, their colors faded, but maybe it's just that the glass fronting the machine has grown cloudy over the decades. Maybe it's only an illusion, and the candy is restocked every day or so.

And then I think about Hana telling me to please hurry and not to dawdle, and so I push open the door marked Ladies and the old theater smell is immediately replaced with an old theater restroom smell, which isn't all that different from the smell of most public restrooms, at least the ones that are kept reasonably clean and have been around for a while. The women's restroom is so small that I can imagine a claustrophobic preferring to piss themselves rather than spend any time at all in here, certainly not as much time as would be necessary to relieve oneself. There are two stalls, though there's hardly room enough for one, and the walls are painted a color that can't seem to decide whether to be beige or some muddy shade of yellow. The floor is covered in a mosaic of tiny black and white ceramic hexagonal tiles.

Just inside the door, there's a mirror so large it seems entirely out of proportion with so small a room, and I pause and squint back at myself. There's a smudge of newsprint on my chin that Hana hadn't bothered to tell me about, and I rub at it until it's mostly not there anymore. And then, staring at my reflection, I think of watching Hana's reflection in our bedroom vanity mirror that morning, and I think of her tail, and I wonder if maybe it was only some trick of the late morning light. I also wonder what she'd have said if I'd had the nerve to just come right out and ask her about it:

"How is it you've never before mentioned that you have a tail?"

"How is it that you've never noticed?"

"I don't know. I can't say. Maybe it wasn't there until now."

"Or maybe whenever you're fucking me, you're too busy thinking about fucking someone else to pay that much attention. One of your exes, maybe. The one who went away to Seattle to go to clown school, for example."

"It wasn't Seattle, it was Portland."

"Like there's a difference. And who does that, anyway? What sort of grown-up adult woman quits her job and leaves her girlfriend to run off and join the circus?"

"Well, even if that were true – and it most certainly isn't – no matter who I might have been fantasizing about all those times, I think I wouldn't have been so consistently and completely distracted that I would have failed to notice that you have a tail."

"Sure. You say that. But remember when I stopped shaving under my arms, and it took you a month to even notice?"

I suspect it would have gone like that, or it would have gone worse.

There's no one else in the restroom, so I have my choice of the two stalls, and I choose the one nearest to the door, which also happens to be slightly larger than the one farthest from the door. I go in, latch it, pull down my pants, and sit there counting the hexagonal tiles at my feet while I piss and try to remember the name of the movie we've come to see on this rainy Wednesday night, because at least if I'm doing that, if my mind is occupied, maybe I won't be thinking about Hana's tail. I'm just about to tear off a piece of the stiff and scratchy toilet paper from the roll on the wall, when I hear a bird. And not just any bird, but what I am fairly certain is the cawing of a raven. Or at least a crow. My first thought is that I'd never before noticed how clearly sound carries through the floor up from the theater auditorium below, and my second thought is that, were that the case, that I was only hearing a raven from one of the movie trailers, I ought to be hearing other things, as well.

Sound can do funny things, I think. And then I think, *For that matter, so can morning light and shadow in a bedroom when you're still groggy from a dream and from sex.* Neither strikes me as a very convincing explanation.

I hear the bird again, and this time I'm quite sure that I'm not hearing a recorded snippet of film soundtrack, not Dolby stereo, but something that is alive and there in the room with me. I wipe and get to my feet, pull up my pants, and then hesitate, one hand on the stall door's latch and the other on the handle. My heart is beating a little too fast and my mouth has gone dry and cottony. I want a cigarette, and I want to be back downstairs with Hana. I realize that I haven't flushed. I'm about to turn around and do just that, when there's another sound, a dry, rustling, fluttering sort of a sound that might be wings or might be something else altogether. And suddenly I feel very goddamn stupid, like I'm five years old and afraid to step on a crack or walk under a ladder or something like that. I take a deep breath, and I open the door. And I see that there's a huge black bird watching me from the mirror, standing on the floor, the floor in the looking-glass version of the Avon's women's room, glaring up at me with beady golden eyes. It looks angry, that bird. It looks dangerous. It occurs to me that I never had realized just how big ravens are. This one's as big as a tomcat, a very big tomcat, and it hops towards me, and I take a step backwards and bump into the stall. Then I look down and realize that there's no corresponding bird standing on the floor in front of me to be casting the reflection, and when I look back up at the mirror again, there's no bird there either.

I think again about early onset Alzheimer's disease.

And then I flush the toilet and wash my hands with gritty pink powder and go back downstairs.

4.

By the time I get back downstairs, the feature has already started, and despite the bird in the mirror and the very real concern that I may be rapidly losing my mind, that I may have lost it already, I'm mostly worrying about how annoyed with me Hana's going to be. "Just like *Auntie Mame*," she'll say. "Just like *The Hateful Eight* all over again." And it's not as if I can use the phantom raven as an excuse. Well, I could, but I know myself well enough to know that I won't. So long as I keep these visions or hallucinations or illusions to myself, they will seem somehow less solid, less real, less *tangible*. The moment I cast them into language and share them with someone else any possibility that I can simply put it all behind me and get on with my life and have, for example, a perfectly ordinary Wednesday, goes right out the window.

The movie we've come to see, whatever its title, is in black and white.

I don't immediately return to my seat and to Hana. Instead, I stand behind the back row, where no one happens to be sitting, and I watch the movie. Up there on the screen there is a forest primeval rendered in infinite shades of grey, dominated by towering pines and spruces that rise up towards an all but unseen night sky, a forest that seems to have been tasked with the unenviable job of keeping Heaven from sagging and crushing Earth flat. Winding its way between the trees there's a brook, the surface glinting faintly in the stingy bit of moonlight leaking down through the boughs, and bordering the brook are boulders and the broken trunks of trees that have fallen and are now quietly rotting away. Here and there, a log fords the brook. There's the sound of wind and calls of night birds. And in the distance, there's a bright flicker, like a campfire.

I'm reminded of two things, almost simultaneously, as near to simultaneously as anyone may have two distinct and independent thoughts. I am reminded of the illustrations of Gustave Doré and of the dream that I woke from just that morning, my own half forgotten dream of a forested place, the dream I immediately tried to lose in sex. I feel the pricking of gooseflesh up and down my arms and legs, and I shiver, and I hug myself as if a sudden draft has blown by, as if maybe I'm standing directly beneath an air-conditioning vent. I think, *You don't have to watch this, whatever this is. You can turn and walk out into the lobby and wait there until it's over or until Hana comes looking for you, whichever happens first.* And then I tell myself how very silly I'm being, that coincidences occur, that they are inevitable aspects of reality, and how that's all this is, a coincidence. At most, it might be chalked up to an instance of synchronicity, a coincidence rendered meaningful only by my subjective emotional reaction and entirely devoid of any causal relationship or connection between my dream and the film, much less any connection with the raven in the restroom or with Hana's tail, both of which I likely only imagined, anyway. This is what I tell myself, and it does nothing at all to dispel my uneasiness and the cliché chill along my spine and down in my gut.

The camera wanders through the forest, and there are close ups of a sleeping doe and her fawn and of a watchful owl and of a hungry, hunting fox. It springs, and the scream of a rabbit briefly shatters the tranquil night. My mouth has gone very dry, and I lick my lips, wishing I had a swallow of something, anything at all. Hana's Dr. Pepper would do just fine.

A woman's voice says, "It must be lonely work," and it takes me a second or two to realize that the voice is part of the movie and not someone standing there beside me.

The film jump cuts then to a wide clearing and a small camp somewhere deep in the forest, and I think that this must be the source of the distant flickering I saw earlier on. At the center of the camp, surrounded by ragged tree stumps, there's a high conical billet formed from dozens of immense logs stood on their ends and leaning in one against all the others, covered over in places with a layer of soil and chunks of turf, forming a sort of smoldering bonfire or oven. There seems only to be a single man watching the fire, and he's standing with his back to the billet, gazing towards the camera, into the ancient forest ringing the clearing. The man is holding some manner of old-fashioned rifle, a flintlock maybe. I don't know shit about guns.

He says, "Who was that? Who goes there?"

And the woman replies, "No one who means you harm. Only someone passing by who thought you might be happy for the company."

"I'm not alone," says the man.

"I know," answers the woman. "But all your companions are sleeping."

"I could wake them quickly enough," he tells her, "if the need arises."

"Of course," she says. "And you have your rifle. And there must be hounds nearby to keep away the wolves."

"Yes," says the man. "There are hounds, three of them, and I'm a *very* good shot. You'd do well to keep that in mind."

"Naturally," says the woman, and the camera pans around as she emerges from between the boles of two especially enormous pines. The woman is smiling for the man, and she's dressed in a traditional Bavarian dirndl that reaches down almost to the ground. Standing there in the Avon theater, I have no idea that's what her dress is called, a dirndl. I'll only find that out later on, by checking with Wikipedia, which describes it as "a light circular cut dress, gathered at the waist, that falls below the knee." She's also wearing a bonnet. The woman is tall to the point that she could fairly be called lanky, and her face is plain and angular, and her ears are a little too big. But despite all of this, I think she may be one of the most singularly beautiful women I have ever seen. I stop hugging myself and, instead, rest my hands on the back of the theater seat in front of me. The worn velveteen feels like moss.

"It must be lonely work," the woman says again. "The life of a charcoal burner, all these long, cold nights spent so far from your home and your wife and your children."

"How do you know I have a wife and children?" he asks.

"Well, don't you?" she replies. "What an awful waste it would be if you didn't. So, I prefer to assume that you do."

The man has dark eyes, a nose that looks as if it has been broken at least once, and there is a ragged scar that bisects his lower lip and runs the length of his chin down onto his throat. He has the face of someone who is still young, but also the face of someone who has been made prematurely old by the circumstances of his life, by the many hardships and losses endured and written in the lines and creases and angles of skin and bones. It's a curiously effective paradox, not so different from the woman who is beautiful despite her awkwardness (or, perhaps, because of it).

"I know who you are," says the man warily. "My grandmother taught me about you when I was still a boy. I know what you are."

"Then you also know I mean you no harm."

"I know the stories I was taught," he replies, neither agreeing nor disagreeing.

"Then you know that this forest is *my* forest," she tells him, and now the woman takes another step nearer to the man. I realize for the first time that she's barefoot. "You know that these trees are *my* trees. If your grand-mother was a wise woman, she taught you that much, surely."

The man, the charcoal burner, crosses himself, and the woman frowns the sort of frown that, more than anything else, is an expression of disap-pointment, as if she'd hoped for more from this man. As if she'd had cause to expect more.

"After a hard winter," she says, "I may bring prosperity, and for so little a price as a loaf of fresh bread or a hen's egg left at the edge of your fields."

The man nods, and he says, "That is true, so far as it goes. But you also bring hardship when the mood suits you. You cause hunters to lose their way on clearly marked trails and to miss shots that ought to have found their marks. You lead children from their homes and into the dens of hun-gry animals, and you drown swimmers whom you fancy have slighted you in some small way or another."

"These are the sorts of tales you were taught?" asks the woman, who I realize now, and must have known all along, is not simply a human woman.

"They are. And there are others."

"Tell me," she says, and so the charcoal burner tells a story about a young man who was walking in the forest late one summer afternoon and happened to catch the briefest glimpse of the woman bathing in a spring. At once, he became so infatuated with her that he withdrew into himself and would speak to no one and would not eat or drink or care for himself in any way.

"He only lived a few weeks," says the man. "He was a man my grand-mother knew when she was a girl, the son of the cooper in the village where she grew up."

"I don't mean to call her a liar," says the beautiful, awkward woman in the dirndl, "but I would have you know your grandmother's tale was only half the truth of the matter. Yes, a cooper's son from her village saw me bathing, and yes, he wasted away because I wished it so. But she did *not* tell you all the tale. She did not say that after he had discovered the spring where I bathe, he returned with iron horseshoes and used them to lay a trap, for *his* grandmother had taught him how cold iron undoes me. She did not tell you how when I was defenseless the cooper's son raped me and cut off a lock of my hair to keep as a souvenir. I do not mean to call your grandmother a liar, but a story told the wrong way round is not the truth."

The woman takes another step nearer the charcoal burner, and this time he takes a step backwards towards the smoldering billet, yielding a foot of earth. And I want now to look away from the screen, though I would not yet be entirely able to explain just exactly why. But this pretend movie forest is too familiar, and I can't shake the feeling that I've heard this woman's voice before. But I do not look away. I want to search for the spot where Hana is sitting, but I don't. I stand there, and I watch. I stand there, and I listen.

"There is another story I know," the charcoal burner says, and I can tell he's trying hard to sound brave, and I can also hear the fear in his voice. Whatever confidence he might have had in his ability to hold this strange woman at bay is withering. Whatever faith he had is leaving him. "A story," he says, "in which you came down out of your wood on a night when the moon was new and the sky was dark save starlight, and you sat beneath the window of a mother nursing her newborn daughter, her first born. She sang lullabies to the baby, but you sang, too, and your song was so much fairer than the mother's that it was as if you alone were singing. Your melody took root in the mind of the infant, and, as she grew, it twisted her, shaping her to your own purposes. The girl became wicked, and where she walked wheat would not grow, and if she looked upon cows and goats their milk would turn sour and curdle in their udders. She was always singing in a tongue that no one knew, and they say that her songs drove dogs mad and could summon flies and toads."

"And what became of this poor unfortunate?" asks the woman.

"What finally became of her," replies the man, "is that she was driven away from her home for being a witch, turned out into the forest where she might do less harm to people who'd never done any harm to her. She was sent back to the huldra who had sung to her as a baby and so stolen her mind and soul. Not even a fortnight passed before her own brothers found her hanging from a tree, strangled by a noose woven from hair the color of water at the bottom of a well. They left her there for the crows and the maggots, fearing your wrath if they dared even to cut her down and bury her."

"And you believe this story?" the woman asks the charcoal burner.

And he answers her, "I've known stranger things to be true."

And I think, *Like a raven that is only a reflection in a mirror. Like seeing for the first time that the woman you love has a tail.*

Onscreen, the woman nods, and she says, "I was passing by, is all, and it occurred to me what lonely work your work must be and how perhaps you would be grateful for my company and for conversation. I meant no offense. I did not mean to cause you such alarm. I'll be on my way. But you'll remember this is *my* forest, and those are *my* trees."

And then the woman turns and walks away, disappearing back into the blackness between the trunks of the two especially enormous pines, and the charcoal burner is left standing alone in the clearing by his billet. The camera leaves him there, moving slowly around the circumference of the burning woodpile, coming at last to the corpses of three dogs, their necks broken and their throats torn open, as if by teeth and claws. Behind the murdered dogs is a lean-to where the bodies of the charcoal burner's companions lie slumped and mangled. It is a massacre.

And then Hana is standing beside me, and she's holding my hand, and she says, "I think we should go home now. I think it was a mistake, bringing you here."

"I'm sorry I took so long," I say.

"Don't worry about it this time. It's a silly sort of film, anyway."

Onscreen, black and white has given way to color, and the forest has been replaced by a modern city, the streets of Berlin crowded with automobiles and pedestrians all staring at their devices, instead of looking where it is they're going. A woman steps in front of a bus, and someone screams. Finally, I look away. Instead of the old theater smell, I can smell pine straw and wood smoke.

"I don't feel well," I say.

"You'll feel better soon," Hana tells me, and then she leads me out of the auditorium and back to the brightly lit lobby. Out on the street, it's stopped raining.

5.

All the way back home to Wood Street, neither of us talks. The radio is on, and there's music, but it seems to come from somewhere very far off. The roads are still wet and shiny, the pavement glimmering dully beneath the garish new LED streetlights the city has recently installed. Hana drives, and I think about the movie and the raven and how I miss the soft yellow luminescence of the old sodium-vapor bulbs. From Thayer to Wickenden, then Point Street and over the bridge that crosses the filthy slate-colored river, then across the interstate to Westminster to Parade Street to home. I sit quietly and gaze out the passenger-side window, and I think how it is like finding your way back along a forest path. The street signs are bread-crumbs. The traffic lights are notches carved in the bark of living trees, electric talismans against losing one's way.

I have a beer, and then I have a second beer. I watch a few minutes of something on television, a news story on an outbreak of cholera in Yemen. Hana asks if I'm coming to bed, so I do. She's sitting up naked, with her back against the oak headboard, her knees pulled up close to her chest, her arms wrapped around them. Her tail hangs limply over the side of the bed. She watches me while I undress, and she waits there while I go to the bathroom and brush and floss my teeth.

When I come back into the bedroom, she says, "You haven't lost your mind. You're not insane."

I sit down on my side of the bed, and it creaks and pops. "We're going to have to bite the bullet and get a new box spring soon," I say. "This thing's over a decade old. One night, it's just going to collapse beneath us." I sit there staring at the open window, smelling all the fresh, clean smells that come after a summer rain, even in so dirty a city as Providence. I think there might yet be more rain to come before sunrise and we shouldn't fall sleep with the window open, so I should get up and close it. But I don't. I just sit there, my feet on the floor, my back to Hana.

"I know it must seem that way," she says, "like you're losing your mind, and I apologize for that. I genuinely do."

I think about all the things I could say in response, and then I think about just lying down and trying to sleep, and then I think about getting up, putting my clothes back on, and going for a long walk.

"I can be an awful coward," she says. "Using the theater that way, because I was afraid of telling you myself."

And I say, "When I was a little girl, maybe ten, maybe eleven years old, I got lost in the woods once. I'm not sure how it happened, but it did. I grew up in the country, and getting lost in the woods wasn't something I worried about. It wasn't something that my parents or my grandparents worried would ever happen to me, because they'd taught me how not to lose my way. But it did happen that once. I got turned around somehow, and I walked for hours and hours, and finally it started getting dark, and that's when I really got scared. As well as I knew those woods by day, I didn't know them at all by twilight. The shadows changed them, changed the trees and the rocks, changed the way sound moved along the valley between the mountains."

"What did you do?" Hana asks.

"What do frightened children lost in the forest pretty much always do?" I reply, trading her a question for a question.

"I've never been lost in a forest," she says.

"Well," I tell her, "they cry and they start calling out for help. Which is what I did. I shouted for my mother and my father and my grandparents. I even called out the names of our three dogs, hoping anyone at all would hear me and come find me and lead me safely back home."

"But they didn't," she says.

"No, *they* didn't. But someone else did." And I want to ask her, *Was that you or maybe a sister of yours? Was that you or some aunt or distant cousin?* But I don't. I stop staring at the window and stare at my feet, instead. "And I followed her back to the pasture at the edge of the road that led to our house, and I never saw her again. At some point, growing up, I decided I'd made her up. I decided that I'd been so afraid I'd invented her as some sort of coping mechanism that had allowed me push back the panic and calm down and remember my own way out of the woods. And I believed that, until this morning, until I dreamed about being lost and found and about a woman with a cow's tail and a raven on her shoulder who sang to me until I stopped crying."

"Would you like me to sing to you tonight?" she asks.

"Why? Am I lost again tonight?"

"No," she says, "not lost. Just a little turned about."

"Sometimes," I tell her, "I'd leave her little gifts. Offerings, I guess, to show my gratitude. A hardboiled egg, half a baloney sandwich, a Twinkie, and once I even left her one of my dolls."

"A doll with yellow hair," says Hana, "yellow like freshly ground corn-meal, and a blue and white checked gingham dress, like Dorothy wore in *The Wizard of Oz*."

"Yes," I say. "Like that. I left them in an hollow tree, like Boo Radley leaving gifts for Scout and Jem in *To Kill a Mockingbird*. I think I got the idea from the book, the idea to leave her gifts."

"And then you stopped," Hana says.

"We moved here. Dad got a different job, and we moved away."

For a moment or two, neither of us says anything more, and then Hana says that it's late and that we should probably get some sleep, that I have work tomorrow and she has errands to run. When I don't reply, when I neither agree nor disagree, she asks me if I'd prefer that she leaves and never comes back.

"If that's what you'd like, I'll go."

"No," I say, without having to consider my answer. "I wouldn't rather you leave."

"Then I'm glad," she says.

"It must be lonely work," I say, remembering the barefoot woman in the dirndl and the charcoal burner.

"Sometimes," Hana tells me, and then she tells me that we probably shouldn't fall asleep with the window open, that she's pretty sure there will be more rain tonight.

"What finally made you decide to show me?" I ask.

"I don't know," she replies. "I think I just got tired of keeping secrets."

I nod, because that seems like a fair enough answer. I have other questions, but they're nothing that can't wait for some other time. I get up and cross the room and close the window. I check to be sure that it's locked, even though we're on the second floor of the old house on Wood Street. Down on the sidewalk, there's a black bird big as a tomcat, and when I tap on the glass, it spreads its wings and flies away.

FAIRY TALE OF WOOD STREET

Yes, I was born with a tail, which was amputated at birth. I was also born with a caul, but that's probably not relevant to this story. And, too, see the video for David Bowie's "Blackstar" (2016) and Aleksander L. Nordaas' film *Thale* (2012), both of which likely were sources of inspiration for "Fairy Tale of Wood Street." It's one of those stories I don't expect anyone to like, and then it draws a bunch of fan mail and is selected for a "year's best" anthology (in this case, Jonathan Strahan's *The Best Science Fiction and Fantasy of the Year, Volume Twelve*, Solaris, 2018). I'm almost always a poor judge of my own work. The story was written in June and July 2017.

The Dinosaur Tourist
(Murder Ballad No. 11)

The South Dakota summer sky is a broken china teacup, and I have the distinct impression that when I finally stop the car and step outside and dare to let go of the handle on the door, I will fall straight up into that broken china sky. And I will not stop falling until the world below me is so small that I can make a circle of my thumb and forefinger and catch it all inside. And hanging there, I will freeze like a rose dripped in liquid nitrogen or my blood will boil, but I'll have captured the world's disc in one hand. There's country music on the radio, George Jones and Tammy Wynette singing "Golden Ring," and I turn the volume up just a little louder, to help take my mind off the smell. On either side of this seemingly eternal highway, there's shortgrass prairie and patches of bare earth pressed flat beneath that brutal, hungry blue broken cup, and I rush past a comical sort of billboard, an old prospector and his cartoon mule, and the mule is luxuriating in a horse trough, and the billboard promises Refreshing! Free Ice Water! at the Wall Drug Store if I just keep going straight ahead twenty more miles. The kid in the passenger seat is still sleeping. I picked him up last night just outside Sioux Falls, just after I'd traded I-29 North for I-90 West, and the kid said he'd blow me for a ride to Rapid City. And I said shit, get in, and I have an empty seat, don't I? You don't have to blow me, if you don't mind that I smoke, and if you don't mind the music. The kid said he'd blow me, anyway, because he didn't like taking anything for free. Yeah, okay, I said, and so we found a truck stop, and he did it in the stall, and I tangled my fingers in his blond hair while he sucked my cock and fondled my balls and, for no extra charge, slipped a pinkie finger up my asshole. I bought him a burger and fries and told him don't worry, it wasn't for free, he could blow me again later on, so we'd be even. But I had to feed the kid. He looked like a stray dog hadn't been fed in a month. And then I drove, and for a while the kid talked about his boyfriend in Rapid City, and I played the radio, and he finally fell asleep. In his sleep, he looked more like a girl than a boy. I pulled over near Murdo, just before four a.m., and I slept a little myself. I dreamed of the White River Badlands. I dreamed of giant tortoises and great beasts like rhinoceri with Y-shaped horns on their snouts. Overhead, the sky was full of stars pinwheeling points of light against indigo heaven, but all the constellations were unfamiliar or they were only in the wrong place. And then I woke at sunrise, had a cigarette, woke the kid, and we drove on to Belvidere, where we stopped for coffee and breakfast at the Dakota Trail Gas Mart. I fed him again, and this time he didn't protest or insist on recompense. He had eggs and ham and fried potatoes, and then I got back on the highway. He asked me, finally, what it is I do for a living, and I told him I used to be a college geology professor. "You're not anymore?" he asked, and I said no, I got fired a couple of months back. Inevitably, he wanted to know why, and so I lied and told him that it was over drugs, but could we please change the subject. The kid said sure, and then he fell asleep again. I started to wonder if there was something wrong with him, sleeping so much. I wondered if it was maybe something contagious that you can catch by having someone who's infected suck your cock. That was maybe an hour ago now. Maybe only forty-five minutes ago. We have passed Badlands Petrified Gardens. I almost stopped, but it actually isn't on my checklist, and the kid was sleeping so soundly, I just kept driving. And then I passed up two exits that would have taken me south to Badlands National Park, even though it's *on* the list. But I figured I'd drive on to Wall, and then I could take 240 down to the badlands. I figured the kid could go with me, or I could leave him at Wall to find another ride on into Rapid City. I decided I could decide which it would be when the time comes. "Hey, kid," I say. "Wake up. Time to stretch our legs and piss." He opens his eyes, which are, I think, almost the same shade of broken china blue as this sky, and he squints at the green-grey prairie and another sign for Wall Drug, and he wants to know where we are. All along the side of the highway there are black-eyed susans growing wild, a thousand little orange sunbursts poking up through the buffalo grass and prickly pear. Farther out, there are a few stunted cottonwood trees dotting the flat, monotonous landscape. "Did you know," I say "that seventy million years ago, this was the bottom of the ocean," and the kid tells me he doesn't believe in all that Noah's Ark stuff, that he stopped going to church when he realized he was a fag, because if he was going to Hell anyway he might as well be able to sleep in on Sundays. "You ever been to Rapid City?" I ask him, and he says no. I ask how it is his boyfriend is in Rapid City when he's never been there himself, and he tells me they met on the internet. "You've never met him face to face?" I ask, and the kid wants to know what difference that makes. "Does he know you're coming?" I ask him, and the kid just shrugs. "That means he doesn't, right?" I ask. "He'll be glad to see me," says the kid, and I let it go at that. "What kind of drugs?" he asks me, and I've already forgotten the lie, so it takes me a second to figure out what he's talking about. "What kind of drugs got you fired from the college?" he prompts, and now he stops watching the prairie and stares at me, instead. "Heroin," I tell him. "Heroin and pills. And a little coke, just to sweeten the deal." And he says, "So you're a junkie. I gave a junkie professor a blow job. What if you gave me AIDS back there? I didn't know you were a junkie." I tell him I don't have AIDS, and he frowns and sighs and wants to know if he's just supposed to take my word for that? Don't I have some sort of papers to prove that I'm clean, and when I say no, I don't have any fucking papers saying I don't have AIDS, he turns off the radio and goes back to staring out the window. "Your car smells like road kill," he says, and I say yeah, I hit a dead skunk back at the state line, just as I was leaving Nebraska. I pulled over at a truck stop and washed off the tires and underneath the car with one of those high-pressure jet nozzles, but I guess I didn't get it all. "It doesn't smell like skunk," he says. "It just smells like road kill. It just smells like rot." So I ask him if he wants me to pull over and let him walk, and he doesn't answer. I turn the radio back on. Hank Williams is crooning "You'll Never Get Out of This World Alive." "You catch shit from your parents?" I ask him, and he says, "I caught shit from everyone, okay? I caught shit from the whole fucking town," and I say fair enough and that I wasn't trying to pry. "It would be just my luck you gave me AIDS back there," he mutters. "People back home would say I got what I deserve." I ask him if he has any open sores inside his mouth or any bad teeth or anything like that, and he says no (and looks sort of offended at the suggestion), and I tell him fine, then he can stop worrying about catching AIDS from giving someone a blow job. We pass a rusting red Ford pickup truck stranded in the black-eyed susans at the side of the highway. The front windshield is busted in and all four tires are flat. "Lucas has a red pickup truck," says the kid, and when I ask if Lucas is his boyfriend in Rapid City, the kid nods and reaches for his pack on the floorboard between his feet. I told him he could toss it in the backseat, but he said no, he'd rather keep it with him. He'd rather keep it close. I didn't argue. The kid lifts it onto his lap, black polyester bulging at the seams with whatever the kid holds sacred enough that he's brought it along on his sojourn west. He unzips the pack, digs about for a moment, then takes out a little snub-nosed .38-caliber Smith & Wesson revolver. The sun through the windshield glints dully off stainless steel. My heart does a little dance in my chest and my mouth goes dry. "That thing loaded?" I ask, trying to sound cool, trying to keep my voice steady, like it's nothing to me if the kid's carrying a gun. I tell myself, shit, if I were hitching in this day and in this age, I'd be carrying a gun, too. "Wouldn't be much point in my having it if it weren't loaded, now would there?" And I say no, no I guess there wouldn't be much point in that at all. He opens up the cylinder to show me there's a round in all five chambers, and then he snaps it shut again. He aims the pistol out his open window. "You any good with it?" I ask, and the kid shrugs. "I'm good enough," he replies. "My brother, he was in the Army, over in Iraq or someplace like that. He came back and taught me how to shoot. And then he killed himself." I glance at myself in the rearview mirror, and then I glance at the kid again, and then I keep my eyes on the road. "Sorry to hear that," I say, and the kid says, "No, you're not. You don't have to pretend you are. I'm sick to death of people pretending shit they don't really feel." We pass another billboard for Wall Drug Store, and the kid pantomimes taking a shot at it. Bang, bang, bang, like he's seven years old, playing cowboys and indians, cops and robbers, with the neighborhood brats. "Baghdad," says the kid. "That's in Iraq, ain't it?" I nod, and I tell him, yeah, that Baghdad is the capital of Iraq. "Then Iraq is where they sent my brother," the kid tells me. "He saw a buddy of his get blown up by a landmine. He saw another buddy of his kill a woman because just maybe she was carrying a bomb. Something like that. He said everyone was afraid all the time, no matter how many guns they carried, and he came back still scared. He had to take pills to sleep. I guess he just eventually got tired of being fucking scared all the time. I know I would. He couldn't get into college, so he got into the Army, instead." I repress that reflexive urge to say *I'm sorry* again. Instead, I say, "We're gonna be stopping just a couple of miles up ahead, so you better put that thing away until we're back on the road again. You never know when there's gonna be a state trooper or something." The kid fires off another imaginary shot or three, and then he says, "Dude, South Dakota's open carry. What the fuck is it to me whether there's police around." And I say fine, whatever, suit yourself, kid. He asks, "Does it make you nervous?"

And I admit that it does. "Just a little," I say. "I've never much cared for guns. I didn't grow up around them, that's all." And now I'm thinking about three nights ago at a motel outside Lincoln, sitting on the hood of the car in a motel parking lot, and I'm thinking about the oddly comforting smell of cooling asphalt and about staring up at an ivory-white moon only one night past full. I crane my neck and look up through the dirty, bug-specked windshield and wish there were a few clouds this morning to break the tyranny of that broken china blue sky pressing down on me. Or if not to break it – because that would be asking an awful lot of a few clouds – at least to pose a challenge, at least to stand as a counterpoint. The kid opens his backpack again, and he puts the .38 away. I allow myself to relax a little, quietly sighing the proverbial sigh of relief. "This is the farthest west I've ever been," says the kid, and then he asks, "What's in Wall?" and he sets the backpack down on the floor between his feet. "Not much at all," I reply. "Less than a thousand people. There's a deactivated minuteman missile launch control facility, just outside town. In fact, just a few miles north of where we are right now." I take my right hand off the steering wheel and point north. "You mean nuclear bombs?" he wants to know, and I say, yeah, I mean nuclear bombs. "But the site was deactivated in 1991, after Bush and Gorbachev signed the START treaty. So, there aren't any bombs there anymore." The kid, he just sorta gazes off into the distance, off the way I've pointed, out across the prairie. "Jesus," he says, and then he laughs a nervous, hard laugh, a brittle laugh that would seem more natural coming from someone much older than however old he is, and the kid runs his fingers through his dirty blond hair. "I wasn't even born yet. There could'a been a war, and those missiles could'a been fired, and I never would have been born. Jesus." And then, to take his mind off an apocalypse that never happened, I say, "There's also a dinosaur in Wall." He stops staring at the prairie and stares at me, instead. "What do you mean? Like a dinosaur skeleton?" he asks, and I say no, not a skeleton. "You'll see," I tell him and I manage a smile, just to spite that sky. There's only an hour left until noon and the day's getting hot, so I tell him to roll up the window and I'll turn on the air conditioning. He does, and I do. We pass a billboard that proclaims in crimson letters ten feet tall that abortion is murder. We pass another broken down truck, this one missing all four of its tires. We pass the turnoff for Philip. A few hundred yards to the north, there's a deeply gullied ridge now, running parallel with the interstate, weathered beds of claystone and siltstone and mudstone laid down thirty million years ago, beds of volcanic ash and layers of sandstone from ancient Oligocene stream-beds, a preview of the vast badlands farther south. I recall my dream from the night before, of titanotheres and lumbering tortoises. In the bright sun-light, the rocks are a dazzling shade of grey that's very nearly white. The kid says he needs to piss. I point at the windshield, and I say, "There it is." He asks, "What? There's what?" But then he sees it, the queerly majestic silhou-ette of the Wall Drug Dinosaur stark against the sky. The kid says, "Wow," like he really means it, like he's someone who can still be amazed by an eighty-foot-long concrete dinosaur, even after all he's been through. That catches me off my guard almost as much as the sight of the Smith & Wesson did. The sun glistens wetly off the brontosaur's painted Kelly green hide, off its sinuous neck and tiny head. I tell the kid how at night the eyes light up, how at night the eyes glow red, and he says he wishes he could see that. I take Exit 110 off the interstate, rushing past the dinosaur, turning right onto Glenn Street. "Last time I was here," I say, "I was still in college. That was back in 1985, when there were still missiles in those silos, aimed at China and the Soviet Union." The kid doesn't take his eyes off the dinosaur, but he asks me what's the Soviet Union. "Russia," I say. "It's what we used to call Russia." The kid frowns and says, "I swear to fuck, dude, sometimes I think people change the names of shit just to make the next generation feel stupid." And I tell him, yeah, that's exactly why we do it. "I'll tell you something else that's changed," I say. "Last time I was here, all this crap hadn't been built yet." And I mean the Day's Inn and the Exxon station, the Conoco and all the convenience stores and a Motel 6, a Subway and a Dairy Queen, something called the Cactus Cafe and Lounge that promises home cooking and "western hospitality." I'd meant to head straight for the venerable Wall Drug Store, the time-honored crown jewel of this exit, a gaudy oasis to mark the dead center of nowhere, but suddenly I'm no longer in the mood for tourist traps. Suddenly, I feel ill and lightheaded, and I pull into the Conoco's parking lot, instead. The kid says, "Hey, ain't we going to see the dinosaur." I wipe perspiration off my forehead, because now I'm sweating despite the AC vents blowing in my face, and I reply, "I thought you had to piss." And he says, "I can piss after," and I tell him, "You can piss first. That dinosaur's been there since 1967. It weighs eighty tons, and it isn't going to run off anytime soon." There's an enormous convenience store attached to the Conoco station, the Wall Auto Livery, and isn't that smart, isn't that clever. I pull into an empty space between two other cars, one with Oregon plates, the other from Kansas, and I shift into park and cut the engine. I know now that I'm going to be sick, and I know that I'm going to be sick very soon. I taste hot bile in the back of my throat. "You get whatever you want," I say to the kid. "Go on and get whatever you need." Then I'm out of the car, and Jesus it's hot beneath that heavy, heavy sky, and for just a second or two I think maybe I'm gonna wind up on my knees, mired in the soft asphalt like a La Brea mastodon, praying for the mercy of vultures and slow suffocation. But then the door jingles and I'm swallowed by a blast of icy, impossibly cold air, and I realize that I'm inside the convenience store. There are people moving and talking all around me, but I don't make the mistake of looking anyone in the eye. I don't care if maybe they're staring. I just keep walking, past long aisles of snack food and coolers filled with row after row of soft drinks and energy drinks, bottled water and fruit juice. I'm lucky, and there's no one in the restroom. I lock the door behind me and vomit into the toilet, revisiting my breakfast. I sit down with my back pressed against cool ceramic tiles and try not to think how dirty the floor must be. I can smell urine even over the pungent, antiseptic stink of pink deodorant cakes, even over the stink of my own puke. I shut my eyes for a moment, fighting another wave of nausea. I've always hated vomiting, and I don't want to do it again. *What the fuck is happening?* I ask myself. *What the fuck is wrong with you? Get it together, man. Get up off this filthy fucking floor and get it together before some nosy SOB starts asking questions.* I'm trying hard not to think about the weight of the sky endeavoring even now to flatten me, even though I can no longer see it. I'm trying harder still not to think about the way the car smells. But you know how that goes, the white bear problem, ironic process theory, fucking Dostoevsky. "Try to pose for yourself this task: not to think of a polar bear, and you will see that the cursed thing will come to mind every minute." So, I puke again. And then someone knocks at the door. I look at my watch and wonder how long I've been in the restroom, and then I get up and straighten my clothes. I brush off the seat of my jeans, and I go to the sink and wash my hands with mint-green powdered soap from a dispenser. I wash my hands three times. I rinse my mouth with water from the faucet. Again, the knock at the door, and I say, "Yeah, okay. Just give me a second." I splash water on my face, then realize that I didn't flush the toilet, so I walk back over to the stall and flush. I jiggle the handle a few times, out of force of habit, because my toilet at home runs if you don't jiggle the handle. I unlock the bathroom door, only to find there's no one waiting. I spot the kid perusing a display of beef jerky, and then I go over to one of the coolers and take out four cans of Coca-Cola. I'll get a bag of ice for the Coleman chest wedged into the floorboard behind the driver's seat. The kid walks over to me, and he asks if I'm okay. "I'm fine," I tell him, because what's one more lie when all is said and done. "You don't look fine," he says. "You got what you need?" I ask him, and I wipe at my lips; my face is rough against the back of my hand. How long has it been since I last shaved? The kid says yeah, he's got what he needs, but he tells me again how he doesn't like taking charity. I tell him to shut up, and we walk together to the cashier and wait in line until it's our turn at the register. The kid has a pack of Starburst fruit chews, a bag of Skittles, some teriyaki-flavored beef jerky, a couple of cans of Red Bull. I ask the cashier for a pack of Marlboro Reds, and the girl behind the counter asks to see my license. She's wearing a tiny gold cross around her neck. "You don't look so fine," the kid says to me again, while the cashier stares at my driver's license like she's never actually seen one before. "I might have gotten a bad sausage or something at breakfast," I tell him. "How about you? You feeling all right?" He says, "Yeah, sure. I'm feeling fine," and I can tell he's not buying the food-poisoning story. "You don't get car sick, do you?" the kid asks, and the question strikes me as so absurd that I almost laugh. Somehow, I manage only to smile, instead. Finally, the cashier figures out that I'm forty-eight years old, so it's legal to sell me cigarettes, and she rings us up. I tell her to add a bag of ice. I pay for everything with my Visa card, because that one's still good, and I tell her I don't need the receipt. She bags the candy and beef jerky, the drinks and my smokes, and I ask the kid, wait, didn't he need to take a leak. "I used the women's room," he tells me. The cashier sort of glares at him. He glares back at her twice as hard. The name printed on her name tag is Brooklyn, and I wonder who the fuck in Wall, South Dakota goes and names her daughter Brooklyn? I tell the kid to grab the ice, and then I go back outside into the broiling day and stand by the dented left front fender of my car, staring westward, back towards the highway. Towards Rapid City and the Black Hills and the Rocky Mountains, towards the goddamn Pacific Ocean, and I wonder how I've gotten this far. The kid comes back with ten pounds of ice, and I see that there's a polar bear wearing a toboggan cap printed on the plastic bag. I think again about Dostoevsky. I contemplate synchronicity and meaningful coincidence. "I was thinking, maybe I'll get a room," I say to the kid, and he sets the bag of ice down on the hood of the car. "I haven't had a good night's sleep in a couple of days now. It would do me good to sleep in an actual bed. You're welcome to join me, if you want." The kid stares at the bag of ice, and he shrugs. "You still going all the way to Rapid City, or should I start looking for another ride?" I ask myself how far I'm gonna go this time, if I'm in for a penny, in for a pound, or if I should let this one walk. "Sure," I say. "I just need to catch a few hours shuteye, that's all. If you want to hang around, we can get dinner tonight, and then you can see the eyes of the dinosaur." I fish out my keys and open the back door on the driver's side. The cooler is a third full with chilly water, and I pour that out onto the hot asphalt. It pools beneath the car with Oregon plates. "Yeah," he says, "I don't know. Maybe I should keep moving. I'm late, as it is." He hands me the bag of ice, and I slam it on the blacktop a couple of times to break it up, and then I rip open the plastic bag and fill the cooler halfway. I dump the rest out on the pavement, and it begins to melt instantly. I put the cans of Coke into the cooler, and I tell the kid, "Whichever. No pressure. I just thought I'd offer. I don't want you to feel like I'm going back on my word. I just gotta get some sleep." He asks if I really think I have food poisoning, and I tell him maybe, I don't know, but, either way, the sleep will do me good. "Probably wouldn't hurt you none, either," I say. "Two beds?" he wants to know. "Sure," I reply. "Of course. Two beds." The kid sighs and gets back in the car, so it's decided. Just like that. I drive back across Glenn Street to the Day's Inn and get a room with twin beds. The clerk looks at me, and then she looks past me out the sheets of dusty plate-glass fronting the lobby. The kid is waiting in the car, sipping on one of the Red Bulls. "Is he your son?" she wants to know, and I can hear the suspicion in her voice, coiled like a rattlesnake, waiting to strike if I give the wrong answer, waiting to say, sorry Mister, but turns out there's no room at the inn, but maybe next door at the Motel 6 they have a vacancy. It's just down the way, and they don't ask so many questions. "No," I say, too tired and hot and queasy to lie. "I picked him up yesterday, hitchhiking. We're both headed the same way, and, you know, there are bad people on the road. Homos and perverts looking to take advantage of unsuspecting innocents. You know how it is." I'm wondering if maybe I laid it on too thick with the bit about perverts and homos, but apparently not, because then she wants to know, "How old is he?" I reply, "I honestly haven't asked. But he said something about graduating high school back in May, so I'm guessing he's not a minor. Look, I really don't want to cause you any grief. If you're not comfortable with this, that's okay. That's totally understandable. I just couldn't keep driving when I saw him. It's not safe out on the road, hitching." The clerk stares out at the kid just a little while longer, and then she says, "Nah, it's fine." She apologizes for being a snoop. That's the way she put it; her words, not mine. I tell her no problem. These days, the way things are, it pays to be on the alert. See something, say something, right? She gives me a keycard for a room on the first floor. She asks if I mind that it faces the interstate, and I say no, not at all. The sound of traffic helps me sleep. "Almost as good as train tracks," I say, and I smile, and she smiles back at me. She's missing a front tooth, a lower incisor. She asks me for the kid's name, and I tell her his first name's Lucas, but I don't know his last name. She tells me when she was a kid she had an uncle named Lucas, died in the Gulf War, and I say how that's a shame. Then I walk back out into the heat and find a place to park, and me and the kid retire to Room 107. It's dingy and smells of pine-scented disinfectant and stale tobacco smoke. But the beds are clean and the bathroom's clean. The kid brings in the cooler, puts his remaining Red Bull in with my four cans of Coke, and then he switches on the television set. He waits until after it's already on and tuned to ESPN to ask if I mind, if the noise is going to annoy me. I say no, just keep the volume down, please. There's a baseball game, the Yankees against the Detroit Tigers in Yankee Stadium. I pull the drapes closed, drink one of the Cokes, and watch the game for a few minutes. I unbutton my shirt and lay down on the bed nearest to the door, not bothering to turn down the comforter or the sheets. I'd like to brush my teeth, maybe even have a shower, but it can wait. I don't feel like going back out to the car for my suitcase, and speaking of luggage, the kid's backpack is sitting across from me on the other bed. I think about the loaded .38 revolver, about the kid aiming out the car window, firing pretend bullets at invisible targets. I wonder if he's ever killed anything, and I wonder if he has the nerve. I ask myself, if I got up and opened the bag and took the gun, would he try to stop me. Would he dare? Then I tell him, "I'm just gonna nod off, okay?" The kid says, yeah, okay, fine, and he tears open the bag of beef jerky. The salty-sweet odor of teriyaki seasoning immediately fills the room, and my stomach rolls. "So, you know all about dinosaurs and stuff?" the kid asks around a mouthful of dehydrated meat. "Yeah," I answer, and I close my eyes. On TV, there's the sharp crack of a baseball bat making contact, and the crowd cheers. "Is that what you do, dig up dinosaur bones?" he asks. "Not exactly," I say, then open my eyes again and stare at the cottage-cheese ceiling. There's a dark stain above the bed, and I figure that's where the mildew smell's coming from. "I study animals that lived at the same time as dinosaurs." He wants to know what sorts of animals, and I sit up again.

I reach for my cigarettes, open the fresh pack, light a Marlboro, and belat-
edly wonder about smoke detectors. I stare at the TV and explain about
plesiosaurs and mosasaurs and extinct species of sea turtles, about marine
reptiles and secondarily aquatic tetrapods, animals that have given up on
land and gone back to the sea. I tell him about my work in the Niobrara
Chalk of Kansas, the Pierre Shale of Wyoming, and the Mooreville Chalk
of Alabama. "Were you telling the truth about getting fired over drugs?" he
asks, and I say yeah, but I'm clean now. Well, mostly clean. Pills don't really
count. He asks where it is I'm headed, and I tell him I'm headed nowhere
in particular, that after a stint in rehab I just needed to get out on the road
and clear my head, figure out my next move. "I thought I'd take a road trip,
visit some places out West that I've never actually seen or haven't seen since
I was in college." The sort of places that are of interest to geologists and
paleontologists, the South Dakota Badlands, Dinosaur National
Monument, the Florrisant Fossil Beds in Colorado and Como Bluff in
Wyoming, a bunch of quarries and museums, and so on and so forth. I tap
ash into the palm of my hand. No smoke alarms have gone off, so I guess
I'm in the clear. The kid asks, "What's there in Rapid City you want to see?"
and I tell him about the museum at the School of Mines. "You're gay?" he
asks. "Yeah," I reply, and he sort of grins and says how he could tell right
off, how he wouldn't have offered me the blow job if he hadn't been sure.
He tells me he'll be nineteen the week before Christmas. I didn't ask. He
volunteered as though it were the next most natural thing to say. "Lucas,"
says the kid, "he's a lot older than me, too. Maybe I just have a thing for
older men." And I reply, "Maybe so, but you should be careful about that.
There are people who will take advantage of that predilection in a young
man. Out in the big wide world, out on the road, there are men whose
appetites get the better of the better angels of their nature." He says I talk
like a college professor, like someone who's read a lot of books, and then he
goes back to watching the ballgame. I return to staring at the water stain on
the cottage-cheese ceiling. I lie there thinking about wolves and Red Riding
Hood, the road of needles and the road of pins, about foolhardy children
straying from the paths set out before them, about Lincoln, Nebraska, and
before that, the inky shadows beneath a highway overpass just outside
Sioux City, Iowa. And then I drift off to sleep, and I dream of a sky above
the prairie that isn't any sort of sky at all, a sky that is, in fact, the waters of
an inland sea, and I drive and I drive and I drive. Gigantic white worms
have plowed the winding, switchback trails that I follow, and I anxiously

check the rearview mirror, again and again, to be sure that I haven't been followed. I roll along between cathedrals that once were the skeletons of leviathans, bare ribs for flying buttresses, an arching line of vertebrae to support the vaulted dome of Heaven. Monstrous reptiles and fish and sharks the size of whales swim and fly and sail the mesopelagic liquid sky laid out above my car, and their shadows move silent across the land, sirens leading me on. Behind the wheel, I recite a protective zoological mantra, Greek and Latin binomena for an infidel's blasphemous benediction, an atheist's string of prehistoric saints and petrified rosary beads – *Tylosaurus, Archelon, Dolichorhynchops, Xiphactinus, Thalassomedon, Cretoxyrhina mantelli*, Good Lord deliver us. I take a wrong turn and stop at a deserted gas station, but all the pumps are out of order. The flyblown windows of the gas station are filled with jackalopes and pyramids made of empty oil cans. A sign nailed to the door reads "We're Open!" but all the doors have been locked against me. I peer inside, and there's an antique Bell & Howell 8 mm. home projector throwing images on a sheetrock wall. Angry men on horseback riding the hills of a rough and wooded country, hunting a wolf, a ruthless murderer of lambs and babes in cribs and travellers caught unawares. The flanks of the horses are encrusted with barnacles. The wolf turns out to be something else altogether, not a proper wolf at all. And then, on the way back to my car, passing the useless, broken-down pumps, I watch a solar eclipse that is really only the circumference of an enormous ammonite's shell passing between me and the sun shining down on the ocean. *Placenticeras, Hoploscaphites, Oxybeloceras, Sphenodiscus pleurisepta,* Our Father who art forsaken, hossannah, amen, amen. I get back in the car, wishing that I could stop smelling that terrible, terrible stench, wishing it were only from having hit a dead skunk, wishing it were only the funk of road kill – though, in a sense, is it not? I drive, wandering out to where the deeps get deeper, and the sky grows darker, and the roof of the car begins to groan and buckle from the weight of all that water pushing down on me. And then the kid is shaking me awake, and he says that I was talking in my sleep. "Sounded like you were having one hell of a nightmare," he says. I say it wasn't as bad as all that, but sure, I have bad dreams. He's opened the drapes, and I see that the sun is down. The kid sits down on his bed, which doesn't look as if it's been slept in. I glance at the clock on the table between the beds and see it's almost midnight. The TV's been switched off, and the only light is coming from the open bathroom door. I smell soap and shampoo and steam, and I ask the kid if he had a shower. He says yeah, he took a shower, and then, he says, he found my keys and went outside and looked in the trunk. His hair's still wet. I sit up and rub my eyes, and now I see that he's holding the revolver from his backpack. *Quel courage.* I see that it's aimed at me. "What I want to know," he says, "I mean, what I most wanna know, is whether or not you're afraid of dying, whether you're afraid of going to Hell for what you've done?" And I reply, "Or maybe just for being a faggot? That would be transgression enough, right?" And I ask him if I can get one of the Cokes from the cooler, and if he minds if I light a cigarette. Isn't that how it works? The condemned man is at least accorded a final cigarette? He tells me to sit still, and he goes to the Coleman icebox and takes out one of the cans of Coca-Cola and drops it on the bed beside me. He lights one of the Marlboros and passes it to me, and I sit smoking and trying to wake up. But the dream still feels more real and less improbable than sitting in a motel room in Wall, South Dakota, staring at the muzzle of the kid's dead brother's gun. I take a long drag on the cigarette, and then I answer his question. "Yeah," I say, "I'm scared of dying. I probably would have stopped a long time ago, if I weren't afraid to just lie down and fucking die." He asks, "You were gonna do for me what you done for them?" and he nods towards the door to Room 107 and towards the car outside and towards the broken things he found in the trunk. "I hadn't yet decided," I tell him, and that's the truth, for whatever the truth might be worth. "Did you fuck them?" he wants to know. "Did you fuck them, and if you did, was it before or after they were dead?" I ask, "Are you going to ask me questions all night long? Is that how this is gonna go? You sitting there, holding that gun on me, satisfying your morbid curiosity." And he tells me, "Yeah, Mister, maybe that's how it's gonna go. Or maybe I already called the cops. Or maybe I'll take the gun and the car and be on my way. Maybe I'll even leave you alive." I laugh and smoke my Marlboro. "Well," I say, "that's an awful lot of choices. How are you ever going to decide which it's going to be?" He says, "You don't sound scared." I shake my head or I shrug or something of the sort. "Kid, I've been afraid so long I don't know anything else. I've been afraid so long I got tired, and I got sloppy, and I'm starting to think it was all on purpose. Maybe you've been sent by the gods to hand down my sentence and be my salvation, both at the self-same time, doom and deliverance wielding a suicide's revolver." The kid looks a little taken aback, either by so many words or by the sentiment. I open the Coke and take a drink, then set the can down beside the clock on the table between the beds. "I'm not afraid of you," he says, and he only almost sounds as if he means it. "Fear isn't anything to be ashamed of," I tell the kid. "Fear isn't cowardice. Fear isn't weakness. Maybe you'll figure that out one day, a little farther down the road." And then I ask him if he really has a boyfriend in Rapid City or if Lucas is nothing more than a useful fiction, a convenient lie. "That ain't really none of your business," he replies, and I agree, but he's not the only one with questions. "Why do you do it?" he asks, and I tell him I don't know. "That's a lie," he says, and I suggest that if he'd called the cops, they'd be here by now. And he tells me that he doesn't believe I was ever really a college professor, and I say fair enough, you believe what you want to believe. "But it's getting late," I say. "And you're holding all the cards." I imagine that I can hear the hooves of the horses from my nightmare, the horses bearing Wild West wolf slayers charged with a holy task of vengeance and retribution. He asks, "How do I know, if I leave you alive, if I leave you free, how do I know you won't come after me? How do I know you won't follow me?" I taste tinfoil and copper and a dozen poisons hiding in the cigarette smoke. Then I glance past him at the window, at the night waiting out there, at the headlights and taillights of cars and trucks racing by out on the interstate. "Kid, you don't know shit, and however I were to answer that question, you still wouldn't know shit. Whatever course you choose," I say, "it's a gamble. Just do me a favor and don't take all goddamn night about it." And he sits there watching me, and the clock strikes twelve midnight without making a sound. I think about the concrete Wall Drug dinosaur gazing out across the plains with its incandescent scarlet eyes, standing guard just as surely as any gargoyle, a sentinel watching for the evil that sometimes comes rolling along on steel belts, padding up to the off-ramp on four rubber paws, inevitable as rain and taxes and death. Then the kid asks me if next time I'll let him tag along and let him watch, if maybe that's one of the choices laid out before him. "If I don't call the cops," he says. "If I don't pull the trigger. If we could come to some sort of understanding." I have to admit, he catches me entirely off my guard. I don't answer right away. I tell the kid with broken china blue eyes and dirty blond hair how I have to think on it a little while, that it's no simple proposition he's making. And he says that's fine by him, that he figures neither of us is in a hurry, that neither of us has anywhere else to be. Then he lights a cigarette for himself, and he waits for whatever I'm going to decide, and the indifferent, all-powerful, unknowing clock starts counting down another day.

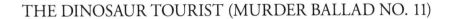

THE DINOSAUR TOURIST (MURDER BALLAD NO. 11)

Sure, it's a serial killer story, but it's also a fond reminiscence of the paleontological field work I did in South Dakota, Nebraska, and Colorado in the mid nineteen eighties. My first visit to the famous Wall Drug Dinosaur was a few days before the 45th annual meeting of the Society of Vertebrate Paleontology, hosted by the South Dakota School of Mines and Technology in Rapid City in October 1985. That was my first SVP. I gave a poster session demonstrating how *Tylosaurus "zangerli"* is a junior synonym of *Tylosaurus proriger,* as well as a talk on a new specimen of *Globidens alabamaensis.* That was also my first trip out west, my first time west of the Mississippi (I was twenty-one), and I loved it, so much so that I moved to Boulder, Colorado less than a year later. Oh, and I should cite Kirk Johnson and Ray Troll's book *Cruisin' the Fossil Freeway* (Fulcrum Publishing, 2007) as another source of inspiration. "The Dinosaur Tourist" was written in August 2017.

Objects in the Mirror

Ere Babylon was dust
The Magus Zoroaster, my dead child,
Met his own image walking in the garden.
        Percy Bysshe Shelley, *Prometheus Unbound*

1.

If I were writing a screenplay, I would begin, I think, with a fade in to a psychiatrist's office. The walls would be that pale shade of blue that puts me in mind of swimming pools, and the sofa where the psychiatrist's patients (she calls them clients) sit would be upholstered in the same shade, as would be the dingy low-pile polyester carpeting. I would note that time and friction have worn the arms and cushions of the sofa thin and shiny. There would be – *are* – framed photographs on the wall, oddly generic seascapes that mirror the walls and the sofa and are no doubt intended to instill a sense of serenity. There's a bookshelf and a small table, and on the table is a box of Kleenex, a silver metal starfish, and a polished nautiloid fossil from the Devonian of Morocco. The psychiatrist's desk is fastidiously neat. There are several careful stacks of papers, a few professional journals (*The American Journal of Psychiatry*, *Psychiatry Research*, and *BJPsych*), a copy of the 69th edition of the *PDR*, a tiny hourglass, a phone, a coffee mug filled with pens, and an electric pencil sharpener shaped like a robotic dog – a small concession to whimsy. There are two windows letting the wan January light into the room, one facing east, the other facing south. The curtains are drawn shut, muting the day. They're a slightly paler blue than the walls, the sofa, and the carpeting. It may be that the sun has faded them. There are fluorescent bulbs in white recessed fixtures set into the dropped ceiling, a stark counterpoint to the afternoon sunlight. On the desk, there's an iPod dock with speakers, but no music is playing at the moment. For now, the only sound is the psychiatrist tap-tap-tapping the eraser end of her pencil against the edge of her spiral-bound notebook. That and the sound of traffic out on the street.

The set decorator and prop master have hit the proverbial nail on its head. There is an almost archetypal tawdriness about the office, clinical prefab ennui; it pulses with the migraine thrum of a low-grade despair. If you weren't suicidal when you showed up for your four p.m., you very well might be by the time the psychiatrist glances at her wristwatch (Daniel Wellington 056DW Classic Southhampton) or the clock mounted on the wall (Ikea) to remind you *"our* hour is almost up." The air smells sickeningly of fake flowers, thanks to a "blooming peony and cherry" Glade Plugin®. The door is shut and locked. It's impossible not the think of Lucy van Pelt: The Doctor is In/Out. 5¢.

And I will play my part.

And she will play hers to perfection, my $125-an-hour, office-park Mother Confessor, my biopsychosocial Virgil. Here we go round the mulberry bush, and if she's worth her salt she'll not believe a single word I say. She will wear an entirely unconvincing mask, two parts sympathy to one part concern, dappled about the edges with phony compassion. Right off, I'm impressed that casting found someone so perfectly fitted to the role, an actress who so deftly communicates mid-life disappointment, the wages of having settled for less, the sour weight of mediocrity. Her hair is brunette, quickly going grey and pulled back in a ponytail that only makes her look older. She's a smoker, and it shows on her teeth and the nicotine stains between her fingers. Her eyes are, appropriately, the color of late autumn. Her clothes are plain, a dingy attempt at business casual. She still wears her wedding ring to the office, though she's been divorced for almost five years. There's cat hair on her skirt and blouse.

Her name is Louise Meriwether, and she mixes alcohol and benzodiazepines.

There's a crescent-shaped scar on the back of her left hand.

Now.

Lights, camera, action. We're only going to get one take, folks. Make it count.

So, here's the scene: I sit on the threadbare blue sofa, she at her desk. She taps that pencil and watches me; I'm paying her to be attentive. I'm staring at the silver starfish and the petrified whorl of the fossil shell. There is a reason that I've chosen Dr. Meriwether. She's written a book on heautoscopy and the problem of reduplicative hallucination in schizophrenics and epileptics, people who see themselves. Let's use the word doppelgänger and avoid the damn psychobabble. There's a copy of the book on her desk, *I Saw a Man Who Wasn't There: Psychopathology and Psychophysiology of the Doppelgänger Phenomenon* (Oxford University Press). The dust jacket has been ripped and Scotch-taped back together.

INT. OFFICE – CONTINUOUS

DR. MERIWETHER
And that was the first time it happened to you?

ME
No. I didn't say that. Not the first time. I doubt that I remember the first time. You might as well ask me to pin down my earliest memory.

DR. MERIWETHER
Because you believe they've always been a part of your life.

I shrug. I nod. I might have said that or I might not. I can't be sure. I've been seeing the psychiatrist once a week for a month now. I've said an awful lot of shit.

DR. MERIWETHER
And you told me you were four then, is that right?

ME
At the bottom of the garden, we wore animal masks.

DR. MERIWETHER
Excuse me?

She stops tapping her pencil and sits up a little straighter. A delivery truck rumbles by outside. I glance at the clock, run my fingers through my oily hair. I can't recall the last time I washed my hair. I can't recall the last time I had a shower.

ME

Yeah, I was four, maybe four and a half. Maybe almost five. We still lived in the big house in Wickford, the house on Elam Street.

DR. MERIWETHER

No, what you said earlier, "At the bottom of the garden, we wore animal masks." What did you mean by that?

CROSSFADE:

There is a big yellow house by the water, and behind the house there is a wide green yard that runs all the way down to the shore of Wickford Cove. The house was built in 1842 by a man named Jabez Bullock. His father had been a captain in the Revolutionary War, but Jabez Bullock was a carpenter and a cabinetmaker.

On this late afternoon in July, the tide is up, and the cove seems as still and flat as a looking glass. Indigo water shimmers beneath the blazing eye of the summer sun, and there are a few sailboats drifting lazily about – sleek hulls, straight black masts, and the sagging white lines of the canvas and rigging. There's hardly any wind today, and the sails hang limply. A pair of mute swans dip their long necks beneath the surface, upending to thrust hungry bills deep into beds of pondweed and eelgrass. Two or three noisy herring gulls swoop low above the cove, then wheel about and head east, towards Narragansett Bay. Behind the house, past the wide green yard, there's a short dock, and there's a dinghy tied up to the weathered pilings. Painted in crimson about its prow are two words: *Flyaway Horse*. Between the house and the cove are a pair of very large oak trees, planted by the second wife of Jabez Bullock; both trees managed somehow to survive the Hurricane of 1938, the infamous Long Island Express. Away from the shadow of the trees are wooden trellises for climbing roses and also beds of blue and pink hydrangeas, sunflowers, snapdragons, and irises. There are bumblebees and honeybees and darting hummingbirds, butterflies and dragonflies to serve as a counterpoint to the oppressive stillness of the day. In the limbs of the oaks, catbirds preen and argue with one another.

Just beyond the moored dinghy, a striped bass leaps from the water, snatching a mayfly in mid air, then falls back with a splash, and the ripples spread out across the cove.

To the mind of a child, this might be Eden.

And there is, as it happens, a child, a four-year-old girl whose mother is a recovering alcoholic and whose father – well, the less said of him, the better. The yellow house belongs to the girl's grandparents, two painters, who bought it cheap back in the late sixties, when the house was in such a dire state of neglect that there was a very real danger of it being condemned and demolished. They fled the squalid confines of Greenwich Village and, with her small inheritance, became nouveau réalisme saviors of gabled pediments and paneled corner pilasters. They're the ones who had the house painted the yellow of Van Gogh's *Wheatfield With Crows*. They restored the white picket fence. They planted this garden on top of the ruins of a much earlier garden.

The girl's mother is reclining in a fold-out lawn chair, white and cornflower-blue webbing inside a dented aluminum frame. She's halfway through Truddi Chase's *When Rabbit Howls,* which she checked out of the North Kingston Free Library the Thursday before. She pauses to light a cigarette and locate her daughter, who's sitting not far away, beneath one of the old oaks. The woman smiles, then goes back to her book:

> *The trouble with multiplicity,*
> *he supposed,*
> *was that to an outsider it did sound "crazy."*

The girl, dressed in dungarees and scuffed-up black Keds, has been occupied collecting handfuls of acorns and arranging them on the ground before her in three neat rows. She might well be making an army of acorns to battle a regiment of dandelions. She's also wearing a plastic Wile E. Coyote mask. It was her mother's mask, many Halloweens ago, and it turned up a few days before while she was looking for something else entirely, hidden in a cardboard box stored in the attic of the yellow house. "Can I have it?" her daughter asked, and "Of course," she said. "Sure, you can have it." The elastic string had dry rotted and snapped, and so she replaced it with sturdy butcher's twine from a kitchen drawer. Since then, the kid's hardly taken the thing off. She's even been falling asleep in it.

Beneath the tree, the girl counts her acorns, though she can only count as high as fifteen, and she's certainly collected twice that many, at least.

Her mother turns a page:

"Rabbit? Rabbit, where'd you put the keys, Girl?"

And the girl looks up to find that she's being watched by someone other than her mother. Standing only ten or fifteen feet away there is another little girl dressed in overalls and sneakers, another girl in a plastic Wile E. Coyote mask. She opens her left hand, and five acorns tumble out into the grass. Her mask isn't precisely the same: this *other* girl's mask has a dent and a crack in the coyote's muzzle.

The standing girl whispers something.

And the girl sitting beneath the oak screams.

CROSSFADE:

Not meaning to, I've allowed an entire three minutes to pass without having answered her question. I check the clock on the wall, and then I glace back down at the whorls of the fossilized nautilus shell. I asked her about it during our first session, and she told me it was a gift from an English college friend who'd become a geologist. She told me it had been collected from the Lesser Atlas Mountains of Morocco, and I thought then, and I think now, how odd that I can hold in my hand a thing so shifted in time and space. This object has traveled across more than thirty-six hundred miles and three hundred and seventy million years to lay on this tabletop in this tawdry office with its robot-dog pencil sharpener, its polyester carpet, and its depressing swimming-pool blue walls. The sheer unlikeliness makes me a little dizzy, if I consider it too closely.

"Back then," explained Dr. Meriwether, "the continents were in different positions than they are now."

"Continental drift," I said. "Plate tectonics."

"Right, exactly. And back in the Devonian, New England and North Africa weren't very far apart, at all. Time divided them."

The sun through the drab blue curtains glistens dully off the fossil, and I look up at the psychiatrist. She's watching me the way she does. I tell her what I'd meant about the garden and animals masks, describing that summer day by Wickford Cove, and she listens, and when I'm done she nods.

DR. MERIWETHER

If it makes you uncomfortable, we can move on.

ME

I didn't say that. I didn't say that it makes me
uncomfortable. I'm fine.

DR. MERIWETHER

Well, then I have a question. If that wasn't the
first time, why do you think you screamed?

FADE TO BLACK

2.

Here in this sheltered place, where freezing meltwater streams gurgle
down from the mountain passes and rivers of ice, the girl clambers over
rocks slick with moss and between deadfall branches. The old people have
two names for this place, one of which is the same word that is used for
becoming lost in the forest at night, and the girl has been warned many
times that she should never come here, and that she should certainly never
come here alone. Late in the spring the floods scour the high granite walls
raw. The evidence of the floods is all about her – the rotting trunks of shattered fir trees, the tumbled boulders, the broken bones of mammoth and
auroch wedged between the stones. But it's almost summer now, and the
time of floods has come and gone. So, she has no fear of drowning today
or of being swept off to wherever it is the floods are always bound in such
a hurry. And she's grown reasonably certain that the tales she's been told of
demons and monsters lurking in this place are only meant to keep clumsy
children away, those too young and inexperienced to know which footholds
are stable and which logs can be counted upon to support your weight. She's
neither a child, nor is she clumsy, and if there truly *are* monsters here, if the
souls of evil people truly do haunt this ravine, she'd like to see them for herself. She's seen starving wolves in winter, and she's seen what an angry bear
can do to a man. She's watched mothers wail over their stillborn infants and
has come upon the grisly leavings of the cannibals who live in the lowland
woods. If there's anything worse waiting for her, she'd be surprised.

Sometimes, says First Mother, speaking from the darkness behind the
girl's eyes, *you are too bold, child. Sometimes, you risk too much for too little.
Or for nothing at all.*

289

"Don't you trouble me today," the girl replies, ducking beneath an enormous log that is too much trouble to climb over, picking and wriggling her way through the narrow darkness underneath, a little cave whose ceiling is decaying wood and whose floor is loose stones, mud, and scuttling black beetles. She almost gets stuck once, but by relaxing and exhaling and making herself just a little bit smaller she squeezes through to the other side.

That might have been something's den, says First Mother disapprovingly. *Something with sharp teeth and sharp claws and young ones to protect.*

"There weren't any tracks," the girl replies, standing upright and dusting herself off, sucking at a scrape on the heel of her left hand. "I checked. There wasn't any scat or bones. I knew it was clear, or I never would have gone in. I'm not a fool."

And yet you do foolish things.

"It was safe."

I only worry for you.

The girl shakes her head, then scrambles up the next line of boulders.

"You want me to be like my sisters and aunts," she says, "like my mother. You want me to be too afraid to go out walking on my own. You'd have me cower at shadows cast by firelight and have no other desire but the birthing sons and daughters."

You don't yet know the world, child, not like you think you do.

"Then I'll see that for myself, won't I? And then I will know."

The girl comes upon the pool sooner than she'd expected, and she almost slips off a low ledge into the deep, still water. But she's quick and steady, and her fingers and toes and the thick pads of her feet find just enough purchase that she doesn't fall.

You see? says First Mother. *That might have been the end of you. You're not an otter or a beaver or a mink. You would drown.*

"I can swim well enough," the girl mutters, then finds her way along the shore to a narrow bit of beach.

They'd never find you. Not here. They'd never come here to search for you.

A tilted slab of granite juts out a little ways above the pool, and the girl climbs up onto it and sits down, dangling her feet over the edge. The stone is cool and damp beneath her, worn smooth by ages of floods and rain, rock the color of raw salmon, flecked with sparkling flakes of white and black.

What is it you risked so much to find here? asks the voice behind her eyes. *What is it here that is worth as much as that?*

"Be quiet and watch, and maybe you'll find out," replies the girl. The truth, though, is that she hasn't come here to find anything in particular, except, perhaps, the reason she's been told she shouldn't. Or to make the point, if only for her own satisfaction, that the stories of demons are merely lies to scare off the children. But when she looks back the direction she's come, gazing up along the gash cut into the mountainside, she shivers, despite herself. The truth is there are very many ways to die here, deaths that sure feet and quick thinking wouldn't spare her from. There are probably lions lurking along those bluffs, and anyone could be unlucky enough to be crushed by a landslide.

Death comes for idiots and the wise alike, First Mother whispers.

"You leave me be, spirit," the girl whispers defiantly back, but she's thinking now of the story that She Who Holds Fire tells, of how the sky plowed this furrow to fuck the earth and make the world pregnant with stars, how the earthborn stars became men and women, bears and mammoth and auroch. Which is why the other name for this place is the same as the word for being taken by force by a man who is not your husband or your husband's brother. The girl squints up at the blue wedge of sky visible between the steep walls of granite, at the white fire of the sun, and she tries to imagine the agony of the whole world, seized by all that emptiness and split open right down the middle. *How would one ever hope to hide themselves away from the lusts of the sky?* she wonders, and then the girl feels that shiver again, and she looks back down at the pool, instead.

Even though the pool is deep, the water is so clear that she can see every pebble lying on the bottom, cradled in folds of silt and sand and sunken leaves. There are tiny fish, shards of living silver light darting to and fro, and she also spots a big crayfish creeping along, its pincers raised defensively, warning away some or another invisible threat. The soles of her feet, her toes, brush the air only inches from the surface.

In the story that She Who Holds Fire tells, the pool was first filled by the tears of the world on the day she was raped by the sky. And even after all this long time, she says, if you happen to taste the water it will still taste salty, so terrible was the world's sorrow and pain. But, she cautions, do not ever dare drink from the pool, for that ache will crawl down into your *own* belly and forevermore will you know what the whole earth felt and how it feels still. Like the pool, you'll become a vessel for its tears and you will be changed utterly and never know comfort again.

Leaning forward slightly, the girl swings her legs, kicking out, and in the instant before her toes and the balls of her feet strike the water, she sees herself reversed, gazing back up from the glistening surface – her mother's bright green-brown eyes, her father's broad nose, the long auburn braids framing her face. And then the image comes apart in a splash and ripples spread across the pool. The water is ice cold, and when she kicks again, her feet scatter bright droplets almost all the way to the other shore.

There, says First Mother, *you have seen it all, all there is here to see. You're satisfied. Go back now, and do not press your luck again, child.*

The girl chews at her lip a moment, kicks a third time at the water, then says aloud, "Spirit, if you are First Mother, as we are taught, then, this is where you were conceived. That would be true, wouldn't it?"

This time First Mother doesn't answer, and there's only the sound of the wind rustling through the limbs of the trees that grow along the edges of the ravine and the soft lapping of small waves against the edges of the pool. *She made the wind,* thinks the girl, *and I made the waves. And waves are only wind on water.*

You assume many things, whispers First Mother, and now there's a meanness in her voice, as brittle and sharp as shards of a freshly broken bone. This is something the girl cannot recall ever having heard before, not for herself, though she's been warned that the spirit can be angered if its advices are too frequently ignored. The change in tone takes the girl by surprise. But it also emboldens her, and she smiles.

And kicks at the pool.

"And if this is where the sky entered the world, this is also where you were born," she says. "Here, by the water, you and First Father and all the others. How can you fear the place where you were born, even if you were sired by the rape of the world?"

The wind is blowing harder now, causing the firs and oaks, the sycamores and elms to creak and sway, and it seems that the ripples are striking the edges of the pool with more force than before. The girl glances very briefly at the cloudless blue stretched out above the ravine. For just a second, she has the distinct sensation that she's falling – not down, but up towards the sky – and she stops kicking her legs and grips the rough granite ledge. She shuts her eyes, and the sensation passes, as quickly as it came.

"Why?" she asks, and when she opens her eyes, the surface of the pool is growing still and flat once more. She can see the little fish again and the drowned leaves and her own face staring back at her. The girl in the water looks shaken and wary, but not afraid. "Tell me, First Mother, why that should be? Maybe this is exactly what I came here to learn, the why of this."

I always knew you were a wicked child, mutters First Mother. *On the day you were shat squealing out into the light, I cried that the People would ever be cursed with the burden of one so very wicked.*

The girl's mouth has gone dry, and she licks at her lips.

"How can it be that it's so easy to make you angry, you who knows the secret souls of every woman who lives or who ever has lived, who knows all the People, every one of us, even the outcasts and the moonstruck and the eaters of men? I've only asked a *question,* and that one question is enough to make me *wicked?*"

I should stop this, the girl thinks, *before it's too late.* And she knows, of course, that First Mother hears that thought, too, as clearly as she hears words fashioned by tongues and teeth and lips.

No one will ever find you here, the spirit whispers.

"Why won't you *tell* me? Why shouldn't I *know?*"

Wicked.

From behind the girl, then, comes the unmistakable sound of heavy paws, very near to her and coming closer. The noise of claws dragged across granite so that she knows it's a bear, a very large bear, and not a lion – you never hear a lion's claws. Already, she can feel the animal's breath against the back of her neck, warm as a morning's coals and fetid as an old kill. And now the girl is more afraid than she's ever been in her entire life, and her heart races, and she jumps to her feet, spinning about to face her attacker, and...

...there is no bear, only boulders, a splintered log, and the vertical wall of the ravine, so close that she could almost reach out and touch it...

...and she loses her balance, sliding backwards off the ledge.

Poor wicked, wicked child, who thinks that she would know the truth of all things.

There's the smallest space of time when the girl seems to hang suspended between the sky and the world, as if maybe both have decided they want nothing more to do with her, and then she hits the water, the water frigid as dark midwinter, and it instantly closes around her, solid as a fist, insubstantial as night. It's like being punched in the chest, in the gut, the sheer force of this cold, a cold that burns like fire, and the girl coughs out, vomits up her breath and watches as it rushes back towards the surface in a spiraling trail of bubbles to be reclaimed by the rapacious sky. When she told First Mother she could swim, that wasn't a lie. But the shock of this chill has already numbed her arms and legs, her hands and feet, and is quickly clouding her mind. She's sinking, surely as any stone would sink. She reaches out, clawing, grasping at that shimmering membrane dividing the world beneath the water from the world above it, summoning what little strength the cold has left to her. But now the day is like a dream, a dream of being chased by wolves or hyenas or an angry bull bison, and no matter how fast you run, you can't run fast enough to get away. The cold is pulling her down and – awake or dreaming – she cannot get away, and soon she'll be nothing but food for those tiny silver fish and for the crayfish and for everything else that lives in the deep pool.

What is it, mutters First Mother, *that you risked so much to find here? That you risked your life?*

What is it here that is worth as much as that, wicked child?

And the spirit's voice behind the girl's eyes is even colder than the water.

This is where I will die, the girl thinks, *and no one will ever come here to look for me, and so no one will ever find me.* And First Mother cackles, and again she says, *You're not an otter or a beaver or a mink.*

The girl swallows water…

…past a long hallway and marble busts of Richard Leakey and Charles Darwin, we enter a darkened gallery, you and I. The only lighting here is held inside the big display cases and set into the floors along the wood-paneled walls. The only lighting here is here for effect. You're talking about the train ride from Berlin to Mettmann and about the other things you want to see before you have to head back, the Goldberger Mill and the birthplace of Konrad Heresbach.

"You're enjoying Germany, then?" I ask, and you smile and nod as we pass mounted skeletons of woolly mammoths, cave bears, and ice age horses.

"I'm terrible about homesickness," you say, "but it's been nice."

We pause before the reconstructed remains of a lion-sized sabre-toothed cat – Homotherium latidens, according the museum label. Its bones have been skillfully wired together so that it appears to be lunging at the fleeing skeleton of an antelope of some sort.

"And good for the book, I would imagine," I say.

And you reply, "Yes, and very good for the book."

"I'm excited to read it."

"I think it'll be much better than the last one."

And, of course, I'm not thinking about the books at all, not the one you published three years ago to resounding indifference or the one you've spent all your time ever since trying to write. I'm thinking about the last time we fucked, and how your skin tasted, and about the smell of your sweat. I'm thinking about your face dimly reflected in the Plexiglas dividing us from those fragile fossil bones. You're talking now about agents and editors, contracts and lunches in Lower Manhattan, and I'm thinking about the last time we were together, the afternoon we visited the Archenhold Observatory. I was giving a lecture there on SETI and the Drake Equation, and then we were taken up onto the roof and treated to a demonstration of the Treptow refracting telescope, installed in 1896 and still the eighth largest in the world. You looked through the antique eyepiece at the starry Northern sky and made a joke about a thousand eyes on a thousand worlds peering through a thousand alien telescopes, looking back at you.

"I very much enjoyed the last one."

"You and no one else."

Then neither of us says anything for maybe half a minute, and I wish it were because we've always been comfortable with one another's silence. But I know it's simply that we're both running out of things to say.

"Poor old fucker," you say, finally, and you tap the Plexiglas.

"Die Katze oder der Hirsch?"

"Oh, die Katze," you smile, "most definitely die Katze."

And then you tug the sleeve of my sweater and we're walking again, leaving behind the sabre-tooth and the deer it will never catch frozen together in a limbo tableau, a limbo for predator and prey alike. The next time we pause, it's before a wide diorama depicting several members of a Neanderthaler tribe outside the mouth of a cave, everyday life thirty-five thousand years ago. There are eleven of the figures, each sculpted and painted with such startling hyper-realism that I wouldn't be entirely taken aback if any one of them should move or speak, if all together they should begin to sing or to dance. Their hair, their eyes, the grime beneath their nails, everything rendered in an all but perfect dermoplastic simulacrum of life. One of the men has a dead boar slung over his shoulders, and another, missing his left forearm, is pointing at the ground with his right index finger. A third man sits before a fire, shaping a tool from flint and an antler, while a male child watches on with an expression that is one part curiosity and one part boredom. Behind them, a young mother nurses her baby, and still farther back, half lost in shadows, there's an old woman kneeling beside a man lying on his back, half covered with an animal pelt, an elder caring for the sick or the dying.

"Do you ever think of coming home to New York?" you ask, and you look at me then, just for a moment, before turning your attention once more to the exhibit.

"Of course," I tell you. "I think about it, but we both know it's not a very practical solution. Don't we?"

"Yeah," you say, not the least bit convincingly. And then you lean nearer to the Plexiglas dividing the two of us from the scene of Paleolithic domesticity. And you say, "Jesus, that's creepy." And you point at something, but at just what I'm not at all sure, and I suppose you can see that from my expression, because you say, "Back there, behind the old woman and the sick guy." And now I do see...

...and it does taste salty, just as She Who Holds Fire said it would. The water is so very cold it hurts the girl's teeth and sears her throat and her belly. She kicks out with all the force she has left, kicking out against the bright panic pouring through her mind, and her feet strike the gravel at the bottom of the deep pool. A cloud of silt rises about her like morning fog or a burial pelt. And that's when she sees the faces in the water, the faces of two women watching her through the veil of sediment whirling all about her.

And you thought there were no ghosts, says First Mother. *You thought there were no demons waiting in this place to haul foolish children down to their well-deserved deaths.*

The women watching her are not of the upland tribes. By their narrow noses and flat brows, by their thin lips and weak chins, she immediately recognizes them as lowlanders, and so here is the awful secret of the pool, the truth of it she has not been told. It's haunted by the spirits of the eaters of men.

One of the women points at her.

Your flesh will be sweet, I'd think, First Mother tells her. *The marrow in your bones will be sweeter. Hear the crackling of your fat over their cooking fire? One of those women will wear your teeth about her throat. The other will weave a pretty belt from your scalp.*

No! the girl screams without opening her mouth. *No, spirit, I will* not *die here!*

And with all the strength left to her she pushes off from the bottom of the pool...

…at the very back of the museum's artificial cave, there's a pool fabricated of some clear resin, and a Neanderthaler girl, no more I would guess than fourteen or fifteen, crouches at its edge, staring down into the water. We're left to guess whatever it is she sees there, and maybe it's meant to be nothing more than her own reflection, but she looks startled, startled and maybe even a little bit afraid. I see the girl before I'm aware of the figure standing behind her, a thinner man than the others in the tribe. There are circular patterns – whorls – drawn on his skin in soot or some other dark pigment, and his face is hidden by a mask – the face and muzzle of a wolf, a wolf's ears and black nose, skinned and fashioned into a headdress for this looming shamanic figure. The man is resting his right hand on the girl's left shoulder.

"What does she see?" you ask. "What is it you think she sees?"

…and then, after what seems like only an instant, the girl breaks the surface of the pool, and she sucks in great mouthfuls of the warm summer air as she splashes her way to shore. With numbed fingers and cramping arms, she hauls herself out onto the rocks, sputtering and gagging and coughing up water that doesn't taste salty after all…

…and I lean in close and whisper, "What big eyes you have."

You turn away from the exhibit just long enough to scowl at me. You turn back, and there's your face reflected in the Plexiglas, superimposed over the diorama.

"All the better to see you with, my dear," you reply.

…rolling over onto her back, staring up at the single brilliant white eye of the sun, here in the place where the sky fucked the world, here where all the People were born. Here, where she will not die to make a feast for the ghosts of hungry lowlanders.

You may learn yet, First Mother whispers.

And the girl closes her eyes and waits for the shivering to pass.

FADE TO:

3.

BLACK
FADE IN:
NEXT SCENE
INT. OFFICE – CONTINUOUS

We still have fifteen minutes remaining on *our* hour, here in the office of the psychiatrist. Neither of us has said anything for almost five minutes, which isn't as unusual as you might think. Sometimes I run out of words. I think sometimes she might even run out of questions. But her time is purchased in tidy one-hour increments, and if I have paid for it, it's mine. The camera captures her face, not as patient as it was when I arrived – she needs a cigarette. It captures the ticking wall clock, blank hands, white face, red Roman numerals. It lingers on the fossil ammonite, which I picked up off the table shortly after she asked me why I screamed on a summer afternoon when I was only four years old, and shortly after I did my best to answer. I do try to tell the truth in here, though the truth has never come naturally to me. I think of it as a foreign language I had to endure in high school and hardly learned at all. She's tapping her eraser again. Outside, a car blaring bass-heavy rock music drives very slowly past the office building. In the past, when sessions have devolved into dead air, we've talked about – twice now – historical accounts of doppelgängers, many seeming to presage calamity: Vice-Admiral Sir George Tryon (Eaton Square, London; 22 June 1893), Emilie Sagee (*Pensionnat Neuwelcke,* Livonia; 1845-1846), the wife of John Donne (Paris; 1612), Percy Bysshe Shelley (Pisa, Italy; 23 June 1822), Sir Gilbert Parker (British Parliament, London; 1906), Guy de Maupassant (Paris; early 1890s), Abraham Lincoln (Washington, D.C.; 6 November 1860), Queen Elizabeth 1 (1603), et alia. But today I am in no mood for history. The camera tracks my hand as I set the fossil back onto the tabletop.

ME
So, how did it start for you?

DR. MERIWETHER
What do you mean? How did what start for me?

ME

I've preferred to imagine that it's not simply aca-
demic, your interest. I find the prospect that
perhaps it's something more personal to be far
more intriguing. Am I wrong? Are you going to
disappoint me now?

I've caught her off guard, and she hesitates. She shifts in her chair,
crossing, then uncrossing her legs. She almost smiles a nervous smile,
but doesn't quite manage to pull it off. Her gaze drifts to the drab blue
curtains.

DR. MERIWETHER

April 1996. I was still in college. I'd taken the
train down to London for the weekend, to see a
play. It was outside the theatre after the show.

And at first I think that's all I'm going to get, a welcomed confirmation
of my suspicion, but nothing more. I nod, then rub my eyes. I haven't been
sleeping again, and I left the Visine in the car.

DR. MERIWETHER (contd.)

There were a lot of people, everyone crowded
together between the curb and the door to the
lobby. And I saw her trying to hail a cab.

ME
(pushing)

Her?

DR. MERIWETHER
(looking at me now)

Her. Me. She was wearing a blue silk scarf that
I'd almost worn. At the very last I'd changed
my mind. It had been a birthday gift from my
mother, that scarf. But everything else was exactly
the same.

I glance at the clock – ten minutes to go – and then back to her. The psychiatrist looks tired and antsy. Suddenly, it occurs to me that everything between us has changed. It occurs to me that we're now coconspirators.

> DR. MERIWETHER (contd.)
> I saw her, and a few seconds later she saw me. I'd
> never seen anyone look that frightened. I mean,
> absolutely terrified.
>
> For that matter, I'm not sure I ever have again.
> We only made eye contact for – I don't know –
> seconds. A cab pulled up and someone opened
> the door for her, and then she was gone.

Dr. Meriwether tells me, almost matter of factly, there was no more to the incident than that. And I'm sure some people would believe her, because I've found the psychiatrist is quite good with feigned sincerity. As I've said, were I writing a screenplay, were this merely light and shadow projected on a wall, then casting would have done an admirable job with my psychiatrist. This drab, weary woman is convincing. I suspect that, as with writers, psychiatrists *must* be skillful liars. After all, if each and every empathetic word and gesture were genuine, they would certainly soon be crushed by the weight of so much borrowed despair, anger, sorrow, fear, confusion, delusion, and et cetera. So, the psychiatrist tells me *that* was *that*, and, on some level, I understand that I probably ought to take her word for it. But I know better. I've spent my life learning what the eyes of a haunted woman look like. I've seen that expression so often in the mirror, and on the faces of my seemingly endless parade of alternate selves, those doppelgängers, the double walkers.

> ME
> And was it the only time, that night outside the
> theatre? Was that your first and last time?

> DR. MERIWETHER
> Yes, that was the only time.
> (pause)
> I haven't told a lot of people that story, you know.

ME
Have you ever wondered why that is?

DR. MERIWETHER
I don't know. My reputation, I suppose. We can't
have shrinks seeing their own ghosts.
(beat)
Anyway, I'm afraid our hour's up. I have you
down for four o'clock next Tuesday. Does that
still work?

And I tell her yes, that still works. That still works just fine. I stand and slip my coat on, and the psychiatrist thoughtfully hands me an appointment card with the date and time scribbled with her tap-tapping pencil. She tells me to be careful, that she's heard there may be snow before nightfall. And if I am only writing a screenplay, then the camera watches with its voyeuristic dedication as I open the office door, step across the threshold into the outer office, then pull the door shut again behind me. And when I have gone, the woman who once saw herself watching herself on a street outside a theatre in London sits in her chair and stares at the fading day leaking in through her curtains and leaking out again.

FADE TO BLACK
ROLL CREDITS

OBJECTS IN THE MIRROR

This story was written in March 2016 for Dave McKean and William Schafer's anthology *The Weight of Words* (Subterranean Press, 2017). Each story in the volume was inspired by a preexisting piece of art by Dave, and then Dave created a new piece of art inspired by each story. I'd worked with Dave before, of course, as he did all the covers for my issues of *The Dreaming* (1997-2001), as well as my first mini-series, *Bast: Eternity Game* (2002).

Publication History

"The Beginning of the Year Without a Summer," first published in *Sirenia Digest* #99, April 2014; reprinted in *The Monstrous,* Ellen Datlow ed., Tachyon Publications, 2015.

"Far From Any Shore," first published in *Sirenia Digest* #101, June 2014; reprinted in *Black Wings V: New Tales of Lovecraftian Horror,* S.T. Joshi ed., PS Publishing, 2016.

"The Cats of River Street (1925)," first published in *Sirenia Digest* #102, July 2014; reprinted in *Innsmouth Nightmares,* Lois H. Gresh ed., PS Publishing, 2015.

"Elegy for a Suicide," first published in *Sirenia Digest* #90, July 2013.

"The Road of Needles," first published in *Once Upon A Time: New Fairy Tales,* Paula Guran ed., Prime Books, 2013.

"Whilst the Night Rejoices Profound and Still," first published in *Sirenia Digest* #83, October 2012; reprinted in *Halloween: Magic, Mystery, and the Macabre,* Paula Guran ed., Prime Books, 2013.

"Ballad of an Echo Whisperer," first published in *Fearful Symmetries,* Ellen Datlow ed., ChiZine Publications, 2014.

"The Cripple and the Starfish," first published in *Sirenia Digest* #108, January 2015; reprinted in *The Year's Best Dark Fantasy and Science Fiction,* Paula Guran ed., Prime Books, 2016.

"Fake Plastic Trees," first published in *After: Nineteen Stories of Apocalypse and Dystopia,* Ellen Datlow and Terri Windling eds., Hyperion Books, 2012.

"Whisper Road (Murder Ballad No. 9)," first published in *Sirenia Digest* #125, July 2016; reprinted in *The Year's Best Dark Fantasy and Science Fiction,* Paula Guran ed., Prime Books, 2017.

"Animals Pull the Night Around Their Shoulders," first published in *Sirenia Digest* #128, September 2016.

"Untitled Psychiatrist #2," first published in *Sirenia Digest* #133, February 2017.

"Excerpts from *An Eschatology Quadrille*," first published in *Children of Lovecraft*, Ellen Datlow ed., Dark Horse Books, 2016.

"Ballad of a Catamite Revolver," first published in *Sirenia Digest* #134, March 2017.

"Untitled Psychiatrist #3," first published in *Sirenia Digest* #136, May 2017.

"Albatross (1994)," first published in *Sirenia Digest* #141, October 2017.

"Fairy Tale of Wood Street," first published in *Sirenia Digest* #137, June 2017; reprinted in *The Best Science Fiction and Fantasy of the Year*, Jonathan Strahan ed., Solaris, 2018.

"The Dinosaur Tourist," first published in *Sirenia Digest* #139, August 2017.

"Objects in the Mirror," first published in *The Weight of Words*, Dave McKean and William Schafer eds., Subterranean Press, 2017.

About the Author

The New York Times has heralded Caitlín R. Kiernan as "one of our essential writers of dark fiction" and S. T. Joshi has declared "...hers is now the voice of weird fiction." Her novels include *Silk, Threshold, Low Red Moon, Daughter of Hounds, The Red Tree* (nominated for the Shirley Jackson and World Fantasy awards), and *The Drowning Girl: A Memoir* (winner of the James Tiptree, Jr. and Bram Stoker awards, nominated for the Nebula, World Fantasy, British Fantasy, Mythopoeic, Locus, and Shirley Jackson awards). To date, her short fiction has been collected in thirteen volumes, including *Tales of Pain and Wonder, From Weird and Distant Shores, Alabaster, A is for Alien, The Ammonite Violin & Others, Confessions of a Five-Chambered Heart, Two Worlds and In Between: The Best of Caitlín R. Kiernan (Volume One), Beneath an Oil-Dark Sea: The Best of Caitlín R. Kiernan (Volume Two)*, the World Fantasy Award winning *The Ape's Wife and Other Stories*, and *Dear Sweet Filthy World*. She has also won a World Fantasy Award for Best Short Fiction for "The Prayer of Ninety Cats." During the 1990s, she wrote *The Dreaming* for DC Comics' Vertigo imprint and recently completed the three-volume *Alabaster* series for Dark Horse Comics. The first third, *Alabaster: Wolves*, received the Bram Stoker Award. She lives in Providence, Rhode Island with her partner, Kathryn Pollnac.